Sphinx with Great and Second
Pyramids of Gizeh
From an original photograph.

From an original photograph.

THE GREAT EVENTS

BY

FAMOUS HISTORIANS

A COMPREHENSIVE AND READABLE ACCOUNT OF THE WORLD'S
HISTORY, EMPHASIZING THE MORE IMPORTANT EVENTS, AND PRE-
SENTING THESE AS COMPLETE NARRATIVES IN THE MASTER-WORDS
OF THE MOST EMINENT HISTORIANS

NON-SECTARIAN   NON-PARTISAN   NON-SECTIONAL

ON THE PLAN EVOLVED FROM A CONSENSUS OF OPINIONS GATH-
ERED FROM THE MOST DISTINGUISHED SCHOLARS OF AMERICA
AND EUROPE, INCLUDING BRIEF INTRODUCTIONS BY SPECIALISTS
TO CONNECT AND EXPLAIN THE CELEBRATED NARRATIVES, AR-
RANGED CHRONOLOGICALLY, WITH THOROUGH INDICES, BIBLIOG-
RAPHIES, CHRONOLOGIES, AND COURSES OF READING

EDITOR-IN-CHIEF

ROSSITER JOHNSON, LL.D

ASSOCIATE EDITORS

CHARLES F. HORNE, Ph.D.
JOHN RUDD, LL.D.

With a staff of specialists

VOLUME I

The National Alumni

CONTENTS

VOLUME I

LIST OF ILLUSTRATIONS

VOLUME I

THE GREAT EVENTS

BY

FAMOUS HISTORIANS

General Introduction

THE GREAT EVENTS BY FAMOUS HISTORIANS is the answer to a problem which has long been agitating the learned world. How shall real history, the ablest and profoundest work of the greatest historians, be rescued from its present oblivion on the dusty shelves of scholars, and made welcome to the homes of the people?

THE NATIONAL ALUMNI, an association of college men, having given this question long and earnest discussion among themselves, sought finally the views of a carefully elaborated list of authorities throughout America and Europe. They consulted the foremost living historians and professors of history, successful writers in other fields, statesmen, university and college presidents, and prominent business men. From this widely gathered consensus of opinions, after much comparison and sifting of ideas, was evolved the following practical, and it would seem incontrovertible, series of plain facts. And these all pointed toward "THE GREAT EVENTS."

In the first place, the entire American public, from top to bottom of the social ladder, are at this moment anxious to read history. Its predominant importance among the varied forms of literature is fully recognized. To understand the past is to understand the future. The successful men in every line of life are those who look ahead, whose keen foresight enables them to probe into the future, not by magic, but by patiently acquired knowledge. To see clearly what the world has done, and why, is to see at least vaguely what the world will do, and when.

Moreover, no man can understand himself unless he understands others; and he cannot do that without some idea of the past, which has produced both him and them. To know his neighbors, he must know something of the country from which they came, the conditions under which they formerly lived. He cannot do his own simple duty by his own country if he does not know through what tribulations that country has passed. He cannot be a good citizen, he cannot even vote honestly, much less intelligently, unless he has read history. Fortunately the point needs little urging. It is almost an impertinence to refer to it. We are all anxious, more than anxious to learn—*if only the path of study be made easy.*

Can this be accomplished? Can the vanishing pictures of the past be made as simply obvious as mathematics, as fascinating as a breezy novel of adventure? Genius has already answered, yes. Hand to a mere boy Macaulay's sketch of Warren Hastings in India, and the lad will see as easily as if laid out upon a map the host of interwoven and elaborate problems that perplexed the great administrator. Offer to the youngest lass the tale told by Guizot of King Robert of France and his struggle to retain his beloved wife Bertha. Its vivid reality will draw from the girl's heart far deeper and truer tears than the most pathetic romance.

We begin to realize that in very truth History has been one vast stupendous drama, world-embracing in its splendor, majestic, awful, irresistible in the insistence of its pointing finger of fate. It has indeed its comic interludes, a Prussian king befuddling ambassadors in his "Tobacco Parliament"; its pauses of intense and cumulative suspense, Queen Louise pleading to Napoleon for her country's life; but it has also its magnificent pageants, its gorgeous culminating spectacles of wonder. Kings and emperors are but the supernumeraries upon its boards; its hero is the common man, its plot his triumph over ignorance, his struggle upward out of the slime of earth.

Yet the great historians are not being widely read. The
ablest and most convincing stories of his own development
seem closed against the ordinary man. Why? In the first
place, the works of the masters are too voluminous. Grote's
unrivalled history of Greece fills ten large and forbidding volumes. Guizot takes thirty-one to tell a portion of the story of
France. Freeman won credit in the professorial world by
devoting five to the detailing of a single episode, the Norman
Conquest. Surely no busy man can gather a general historic
knowledge, if he must read such works as these! We are told
that the great library of Paris contains over four hundred thousand volumes and pamphlets on French history alone. The
output of historic works in all languages approaches ten thousand volumes every year. No scholar, even, can peruse more
than the smallest fraction of this enormously increasing mass.
Herodotus is forgotten, Livy remains to most of us but a recollection of our school-days, and Thucydides has become an exercise in Greek.

There is yet another difficulty. Even the honest man who
tries, who takes down his Grote or Freeman, heroically resolved
to struggle through it at all speed, fails often in his purpose.
He discovers that the greatest masters nod. Sometimes in
their slow advance they come upon a point that rouses their
enthusiasm; they become vigorous, passionate, sarcastic, fascinating, they are masters indeed. But the fire soon dies, the in-
spiration flags, "no man can be always on the heights," and
the unhappy reader drowses in the company of his guide.

This leads us then to one clear point. From these justly
famous works a selection should be made. Their length should
be avoided, their prosy passages eliminated; the one picture, or
perhaps the many pictures, which each master has painted better than any rival before or since, that and that alone should
be preserved.

Read in this way, history may be sought with genuine pleasure. It is only pedantry has made it dreary, only blindness has
left it dull. The story of man is the most wonderful ever conceived. It can be made the most fascinating ever written.

With this idea firmly established in mind, we seek another
line of thought. The world grows smaller every day. Russia

fights huge battles five thousand miles from her capital. England governs India. Spain and the United States contend for empire in the antipodes. Our rapidly improving means of communication, electric trains, and, it may be, flying machines, cables, and wireless telegraphy, link lands so close together that no man lives to-day the subject of an isolated state. Rather, indeed, do all the kingdoms seem to shrink, to become but districts in one world-including commonwealth.

To tell the story of one nation by itself is thus no longer possible. Great movements of the human race do not stop for imaginary boundary lines thrown across a map. It was not the German students, nor the Parisian mob, nor the Italian peasants who rebelled in 1848; it was the "people of Europe" who arose against their oppressors. To read the history of one's own country only is to get distorted views, to exaggerate our own importance, to remain often in densest ignorance of the real meaning of what we read. The ideas American schoolboys get of the Revolution are in many cases simply absurd, until they have been modified by wider reading.

From this it becomes very evident that a good history now must be, not a local, but a world history. The idea of such a work is not new. Diodorus penned one two hundred years before Christ. But even then the tale took forty books; and we have been making history rather rapidly since Diodorus' time. Of the many who have more recently attempted his task, few have improved upon his methods; and the best of these works only shows upon a larger scale the same dreariness that we have found in other masters.

Let us then be frank and admit that no one man can make a thoroughly good world history. No one man could be possessed of the almost infinite learning required; none could have the infinite enthusiasm to delight equally in each separate event, to dwell on all impartially and yet ecstatically. So once more we are forced back upon the same conclusion. We will take what we already have. We will appeal to each master for the event in which he did delight, the one in which we find him at his best.

This also has been attempted before, but perhaps in a manner too lengthy, too exact, too pedantic to be popular. The

aim has been to get in everything. Everything great or small
has been narrated, and so the real points of value have been
lost in the multiplicity of lesser facts, about which no ordinary
reader cares or needs to care. After all, what we want to
know and remember are the Great Events, the ones which
have really changed and influenced humanity. How many of
us do really know about them? or even know what they are?
or one-twentieth part of them? And until we know, is it not
a waste of time to pore over the lesser happenings between?

Yet the connection between these events must somehow
be shown. They must not stand as separate, unrelated fragments. If the story of the world is indeed one, it must be
shown as one, not even broken by arbitrary division into countries, those temporary political constructions, often separating
a single race, lines of imaginary demarcation, varying with the
centuries, invisible in earth's yesterday, sure to change if not
to perish in her to-morrow. Moreover, such a system of division necessitates endless repetition. Each really important
occurrence influences many countries, and so is told of again
and again with monotonous iteration and extravagant waste of
space.

It may, however, be fairly urged that the story should vary
according to the country for which it is designed. To our individual lives the events happening nearest prove most important. Great though others be, their influence diminishes with
their increasing distance in space and time. For the people of
North America the story of the world should have the part
taken by America written large across the pages.

From all these lines of reasoning arose the present work,
which the National Alumni believe has solved the problem. It
tells the story of the world, tells it in the most famous words of
the most famous writers, makes of it a single, continued story,
giving the results of the most recent research. Yet all dry
detail has been deliberately eliminated; the tale runs rapidly
and brightly. Whatever else may happen, the reader shall not
yawn. Only important points are dwelt on, and their relative
value is made clear.

Each volume of THE GREAT EVENTS opens with a brief
survey of the period with which it deals. The broad world

movements of the time are pointed out, their importance is emphasized, their mutual relationship made clear. If the reader finds his interest specially roused in one of these events, and he would learn more of it, he is aided by a directing note, which, in each case, tells him where in the body of the volume the subject is further treated. Turning thither he may plunge at once into the fuller account which he desires, sure that it will be both vivid and authoritative; in short, the best-known treatment of the subject.

Meanwhile the general survey, being thus relieved from the necessity of constant explanation, expansion, and digression, is enabled to flow straight onward with its story, rapidly, simply, entertainingly. Indeed, these opening sketches, written especially for this series, and in a popular style, may be read on from volume to volume, forming a book in themselves, presenting a bird's-eye view of the whole course of earth, an ideal world history which leaves the details to be filled in by the reader at his pleasure. It is thus, we believe, and thus only, that world history can be made plain and popular. The great lessons of history can thus be clearly grasped. And by their light all life takes on a deeper meaning.

The body of each volume, then, contains the Great Events of the period, ranged in chronological order. Of each event there are given one, perhaps two, or even three complete accounts, not chosen hap-hazard, but selected after conference with many scholars, accounts the most accurate and most celebrated in existence, gathered from all languages and all times. Where the event itself is under dispute, the editors do not presume to judge for the reader; they present the authorities upon both sides. The Reformation is thus portrayed from the Catholic as well as the Protestant standpoint. The American Revolution is shown in part as England saw it; and in the American Civil War, and the causes which produced it, the North and the South speak for themselves in the words of their best historians.

To each of these accounts is prefixed a brief introduction, prepared for this work by a specialist in the field of history of which it treats. This introduction serves a double purpose. In the first place, it explains whatever is necessary for the understanding and appreciation of the story that follows. Unfortunately, many a striking bit of historic writing has become antiquated in the present day. Scholars have discovered that it blunders here and there, perhaps is prejudiced, perhaps extravagant. Newer writers, therefore, base a new book upon the old one, not changing much, but paraphrasing it into deadly dulness by their efforts after accuracy. Thanks to our introduction we can revive the more spirited account, and, while pointing out its value to the reader, can warn him of its errors. Thus he secures in briefest form the results of the most recent research.

Another purpose of the introduction is to link each event with the preceding ones in whatever countries it affects. Thus if one chooses he may read by countries after all, and get a completed story of a single nation. That is, he may peruse the account of the battle of Hastings and then turn onward to the making of the *Domesday Book*, where he will find a few brief lines to cover the intervening space in England's history. From the struggles of Stephen and Matilda he is led to the quarrel of her son, King Henry, with Thomas Becket, and so onward step by step.

Starting with this ground plan of the design in mind, the reader will see that its compilation was a work of enormous labor. This has been undertaken seriously, patiently, and with earnest purpose. The first problem to be confronted was, What were the Great Events that should be told? Almost every writer and teacher of history, every well-known authority, was appealed to; many lists of events were compiled, revised, collated, and compared; and so at last our final list was evolved, fitted to bear the brunt of every criticism.

Then came the heavier problem of what authorities to quote for each event. And here also the editors owe much to the capable aid of many generous, unremunerated advisers. Thus, for instance, they sought and obtained from the Hon. Joseph Chamberlain his advice as to the authorities to be used for the Jameson raid and the Boer war. The account presented may therefore be fairly regarded as England's own authoritative presentment of those events. Several little known and wholly unused Russian sources were pointed out by Professor Ram-

baud, the French Academician. But this is mentioned only to
illustrate the impartiality with which the editors have endeavored to cover all fields. If, under the plea of expressing gratitude
to all those who have lent us courteous assistance, we were to
spread across these pages the long roll of their distinguished
names, it would sound too much like boasting of their condescension.

The work of selecting the accounts has been one of time
and careful thought. Many thousands of books have been read
and read again. The cardinal points of consideration in the
choice have been: (1) Interest, that is, vividness of narration;
(2) simplicity, for we aim to reach the people, to make a book
fit even for a child; (3) the fame of the author, for everyone
is pleased to be thus easily introduced to some long-heard-of
celebrity, distantly revered, but dreaded; and (4) accuracy, a
point set last because its defects could be so easily remedied
by the specialist's introduction to each event.

These considerations have led occasionally to the selection
of very ancient documents, the original "sources" of history
themselves, as, for instance, Columbus' own story of his voyage, rather than any later account built up on this; Pliny's
picture of the destruction of Pompeii, for Pliny was there and
saw the heavens rain down fire, and told of it as no man has
done since. So, too, we give a literal translation of the earliest
known code of laws, antedating those of Moses by more than
a thousand years, rather than some modern commentary on
them. At other times the same principles have led to the
other extreme, and on modern events, where there seemed no
wholly satisfactory or standard accounts, we have had them written for us by the specialists best acquainted with the field.

As the work thus grew in hand, it became manifest that it
would be, in truth, far more than a mere story of events.
With each event was connected the man who embodied it.
Often his life was handled quite as fully as the event, and so
we had biography. Lands had to be described — geography.
Peoples and customs — sociology. Laws and the arguments
concerning them — political economy. In short, our history
proved a universal cyclopædia as well.

To give it its full value, therefore, an index became obviously necessary — and no ordinary index. Its aim must be to anticipate every possible question with which a reader might approach the past, and direct him to the answer. Even, it might be, he would want details more elaborate than we give. If so, we must direct him where to find them.

Professional index-makers were therefore summoned to our help, a complete and readable chronology was appended to each volume, and the final volume of the series was turned over to the indexers entirely. We believe their work will prove not the least valuable feature of the whole. Briefly, the Index Volume contains:

1. A complete list of the Great Events of the world's history. Opposite each event are given the date, the name of the author and standard work from which our account is selected, and a number of references to other works and to a short discussion of these in our Bibliography. Thus the reader may pursue an extended course of study on each particular event.

2. A bibliography of the best general histories of ancient, mediæval, and modern times, and of important political, religious, and educational movements; also a bibliography of the best historical works dealing with each nation, and arranged under the following subdivisions: (*a*) The general history of the nation; (*b*) special periods in its career; (*c*) the descriptions of the people, their civilization and institutions. On each work thus mentioned there is a critical comment with suggestions to readers. This bibliography is designed chiefly for those who desire to pursue more extended courses of reading, and it offers them the experience and guidance of those who have preceded them on their special field.

3. A classified index of famous historic characters. The names are grouped under such headings as "Rulers, Statesmen, and Patriots," "Famous Women," "Military and Naval Commanders," "Philosophers and Teachers," "Religious Leaders," etc. Under each person's name is given a biographical chronology of his career, showing every important event in which he played a part, together with the date of the event, and the volume and page of this series where a full account of it may be found. This plan provides a new and very valuable

means of reading the biography of any noted personage, one of the great advantages being that the accounts of the various events in his life are not all in the language of the same author, not written by a man anxious to bring out the importance of his special hero. The writers are mainly interested in the event, and show the hero only in his true and unexaggerated relation to it. Under each name will also be found references to such further authorities on the biography of the personage as may be consulted with profit by those students and scholars who wish to pursue an exhaustive study of his career.

4. A biographical index of the authors represented in the series. This consists of brief sketches of the many writers whose work has been drawn upon for the narratives of Great Events. It is intended for ready reference, and gives only the essential facts. This index serves a double purpose. Suppose, for instance, that a reader is familiar with the name of John Lothrop Motley, but happens not to know whether he is still living, whether he had other occupation than writing, or what offices he held. This index will answer these questions. On the other hand, an admirer of Thomas Jefferson or Theodore Roosevelt may wish to know whether we have taken anything —and, if so, what—from their writings. This index will answer at once.

5. A general index covering every reference in the series to dates, events, persons, and places of historic importance. These are made easily accessible by a careful and elaborate system of cross-references.

6. A separate and complete chronology of each nation of ancient, mediæval, and modern times, with references to the volume and page where each item is treated, either as an entire article or as part of one; so that the history of any one nation may be read in its logical order and in the language of its best historians.

Such, as the National Alumni regard it, are the general character, wide scope, and earnest purpose of THE GREAT EVENTS BY FAMOUS HISTORIANS. Let us end by saying, in the friendly fashion of the old days when bookmakers and their readers were more intimate than now: "Kind reader, if this our performance doth in aught fall short of promise, blame not our good intent, but our unperfect wit."

THE NATIONAL ALUMNI.

AN OUTLINE NARRATIVE

TRACING BRIEFLY THE CAUSES, CONNECTIONS, AND CONSEQUENCES OF

THE GREAT EVENTS

A GENERAL SURVEY OF THE PROGRESS OF THE
HUMAN RACE, ITS ADVANCE IN KNOWLEDGE
AND CIVILIZATION, AND THE BROAD WORLD-
MOVEMENTS WHICH HAVE SHAPED ITS DESTINY

CHARLES F. HORNE, Ph.D.

CONTINUED THROUGH THE SUCCESSIVE VOLUMES
AND COVERING THE SUCCESSIVE PERIODS OF

THE GREAT EVENTS BY FAMOUS HISTORIANS

AN OUTLINE NARRATIVE

TRACING BRIEFLY THE CAUSES, CON-
NECTIONS, AND CONSEQUENCES OF

THE GREAT EVENTS

(FROM THE BEGINNING TO THE OVERTHROW OF THE PERSIANS)

CHARLES F. HORNE

HISTORY, if we define it as the mere transcription of the written records of former generations, can go no farther back than the time such records were first made, no farther than the art of writing. But now that we have come to recognize the great earth itself as a story-book, as a keeper of records buried one beneath the other, confused and half obliterated, yet not wholly beyond our comprehension, now the historian may fairly be allowed to speak of a far earlier day.

For unmeasured and immeasurable centuries man lived on earth a creature so little removed from "the beasts that die," so little superior to them, that he has left no clearer record than they of his presence here. From the dry bones of an extinct mammoth or a plesiosaur, Cuvier reconstructed the entire animal and described its habits and its home. So, too, looking on an ancient, strange, scarce human skull, dug from the deeper strata beneath our feet, anatomists tell us that the owner was a man indeed, but one little better than an ape. A few æons later this creature leaves among his bones chipped flints that narrow to a point; and the archæologist, taking up the tale, explains that man has become tool-using, he has become intelligent beyond all the other animals of earth. Physically he is but a mite amid the beast monsters that surround him, but by value of his brain he conquers them. He has begun his career of mastery.

If we delve amid more recent strata, we find the flint weapons have become bronze. Their owner has learned to handle a ductile metal, to draw it from the rocks and fuse it in the fire. Later still he has discovered how to melt the harder and more useful iron. We say roughly, therefore, that man passed through a stone age, a bronze age, and then an iron age.

Somewhere, perhaps in the earliest of these, he began to build rude houses. In the next, he drew pictures. During the latest, his pictures grew into an alphabet of signs, his structures developed into vast and enduring piles of brick or stone. Buildings and inscriptions became his relics, more like to our own, more fully understandable, giving us a sense of closer kinship with his race.

SOURCES OF EARLY KNOWLEDGE

There are three different lines along which we have succeeded in securing some knowledge of these our distant ancestors, three telephones from the past, over which they send to us confused and feeble murmurings, whose fascination makes only more maddening the vagueness of their speech.

First, we have the picture-writings, whether of Central America, of Egypt, of Babylonia, or of other lands. These when translatable bring us nearest of all to the heart of the great past. It is the mind, the thought, the spoken word, of man that is most intimately he; not his face, nor his figure, nor his clothes. Unfortunately, the translation of these writings is no easy task. Those of Central America are still an unsolved riddle. Those of Babylon have been slowly pieced together like a puzzle, a puzzle to which the learned world has given its most able thought. Yet they are not fully understood. In Egypt we have had the luck to stumble on a clew, the Rosetta Stone, which makes the ancient writing fairly clear.[1]

Where this mode of communication fails, we turn to another which carries us even farther into the past. The records which

---

[1] See page 1 for an engraving and account of this famous stone. It was found over a century ago and its value was instantly recognized, but many years passed before its secrets were deciphered. It contains an inscription repeated in three forms of writing: the early Egyptian of the hieroglyphics, a later Egyptian (the demotic), and Greek.

have been less intentionally preserved, not only the buildings themselves, but their decorations, the personal ornaments of men, idols, coins, every imaginable fragment, chance escaped from the maw of time, has its own story for our reading. In Egypt we have found deep-hidden, secret tombs, and, intruding on their many centuries of silence, have reaped rich harvests of knowledge from the garnered wealth. In Babylonia the rank vegetation had covered whole cities underneath green hillocks, and preserved them till our modern curiosity delved them out. To-day, he who wills, may walk amid the halls of Sennacherib, may tread the streets whence Abraham fled, ay, he may gaze upon the handiwork of men who lived perhaps as far before Abraham as we ourselves do after him.

Nor are our means of penetrating the past even thus exhausted. A third chain yet more subtle and more marvellous has been found to link us to an ancestry immeasurably remote. This unbroken chain consists of the words from our own mouths. We speak as our fathers spoke; and they did but follow the generations before. Occasional pronunciations have altered, new words have been added, and old ones forgotten; but some basal sounds of names, some root-thoughts of the heart, have proved as immutable as the superficial elegancies are changeful. "Father" and "mother" mean what they have meant for uncounted ages.

Comparative philology, the science which compares one language with another to note the points of similarity between them, has discovered that many of these root-sounds are alike in almost all the varied tongues of Europe. The resemblance is too common to be the result of coincidence, too deep-seated to be accounted for by mere communication between the nations. We have gotten far beyond the possibility of such explanations; and science says now with positive confidence that there must have been a time when all these nations were but one, that their languages are all but variations of the tongue their distant ancestors once held in common.

Study has progressed beyond this point, can tell us far more intricate and fainter facts. It argues that one by one the various tribes left their common home and became completely separated; and that each root-sound still used by all the na-

tions represents an idea, an object, they already possessed before their dispersal.   Thus we can vaguely reconstruct that ancient, aboriginal civilization.   We can even guess which tribes
first broke away, and where again these wanderers subdivided,
and at what stage of progress.   Surely a fascinating science
this!   And in its infancy!   If its later development shall justify
present promise, it has still strange tales to tell us in the future.

THE RACES OF MAN

Turn now from this tracing of our means of knowledge, to
speak of the facts they tell us.   When our humankind first become clearly visible they are already divided into races, which
for convenience we speak of as white, yellow, and black.   Of
these the whites had apparently advanced farthest on the road
to civilization; and the white race itself had become divided
into at least three varieties, so clearly marked as to have per-
sisted through all the modern centuries of communication and
intermarriage.   Science is not even able to say positively that
these varieties or families had a common origin.   She inclines
to think so; but when all these later ages have failed to oblit-
erate the marks of difference, what far longer period of separation must have been required to establish them!

These three clearly outlined families of the whites are the
Hamites, of whom the Egyptians are the best-known type;
the Semites, as represented by ancient Babylonians and modern
Jews and Arabs; and the great Aryan or Indo-European family, once called the Japhites, and including Hindus, Persians,
Greeks, Latins, the modern Celtic and Germanic races, and even
the Slavs or Russians.

The Egyptians, when we first see them, are already well
advanced toward civilization.[1]   To say that they were the first
people to emerge from barbarism is going much further than
we dare.   Their records are the most ancient that have come
clearly down to us; but there may easily have been other social
organisms, other races, to whom the chances of time and nature
have been less gentle.   Cataclysms may have engulfed more than
one Atlantis; and few climates are so fitted for the preserva-
tion of man's buildings as is the rainless valley of the Nile.

[1] See the *Dawn of Civilization*, page 1.

Moreover, the Egyptians may not have been the earliest inhabitants even of their own rich valley. We find hints that they
were wanderers, invaders, coming from the East, and that
with the land they appropriated also the ideas, the inventions,
of an earlier negroid race. But whatever they took they added
to, they improved on. The idea of futurity, of man's existence
beyond the grave, became prominent among them; and in the
absence of clearer knowledge we may well take this idea as the
groundwork, the starting-point, of all man's later and more striking progress.

Since the Egyptians believed in a future life they strove to
preserve the body for it, and built ever stronger and more
gigantic tombs. They strove to fit the mind for it, and cultivated virtues, not wholly animal such as physical strength, nor
wholly commercial such as cunning. They even carved around
the sepulchre of the departed a record of his doings, lest they
—and perhaps he too in that next life—forget. There were
elements of intellectual growth in all this, conditions to stimulate the mind beyond the body.

And the Egyptians did develop. If one reads the tales, the
romances, that have survived from their remoter periods, he
finds few emotions higher than childish curiosity or mere animal rage and fear. Amid their latest stories, on the contrary,
we encounter touches of sentiment, of pity and self-sacrifice,
such as would even now be not unworthy of praise. But, alas!
the improvement seems most marked where it was most distant.
Perhaps the material prosperity of the land was too great, the
conditions of life too easy; there was no stimulus to effort, to
endeavor. By about the year 2200 B.C. we find Egypt fallen into
the grip of a cold and lifeless formalism. Everything was fixed
by law; even pictures must be drawn in a certain way, thoughts
must be expressed by stated and unvariable symbols. Advance
became wellnigh impossible. Everything lay in the hands of
a priestly caste the completeness of whose dominion has perhaps never been matched in history. The leaders lived lives
of luxurious pleasure enlightened by scientific study; but the
people scarce existed except as automatons. The race was
dead; its true life, the vigor of its masses, was exhausted, and
the land soon fell an easy prey to every spirited invader.

Meanwhile a rougher, stronger civilization was growing in the river valleys eastward from the Nile. The Semitic tribes, who seem to have had their early seat and centre of dispersion somewhere in this region, were coalescing into nations, Babylonians along the lower Tigris and Euphrates, Assyrians later along the upper rivers, Hebrews under David and Solomon[1] by the Jordan, Phœnicians on the Mediterranean coast.

The early Babylonian civilization may antedate even the Egyptian; but its monuments were less permanent, its rulers less anxious for the future. The "appeal to posterity," the desire for a posthumous fame, seems with them to have been slower of conception. True, the first Babylonian monarchs of whom we have any record, in an era perhaps over five thousand years before Christianity, stamped the royal signet on every brick of their walls and temples. But common-sense suggests that this was less to preserve their fame than to preserve their bricks. Theft is no modern innovation.

They were a mathematical race, these Babylonians. In fact, Semite and mathematician are names that have been closely allied through all the course of history, and one cannot help but wish our Aryan race had somewhere lived through an experience which would produce in them the exactitude in balance and measurement of facts that has distinguished the Arabs and the Jews. The Babylonians founded astronomy and chronology; they recorded the movements of the stars, and divided their year according to the sun and moon. They built a vast and intricate network of canals to fertilize their land; and they arranged the earliest system of legal government, the earliest code of laws, that has come down to us.[2]

The sciences, then, arise more truly here than with the Egyptians. Man here began to take notice, to record and to classify the facts of nature. We may count this the second visible step in his great progress. Never again shall we find him in a childish attitude of idle wonder. Always is his brain alert, striving to understand, self-conscious of its own power over nature.

It may have been wealth and luxury that enfeebled the Bab-

[1] See *Accession of Solomon*, page 92.
[2] See *Compilation of the Earliest Code*, page 14.

ylonians as it did the Egyptians. At any rate, their empire was overturned by a border colony of their own, the Assyrians, a rough and hardy folk who had maintained themselves for centuries battling against tribes from the surrounding mountains. It was like a return to barbarism when about B.C. 880 the Assyrians swept over the various Semite lands. Loud were the laments of the Hebrews; terrible the tales of cruelty; deep the scorn with which the Babylonians submitted to the rude conquerors. We approach here a clearer historic period; we can trace with plainness the devastating track of war;[1] we can read the boastful triumph of the Assyrian chiefs, can watch them step by step as they adopt the culture and the vices of their new subjects, growing ever more graceful and more enfeebled, until they too are overthrown by a new and hardier race, the Persians, an Aryan folk.

Before turning to this last and most prominent family of humankind, let us look for a moment at the other, darker races, seen vaguely as they come in contact with the whites. The negroes, set sharply by themselves in Africa, never seem to have created any progressive civilization of their own, never seem to have advanced further than we find the wild tribes in the interior of the country to-day. But the yellow or Turanian races, the Chinese and Japanese, the Turks and the Tartars, did not linger so helplessly behind. The Chinese, at least, established a social world of their own, widely different from that of the whites, in some respects perhaps superior to it. But the fatal weakness of the yellow civilization was that it was not ennobling like the Egyptian, not scientific like the Babylonian, not adventurous and progressive as we shall find the Aryan.

This, of course, is speaking in general terms. Something somewhat ennobling there may be in the contemplations of Confucius;[2] but no man can favorably compare the Chinese character to-day with the European, whether we regard either intensity of feeling, or variety, range, subtlety, and beauty of emotion. So, also, the Chinese made scientific discoveries—but knew not how to apply them or improve them. So also

[1] See *Rise and Fall of Assyria*, page 105.
[2] See *Rise of Confucius*, page 270.

they made conquests—and abandoned them; toiled—and sank back into inertia.

The Japanese present a separate problem, as yet little understood in its earlier stages.[1] As to the Tartars, wild and hardy horsemen roaming over Northern Asia, they kept for ages their independent animal strength and fierceness. They appear and disappear like flashes. They seem to seek no civilization of their own; they threaten again and again to destroy that of all the other races of the globe. Fitly, indeed, was their leader Attila once termed "the Scourge of God."

THE ARYANS

Of our own progressive Aryan race, we have no monuments nor inscriptions so old as those of the Hamites and the Semites. What comparative philology tells is this: An early, if not the original, home of the Aryans was in Asia, to the eastward of the Semites, probably in the mountain district back of modern Persia. That is, they were not, like the other whites, a people of the marsh lands and river valleys. They lived in a higher, hardier, and more bracing atmosphere. Perhaps it was here that their minds took a freer bent, their spirits caught a bolder tone. Wherever they moved they came as conquerors among other races.

In their primeval home and probably before the year B.C. 3000, they had already acquired a fair degree of civilization. They built houses, ploughed the land, and ground grain into flour for their baking. The family relations were established among them; they had some social organization and simple form of government; they had learned to worship a god, and to see in him a counterpart of their tribal ruler.

From their upland farms they must have looked eastward upon yet higher mountains, rising impenetrable above the snow-line; but to north and south and west they might turn to lower regions; and by degrees, perhaps as they grew too numerous for comfort, a few families wandered off along the more inviting routes. Whichever way they started, their adventurous spirit led them on. We find no trace of a single case where hearts failed or strength grew weary and the movement

[1] See *Prince Jimmu*, page 140.

became retrograde, back toward the ancient home. Spreading out, radiating in all directions, it is they who have explored the earth, who have measured it and marked its bounds and penetrated almost to its every corner. It is they who still pant to complete the work so long ago begun.

Before B.C. 2000 one of these exuded swarms had penetrated India, probably by way of the Indus River. In the course of a thousand years or so, the intruders expanded and fought their way slowly from the Indus to the Ganges. The earlier and duskier inhabitants gave way before them or became incorporated in the stronger race. A mighty Aryan or Hindu empire was formed in India and endured there until well within historic times.

Yet its power faded. Life in the hot and languid tropics tends to weaken, not invigorate, the sinews of a race. Then, too, a formal religion, a system of castes [1] as arbitrary as among the Egyptians, laid its paralyzing grip upon the land. About B.C. 600 Buddhism, a new and beautiful religion, sought to revive the despairing people; but they were beyond its help.[2] Their slothful languor had become too deep. From having been perhaps the first and foremost and most civilized of the Aryan tribes, the Hindus sank to be degenerate members of the race. We shall turn to look on them again in a later period; but they will be seen in no favorable light.

Meanwhile other wanderers from the Aryan home appear to the north and west. Perhaps even the fierce Tartars are an Aryan race, much altered from long dwelling among the yellow peoples. One tribe, the Persians, moved directly west, and became neighbors of the already noted Semitic group. After long wars backward and forward, bringing us well within the range of history, the Persians proved too powerful for the whole Semite group. They helped destroy Assyria,[3] they overthrew the second Babylonian empire which Nebuchadnezzar had built up, and then, pressing on to the conquest of Egypt, they swept the Hamites too from their place of sovereignty.[4]

---

[1] See *The Formation of the Castes*, page 52.
[2] See *The Foundation of Buddhism*, page 160.
[3] See *Destruction of Nineveh*, page 105.
[4] See *Conquests of Cyrus*, page 250.

How surely do those tropic lands avenge themselves on each new savage horde of invaders from the hardy North. It is not done in a generation, not in a century, perhaps. But drop by drop the vigorous, tingling, Arctic blood is sapped away. Year after year the lazy comfort, the loose pleasure, of the south land fastens its curse upon the mighty warriors. As we watch the Persians, we see their kings go mad, or become effeminate tyrants sending underlings to do their fighting for them. We see the whole race visibly degenerate, until one questions if Marathon [1] were after all so marvellous a victory, and suspects that at whatever point the Persians had begun their advance on Europe they would have been easily hurled back.

It was in Europe only that the Aryan wanderers found a temperate climate, a region similar to that in which they had been bred. Recent speculation has even suggested that Europe was their primeval home, from which they had strayed toward Asia, and to which they now returned. Certainly it is in Europe that the race has continued to develop. Earliest of these Aryan waves to take possession of their modern heritage, were the Celts, who must have journeyed over the European continent at some dim period too remote even for a guess. Then came the Greeks and Latins, closely allied tribes, representing possibly a single migration, that spread westward along the islands and peninsulas of the Mediterranean. The Teutons may have left Asia before B.C. 1000, for they seem to have reached their German forests by three centuries beyond that time, and these vast migratory movements were very slow. The latest Aryan wave, that of the Slavs, came well within historic times. We almost fancy we can see its movement. Russian statesmen, indeed, have hopes that this is not yet completed. They dream that they, the youngest of the peoples, are yet to dominate the whole.

THE GREEKS AND LATINS

Of these European Aryans the only branches that come within the limits of our present period, that become noteworthy before B.C. 480, are the Greeks and Latins.

---

[1] See *The Battle of Marathon*, page 322.

Their languages tell us that they formed but a single tribe long after they became separated from the other peoples of their race. Finally, however, the Latins, journeying onward, lost sight of their friends, and it must have taken many centuries of separation for the two tongues to grow so different as they were when Greeks and Romans, each risen to a mighty nation, met again.

The Greeks, or Hellenes as they called themselves, seem to have been only one of a number of kindred tribes who occupied not only the shores of the Ægean, but Thrace, Macedonia, a considerable part of Asia Minor, and other neighboring regions. The Greeks developed in intellect more rapidly than their neighbors, outdistanced them in the race for civilization, forgot these poor relations, and grouped them with the rest of outside mankind under the scornful name "barbarians."

Why it was that the Greeks were thus specially stimulated beyond their brethren we do not know. It has long been one of the commonplaces of history to declare them the result of their environment. It is pointed out that in Greece they lived amid precipitous mountains, where, as hunters, they became strong and venturesome, independent and self-reliant. A sea of islands lay all around; and while an open ocean might only have awed and intimidated them, this ever-luring prospect of shore beyond shore rising in turn on the horizon made them sailors, made them friendly traffickers among themselves. Always meeting new faces, driving new bargains, they became alert, quick-witted, progressive, the foremost race of all the ancient world.

They do not seem to have been a creative folk. They only adapted and carried to a higher point what they learned from the older nations with whom they now came in contact. Phœnicia supplied them with an alphabet, and they began the writing of books. Egypt showed them her records, and, improving on her idea, they became historians. So far as we know, the earliest real "histories" were written in Greece; that is, the earliest accounts of a whole people, an entire series of events, as opposed to the merely individual statements on the Egyptian monuments, the personal, boastful clamor of some king.

Before we reach this period of written history we know that the Greeks had long been civilized. Their own legends scarce reach back farther than the first founding of Athens,[1] which they place about B.C. 1500. Yet recent excavations in Crete have revealed the remains of a civilization which must have antedated that by several centuries.

But we grope in darkness! The most ancient Greek book that has come down to us is the *Iliad*, with its tale of the great war against Troy.[2] Critics will not permit us to call the *Iliad* a history, because it was not composed, or at least not written down, until some centuries after the events of which it tells. Moreover, it poetizes its theme, doubtless enlarges its pictures, brings gods and goddesses before our eyes, instead of severely excluding everything except what the blind bard perchance could personally vouch for.

Still both the *Iliad* and the *Odyssey* are good enough history for most of us, in that they give a full outline of Grecian life and society as Homer knew it. We see the little, petty states, with their chiefs all-powerful, and the people quite ignored. We see the heroes driving to battle in their chariots, guarded by shield and helmet, flourishing sword and spear. We learn what Ulysses did not know of foreign lands. We hear Achilles' famed lament amid the dead, and note the vague glimmering idea of a future life, which the Greeks had caught perhaps from the Egyptians, perhaps from the suggestive land of dreams.

With the year B.C. 776 we come in contact with a clear marked chronology. The Greeks themselves reckoned from that date by means of olympiads or intervals between the Olympic games. The story becomes clear. The autocratic little city kings, governing almost as they pleased, have everywhere been displaced by oligarchies. The few leading nobles may name one of themselves to bear rule, but the real power lies divided among the class. Then, with the growing prominence of the Pythian games[3] we come upon a new stage of national development. The various cities begin to form alliances, to recognize the fact that they may be made safer and happier

[1] See *Theseus Founds Athens*, page 45.
[2] See *Fall of Troy*, page 70.
[3] See *Pythian Games at Delphi*, page 181.

by a larger national life. The sense of brotherhood begins to extend beyond the circle of personal acquaintance.

This period was one of lawmaking, of experimenting. The traditions, the simple customs of the old kingly days, were no longer sufficient for the guidance of the larger cities, the more complicated circles of society, which were growing up. It was no longer possible for a man who did not like his tribe to abandon it and wander elsewhere with his family and herds. The land was too fully peopled for that. The dissatisfied could only endure and grumble and rebel. One system of law after another was tried and thrown aside. The class on whom in practice a rule bore most hard, would refuse longer assent to it. There were uprisings, tumults, bloody frays.

Sparta, at this time the most prominent of the Greek cities, evolved a code which made her in some ways the wonder of ancient days. The state was made all-powerful; it took entire possession of the citizen, with the purpose of making him a fighter, a strong defender of himself and of his country. His home life was almost obliterated, or, if you like, the whole city was made one huge family. All men ate in common; youth was severely restrained; its training was all for physical hardihood. Modern socialism, communism, have seldom ventured further in theory than the Spartans went in practice. The result seems to have been the production of a race possessed of tremendous bodily power and courage, but of stunted intellectual growth. The great individual minds of Greece, the thinkers, the creators, did not come from Sparta.

In Athens a different *régime* was meanwhile developing Hellenes of another type. A realization of how superior the Greeks were to earlier races, of what vast strides man was making in intelligence and social organization, can in no way be better gained than by comparing the law code of the Babylonian Hammurabi with that of Solon in Athens.[1] A period of perhaps sixteen hundred years separates the two, but the difference in their mental power is wider still.

While the Greeks were thus forging rapidly ahead, their ancient kindred, the Latins, were also progressing, though at a

[1] See *Solon's Legislation*, page 203, and *Compilation of the Earliest Code*, page 14.

rate less dazzling. The true date of Rome's founding we do not know. Her own legends give B.C. 753.[1] But recent excavations on the Palatine hill show that it was already fortified at a much earlier period. Rome, we believe, was originally a frontier fortress erected by the Latins to protect them from the attacks of the non-Aryan races among whom they had intruded. This stronghold became ever more numerously peopled, until it grew into an individual state separate from the other Latin cities.

The Romans passed through the vicissitudes which we have already noted in Greece as characteristic of the Aryan development. The early war leader became an absolute king, his power tended to become hereditary, but its abuse roused the more powerful citizens to rebellion, and the kingdom vanished in an oligarchy.[2] This last change occurred in Rome about B.C. 510, and it was attended by such disasters that the city sank back into a condition that was almost barbarous when compared with her opulence under the Tarquin kings.

It was soon after this that the Persians, ignorant of their own decadence, and dreaming still of world power, resolved to conquer the remaining little states lying scarce known along the boundaries of their empire. They attacked the Greeks, and at Marathon (B.C. 490) and Salamis (B.C. 480) were hurled back and their power broken.[3]

This was a world event, one of the great turning points, a decision that could not have been otherwise if man was really to progress. The degenerate, enfeebled, half-Semitized Aryans of Asia were not permitted to crush the higher type which was developing in Europe. The more vigorous bodies and far abler brains of the Greeks enabled them to triumph over all the hordes of their opponents. The few conquered the many; and the following era became one of European progress, not of Asiatic stagnation.

[1] See *The Foundation of Rome*, page 116.
[2] See *Rome Established as a Republic*, page 300.
[3] See *Battle of Marathon*, page 322, and *Invasion of Greece*, page 354.

[FOR THE NEXT SECTION OF THIS GENERAL SURVEY SEE VOLUME II.]

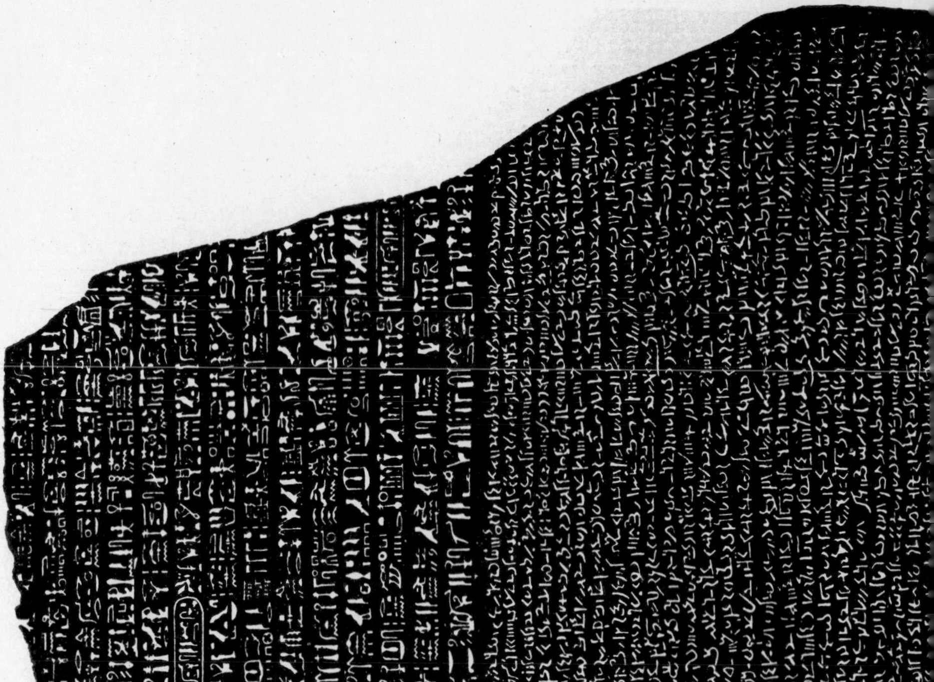

THE TRILINGUAL INSCRIPTION OF THE ROSETTA STONE. IN HIEROGLYPHIC, DEMOTIC, AND GREEK CHARACTERS. BRITISH MUSEUM, LONDON.

(FOR DESCRIPTION OF THIS CUT, SEE OTHER SIDE.)

THE ROSETTA STONE

Almost as interesting as the Rosetta Stone itself is the story of its discovery. During the French occupation of Egypt soldiers were digging out the foundations of a fort, and in the trench the famous tablet was found. At the peace of Alexandra the Rosetta Stone passed to the English, who (1801) housed it in the British Museum, where it remains. The text when translated showed that the inscription is a "decree of the priests of Memphis, conferring divine honors on Ptolemy V, Epiphanes, King of Egypt, B.C. 195," on the occasion of his coronation. Further it commands that the decree be inscribed in the sacred letters (hieroglyphics); the alphabet of the people (enchorial or demotic); and Greek.

It was recognized by the trustees of the British Museum that the problem of the Rosetta Stone was one which would test the ingenuity of the scientists of the world to unfathom, and they promptly published a carefully prepared copy of the entire inscription. Scholars of every nation exhausted their learning to unravel the riddle, but beyond a few shrewd guesses (afterward proved to be quite incorrect) nothing was accomplished for a dozen years. The key was there, but its application required the inspired insight of genius.

Dr. Thomas Young, the demonstrator of the vibratory nature of light, who had perhaps the most versatile profundity of knowledge and the keenest scientific imagination of his generation, undertook the task.

Accident had called Young's attention to the Rosetta Stone, and his rapacity for knowledge led him to speculate as to the possible aid this trilingual inscription might offer in the solution of Egyptian problems. Having an amazing faculty for the acquisition of languages, he, in one short year, had mastered Coptic, after having assured himself that it was the nearest existing approach to the ancient Egyptian language, and had even made a tentative attempt at the translation of the Egyptian scroll. This was the very beginning of our knowledge of the meaning of hieroglyphics.

The specific discoveries that Dr. Young made were : 1, That some of the pictures of the hieroglyphics stand for the names of the objects delineated; 2, that other pictures are at times only symbolic; 3, that plural numbers are represented by repetition; 4, that numerals are represented by dashes; 5, that hieroglyphics may read either from the right or from the left, but always from the direction in which the animals and human figures face : 6, that a graven oval ring surrounds proper names, making a cartouche; 7, that the cartouches of the Rosetta Stone stand for the name of Ptolemy alone; 8, that the presence of a female figure after such cartouches always denotes the female sex; 9, that within the cartouches the hieroglyphic symbols have an actual phonetic value, either alphabetic or syllabic; and 10, that several dissimilar characters may have the same phonetic value.

K A L A Re Sa W Sa Re M Ha Her Re M T

Kaharesapusaremkaherremt.

AN EGYPTIAN PROPER NAME SPELLED OUT IN FULL BY MEANS OF ALPHABETICAL AND SYLLABIC SIGNS.

Dr. Young was certainly on the right track, and very near the complete discovery; unfortunately he failed to take the next step, which was to learn that the use of an alphabet was not confined to proper names. This grand secret Young missed; his French successor, Champollion, ferreted it out from the foundation he had laid. The "Enigma of the Sphinx" was practically solved, and the secrets held by the monuments of Egypt for so many centuries were disclosed to the world. Champollion proved that the Egyptians had developed an alphabet—neglecting the vowels, as did also the early Semitic alphabet—centuries before the Phœnicians were heard of in history. Some of these pictures are purely alphabetical in character, some are otherwise symbolic. Some characters represent syllables, others again stand as representatives of sounds, and once again, as representatives of things; hence the difficulties and complications it presented.

DAWN OF CIVILIZATION

B.C. 5867 [1]

G. C. C. MASPERO

It is a far cry to hark back to 11,000 years before Christ, yet borings in the valley of the Nile, whence comes the first recorded history of the human race, have unveiled to the light pottery and other relics of civilization that, at the rate of deposits of the Nile, must have taken at least that number of years to cover.

Nature takes countless thousands of years to form and build up her limestone hills, but buried deep in these we find evidences of a stone age wherein man devised and made himself edged tools and weapons of rudely chipped stone. These shaped, edged implements, we have learned, were made by white-heating a suitable flint or stone and tracing thereon with cold water the pattern desired, just as practised by the Indians of the American continent, and in our day by the manufacturers of ancient (*sic*) arrow-, spear-, and axe-heads. This shows a civilization that has learned the method of artificially producing fire, and its uses.

Egypt is the monumental land of the earth, as the Egyptians are the monumental people of history. The first human monarch to reign over all Egypt was Menes, the founder of Memphis. As the gate of Africa, Egypt has always held an important position in world-politics. Its ancient wealth and power were enormous. Inclusive of the Soudan, its population is now more than eight millions. Its present importance is indicated by its relations to England. Historians vary in their compilations of Egyptian chronology. The epoch of Menes is fixed by Bunsen at B.C. 3643, by Lepsius at B.C. 3892, and by Poole at B.C. 2717. Before Menes Egypt was divided into independent kingdoms. It has always been a country of mysteries, with the mighty Nile, and its inundations, so little understood by the ancients; its trackless desert; its camels and caravans; its tombs and temples; its obelisks and pyramids, its groups of gods: Ra, Osiris, Isis, Apis, Horus, Hathor—the very names breathe suggestions of mystery, cruelty, pomp, and power. In the sciences and in the industrial arts the ancient Egyptians were highly cultivated. Much Egyptian literature has come down to us, but it is unsystematic and entirely devoid of style, being without lofty ideas or charms. In art, however, Egypt may be placed next to Greece, particularly in architecture.

The age of the Pyramid-builders was a brilliant one. They prove the magnificence of the kings and the vast amount of human labor at their

[1] Champollion.

disposal. The regal power at that time was very strong. The reign of Khufu or Cheops is marked by the building of the great pyramid. The pyramids were the tombs of kings, built in the necropolis of Memphis, ten miles above the modern Cairo. Security was the object as well as splendor.

As remarked by a great Egyptologist, the whole life of the Egyptian was spent in the contemplation of death; thus the tomb became the concrete thought. The belief of the ancient Egyptian was that so long as his body remained intact so was his immortality; whence arose the embalming of the great, and hence the immense structures of stone to secure the inviolability of the entombed monarch.

THE monuments have as yet yielded no account of the events which tended to unite Egypt under the rule of one man; we can only surmise that the feudal principalities had gradually been drawn together into two groups, each of which formed a separate kingdom. Heliopolis became the chief focus in the north, from which civilization radiated over the wet plain and the marshes of the Delta.

Its colleges of priests had collected, condensed, and arranged the principal myths of the local regions; the Ennead to which it gave conception would never have obtained the popularity which we must acknowledge it had, if its princes had not exercised, for at least some period, an actual suzerainty over the neighboring plains. It was around Heliopolis that the kingdom of Lower Egypt was organized; everything there bore traces of Heliopolitan theories—the protocol of the kings, their supposed descent from Ra, and the enthusiastic worship which they offered to the sun.

The Delta, owing to its compact and restricted area, was aptly suited for government from one centre; the Nile valley proper, narrow, tortuous, and stretching like a thin strip on either bank of the river, did not lend itself to so complete a unity. It, too, represented a single kingdom, having the reed and the lotus for its emblems; but its component parts were more loosely united, its religion was less systematized, and it lacked a well-placed city to serve as a political and sacerdotal centre. Hermopolis contained schools of theologians who certainly played an important part in the development of myths and dogmas; but the influence of its rulers was never widely felt.

In the south, Siut disputed their supremacy, and Heracleopolis stopped their road to the north. These three cities thwarted and neutralized one another, and not one of them ever succeeded in obtaining a lasting authority over Upper Egypt. Each of the two kingdoms had its own natural advantages and its system of government, which gave to it a peculiar character, and stamped it, as it were, with a distinct personality down to its latest days. The kingdom of Upper Egypt was more powerful, richer, better populated, and was governed apparently by more active and enterprising rulers. It is to one of the latter, Mini or Menes of Thinis, that tradition ascribes the honor of having fused the two Egypts into a single empire, and of having inaugurated the reign of the human dynasties.

Thinis figured in the historic period as one of the least of Egyptian cities. It barely maintained an existence on the left bank of the Nile, if not on the exact spot now occupied by Girgeh, at least only a short distance from it. The principality of the Osirian Reliquary, of which it was the metropolis, occupied the valley from one mountain to the other, and gradually extended across the desert as far as the Great Theban Oasis. Its inhabitants worshipped a sky-god, Anhuri, or rather two twin gods, Anhuri-shu, who were speedily amalgamated with the solar deities and became a warlike personification of Ra.

Anhuri-shu, like all other solar manifestations, came to be associated with a goddess having the form or head of a lioness —a Sokhit, who took for the occasion the epithet of Mîhît, the northern one. Some of the dead from this city are buried on the other side of the Nile, near the modern village of Mesheikh, at the foot of the Arabian chain, whose deep cliffs here approach somewhat near the river: the principal necropolis was at some distance to the east, near the sacred town of Abydos. It would appear that, at the outset, Abydos was the capital of the country, for the entire nome bore the same name as the city, and had adopted for its symbol the representation of the reliquary in which the god reposed.

In very early times Abydos fell into decay, and resigned its political rank to Thinis, but its religious importance remained unimpaired. The city occupied a long and narrow strip between the canal and the first slopes of the Libyan mountains. A brick fortress defended it from the incursions of the Bedouin, and beside it the temple of the god of the dead reared its naked walls. Here Anhuri, having passed from life to death, was worshipped under the name of Khontamentit, the chief of that western region whither souls repair on quitting this earth.

It is impossible to say by what blending of doctrines or by what political combinations this Sun of the Night came to be identified with Osiris of Mendes, since the fusion dates back to a very remote antiquity; it had become an established fact long before the most ancient sacred books were compiled. Osiris Khontamentit grew rapidly in popular favor, and his temple attracted annually an increasing number of pilgrims. The Great Oasis had been considered at first as a sort of mysterious paradise, whither the dead went in search of peace and happiness. It was called Uit, the Sepulchre; this name clung to it after it had become an actual Egyptian province, and the remembrance of its ancient purpose survived in the minds of the people, so that the "cleft," the gorge in the mountain through which the doubles journeyed toward it, never ceased to be regarded as one of the gates of the other world.

At the time of the New Year festivals, spirits flocked thither from all parts of the valley; they there awaited the coming of the dying sun, in order to embark with him and enter safely the dominions of Khontamentit. Abydos, even before the historic period, was the only town, and its god the only god, whose worship, practised by all Egyptians, inspired them all with an equal devotion.

Did this sort of moral conquest give rise, later on, to a belief in a material conquest by the princes of Thinis and Abydos, or is there an historical foundation for the tradition which ascribes to them the establishment of a single monarchy? It is the Thinite Menes, whom the Theban annalists point out as the ancestor of the glorious Pharaohs of the XVIII dynasty: it is he also who is inscribed in the Memphite chronicles, followed by Manetho, at the head of their lists of human kings, and all Egypt for centuries acknowledged him as its first mortal ruler.

It is true that a chief of Thinis may well have borne such a name, and may have accomplished feats which rendered him famous; but on closer examination his pretensions to reality disappear, and his personality is reduced to a cipher.

"This Menes, according to the priests, surrounded Memphis with dikes. For the river formerly followed the sand-hills for some distance on the Libyan side. Menes, having dammed up the reach about a hundred stadia to the south of Memphis, caused the old bed to dry up, and conveyed the river through an artificial channel dug midway between the two mountain ranges.

"Then Menes, the first who was king, having enclosed a space of ground with dikes, founded that town which is still called Memphis: he then made a lake around it to the north and west, fed by the river; the city he bounded on the east by the Nile." The history of Memphis, such as it can be gathered from the monuments, differs considerably from the tradition current in Egypt at the time of Herodotus.

It appears, indeed, that at the outset the site on which it subsequently arose was occupied by a small fortress, Anbu-hazu —the white wall—which was dependent on Heliopolis and in which Phtah possessed a sanctuary. After the "white wall" was separated from the Heliopolitan principality to form a nome by itself it assumed a certain importance, and furnished, so it was said, the dynasties which succeeded the Thinite. Its prosperity dates only, however, from the time when the sovereigns of the V and VI dynasties fixed on it for their residence; one of them, Papi I, there founded for himself and for his "double" after him, a new town, which he called Minnofiru, from his tomb. Minnofiru, which is the correct pronunciation and the origin of Memphis, probably signified "the good refuge," the haven of the good, the burying-place where the blessed dead came to rest beside Osiris.

The people soon forgot the true interpretation, or probably it did not fall in with their taste for romantic tales. They rather despised, as a rule, to discover in the beginnings of history individuals from whom the countries or cities with which they were familiar took their names: if no tradition supplied them with this, they did not experience any scruples in inventing one. The Egyptians of the time of the Ptolemies, who were guided in their philological speculations by the pronunciation in vogue around them, attributed the patronship of their city to a Princess Memphis, a daughter of its founder, the fabu-

lous Uchoreus; those of preceding ages before the name had
become altered thought to find in Minnofiru or "Mini Nofir,"
or "Menes the Good," the reputed founder of the capital of the
Delta.   Menes the Good, divested of his epithet, is none other
than Menes, the first king of all Egypt, and he owes his existence to a popular attempt at etymology.

The legend which identifies the establishment of the kingdom with the construction of the city, must have originated at
a time when Memphis was still the residence of the kings and
the seat of government, at latest about the end of the Memphite period.   It must have been an old tradition at the time of
the Theban dynasties, since they admitted unhesitatingly the
authenticity of the statements which ascribed to the northern
city so marked a superiority over their own country.   When
the hero was once created and firmly established in his position, there was little difficulty in inventing a story about him
which would portray him as a paragon and an ideal sovereign.

He was represented in turn as architect, warrior, and statesman; he had founded Memphis, he had begun the temple of
Phtah, written laws and regulated the worship of the gods, particularly that of Hapis, and he had conducted expeditions
against the Libyans.   When he lost his only son in the flower
of his age, the people improvised a hymn of mourning to con-
sole him—the "Maneros"—both the words and the tune of
which were handed down from generation to generation.

He did not, moreover, disdain the luxuries of the table, for
he invented the art of serving a dinner, and the mode of eating
it in a reclining posture.   One day, while hunting, his dogs, excited by something or other, fell upon him to devour him.   He
escaped with difficulty and, pursued by them, fled to the shore
of Lake Mœris, and was there brought to bay; he was on the
point of succumbing to them, when a crocodile took him on his
back and carried him across to the other side.   In gratitude he
built a new town, which he called Crocodilopolis, and assigned
to it for its god the crocodile which had saved him; he then
erected close to it the famous labyrinth and a pyramid for his
tomb.

Other traditions show him in a less favorable light.   They
accuse him of having, by horrible crimes, excited against him

the anger of the gods, and allege that after a reign of sixty-two years he was killed by a hippopotamus which came forth from the Nile. They also relate that the Saite Tafnakhti, returning from an expedition against the Arabs, during which he had been obliged to renounce the pomp and luxuries of life, had solemnly cursed him, and had caused his imprecations to be inscribed upon a "stele" [1] set up in the temple of Amon at Thebes. Nevertheless, in the memory that Egypt preserved of its first Pharaoh, the good outweighed the evil. He was worshipped in Memphis, side by side with Phtah and Ramses II.; his name figured at the head of the royal lists, and his cult continued till the time of the Ptolemies.

His immediate successors have only a semblance of reality, such as he had. The lists give the order of succession, it is true, with the years of their reigns almost to a day, sometimes the length of their lives, but we may well ask whence the chroniclers procured so much precise information. They were in the same position as ourselves with regard to these ancient kings: they knew them by a tradition of a later age, by a fragment papyrus fortuitously preserved in a temple, by accidentally coming across some monument bearing their name, and were reduced, as it were, to put together the few facts which they possessed, or to supply such as were wanting by conjectures, often in a very improbable manner. It is quite possible that they were unable to gather from the memory of the past the names of those individuals of which they made up the first two dynasties. The forms of these names are curt and rugged, and indicative of a rude and savage state, harmonizing with the semi-barbaric period to which they are relegated: Ati the Wrestler, Teti the Runner, Qeunqoni the Crusher, are suitable rulers for a people the first duty of whose chief was to lead his followers into battle, and to strike harder than any other man in the thickest of the fight.

The inscriptions supply us with proofs that some of these princes lived and reigned:—Sondi, who is classed in the II dynasty, received a continuous worship toward the end of the III dynasty. But did all those who preceded him, and those

[1] The burned tile showing the impression of the stylus, made on the clay while plastic.—ED.

who followed him, exist as he did? And if they existed, do the order and relation agree with actual truth? The different lists do not contain the same names in the same position; certain Pharaohs are added or suppressed without appreciable reason. Where Manetho inscribes Kenkenes and Ouenephes, the tables of the time of Seti I give us Ati and Ata; Manetho reckons nine kings to the II dynasty, while they register only five. The monuments, indeed, show us that Egypt in the past obeyed princes whom her annalists were unable to classify: for instance, they associated with Sondi a Pirsenu, who is not mentioned in the annals. We must, therefore, take the record of all this opening period of history for what it is—namely, a system invented at a much later date, by means of various artifices and combinations—to be partially accepted in default of a better, but without, according to it, that excessive confidence which it has hitherto received. The two Thinite dynasties, in direct descent from the fabulous Menes, furnish, like this hero himself, only a tissue of romantic tales and miraculous legends in the place of history. A double-headed stork, which had appeared in the first year of Teti, son of Menes, had foreshadowed to Egypt a long prosperity, but a famine under Ouenephes, and a terrible plague under Semempses, had depopulated the country; the laws had been relaxed, great crimes had been committed, and revolts had broken out.

During the reign of the Boethos a gulf had opened near Bubastis, and swallowed up many people, then the Nile had flowed with honey for fifteen days in the time of Nephercheres, and Sesochris was supposed to have been a giant in stature. A few details about royal edifices were mixed up with these prodigies. Teti had laid the foundation of the great palace of Memphis, Ouenephes had built the pyramids of Ko-kome near Saqqara. Several of the ancient Pharaohs had published books on theology, or had written treatises on anatomy and medicine; several had made laws called Kakôû, the male of males, or the bull of bulls. They explained his name by the statement that he had concerned himself about the sacred animals; he had proclaimed as gods, Hapis of Memphis, Mnevis of Heliopolis, and the goat of Mendes.

After him, Binothris had conferred the right of succession

upon all women of the blood-royal. The accession of the III dynasty, a Memphite one according to Manetho, did not at first change the miraculous character of this history. The Libyans had revolted against Necherophes, and the two armies were encamped before each other, when one night the disk of the moon became immeasurably enlarged, to the great alarm of the rebels, who recognized in this phenomenon a sign of the anger of heaven, and yielded without fighting. Tosorthros, the successor of Necherophes, brought the hieroglyphs and the art of stone-cutting to perfection. He composed, as Teti did, books of medicine, a fact which caused him to be identified with the healing god Imhotpu. The priests related these things seriously, and the Greek writers took them down from their lips with the respect which they offered to everything emanating from the wise men of Egypt.

What they related of the human kings was not more detailed, as we see, than their accounts of the gods. Whether the legends dealt with deities or kings, all that we know took its origin, not in popular imagination, but in sacerdotal dogma: they were invented long after the times they dealt with, in the recesses of the temples, with an intention and a method of which we are enabled to detect flagrant instances on the monuments.

Toward the middle of the third century before our era the Greek troops stationed on the southern frontier, in the forts at the first cataract, developed a particular veneration for Isis of Philæ. Their devotion spread to the superior officers who came to inspect them, then to the whole population of the Thebaid, and finally reached the court of the Macedonian kings. The latter, carried away by force of example, gave every encouragement to a movement which attracted worshippers to a common sanctuary, and united in one cult two races over which they ruled. They pulled down the meagre building of the Saite period, which had hitherto sufficed for the worship of Isis, constructed at great cost the temple which still remains almost intact, and assigned to it considerable possessions in Nubia, which, in addition to gifts from private individuals, made the goddess the richest land-owner in Southern Egypt. Knumu and his two wives, Anukit and Satit, who, before Isis, had been the undisputed suzerains of the cataract, perceived with jealousy their neighbor's prosperity: the civil wars and invasions of the centuries immediately preceding had ruined their temples, and their poverty contrasted painfully with the riches of the new-comer.

The priests resolved to lay this sad state of affairs before King Ptolemy, to represent to him the services which they had rendered and still continued to render to Egypt, and above all to remind him of the generosity of the ancient Pharaohs, whose example, owing to the poverty of the times, the recent Pharaohs had been unable to follow. Doubtless authentic documents were wanting in their archives to support their pretensions: they therefore inscribed upon a rock, in the island of Sehel, a long inscription which they attributed to Zosiri of the III dynasty. This sovereign had left behind him a vague reputation for greatness. As early as the XII dynasty Usirtasen III had claimed him as "his father"—his ancestor—and had erected a statue to him; the priests knew that, by invoking him, they had a chance of obtaining a hearing.

The inscription which they fabricated set forth that in the eighteenth year of Zosiri's reign he had sent to Madir, lord of Elephantine, a message couched in these terms: "I am overcome with sorrow for the throne, and for those who reside in the palace, and my heart is afflicted and suffers greatly because the Nile has not risen in my time, for the space of eight years. Corn is scarce, there is a lack of herbage, and nothing is left to eat: when any one calls upon his neighbors for help, they take pains not to go. The child weeps, the young man is uneasy, the hearts of the old men are in despair, their limbs are bent, they crouch on the earth, they fold their hands; the courtiers have no further resources; the shops formerly furnished with rich wares are now filled only with air, all that was within them has disappeared. My spirit also, mindful of the beginning of things, seeks to call upon the savior who was here where I am, during the centuries of the gods, upon Thot-Ibis, that great wise one, upon Imhotpu, son of Phtah of Memphis. Where is the place in which the Nile is born? Who is the god or goddess concealed there? What is his likeness?"

The lord of Elephantine brought his reply in person. He

described to the king, who was evidently ignorant of it, the situation of the island and the rocks of the cataract, the phenomena of the inundation, the gods who presided over it, and who alone could relieve Egypt from her disastrous plight.

Zosiri repaired to the temple of the principality and offered the prescribed sacrifices; the god arose, opened his eyes, panted, and cried aloud, "I am Khnumu who created thee!" and promised him a speedy return of a high Nile and the cessation of the famine.

Pharaoh was touched by the benevolence which his divine father had shown him; he forthwith made a decree by which he ceded to the temple all his rights of suzerainty over the neighboring nomes within a radius of twenty miles.

Henceforward the entire population, tillers and vinedressers, fishermen and hunters, had to yield the tithe of their income to the priests; the quarries could not be worked without the consent of Khnumu, and the payment of a suitable indemnity into his coffers; finally, metals and precious woods, shipped thence for Egypt, had to submit to a toll on behalf of the temple.

Did the Ptolemies admit the claims which the local priests attempted to deduce from this romantic tale? and did the god regain possession of the domains and dues which they declared had been his right? The stele shows us with what ease the scribes could forge official documents when the exigencies of daily life forced the necessity upon them; it teaches us at the same time how that fabulous chronicle was elaborated, whose remains have been preserved for us by classical writers. Every prodigy, every fact related by Manetho, was taken from some document analogous to the supposed inscription of Zosiri.

The real history of the early centuries, therefore, eludes our researches, and no contemporary record traces for us those vicissitudes which Egypt passed through before being consolidated into a single kingdom, under the rule of one man. Many names, apparently of powerful and illustrious princes, had survived in the memory of the people; these were collected, classified, and grouped in a regular manner into dynasties, but the people were ignorant of any exact facts connected with the names, and the historians, on their own account, were reduced to collect apocryphal traditions for their sacred archives.

The monuments of these remote ages, however, cannot have entirely disappeared: they existed in places where we have not as yet thought of applying the pick, and chance excavations will some day most certainly bring them to light. The few which we do possess barely go back beyond the III dynasty: namely, the hypogeum of Shiri, priest of Sondi and Pirsenu; possibly the tomb of Khuithotpu at Saqqara; the Great Sphinx of Gizeh; a short inscription on the rocks of Wady Maghara, which represents Zosiri (the same king of whom the priests of Khnumu in the Greek period made a precedent) working the turquoise or copper mines of Sinai; and finally the step pyramid where this Pharaoh rests. It forms a rectangular mass, incorrectly oriented, with a variation from the true north of 4° 35′, 393 ft., 8 in. long from east to west, and 352 ft. deep, with a height of 159 ft. 9 in. It is composed of six cubes, with sloping sides, each being about 13 ft. less in width than the one below it; that nearest to the ground measures 37 ft. 8 in. in height, and the uppermost one 29 ft. 2 in.

It was entirely constructed of limestone from neighboring mountains. The blocks are small and badly cut, the stone courses being concave, to offer a better resistance to downward thrust and to shocks of earthquake. When breaches in the masonry are examined, it can be seen that the external surface of the steps has, as it were, a double stone facing, each facing being carefully dressed. The body of the pyramid is solid, the chambers being cut in the rock beneath. These chambers have often been enlarged, restored, and reworked in the course of centuries, and the passages which connect them form a perfect labyrinth into which it is dangerous to venture without a guide. The columned porch, the galleries and halls, all lead to a sort of enormous shaft, at the bottom of which the architect had contrived a hiding-place, destined, no doubt, to contain the more precious objects of the funerary furniture. Until the beginning of this century the vault had preserved its original lining of glazed pottery. Three quarters of the wall surface was covered with green tiles, oblong and lightly convex on the outer side, but flat on the inner: a square projection pierced with a hole served to fix them at the back in a horizontal line by means of flexible wooden rods. Three bands which frame one of the doors are inscribed with the titles of the Pharaoh. The hieroglyphs are raised in either blue, red, green, or yellow, on a fawn-colored ground.

The towns, palaces, temples, all the buildings which princes and kings had constructed to be witnesses of their power or piety to future generations, have disappeared in the course of ages, under the feet and before the triumphal blasts of many invading hosts: the pyramid alone has survived, and the most ancient of the historic monuments of Egypt is a tomb.

COMPILATION OF THE EARLIEST CODE

B.C. 2250

HAMMURABI

The foundation of all law-making in Babylonia from about the middle of the twenty-third century B.C. to the fall of the empire was the code of Hammurabi, the first king of all Babylonia. He expelled invaders from his dominions, cemented the union of north and south Babylonia, made Babylon the capital, and thus consolidated an empire which endured for almost twenty centuries. The code which he compiled is the oldest known in history, older by nearly a thousand years than the Mosaic, and of earlier date than the so-called Laws of Manu. It is one of the most important historical landmarks in existence, a document which gives us knowledge not otherwise furnished of the country and people, the civilization and life of a great centre of human action hitherto almost hidden in obscurity. Hammurabi, who is supposed to be identical with Amraphel, a contemporary of Abraham, is regarded as having certainly contributed through his laws to the Hebrew traditions. The discovery of this code has, therefore, a special value in relation to biblical studies, upon which so many other important side-lights have recently been thrown.

The discovery was made at Susa, Persia, in December and January, 1901-2, by M. de Morgan's French excavating expedition. The monument on which the laws are inscribed, a stele of black diorite nearly eight feet high, has been fully described by Assyriologists, and the inscription transcribed. It has been completely translated by Dr. Hugo Winckler, whose translation (in *Die Gesetze Hammurabis*, Band IV, Heft 4, of *Der Alte Orient*) furnishes the basis of the version herewith presented. Following an autobiographic preface, the text of the code contains two hundred and eighty edicts and an epilogue. To readers of the code who are familiar with the Hebrew Scriptures many biblical parallels will occur.

WHEN Anu the Sublime, king of the Anunaki, and Bel [god of the earth], the Lord of Heaven and earth, who decreed the fate of the land, assigned to Marduk [or Merodach, the great god of Babylon] the over-ruling son of Ea [god of the waters], God of righteousness, dominion over earthly man, and made him great among the Igigi, they called Babylon by his illustrious name, made it great on earth, and founded an ever-lasting kingdom in it [Babylon], whose foundations are laid so solidly as those of heaven and earth; then Anu and Bel called by name me, Hammurabi, the exalted prince, who feared God, to bring about the rule of righteousness in the land, to destroy the wicked and the evil-doers; so that the strong should not harm the weak; so that I should rule over the black-headed people like Shamash [the sun-god], and enlighten the land, to further the well-being of mankind.

Hammurabi, the prince, called of Bel am I, making riches and increase, enriching Nippur and Dur-ilu beyond compare, sublime patron of E-kur [temple of Bel in Nippur, the seat of Bel's worship]; who reëstablished Eridu and purified the worship of E-apsu [temple of Ea, at Eridu, the chief seat of Ea's worship]; who conquered the four quarters of the world, made great the name of Babylon, rejoiced the heart of Marduk, his lord who daily pays his devotions in Saggil [Marduk's temple in Babylon]; the royal scion whom Sin made; who enriched Ur [Abraham's birthplace, the seat of the worship of Sin, the moon-god]; the humble, the reverent, who brings wealth to Gish-shir-gal; the white king, heard of Shamash, the mighty, who again laid the foundations of Sippana [seat of worship of Shamash and his wife, Malkat]; who clothed the gravestones of Malkat with green [symbolizing the resurrection of nature]; who made E-babbar [temple of the sun in Sippara] great, which is like the heavens; the warrior who guarded Larsa and re-newed E-babbar [temple of the sun in Larsa, biblical Elassar, in Southern Babylonia], with Shamash as his helper; the lord who granted new life to Uruk [biblical Erech], who brought plenteous water to its inhabitants, raised the head of E-anna [temple of Ishtar-Nana at Uruk], and perfected the beauty of Anu and Nana; shield of the land, who reunited the scattered inhabitants of Isin; who richly endowed E-gal-mach [temple of Isin]; the protecting king of the city, brother of the god Zamama [god of Kish]; who firmly founded the farms of Kish, crowned E-me-te-ursag [sister city of Kish] with glory, re-doubled the great holy treasures of Nana, managed the temple of Harsag-kalama [temple of Nergal at Cuthah]; the grave of the enemy, whose help brought about the victory; who in-

creased the power of Cuthah; made all glorious in E-shidlam
[a temple], the black steer [title of Marduk] who gored the
enemy; beloved of the god Nebo, who rejoiced the inhabitants
of Borsippa, the Sublime; who is indefatigable for E-zida [tem-
ple of Nebo in Babylon]; the divine king of the city; the
White, Wise; who broadened the fields of Dilbat, who heaped
up the harvests for Urash; the Mighty, the lord to whom come
sceptre and crown, with which he clothes himself; the Elect
of Ma-ma; who fixed the temple bounds of Kesh, who made
rich the holy feasts of Nin-tu [goddess of Kesh]; the provident, solicitous, who provided food and drink for Lagash and
Girsu, who provided large sacrificial offerings for the temple
of Ningirsu [at Lagash]; who captured the enemy, the Elect
of the oracle who fulfilled the prediction of Hallab, who rejoiced the heart of Anunit [whose oracle had predicted vic-
tory]; the pure prince, whose prayer is accepted by Adad [god
of Hallab, with goddess Anunit]; who satisfied the heart of
Adad, the warrior, in Karkar, who restored the vessels for
worship in E-ud-gal-gal; the king who granted life to the city
of Adab; the guide of E-mach; the princely king of the city,
the irresistible warrior, who granted life to the inhabitants of
Mashkanshabri, and brought abundance to the temple of Shid-
lam; the White, Potent, who penetrated the secret cave of the
bandits, saved the inhabitants of Malka from misfortune, and
fixed their home fast in wealth; who established pure sacrificial gifts for Ea and Dam-gal-nun-na, who made his kingdom
everlastingly great; the princely king of the city, who subjected the districts on the Ud-kib-nun-na Canal [Euphrates?]
to the sway of Dagon, his Creator; who spared the inhabitants
of Mera and Tutul; the sublime prince, who makes the face of
Ninni shine; who presents holy meals to the divinity of Nin-
a-zu, who cared for its inhabitants in their need, provided a
portion for them in Babylon in peace; the shepherd of the oppressed and of the slaves; whose deeds find favor before
Anunit, who provided for Anunit in the temple of Dumash in
the suburb of Agade; who recognizes the right, who rules by
law; who gave back to the city of Assur its protecting god;
who let the name of Istar of Nineveh remain in E-mish-mish;
the Sublime, who humbles himself before the great gods; suc-

cessor of Sumula-il; the mighty son of Sin-muballit; the royal scion of Eternity; the mighty monarch, the sun of Babylon, whose rays shed light over the land of Sumer and Akkad; the king, obeyed by the four quarters of the world; Beloved of Ninni, am I.

When Marduk sent me to rule over men, to give the protection of right to the land, I did right and righteousness in . . . . ., and brought about the well-being of the oppressed.

CODE OF LAWS

1. If any one ensnare another, putting a ban upon him, but he cannot prove it, then he that ensnared him shall be put to death.

2. If any one bring an accusation against a man, and the accused go to the river and leap into the river, if he sink in the river his accuser shall take possession of his house. But if the river prove that the accused is not guilty, and he escape unhurt, then he who had brought the accusation shall be put to death, while he who leaped into the river shall take possession of the house that had belonged to his accuser.

3. If any one bring an accusation of any crime before the elders, and does not prove what he has charged, he shall, if it be a capital offence charged, be put to death.

4. If he satisfy the elders to impose a fine of grain or money, he shall receive the fine that the action produces.

5. If a judge try a case, reach a decision and present his judgment in writing; if later error shall appear in his decision, and it be through his own fault, then he shall pay twelve times the fine set by him in the case, and he shall be publicly removed from the judge's bench, and never again shall he sit there to render judgment.

6. If any one steal the property of a temple or of the court, he shall be put to death, and also the one who receives the stolen thing from him shall be put to death

7. If any one buy from the son or the slave of another man, without witnesses or a contract, silver or gold, a male or female slave, an ox or a sheep, an ass or anything, or if he take it in charge, he is considered a thief and shall be put to death.

8. If any one steal cattle or sheep, or an ass, or a pig or a goat, if it belong to a god or to the court, the thief shall pay thirtyfold therefor; if they belonged to a freed man (of the king) he shall pay tenfold; if the thief has nothing with which to pay he shall be put to death.

9. If any one lose an article, and find it in the possession of another: if the person in whose possession the thing is found say "A merchant sold it to me, I paid for it before witnesses," and if the owner of the thing say "I will bring witnesses who know my property," then shall the purchaser bring the merchant who sold it to him, and the witnesses before whom he bought it, and the owner shall bring witnesses who can identify his property. The judge shall examine their testimony— both of the witnesses before whom the price was paid, and of the witnesses who identify the lost article on oath. The merchant is then proven to be a thief and shall be put to death. The owner of the lost article receives his property, and he who bought it receives the money he paid from the estate of the merchant.

10. If the purchaser does not bring the merchant and the witnesses before whom he bought the article, but its owner bring witnesses who identify it, then the buyer is the thief and shall be put to death, and the owner receives the lost article.

11. If the owner do not bring witnesses to identify the lost article, he is an evil-doer, he has traduced, and shall be put to death.

12. If the witnesses be not at hand, then shall the judge set a limit, at the expiration of six months. If his witnesses have not appeared within the six months, he is an evil-doer, and shall bear the fine of the pending case.

14. If any one steal the minor son of another, he shall be put to death.

15. If any one take a male or female slave of the court, or a male or female slave of a freed man, outside the city gates, he shall be put to death.

16. If any one receive into his house a runaway male or female slave of the court, or of a freedman, and does not bring it out at the public proclamation of the major domus, the master of the house shall be put to death.

17. If any one find a runaway male or female slave in the open country and bring them to their masters, the master of the slaves shall pay him two shekels of silver.

18. If the slave will not give the name of the master, the finder shall bring him to the palace; a further investigation must follow and the slave shall be returned to his master.

19. If he hold the slaves in his house, and they are caught there, he shall be put to death.

20. If the slave that he caught run away from him, then shall he swear to the owners of the slave, and he is free of all blame.

21. If any one break a hole into a house [break in to steal], he shall be put to death before that hole and be buried.

22. If any one is committing a robbery and is caught, then he shall be put to death.

23. If the robber is not caught, then shall he who was robbed claim under oath the amount of his loss; then shall the community, and . . . . . on whose ground and territory and in whose domain it was compensate him for the goods stolen.

24. If persons are stolen, then shall the community and . . . . . . pay one mina of silver to their relatives.

25. If fire break out in a house, and some one who comes to put it out, cast his eye upon the property of the owner of the house, and take the property of the master of the house, he shall be thrown into that self-same fire.

26. If a chieftain or a man [common soldier], who has been ordered to go upon the king's highway [for war] does not go, but hires a mercenary, if he withholds the compensation, then shall this officer or man be put to death, and he who represented him shall take possession of his house.

27. If a chieftain or man be caught in the misfortune of the king [captured in battle], and if his fields and garden be given to another and he take possession, if he return and reaches his place, his field and garden shall be returned to him, he shall take it over again.

28. If a chieftain or a man be caught in the misfortune of a king, if his son is able to enter into possession, then the field and garden shall be given to him, he shall take over the fee of his father.

29. If his son is still young, and cannot take possession, a third of the field and garden shall be given to his mother, and she shall bring him up.

30. If a chieftain or a man leave his house, garden and field and hires it out, and some one else takes possession of his house, garden and field and uses it for three years: if the first owner return and claims his house, garden and field, it shall not be given to him, but he who has taken possession of it and used it shall continue to use it.

31. If he hire it out for one year and then return, the house, garden and field shall be given back to him, and he shall take it over again.

32. If a chieftain or a man is captured on the " Way of the King" [in war], and a merchant buy him free, and bring him back to his place; if he have the means in his house to buy his freedom, he shall buy himself free: if he have nothing in his house with which to buy himself free, he shall be bought free by the temple of his community; if there be nothing in the temple with which to buy him free, the court shall buy his freedom. His field, garden and house shall not be given for the purchase of his freedom.

33. If a . . . . . or a . . . . . [from the connection, some man higher in rank than a chieftain] enter himself as withdrawn from the " Way of the King," and send a mercenary as substitute, but withdraw him, then the . . . . or . . . shall be put to death.

34. If a . . . . . [same as in 33] or a . . . . . harm the property of a captain, injure the captain, or take away from the captain a gift presented to him by the king then the . . . . or . . . . shall be put to death.

35. If any one buy the cattle or sheep which the king has given to chieftains from him he loses his money.

35. The field, garden and house of a chieftain, of a man, or of one subject to quit-rent, cannot be sold.

37. If any one buy the field, garden and house of a chieftain, man or one subject to quit-rent, his contract tablet of sale shall be broken [declared invalid] and he loses his money. The field, garden and house return to their owners.

38. A chieftain, man or one subject to quit-rent cannot as-

sign his tenure of field, house and garden to his wife or daughter, nor can he assign it for a debt.

39. He may, however, assign a field, garden or house which he has bought, and holds as property, to his wife or daughter or give it for debt.

40. He may sell field, garden and house to a merchant [royal agents] or to any other public official, the buyer holding field, house and garden for its usufruct.

41. If any one fence in the field, garden and house of a chieftain, man or one subject to quit-rent, furnishing the palings therefor; if the chieftain, man or one subject to quit-rent return to field, garden and house, the palings which were given to him become his property.

42. If any one take over a field to till it, and obtain no harvest therefrom, it must be proved that he did no work on the field, and he must deliver grain, just as his neighbor raised, to the owner of the field.

43. If he do not till the field, but let it lie fallow, he shall give grain like his neighbor's to the owner of the field, and the field which he let lie fallow he must plow and sow and return to its owner.

44. If any one take over a waste-lying field to make it arable, but is lazy, and does not make it arable, he shall plow the fallow field in the fourth year, harrow it and till it, and give it back to its owner and for each ten *gan* [a measure of area] ten *gur* [dry measure] of grain shall be paid.

45. If a man rent his field for tillage for a fixed rental, and receive the rent of his field, but bad weather come and destroy the harvest, the injury falls upon the tiller of the soil.

46. If he do not receive a fixed rental for his field, but lets it on half or third shares of the harvest, the grain on the field shall be divided proportionately between the tiller and the owner.

47. If the tiller, because he did not succeed in the first year, has had the soil tilled by others, the owner may raise no objection; the field has been cultivated and he receives the harvest according to agreement.

48. If any one owe a debt for a loan, and a storm prostrates the grain, or the harvest fail, or the grain does not grow for

lack of water; in that year he need not give his creditor any grain, he washes his debt-tablet in water [a symbolic action indicating the inability to pay] and pays no rent for this year.

49. If any one take money from a merchant, and give the merchant a field tillable for corn or sesame and order him to plant corn or sesame in the field, and to harvest the crop; if the cultivator plant corn or sesame in the field, at the harvest the corn or sesame that is in the field shall belong to the owner of the field and he shall pay corn as rent, for the money he received from the merchant, and the livelihood of the cultivator shall he give to the merchant.

50. If he give a cultivated corn-field or a cultivated sesame-field, the corn or sesame in the field shall belong to the owner of the field, and he shall return the money to the merchant as rent.

51. If he have no money to repay, then he shall pay in corn or sesame in place of the money as rent for what he received from the merchant, according to the royal tariff.

52. If the cultivator do not plant corn or sesame in the field, the debtor's contract is not weakened.

53. If any one be too lazy to keep his dam in proper condition, and does not so keep it; if then the dam break and all the fields be flooded, then shall he in whose dam the break occurred be sold for money, and the money shall replace the corn which he has caused to be ruined.

54. If he be not able to replace the corn, then he and his possessions shall be divided among the farmers whose corn he has flooded.

55. If any one open his ditches to water his crop, but is careless, and the water flood the field of his neighbor, then he shall pay his neighbor corn for his loss.

56. If a man let in the water, and the water overflow the plantation of his neighbor, he shall pay ten *gur* of corn for every ten *gan* of land.

57. If a shepherd, without the permission of the owner of the field, and without the knowledge of the owner of the sheep, lets the sheep into a field to graze, then the owner of the field shall harvest his crop, and the shepherd, who had pastured his

flock there without permission of the owner of the field, shall pay to the owner twenty *gur* of corn for every ten *gan*.

58. If after the flocks have left the pasture and been shut up in the common fold at the city gate, any shepherd let them into a field and they graze there, this shepherd shall take possession of the field which he has allowed to be grazed on, and at the harvest he must pay sixty *gur* of corn for every ten *gan*.

59. If any man, without the knowledge of the owner of a garden, fell a tree in a garden he shall pay half a mina in money.

60. If any one give over a field to a gardener, for him to plant it as a garden, if he work at it, and care for it for four years, in the fifth year the owner and the gardener shall divide it, the owner taking his part in charge.

61. If the gardener has not completed the planting of the field, leaving one part unused, this shall be assigned to him as his.

62. If he do not plant the field that was given over to him as a garden, if it be arable land [for corn or sesame] the gardener shall pay the owner the produce of the field for the years that he let it lie fallow, according to the product of neighboring fields, put the field in arable condition and return it to its owner.

63. If he transform waste land into arable fields and return it to its owner, the latter shall pay him for one year ten *gur* for ten *gan*.

64. If any one hand over his garden to a gardener to work, the gardener shall pay to its owner two-thirds of the produce of the garden, for so long as he has it in possession, and the other third shall he keep.

65. If the gardener do not work in the garden and the product fall off, the gardener shall pay in proportion to other neighboring gardens.

[Here a portion of the text is missing, apparently comprising thirty-five paragraphs.]

100. . . . interest for the money, as much as he has received, he shall give a note therefor, and on the day, when they settle, pay to the merchant.

101. If there are no mercantile arrangements in the place whither he went, he shall leave the entire amount of money which he received with the broker to give to the merchant.

102. If a merchant intrust money to an agent [broker] for some investment, and the broker suffer a loss in the place to which he goes, he shall make good the capital to the merchant.

103. If, while on the journey, an enemy take away from him anything that he had, the broker shall swear by God [take an oath] and be free of obligation.

104. If a merchant give an agent corn, wool, oil or any other goods to transport, the agent shall give a receipt for the amount, and compensate the merchant therefor. Then he shall obtain a receipt from the merchant for the money that he gives the merchant.

105. If the agent is careless, and does not take a receipt for the money which he gave the merchant, he cannot consider the unreceipted money as his own.

106. If the agent accept money from the merchant, but have a quarrel with the merchant [denying the receipt], then shall the merchant swear before God and witnesses that he has given this money to the agent, and the agent shall pay him three times the sum.

107. If the merchant cheat the agent, in that as the latter has returned to him all that had been given him, but the merchant denies the receipt of what had been returned to him, then shall this agent convict the merchant before God and the judges, and if he still deny receiving what the agent had given him shall pay six times the sum to the agent.

108. If a tavern-keeper [feminine] does not accept corn according to gross weight in payment of drink, but takes money, and the price of the drink is less than that of the corn, she shall be convicted and thrown into the water.

109. If conspirators meet in the house of a tavern-keeper, and these conspirators are not captured and delivered to the court, the tavern-keeper shall be put to death.

110. If a "sister of a god" [one devoted to the temple] open a tavern, or enter a tavern to drink, then shall this woman be burned to death.

111. If an inn-keeper furnish sixty *ka* of *usakani*-drink to .... she shall receive fifty *ka* of corn at the harvest.

112. If any one be on a journey and intrust silver, gold, precious stones, or any movable property to another, and wish to recover it from him; if the latter do not bring all of the property to the appointed place, but appropriate it to his own use, then shall this man, who did not bring the property to hand it over be convicted, and he shall pay fivefold for all that had been intrusted to him.

113. If any one have a consignment of corn or money, and he take from the granary or box, without the knowledge of the owner, then shall he who took corn without the knowledge of the owner out of the granary or money out of the box be legally convicted, and repay the corn he has taken. And he shall lose whatever commission was paid to him, or due him.

114. If a man have no claim on another for corn and money, and try to demand it by force, he shall pay one-third of a mina of silver in every case.

115. If any one have a claim for corn or money upon another and imprison him; if the prisoner die in prison a natural death, the case shall go no further.

116. If the prisoner die in prison from blows or maltreatment, the master of the prisoner shall convict the merchant before the judge. If he was a free-born man, the son of the merchant shall be put to death; if it was a slave, he shall pay one-third of a mina of gold, and all that the master of the prisoner gave he shall forfeit.

117. If any one fail to meet a claim for debt, and sell himself, his wife, his son and daughter for money or give them away to forced labor: they shall work for three years in the house of the man who bought them or the proprietor and in the fourth year they shall be set free.

118. If he give a male or female slave away for forced labor, and the merchant sublease them, or sell them for money, no objection can be raised.

119. If any one fail to meet a claim for debt, and he sell the maid servant who has borne him children, for money, the money which the merchant has paid shall be repaid to him by the owner of the slave and she shall be freed.

120. If any one store corn for safe keeping in another person's house, and any harm happen to the corn in storage, or if the owner of the house open the granary and take some of the corn, or if especially he deny that the corn was stored in his house: then the owner of the corn shall claim his corn before God [on oath], and the owner of the house shall pay its owner for all of the corn that he took..

121. If any one store corn in another man's house he shall pay him storage at the rate of one *gur* for every five *ka* of corn per year.

122. If any one give another silver, gold or anything else to keep, he shall show everything to some witness, draw up a contract, and then hand it over for safe keeping.

123. If he turn it over for safe keeping without witness or contract, and if he to whom it was given deny it, then he has no legitimate claim.

124. If any one deliver silver, gold or anything else to another for safe keeping, before a witness, but he deny it, he shall be brought before a judge, and all that he has denied he shall pay in full.

125. If any one place his property with another for safe keeping, and there, either through thieves or robbers, his property and the property of the other man be lost, the owner of the house, through whose neglect the loss took place, shall compensate the owner for all that was given to him in charge. But the owner of the house shall try to follow up and recover his property, and take it away from the thief.

126. If any one who has not lost his goods, state that they have been lost, and make false claims: if he claim his goods and amount of injury before God, even though he has not lost them, he shall be fully compensated for all his loss claimed [*i.e.*, the oath is all that is needed].

127. If any one point the finger [slander] at a sister of a god or the wife of any one, and cannot prove it, this man shall be taken before the judges and his brow shall be marked [by cutting the skin, or perhaps hair].

128. If a man take a woman to wife, but have no intercourse with her, this woman is no wife to him.

129. If a man's wife be surprised with another man, both

shall be tied and thrown into the water, but the husband may pardon his wife and the king his slaves.

130. If a man violate the wife [betrothed or child-wife] of another man, who has never known a man, and still lives in her father's house, and sleep with her and be surprised, this man shall be put to death, but the wife is blameless.

131. If a man bring a charge against one's wife, but she is not surprised with another man [*delit flagrant* is necessary for divorce], she must take an oath and then may return to her house.

132. If the "finger is pointed" at a man's wife about another man, but she is not caught sleeping with the other man, she shall jump into the river for her husband [prove her innocence by this test].

133. If a man is taken prisoner in war, and there is a sustenance in his house, but his wife leave house and court, and go to another house: because this wife did not keep her court, and went to another house, she shall be judicially condemned and thrown into the water.

134. If any one be captured in war and there is no sustenance in his house, if then his wife go to another house, this woman shall be held blameless.

135. If a man be taken prisoner in war and there be no sustenance in his house and his wife go to another house and bear children; and if later her husband return and come to his home: then this wife shall return to her husband, but the children follow their father.

136. If any one leave his house, run away, and then his wife go to another house, if then he return, and wishes to take his wife back: because he fled from his home and ran away, the wife of this runaway shall not return to her husband.

137. If a man wish to separate from a woman who has borne him children, or from his wife who has borne him children: then he shall give that wife her dowry, and a part of the usufruct of field, garden and property, so that she can rear her children. When she has brought up her children, a portion of all that is given to the children, equal as that of one son, shall be given to her. She may then marry the man of her heart.

138. If a man wishes to separate from his wife who has

borne him no children, he shall give her the amount of her purchase money [amount formerly paid to the bride's father] and the dowry which she brought from her father's house, and let her go.

139. If there was no purchase price he shall give her one mina of gold as a gift of release.

140. If he be a freed man he shall give her one-third of a mina of gold.

141. If a man's wife, who lives in his house, wishes to leave it, plunges into debt, tries to ruin her house, neglects her husband, and is judicially convicted: if her husband offer her release, she may go on her way, and he gives her nothing as a gift of release. If her husband does not wish to release her, and if he take another wife, she shall remain as servant in her husband's house.

142. If a woman quarrel with her husband, and say: "You are not congenial to me," the reasons for her prejudice must be presented. If she is guiltless, and there is no fault on her part, but he leaves and neglects her, then no guilt attaches to this woman, she shall take her dowry and go back to her father's house.

143. If she is not innocent, but leaves her husband, and ruins her house, neglecting her husband, this woman shall be cast into the water.

144. If a man take a wife and this woman give her husband a maid-servant, and she bear him children, but this man wishes to take another wife, this shall not be permitted to him; he shall not take a second wife.

145. If a man take a wife, and she bear him no children, and he intend to take another wife: if he take this second wife, and bring her into the house, this second wife shall not be allowed equality with his wife.

146. If a man take a wife and she give this man a maid servant as wife and she bear him children, and then this maid assume equality with the wife: because she has borne him children her master shall not sell her for money, but he may keep her as a slave, reckoning her among the maid-servants.

147. If she have not borne him children, then her mistress may sell her for money.

148. If a man take a wife, and she be seized by disease, if he then desire to take a second wife he shall not put away his wife, who has been attacked by disease, but he shall keep her in the house which he has built and support her so long as she lives.

149. If this woman does not wish to remain in her husband's house, then he shall compensate her for the dowry that she brought with her from her father's house, and she may go.

150. If a man give his wife a field, garden and house and a deed therefor, if then after the death of her husband the sons raise no claim, then the mother may bequeath all to one of her sons whom she prefers, and need leave nothing to his brothers.

151. If a woman who lived in a man's house, made an agreement with her husband, that no creditor can arrest her, and has given a document therefor: if that man, before he married that woman, had a debt, the creditor cannot hold the woman for it.   But if the woman, before she entered the man's house, had contracted a debt, her creditor cannot arrest her husband therefor.

152. If after the woman had entered the man's house, both contracted a debt, both must pay the merchant.

153. If the wife of one man on account of another man has their mates [her husband and the other man's wife] murdered, both of them shall be impaled.

154. If a man be guilty of incest with his daughter, he shall be driven from the place [exiled].

155. If a man betroth a girl to his son, and his son have intercourse with her, but he [the father] afterward defile her, and be surprised, then he shall be bound and cast into the water [drowned].

156. If a man betroth a girl to his son, but his son has not known her, and if then he defile her, he shall pay her half a gold mina, and compensate her for all that she brought out of her father's house.   She may marry the man of her heart.

157. If any one be guilty of incest with his mother after his father, both shall be burned.

158. If any one be surprised after his father with his chief wife, who has borne children, he shall be driven out of his father's house.

159. If any one, who has brought chattels into his father-in-law's house, and has paid the purchase-money, looks for another wife, and says to his father-in-law: "I do not want your daughter," the girl's father may keep all that he had brought.

160. If a man bring chattels into the house of his father-in-law, and pay the "purchase price" [for his wife]: if then the father of the girl say: "I will not give you my daughter," he shall give him back all that he brought with him.

161. If a man bring chattels into his father-in-law's house and pay the "purchase price," if then his friend slander him, and his father-in-law say to the young husband: "You shall not marry my daughter," then he shall give back to him undiminished all that he had brought with him; but his wife shall not be married to the friend.

162. If a man marry a woman, and she bear sons to him; if then this woman die, then shall her father have no claim on her dowry; this belongs to her sons.

163. If a man marry a woman and she bear him no sons; if then this woman die, if the "purchase price" which he had paid into the house of his father-in-law is repaid to him, her husband shall have no claim upon the dowry of this woman; it belongs to her father's house.

164. If his father-in-law do not pay back to him the amount of the "purchase price" he may subtract the amount of the "purchase price" from the dowry, and then pay the remainder to her father's house.

165. If a man give to one of his sons whom he prefers, a field, garden and house and a deed therefor: if later the father die, and the brothers divide [the estate], then they shall first give him the present of his father, and he shall accept it; and the rest of the paternal property shall they divide.

166. If a man take wives for his sons, but take no wife for his minor son, and if then he die: if the sons divide the estate, they shall set aside besides his portion the money for the "purchase price" for the minor brother who had taken no wife as yet, and secure a wife for him.

167. If a man marry a wife and she bear him children: if this wife die and he then take another wife and she bear him children: if then the father die, the sons must not partition

the estate according to the mothers, they shall divide the dowries of their mothers only in this way; the paternal estate they shall divide equally with one another.

168. If a man wish to put his son out of his house, and declare before the judge: "I want to put my son out," then the judge shall examine into his reasons. If the son be guilty of no great fault, for which he can be rightfully put out, the father shall not put him out.

169. If he be guilty of a grave fault, which should rightfully deprive him of the filial relationship, the father shall forgive him the first time; but if he be guilty of a grave fault a second time the father may deprive his son of all filial relation.

170. If his wife bear sons to a man, or his maid-servant have borne sons, and the father while still living says to the children whom his maid-servant has borne: "My sons," and he count them with the sons of his wife; if then the father die, then the sons of the wife and of the maid-servant shall divide the paternal property in common. The son of the wife is to partition and choose.

171. If, however, the father while still living did not say to the sons of the maid-servant: "My sons," and then the father dies, then the sons of the maid-servant shall not share with the sons of the wife, but the freedom of the maid and her sons shall be granted. The sons of the wife shall have no right to enslave the sons of the maid; the wife shall take her dowry [from her father], and the gift that her husband gave her and deeded to her [separate from dowry, or the purchase money paid her father], and live in the home of her husband: so long as she lives she shall use it, it shall not be sold for money. Whatever she leaves shall belong to her children.

172. If her husband made her no gift, she shall be compensated for her gift, and she shall receive a portion from the estate of her husband, equal to that of one child. If her sons oppress her, to force her out of the house, the judge shall examine into the matter, and if the sons are at fault the woman shall not leave her husband's house. If the woman desire to leave the house, she must leave to her sons the gift which her husband gave her, but she may take the dowry of her father's house. Then she may marry the man of her heart.

173. If this woman bear sons to her second husband, in the place to which she went, and then die, her earlier and later sons shall divide the dowry between them.

174. If she bear no sons to her second husband, the sons of her first husband shall have the dowry.

175. If a state slave or the slave of a freed man marry the daughter of a free man, and children are born, the master of the slave shall have no right to enslave the children of the free.

176. If, however, a state slave or the slave of a freed man marry a man's daughter, and after he married her she bring a dowry from a father's house, if then they both enjoy it and found a household, and accumulate means, if then the slave die, then she who was free born may take her dowry, and all that her husband and she had earned; she shall divide them into two parts, one-half the master for the slave shall take, and the other half shall the free-born woman take for her children. If the free-born woman had no gift she shall take all that her husband and she had earned and divide it into two parts; and the master of the slave shall take one-half and she shall take the other for her children.

177. If a widow, whose children are not grown, wishes to enter another house [remarry], she shall not enter it without the knowledge of the judge. If she enter another house the judge shall examine the estate of the house of her first husband. Then the house of her first husband shall be intrusted to the second husband and the woman herself as managers. And a record must be made thereof. She shall keep the house in order, bring up the children, and not sell the household utensils. He who buys the utensils of the children of a widow shall lose his money, and the goods shall return to their owners.

178. If a "devoted woman" or a prostitute [connected with the temple neither can marry] to whom her father has given a dowry and a deed therefor, but if in this deed it is not stated that she may bequeath it as she pleases, and has not explicitly stated that she has the right of disposal; if then her father die, then her brothers shall hold her field and garden, and give her corn, oil and milk according to her portion, and

satisfy her. If her brothers do not give her corn, oil and milk according to her share, then her field and garden shall be given to a farmer whom she chooses and the farmer shall support her. She shall have the usufruct of field and garden and all that her father gave her so long as she lives, but she cannot sell or assign it to others. Her position of inheritance belongs to her brothers.

179. If a " sister of a god " [whose hire went to the revenue of the temple, counterpart to the public prostitute], or a prostitute, receive a gift from her father, and a deed in which it has been explicitly stated that she may dispose of it as she pleases, and give her complete disposition thereof: if then her father die, then she may leave her property to whomsoever she pleases. Her brothers can raise no claim thereto.

180. If a father give a present to his daughter—either marriageable or a prostitute [unmarriageable]—and then die, then she is to receive a portion as a child from the paternal estate, and enjoy its usufruct so long as she lives. Her estate belongs to her brothers.

181. If a father devote a temple-maid or temple-virgin to God and give her no present: if then the father die, she shall receive the third of a child's portion from the inheritance of her father's house, and enjoy its usufruct so long as she lives. Her estate belongs to her brothers.

182. If a father devote his daughter as a wife of Marduk of Babylon [as in 181], and give her no present, nor a deed; if then her father die, then shall she receive one-third of her portion as a child of her father's house from her brothers, but she shall not have the management thereof. A wife of Marduk may leave her estate to whomsoever she wishes.

183. If a man give his daughter by a concubine a dowry, and a husband, and a deed; if then her father die, she shall receive no portion from the paternal estate.

184. If a man do not give a dowry to his daughter by a concubine, and no husband; if then her father die then her brother shall give her a dowry according to her father's wealth and secure a husband for her.

185. If a man adopt a child and to his name as son, and rear him, this grown son cannot be demanded back again.

186. If a man adopt a son, and if after he has taken him he injure his foster father and mother, then this adopted son shall return to his father's house.

187. The son of a paramour in the palace service, or of a prostitute, cannot be demanded back.

188. If an artisan has undertaken to rear a child and teaches him his craft, he cannot be demanded back.

189. If he has not taught him his craft, this adopted son may return to his father's house.

190. If a man does not maintain a child that he has adopted as son and reared with his other children, then his adopted son may return to his father's house.

191. If a man, who had adopted a son and reared him, founded a household, and had children, wish to put this adopted son out, then this son shall not simply go his way. His adoptive father shall give him of his wealth one-third of a child's portion, and then he may go. He shall not give him of the field, garden and house.

192. If a son of a paramour or a prostitute say to his adoptive father or mother: "You are not my father, or my mother," his tongue shall be cut off.

193. If the son of a paramour or a prostitute desire his father's house, and desert his adoptive father and adoptive mother, and goes to his father's house, then shall his eye be put out.

194. If a man give his child to a nurse and the child die in her hands, but the nurse unbeknown to the father and mother nurse another child, then they shall convict her of having nursed another child without the knowledge of the father and mother and her breasts shall be cut off.

195. If a son strike his father, his hands shall be hewn off.

196. If a man put out the eye of another man, his eye shall be put out.

197. If he break another man's bone, his bone shall be broken.

198. If he put out the eye of a freed man, or break the bone of a freed man, he shall pay one gold mina.

199. If he put out the eye of a man's slave, or break the bone of a man's slave, he shall pay one-half of its value.

200. If a man knock out the teeth of his equal, his teeth shall be knocked out.

201. If he knock out the teeth of a freed man, he shall pay one-third of a gold mina.

202. If any one strike the body of a man higher in rank than he, he shall receive sixty blows with an ox-hide whip in public.

203. If a free-born man strike the body of another free-born man of equal rank, he shall pay one gold mina.

204. If a freed man strike the body of another freed man, he shall pay ten shekels in money.

205. If the slave of a freed man strike the body of a freed man, his ear shall be cut off.

206. If during a quarrel one man strike another and wound him, then he shall swear, "I did not injure him wittingly," and pay the physician.

207. If the man die of his wound, he shall swear similarly, and if he [the deceased] was a free-born man, he shall pay half a mina in money.

208. If he was a freed man, he shall pay one-third of a mina.

209. If a man strike a free-born woman so that she lose her unborn child, he shall pay ten shekels for her loss.

210. If the woman die, his daughter shall be put to death.

211. If a woman of the freed class lose her child by a blow, he shall pay five shekels in money.

212. If this woman die, he shall pay half a mina.

213. If he strike the maid-servant of a man, and she lose her child, he shall pay two shekels in money.

214. If this maid-servant die, he shall pay one-third of a mina.

215. If a physician make a large incision with a operating knife and cure it, or if he open a tumor [over the eye] with an operating knife, and saves the eye, he shall receive ten shekels in money.

216. If the patient be a freed man, he receives five shekels.

217. If he be the slave of some one, his owner shall give the physician two shekels.

218. If a physician make a large incision with the operat-

ing knife, and kill him, or open a tumor with the operating knife, and cut out the eye, his hands shall be cut off.

219. If a physician make a large incision in the slave of a freed man, and kill him, he shall replace the slave with another slave.

220. If he had opened a tumor with the operating knife, and put out his eye, he shall pay half his value.

221. If a physician heal the broken bone or diseased soft part of a man, the patient shall pay the physician five shekels in money.

222. If he were a freed man he shall pay three shekels.

223. If he were a slave his owner shall pay the physician two shekels.

224. If a veterinary surgeon perform a serious operation on an ass or an ox, and cure it, the owner shall pay the surgeon one-sixth of a shekel as fee.

225. If he perform a serious operation on an ass or ox, and kill it, he shall pay the owner one-fourth of its value.

226. If a barber, without the knowledge of his master, cut the sign of a slave on a slave not to be sold, the hands of this barber shall be cut off.

227. If any one deceive a barber, and have him mark a slave not for sale with the sign of a slave, he shall be put to death, and buried in his house. The barber shall swear: "I did not mark him wittingly," and shall be guiltless.

228. If a builder build a house for some one and complete it, he shall give him a fee of two shekels in money for each *sar* of surface.

229. If a builder build a house for some one, and does not construct it properly, and the house which he built fall in and kill its owner, then that builder shall be put to death.

230. If it kill the son of the owner the son of that builder shall be put to death.

231. If it kill a slave of the owner, then he shall pay slave for slave to the owner of the house.

232. If it ruin goods, he shall make compensation for all that has been ruined, and inasmuch as he did not construct properly this house which he built and it fell, he shall reërect the house from his own means.

233. If a builder build a house for some one, even though he has not yet completed it; if then the walls seem toppling, the builder must make the walls solid from his own means.

234. If a shipbuilder build a boat of sixty *gur* for a man, he shall pay him a fee of two shekels in money.

235. If a shipbuilder build a boat for some one, and do not make it tight, if during that same year that boat is sent away and suffers injury, the shipbuilder shall take the boat apart and put it together tight at his own expense. The tight boat he shall give to the boat owner.

236. If a man rent his boat to a sailor, and the sailor is careless, and the boat is wrecked or goes aground, the sailor shall give the owner of the boat another boat as compensation.

237. If a man hire a sailor and his boat, and provide it with corn, clothing, oil and dates, and other things of the kind needed for fitting it: if the sailor is careless, the boat is wrecked, and its contents ruined, then the sailor shall compensate for the boat which was wrecked and all in it that he ruined.

238. If a sailor wreck any one's ship, but saves it, he shall pay the half of its value in money.

239. If a man hire a sailor, he shall pay him six *gur* of corn per year.

240. If a merchantman run against a ferryboat, and wreck it, the master of the ship that was wrecked shall seek justice before God; the master of the merchantman, which wrecked the ferryboat, must compensate the owner for the boat and all that he ruined.

241. If any one impresses an ox for forced labor, he shall pay one-third of a mina in money.

242. If any one hire oxen for a year, he shall pay four *gur* of corn for plow-oxen.

243. As rent of herd cattle he shall pay three *gur* of corn to the owner.

244. If any one hire an ox or an ass, and a lion kill it in the field, the loss is upon its owner.

245. If any one hire oxen, and kill them by bad treatment or blows, he shall compensate the owner, oxen for oxen.

246. If a man hire an ox, and he break its leg or cut the

ligament of its neck, he shall compensate the owner with ox for ox.

247. If any one hire an ox, and put out its eye, he shall pay the owner one-half of its value.

248. If any one hire an ox, and break off a horn, or cut off its tail or hurt its muzzle, he shall pay one-fourth of its value in money.

249. If any one hire an ox, and God strike it that it die, the man who hired it shall swear by God and be considered guiltless.

250. If while an ox is passing on the street [market?] some one push it, and kill it, the owner can set up no claim in the suit [against the hirer].

251. If an ox be a goring ox, and it is shown that he is a gorer, and he do not bind his horns, or fasten the ox up, and the ox gore a free-born man and kill him, the owner shall pay one-half a mina in money.

252. If he kill a man's slave, he shall pay one-third of a mina.

253. If any one agree with another to tend his field, give him seed, intrust a yoke of oxen to him, and bind him to cultivate the field, if he steal the corn or plants, and take them for himself, his hands shall be hewn off.

254. If he take the seed-corn for himself, and do not use the yoke of oxen, he shall compensate him for the amount of the seed-corn.

255. If he sublet the man's yoke of oxen or steal the seed-corn, planting nothing in the field, he shall be convicted, and for each one hundred *gan* he shall pay sixty *gur* of corn.

256. If his community will not pay for him, then he shall be placed in that field with the cattle [at work].

257. If any one hire a field laborer, he shall pay him eight *gur* of corn per year.

258. If any one hire an ox-driver, he shall pay him six *gur* of corn per year.

259. If any one steal a water-wheel from the field, he shall pay five shekels in money to its owner.

260. If any one steal a *shadduf* [used to draw water from the river or canal] or a plow, he shall pay three shekels in money.

261. If any one hire a herdsman for cattle or sheep, he shall pay him eight *gur* of corn per annum.

262. If any one, a cow or a sheep . . . . . [broken off].

263. If he kill the cattle or sheep that were given to him, he shall compensate the owner with cattle for cattle and sheep for sheep.

264. If a herdsman, to whom cattle or sheep have been intrusted for watching over, and who has received his wages as agreed upon, and is satisfied, diminish the number of the cattle or sheep, or make the increase by birth less, he shall make good the increase and profit which was lost in the terms of settlement.

265. If a herdsman, to whose care cattle or sheep have been intrusted, be guilty of fraud and make false returns of the natural increase, or sell them for money, then shall he be convicted and pay the owner ten times the loss.

266. If the animal be killed in the stable by God [an accident], or if a lion kill it, the herdsman shall declare his innocence before God, and the owner bears the accident in the stable.

267. If the herdsman overlook something, and an accident happen in the stable, then the herdsman is at fault for the accident which he has caused in the stable, and he must compensate the owner for the cattle or sheep.

268. If any one hire an ox for threshing, the amount of the hire is twenty *ka* of corn.

269. If he hire an ass for threshing, the hire is twenty *ka* of corn.

270. If he hire a young animal for threshing, the hire is ten *ka* of corn.

271. If any one hire oxen, cart and driver, he shall pay one hundred and eighty *ka* of corn per day.

272. If any one hire a cart alone, he shall pay forty *ka* of corn per day.

273. If any one hire a day laborer, he shall pay him from the New Year until the fifth month [April to August, when days are long and work hard] six gerahs in money per day; from the sixth month to the end of the year he shall give him five gerahs per day.

274. If any one hire a skilled artisan, he shall pay as wages of the . . . . . . five gerahs, as wages of the potter five gerahs, of a tailor five gerahs, of . . . . . . gerahs, ... of . . . . . gerahs . . . . . of . . . . . gerahs, of a carpenter four gerahs, of a rope-maker four gerahs, of . . . . . gerahs, of a mason . . . . . . gerahs per day.

275. If any one hire a ferryboat, he shall pay three gerahs in money per day

276. If he hire a freight-boat, he shall pay two and one-half gerahs per day.

277. If any one hire a ship of sixty *gur*, he shall pay one-sixth of a shekel in money as its hire per day.

278. If any one buy a male or female slave, and before a month has elapsed the *benu*-disease be developed, he shall return the slave to the seller, and receive the money which he had paid.

279. If any one buy a male or female slave, and a third party claim it, the seller is liable for the claim.

280. If while in a foreign country a man buy a male or female slave belonging to another [of his own country]: if when he return home the owner of the male or female slave recognize it: if the male or female slave be a native of the country, he shall give them back without any money.

281. If they are from another country, the buyer shall declare the amount of money he paid before God, and the owner shall give the money paid therefor to the merchant, and keep the male or female slave.

282. If a slave say to his master: "You are not my master," if they convict him his master shall cut off his ear.

THE EPILOGUE

Laws of justice which Hammurabi, the wise king, established. A righteous law, and pious statute did he teach the land. Hammurabi, the protecting king am I. I have not withdrawn myself from the men, whom Bel gave to me, the rule over whom Marduk gave to me, I was not negligent, but I made them a peaceful abiding place. I expounded all great difficulties, I made the light shine upon them. With the mighty weapons which Zamama and Ishtar intrusted to me, with the keen vision with which Ea endowed me, with the wisdom that Marduk gave me, I have uprooted the enemy above and below [in north and south], subdued the earth, brought prosperity to the land, guaranteed security to the inhabitants in their homes; a disturber was not permitted The great gods have called me, I am the salvation-bearing shepherd [ruler], whose staff [sceptre] is straight [just], the good shadow that is spread over my city; on my breast I cherish the inhabitants of the land of Sumer and Akkad [Babylonia]; in my shelter I have let them repose in peace; in my deep wisdom have I inclosed them. That the strong might not injure the weak, in order to protect the widows and orphans, I have in Babylon the city where Anu and Bel raise high their head, in E-Sagil, the Temple, whose foundations stand firm as heaven and earth, in order to bespeak justice in the land, to settle all disputes, and heal all injuries, set up these my precious words, written upon my memorial stone, before the image of me, as king of righteousness.

The king who ruleth among the kings of the cities am I. My words are well considered; there is no wisdom like unto mine. By the command of Shamash [the sun-god], the great judge of heaven and earth, let righteousness go forth in the land: by the order of Marduk, my lord, let no destruction befall my monument. In E-Sagil, which I love, let my name be ever repeated; let the oppressed, who has a case at law, come and stand before this my image as king of righteousness; let him read the inscription, and understand my precious words: the inscription will explain his case to him; he will find out what is just, and his heart will be glad [so that he will say]:

"Hammurabi is a ruler, who is as a father to his subjects, who holds the words of Marduk in reverence, who has achieved conquest for Marduk over the north and south, who rejoices the heart of Marduk, his lord, who has bestowed benefits forever and ever on his subjects, and has established order in the land."

When he reads the record, let him pray with full heart to Marduk, my lord, and Zarpanit, my lady; and then shall the protecting deities and the gods, who frequent E-Sagil, graciously grant the desires daily presented before Marduk, my lord, and Zarpanit, my lady.

In future time, through all coming generations, let the king, who may be in the land, observe the words of righteousness which I have written on my monument; let him not alter the law of the land which I have given, the edicts which I have enacted; my monument let him not mar. If such a ruler have wisdom, and be able to keep his land in order, he shall observe the words which I have written in this inscription; the rule, statute and law of the land which I have given; the decisions which I have made will this inscription show him; let him rule his subjects accordingly, speak justice to them, give right decisions, root out the miscreants and criminals from his land, and grant prosperity to his subjects.

Hammurabi, the king of righteousness, on whom Shamash has conferred right [or law] am I. My words are well considered, my deeds are not equaled, to bring low those that were high, to humble the proud, to expel insolence. If a succeeding ruler considers my words, which I have written in this my inscription, if he do not annul my law, nor corrupt my words, nor change my monument, then may Shamash lengthen that king's reign, as he has that of me, the king of righteousness, that he may reign in righteousness over his subjects. If this ruler do not esteem my words, which I have written in my inscription, if he despise my curses, and fear not the curse of God, if he destroy the law which I have given, corrupt my words, change my monument, efface my name, write his name there, or on account of the curses commission another so to do, that man, whether king or ruler, patesi [priest-viceroy] or commoner, no matter what he be, may the great God [Anu], the Father of the gods, who has ordered my rule, withdraw from him the glory of royalty, break his sceptre, curse his destiny. May Bel, the lord, who fixeth destiny, whose command cannot be altered, who has made my kingdom great, order a rebellion which his hand cannot control; may he let the wind of the overthrow of his habitation blow, may he ordain the years of his rule in groaning, years of scarcity, years of famine, darkness without light, death with seeing eyes be fated to him; may he [Bel] order with his potent mouth the destruction of his city, the dispersion of his subjects, the cutting off of his rule, the removal of his name and memory from the land. May Belit, the great Mother, whose command is potent in E-Kur [the Babylonian Olympus], the Mistress, who hearkens graciously to my petitions, in the seat of judgment and decision [where Bel fixes destiny], turn his affairs evil before Bel, and put the devastation of his land, the destruction of his subjects, the pouring out of his life like water into the mouth of King Bel. May Ea, the great ruler, whose fated decrees come to pass, the thinker of the gods, the omniscient, who maketh long the days of my life, withdraw understanding and wisdom from him, lead him to forgetfulness, shut up his rivers at their sources, and not allow corn or sustenance for man to grow in his land. May Shamash, the great Judge of heaven and earth, who supporteth all means of livelihood, Lord of life-courage, shatter his dominion, annul his law, destroy his way, make vain the march of his troops, send him in his visions forecasts of the uprooting of the foundations of his throne and of the destruction of his land. May the condemnation of Shamash overtake him forthwith; may he be deprived of water above among the living, and his spirit below in the earth. May Sin [the moon-god], the Lord of Heaven, the divine father, whose crescent gives light among the gods, take away the crown and regal throne from him; may he put upon him heavy guilt, great decay, that nothing may be lower than he. May he destine him as fated, days, months and years of dominion filled with sighing and tears, increase of the burden of dominion, a life that is like unto death. May Adad, the lord of fruitfulness, ruler of heaven and earth, my helper, withhold from him rain from heaven, and the flood of water from the springs, destroying his land by famine and want; may he rage mightily over his city, and make his land into flood-hills [heaps of ruined cities]. May Zamama, the great warrior, the first born son of E-Kur, who goeth at my right hand, shatter his weapons on the field of battle, turn day into night for him, and let his foe triumph over him. May Ishtar, the goddess of fighting and war, who unfetters my weapons, my gracious protecting spirit, who loveth my dominion, curse his kingdom in her angry heart; in her great wrath, change his grace into evil, and shatter his weapons on the place of fighting and war. May she create disorder and sedition for him, strike down his warriors, that the earth may drink their blood, and throw down the piles of corpses of his warriors on the field; may she not grant him a life of mercy, deliver him into the hands of his enemies, and imprison him in the land of his enemies. May Nergal, the mighty among the gods, whose contest is irresistible, who grants me victory, in his great might burn up his subjects like a slender reed-stalk, cut off his limbs with his mighty weapons, and shatter him like an earthen image. May Nin-tu, the sublime mistress of the lands, the fruitful mother, deny him a son, vouchsafe him no name, give him no successor among men. May Nin-karak, the daughter of Anu, who adjudges grace to me, cause to come upon his members in E-kur, high fever, severe wounds, that cannot be healed, whose nature the physician does not understand, which he cannot treat with dressing, which, like the bite of death, cannot be removed, until they have sapped away his life.

May he lament the loss of his life–power, and may the great gods of heaven and earth, the Anunnaki altogether inflict a curse and evil upon the confines of the temple, the walls of this E-barra [the Sun temple of Sippara], upon his dominion, his land, his warriors, his subjects and his troops. May Bel curse him with the potent curses of his mouth that cannot be altered, and may they come upon him forthwith

THESEUS FOUNDS ATHENS

B.C. 1235

PLUTARCH

The founding of the city of Athens, apart from the mythological lore which ascribes its name to Athené, the goddess, is credited by the Greeks to Sais, a native of Egypt. The real founder of Athens, the one who made it a city and kingdom, was Theseus; an unacknowledged illegitimate child. The usual myth surrounds his birth and upbringing.

King Ægeus, of Attica, his father, had an intrigue with Æthra. Before leaving, Ægeus informed her that he had hidden his sword and sandals beneath a great stone, hollowed out to receive them. She was charged that should a son be born to them and, on growing to man's estate, be able to lift the stone, Æthra must send him to his father, with these things under it, in all secrecy. These happenings were in Trœzen, in which place Ægeus had been sojourning.

All came about as expected. Theseus, the son, lifted the stone, took thence the deposit and departed for Attica, his father's home. On his way Theseus had a number of adventures which proved his prowess, not the least being his encounter with and defeat of Periphetes, the " clubbearer," so called from the weapon he used.

Theseus had complied with the custom of his country by journeying to Delphi and offering the first-fruits of his hair, then cut for the first time. This first cutting of the hair was always an occasion of solemnity among the Greeks, the hair being dedicated to some god. It will be remembered that Homer speaks of this in the *Iliad*.

One salient fact must be borne in mind in Grecian history, which is that it was a settled maxim that each city should have an independent sovereignty. " The patriotism of a Greek was confined to his city, and rarely kindled into any general love for the common welfare of Hellas." [1]

A Greek citizen of Athens was an alien in any other city of the peninsula. This political disunion caused the various cities to turn against each other, and laid them open to conquest by the Macedonians.

A S he [Theseus] proceeded on his way, and reached the river Cephisus, men of the Phytalid race were the first to meet and greet him. He demanded to be purified from the guilt of bloodshed, and they purified him, made propitiatory offerings,

[1] Smith.

45

and also entertained him in their houses, being the first persons
from whom he had received any kindness on his journey.

It is said to have been on the eighth day of the month Cro-
nion, which is now called Hecatombaion, that he came to his
own city. On entering it he found public affairs disturbed by
factions, and the house of Ægeus in great disorder; for Medea,
who had been banished from Corinth, was living with Ægeus,
and had engaged by her drugs to enable Ægeus to have children. She was the first to discover who Theseus was, while
Ægeus, who was an old man, and feared every one because of
the disturbed state of society, did not recognize him. Consequently she advised Ægeus to invite him to a feast, that she
might poison him.

Theseus accordingly came to Ægeus's table. He did not
wish to be the first to tell his name, but, to give his father an
opportunity of recognizing him, he drew his sword, as if he
meant to cut some of the meat with it, and showed it to Ægeus.
Ægeus at once recognized it, overset the cup of poison, looked
closely at his son, and embraced him. He then called a public
meeting and made Theseus known as his son to the citizens,
with whom he was already very popular because of his bravery.
It is said that when the cup was overset the poison was spilt in
the place where now there is the enclosure in the Delphinium,
for there Ægeus dwelt; and the Hermes to the east of the
temple there they call the one who is "at the door of Ægeus."

But the sons of Pallas, who had previously to this expected
that they would inherit the kingdom on the death of Ægeus
without issue, now that Theseus was declared the heir, were
much enraged, first that Ægeus should be king, a man who was
merely an adopted child of Pandion, and had no blood relationship to Erechtheus, and next that Theseus, a stranger and a
foreigner, should inherit the kingdom. They consequently
declared war.

Dividing themselves into two bodies, the one proceeded to
march openly upon the city from Sphettus, under the command
of Pallas their father, while the other lay in ambush at Garget-
tus, in order that they might fall upon their opponents on two
sides at once. But there was a herald among them named
Leos, of the township of Agnus, who betrayed the plans of the

sons of Pallas to Theseus. He suddenly attacked those who were in ambush, and killed them all, hearing which the other body under Pallas dispersed. From this time forth they say that the township of Pallene has never intermarried with that of Agnus, and that it is not customary amongst them for heralds to begin a proclamation with the words "Acouete Leo," (Oyez) for they hate the name of Leo because of the treachery of that man.

Shortly after this the ship from Crete arrived for the third time to collect the customary tribute. Most writers agree that the origin of this was, that on the death of Androgeus, in Attica, which was ascribed to treachery, his father Minos went to war, and wrought much evil to the country, which at the same time was afflicted by scourges from heaven (for the land did not bear fruit, and there was a great pestilence, and the rivers sank into the earth).

So that as the oracle told the Athenians that, if they propitiated Minos and came to terms with him, the anger of heaven would cease and they should have a respite from their sufferings, they sent an embassy to Minos and prevailed on him to make peace, on the condition that every nine years they should send him a tribute of seven youths and seven maidens. The most tragic of the legends states these poor children when they reached Crete were thrown into the Labyrinth, and there either were devoured by the Minotaur or else perished with hunger, being unable to find the way out. The Minotaur, as Euripides tells us, was

"A form commingled, and a monstrous birth,
 Half man, half bull, in twofold shape combined."

So when the time of the third payment of the tribute arrived, and those fathers who had sons not yet grown up had to submit to draw lots, the unhappy people began to revile Ægeus, complaining that he, although the author of this calamity, yet took no share in their affliction, but endured to see them left childless, robbed of their own legitimate offspring, while he made a foreigner and a bastard the heir to his kingdom.

This vexed Theseus, and determining not to hold aloof, but to share the fortunes of the people, he came forward and offered himself without being drawn by lot. The people all admired his courage and patriotism, and Ægeus finding that his prayers and entreaties had no effect on his unalterable resolution, proceeded to choose the rest by lot. Hellanicus says that the city did not select the youths and maidens by lot, but that Minos himself came thither and chose them, and that he picked out Theseus first of all, upon the usual conditions, which were that the Athenians should furnish a ship, and that the youths should embark in it and sail with him, not carrying with them any weapon of war; and that when the Minotaur was slain, the tribute should cease.

Formerly, no one had any hope of safety; so they used to send out the ship with a black sail, as if it were going to a certain doom; but now Theseus so encouraged his father, and boasted that he would overcome the Minotaur, that he gave a second sail, a white one, to the steersman, and charged him on his return, if Theseus were safe, to hoist the white one, if not, the black one as a sign of mourning. But Simonides says that it was not a white sail which was given by Ægeus, but "a scarlet sail embrued in holm oak's juice," and that this was agreed on by him as the signal of safety. The ship was steered by Phereclus, the son of Amarsyas, according to Simonides.

When they reached Crete, according to most historians and poets, Ariadne fell in love with Theseus, and from her he received the clew of string, and was taught how to thread the mazes of the Labyrinth. He slew the Minotaur, and, taking with him Ariadne and the youths, sailed away. Pherecydes also says that Theseus also knocked out the bottoms of the Cretan ships, to prevent pursuit. But Demon says that Taurus, Minos' general, was slain in a sea-fight in the harbor, when Theseus sailed away.

But according to Philochorus, when Minos instituted his games, Taurus was expected to win every prize, and was grudged this honor; for his great influence and his unpopular manners made him disliked, and scandal said that he was too intimate with Pasiphaë. On this account, when Theseus offered to contend with him, Minos agreed. And, as it was the custom in Crete for women as well as men to be spectators of the games, Ariadne was present, and was struck with the appearance of Theseus, and his strength, as he conquered all competitors. Minos was especially pleased, in the wrestling match, at Taurus's defeat and shame, and, restoring the children to Theseus, remitted the tribute for the future.

As he approached Attica, on his return, both he and his steersman in their delight forgot to hoist the sail which was to be a signal of their safety to Ægeus; and he in his despair flung himself down the cliffs and perished. Theseus, as soon as he reached the harbor, performed at Phalerum the sacrifices which he had vowed to the gods if he returned safe, and sent off a herald to the city with the news of his safe return.

This man met with many who were lamenting the death of the king, and, as was natural, with others who were delighted at the news of their safety, and who congratulated him and wished to crown him with garlands. These he received, but placed them on his herald's staff, and when he came back to the seashore, finding that Theseus had not completed his libation, he waited outside the temple, not wishing to disturb the sacrifice. When the libation was finished he announced the death of Ægeus, and then they all hurried up to the city with loud lamentations: wherefore to this day, at the Oschophoria, they say that it is not the herald that is crowned, but his staff, and that at the libations the bystanders cry out, "Eleleu, Iou, Iou!" of which cries the first is used by men in haste, or raising the pæan for battle, while the second is used by persons in surprise and trouble.

Theseus, after burying his father, paid his vow to Apollo, on the seventh day of the month Pyanepsion; for on this day it was that the rescued youths went up into the city. The boiling of pulse, which is customary on this anniversary, is said to be done because the rescued youths put what remained of their pulse together into one pot, boiled it all, and merrily feasted on it together. And on this day also the Athenians carry about the Eiresione, a bough of the olive tree garlanded with wool, just as Theseus had before carried the suppliants' bough, and covered with first-fruits of all sorts of produce, because the barrenness of the land ceased on that day; and they sing,

> "Eiresione, bring us figs,
> And wheaten loaves, and oil,
> And wine to quaff, that we may all
> Rest merrily from toil."

However, some say that these ceremonies are performed in memory of the Heracleidæ, who were thus entertained by the Athenians; but most writers tell the tale as I have told it.

After the death of Ægeus, Theseus conceived a great and important design. He gathered together all the inhabitants of Attica and made them citizens of one city, whereas before they had lived dispersed, so as to be hard to assemble together for the common weal, and at times even fighting with one another.

He visited all the villages and tribes, and won their consent, the poor and lower classes gladly accepting his proposals, while he gained over the more powerful by promising that the new constitution should not include a king, but that it should be a pure commonwealth, with himself merely acting as general of its army and guardian of its laws, while in other respects it would allow perfect freedom and equality to every one. By these arguments he convinced some of them, and the rest knowing his power and courage chose rather to be persuaded than forced into compliance.

He therefore destroyed the prytanea, the senate house, and the magistracy of each individual township, built one common prytaneum and senate house for them all on the site of the present acropolis, called the city Athens, and instituted the Panathenaic festival common to all of them. He also instituted a festival for the resident aliens, on the sixteenth of the month, Hecatombaion, which is still kept up. And having, according to his promise, laid down his sovereign power, he arranged the new constitution under the auspices of the gods; for he made inquiry at Delphi as to how he should deal with the city, and received the following answer:

> "Thou son of Ægeus and of Pittheus' maid,
> My father hath within thy city laid
> The bounds of many cities; weigh not down
> Thy soul with thought; the bladder cannot drown."

The same thing they say was afterward prophesied by the Sibyl concerning the city, in these words:

"The bladder may be dipped, but cannot drown."

Wishing still further to increase the number of his citizens, he invited all strangers to come and share equal privileges, and they say that the words now used, "Come hither all ye peoples," was the proclamation then used by Theseus, establishing as it were a commonwealth of all nations. But he did not permit his state to fall into the disorder which this influx of all kinds of people would probably have produced, but divided the people into three classes, of Eupatridæ or nobles, Geomori or farmers, Demiurgi or artisans.

To the Eupatridæ he assigned the care of religious rites, the supply of magistrates for the city, and the interpretation of the laws and customs sacred or profane; yet he placed them on an equality with the other citizens, thinking that the nobles would always excel in dignity, the farmers in usefulness, and the artisans in numbers. Aristotle tells us that he was the first who inclined to democracy, and gave up the title of king; and Homer seems to confirm this view by speaking of the people of the Athenians alone of all the states mentioned in his catalogue of ships.

Theseus also struck money with the figure of a bull, either alluding to the bull of Marathon, or Taurus, Minos' general, or else to encourage farming among the citizens. Hence, they say, came the words, "worth ten," or "worth a hundred oxen." He permanently annexed Megara to Attica, and set up the famous pillar on the Isthmus, on which he wrote the distinction between the countries in two trimeter lines, of which the one looking east says,

"This is not Peloponnesus, but Ionia,

and the one looking west says,

"This is Peloponnesus, not Ionia."

And also he instituted games there, in emulation of Heracles; that, just as Heracles had ordained that the Greeks should celebrate the Olympic games in honor of Zeus, so by Theseus' appointment they should celebrate the Isthmian games in honor of Poseidon.

THE FORMATION OF THE CASTES IN INDIA

B.C. 1200

GUSTAVE LE BON[1]   W. W. HUNTER

The institution of caste was not peculiar to India. In Rome there was a long struggle over the connubium. Among the Greeks the right of commensality, or eating together, was restricted. In fact, the phenomena of caste are world-wide in their extent. In India the priests and nobles contended for the first place. India had progressed along the line of ethnic evolution from a loose confederacy of tribes into several nations, ruled by kings and priests, and the iron fetters of caste were becoming more rigidly welded. At first the father of the family was the priest. Then the chiefs and sages took the office of spiritual guide, and conducted the sacrifices. As writing was unknown, the liturgies were learned by heart, and handed down in families. The exclusive knowledge of the ancient hymns became hereditary, as it were. The ministrants increased in number, and thus sprang up the powerful priestly caste.

Then the warrior class arose and grew strong in numbers and power, becoming differentiated from the agriculturists, and forming the military caste. The husbandmen drifted into another caste, and the three orders were rigidly separated by a cessation of intermarriage.

At the bottom came the Sudras, or slave bands, the servile dregs of the population. In course of time, from various influences, the third class became almost eliminated in many provinces. From the cradle to the grave these cruel barriers still intervene between the strata of the people, relentless as fate and insurmountable as death.

GUSTAVE LE BON

IN ancient times the power of kings [in India] was only nominal. In the Aryan village, forming a little republic, the chief, bearing the name of rajah, was secure in his fortress, exercising full sway. Such was the political system prevailing in India through all the ages, and which has always been respected by the conquerors, whoever they might be. So, for so

---

[1] Translated from the French by Chauncey C. Starkweather.

many centuries back we see arise the first elements of an organization which still endures.

We find here also the beginnings of that system of castes, which, at first indistinct and floating, when the classes sought only to be distinguished from each other, was to become so rigid, when it was constituted under the influence of ethnological reasons, as to dig fathomless abysses between the races.

In the Vedas may be traced the progression of the distance between the priests and the warriors, at first slight, and then increasing more and more. The division of functions did not stop there. While the sacrificing priest was consecrating himself more exclusively day by day to the accomplishment of the sacred rites and to the composition of hymns; while the warrior passed his days in adventurous expeditions or daring feats, what would have become of the land and what would it have produced if others had not applied themselves without ceasing, to cultivate it? A third class became distinct, the agriculturists.

In one of the last hymns of Rig Veda these three classes appear, absolutely separated and already designated by the three words Brahmans, Kchatryas, Vaisyas.

The fourth class, that of the Sudras, was to arise later and to include the mass of conquered peoples when the latter joined the circle of Aryan civilization. The classes, hitherto mingling, now became rigidly separated castes.

The most important of these divisions, and that which was first formed, was the one between the priests and the warriors. The Brahmans, intermediaries between men and the gods, soon became more and more exacting, and finally considered themselves as entirely superior beings and were accepted as such.

The distinction between the warriors and the agriculturists also soon became marked, arising doubtless rather from a difference in fortune than in functions.

The war chief, who returned laden with booty, covered himself with rings of gold, rich vestments, and gleaming arms. He became "rajah," that is to say "shining," for such was the meaning of the word at the Vedic epoch.

Still no absolute barrier between the classes had arisen. They mingled to offer sacrifices, and sometimes ate in common

Heredity of office and profession began to be established. The sacred songs were handed down in families, as were also the functions of the sacrificers. And here among the Vedic Aryans are seen in process of elaboration the germs of the institution which later gained so much power in India and which dominates it still with apparent immutability.

The system of castes has been the corner-stone of all the institutions of India for two thousand years. Such is its importance, and so generally is it misunderstood, that it will be well briefly to explain its origins, sources, and consequences. A system, the result of which is to permit a handful of Europeans to hold sway over two hundred and fifty millions of men deserves the attention of the observer.

The system of castes has existed for more than twenty centuries in India. It doubtless had its origin in the recognition of the inevitable laws of heredity. When the white-skinned conquerors, whom we call Aryans, penetrated India, they found, in addition to other invaders of Turanian origin, black, half-savage populations whom they subjugated. The conquerors were half-pastoral, half-stationary tribes, under chiefs whose authority was counterbalanced by the all-powerful influence of the priests whose duty it was to secure the protection of the gods. Their occupations were divided into classes, that of Brahmans or priests, Kchatryas or warriors, and Vaisyas, laborers or artisans. The last class was perhaps formed by the invaders anterior to the Aryans, whom we have just mentioned.

These divisions corresponded, as is evident, to our three ancient castes, the clergy, the nobility, and the third estate. Beneath these classes was the aboriginal population, the Sudras, forming three quarters of the whole population.

Experience soon revealed the inconveniences which might rise from the mixture of the superior race with the inferior ones, and all the proscriptions of religion tended thereafter to prevent it. "Every country which gives birth to men of mixed races," said the ancient law-giver of the Hindus, the sage Manu, "is soon destroyed together with those who inhabit it." The decree is harsh, but it is impossible not to recognize its truth. Every superior race which has mingled with another too inferior has speedily been degraded or absorbed by it.

The Spaniards in America, the Portuguese in India, are proofs of the sad results produced by such mixtures. The descendants of the brave Portuguese adventurers, who in other days conquered part of India, fill to-day the employments of servants, and the name of their race has become a term of contempt.

Imbued with the importance of this anthropological truth, the Code of Manu, which has been the law of India for so many centuries, and which, like all codes, is the result of long anterior experiences, neglects nothing to preserve the purity of blood.

It pronounces severe penalties against all intermingling of the superior castes between themselves, and especially with the caste of the Sudras. There are no frightful threats which it does not employ to keep the latter apart.

But in the course of the centuries nature triumphed over these formidable prohibitions. Woman always has her charms, no matter how inferior she may be in caste. In spite of Manu, crossings of caste were numerous, and one need not travel India throughout to perceive that, to-day, the populations of all the races are mixed to a large extent. The number of individuals white enough to prove that their blood is quite pure is very restricted. The word caste, taken in its primitive sense, is no longer a synonym of color, as it used to be in Sanscrit, and, if caste had had only formerly prevailing ethnological reasons to invoke, it would have had no reason for continuing. In fact, the primitive divisions of caste have long since disappeared. They were replaced by new divisions, the origin of which is other than the difference of races, except in the case of the Brahmans, who still form the less mixed portion of the population.

Among the causes which have perpetuated the system of castes, the law of heredity has furthermore continued to play a fundamental part. Aptness is inevitably hereditary among the Hindus, and, also inevitably, the son follows the profession of the father. The principle of heredity of the professions being universally admitted, there has resulted the formation of castes as numerous as the professions themselves, and to-day in India castes are numbered by the thousand. Each new profession has for an immediate consequence the formation of a new caste.

The European who comes to India to live soon perceives to what an extent the castes have multiplied in observing the number of different persons whom he is obliged to hire to wait on him. To the two preceding causes of the formations of castes, the ethnological cause, now very weak, and the professional, which is still very strong, are added political office, and the heterogeneity of religious beliefs.

The castes springing from political office might, strictly speaking, be placed in the category of professional castes, but those produced by diversity of religious beliefs should be attached to none of the preceding causes. In theory, that is, only judged by the reading of books, all India would be divided into two or three great religions only. But practically these religions are very numerous. New gods, considered as simple incarnations of ancient ones, are born and die every day, and their votaries soon form a new caste as rigid in its exclusions as the others.

Two fundamental signs mark the conformity of castes, and separate from all the others the persons belonging to them. The first is that the individuals of the same caste cannot eat except among themselves. The second is that they can only marry among themselves.

These two proscriptions are quite fundamental, and the first not less than the second. You may meet by the hundreds in India Brahmans who are employed by the government in the post-office and railway service, or even Brahmans who are beggars. But the humble functionary or wretched mendicant would rather die than sit at table with the viceroy of India.

The quality of Brahmans is hereditary, like a title of nobility in Europe. It is not a synonym of priest, as is generally believed, because it is from this caste that priests are recruited. This caste was formerly so exalted that the rank of royalty was not sufficient to enable one to aspire to the hand of a Brahman's daughter.

The Hindu would rather die than violate the laws of his caste. Nothing is more terrible than for him to lose it. Such loss may be compared to excommunication in the middle ages, or to a condemnation for an infamous crime in modern Europe. To lose his caste is to lose everything at one blow, parents, relations, and fortune. Every one turns his back upon the culprit and refuses to have any dealings with him. He must enter the casteless category, which is employed only for the most abject functions.

As to the social and political consequences of such a system, the only social bond among the Hindus is caste. Outside of caste the world does not exist for him. He is separated from persons of another caste by an abyss much deeper than that which separates Europeans of the most different nationalities. The latter may intermarry, but persons of different castes cannot. The result is that every village possesses as many groups as there are castes represented.

With such a system union against a master is impossible. This system of caste explains the phenomenon of two hundred and fifty millions of men obeying, without a murmur, sixty or seventy thousand strangers[1] whom they detest. The only fatherland of the Hindu is his caste. He has never had another. His country is not a fatherland to him, and he has never dreamed of its unity.

W. W. HUNTER

At a very early period we catch sight of a nobler race from the northwest, forcing its way in among the primitive peoples of India. This race belonged to the splendid Aryan or Indo-Germanic stock from which the Brahman, the Rajput, and the Englishman alike descend. Its earliest home seems to have been in Western Asia. From that common camping-ground certain branches of the race started for the east, others for the farther west. One of the western offshoots built Athens and Sparta, and became the Greek nation; another went on to Italy, and reared the city on the Seven Hills, which grew into Imperial Rome. A distant colony of the same race excavated the silver ores of prehistoric Spain; and when we first catch a sight of ancient England, we see an Aryan settlement fishing in wattle canoes, and working the tin mines of Cornwall. Meanwhile other branches of the Aryan stock had gone forth from the primitive Asiatic home to the east. Powerful bands found

[1] English.

their way through the passes of the Himalayas into the Punjab, and spread themselves, chiefly as Brahmans and Rajputs,
over India.

The Aryan offshoots, alike to the east and to the west, asserted their superiority over the earlier peoples whom they
found in possession of the soil. The history of ancient Europe
is the story of the Aryan settlements around the shores of the
Mediterranean; and that wide term, modern civilization, merely
means the civilization of the western branches of the same race.
The history of India consists in like manner of the history of
the eastern offshoots of the Aryan stock who settled in that
land.

We know little regarding these noble Aryan tribes in their
early camping-ground in Western Asia. From words preserved
in the languages of their long-separated descendants in Europe
and India, scholars infer that they roamed over the grassy
steppes with their cattle, making long halts to raise crops of
grain. They had tamed most of the domestic animals; were
acquainted with iron; understood the arts of weaving and sew-
ing; wore clothes, and ate cooked food. They lived the hardy
life of the comparatively temperate zone; and the feeling of
cold seems to be one of the earliest common remembrances of
the eastern and the western branches of the race.

The forefathers of the Greek and the Roman, of the English and the Hindu, dwelt together in Western Asia, spoke the
same tongue, worshipped the same gods. The languages of
Europe and India, although at first sight they seem wide apart,
are merely different growths from the original Aryan speech.
This is especially true of the common words of family life. The
names for *father, mother, brother, sister,* and *widow* are the
same in most of the Aryan languages, whether spoken on the
banks of the Ganges, of the Tiber, or of the Thames. Thus
the word *daughter,* which occurs in nearly all of them, has been
derived from the Aryan root *dugh,* which in Sanscrit has the
form of *duh,* to milk; and perhaps preserves the memory of the
time when the daughter was the little milkmaid in the primitive
Aryan household.

The ancient religions of Europe and India had a common
origin. They were to some extent made up of the sacred

stories or myths which our joint ancestors had learned while dwelling together in Asia. Several of the Vedic gods were also the gods of Greece and Rome; and to this day the Divinity is adored by names derived from the same old Aryan word (*deva*, the Shining One), by Brahmans in Calcutta, by the Protestant clergy of England, and by Roman Catholic priests in Peru.

The Vedic hymns exhibit the Indian branch of the Aryans on their march to the southeast, and in their new homes. The earliest songs disclose the race still to the north of the Khaibar pass, in Kabul; the later ones bring them as far as the Ganges. Their victorious advance eastward through the intermediate tract can be traced in the Vedic writings almost step by step. The steady supply of water among the five rivers of the Punjab led the Aryans to settle down from their old state of wandering half-pastoral tribes into regular communities of husbandmen. The Vedic poets praised the rivers which enabled them to make this great change—perhaps the most important step in the progress of a race. "May the Indus," they sang, "the far-famed giver of wealth, hear us; [fertilizing our] broad fields with water." The Himalayas, through whose southwestern passes they had reached India, and at whose southern base they long dwelt, made a lasting impression on their memory. The Vedic singer praised "Him whose greatness the snowy ranges, and the sea, and the aerial river declare." The Aryan race in India never forgot its northern home. There dwelt its gods and holy singers; and there eloquence descended from heaven among men; while high amid the Himalayan mountains lay the paradise of deities and heroes, where the kind and the brave forever repose.

The Rig-Veda forms the great literary memorial of the early Aryan settlements in the Punjab. The age of this venerable hymnal is unknown. Orthodox Hindus believe, without evidence, that it existed "from before all time," or at least from 3001 years B.C. European scholars have inferred from astronomical data that its composition was going on about 1400 B.C. But the evidence might have been calculated backward, and inserted later in the Veda. We only know that the Vedic religion had been at work long before the rise of Buddhism in the sixth century B.C. The Rig-Veda is a very old collection of 1017

short poems, chiefly addressed to the gods, and containing 10,-
580 verses.   Its hymns show us the Aryans on the banks of
the Indus, divided into various tribes, sometimes at war with
each other, sometimes united against the "black-skinned"
aborigines.   Caste, in its later sense, is unknown.   Each
father of a family is the priest of his own household.   The
chieftain acts as father and priest to the tribe; but at the
greater festivals he chooses some one specially learned in holy
offerings to conduct the sacrifice in the name of the people.
The king himself seems to have been elected; and his title of
Vis-pat, literally "Lord of the Settlers," survives in the old
Persian Vis-paiti, and as the Lithuanian Wiez-patis in east-cen-
tral Europe at this day.   Women enjoyed a high position; and
some of the most beautiful hymns were composed by ladies and
queens.   Marriage was held sacred.   Husband and wife were
both "rulers of the house" (*dampati*); and drew near to the
gods together in prayer.   The burning of widows on their husbands' funeral pile was unknown; and the verses in the Veda
which the Brahmans afterwards distorted into a sanction for the
practice, have the very opposite meaning.   "Rise, woman,"
says the Vedic text to the mourner; "come to the world of
life.   Come to us.   Thou hast fulfilled thy duties as a wife to
thy husband."

The Aryan tribes in the Veda have blacksmiths, copper-
smiths, and goldsmiths among them, besides carpenters, bar-
bers, and other artisans.   They fight from chariots, and freely
use the horse, although not yet the elephant, in war.   They
have settled down as husbandmen, till their fields with the
plough, and live in villages or towns.   But they also cling to
their old wandering life, with their herds and "cattle-pens."
Cattle, indeed, still form their chief wealth—the coin in which
payment of fines is made—reminding us of the Latin word for
money, *pecunia*, from *pecus*, a herd.   One of the Vedic words
for war literally means "a desire for cows."   Unlike the modern Hindus, the Aryans of the Veda ate beef; used a fermented
liquor or beer, made from the *soma* plant; and offered the same
strong meat and drink to their gods.   Thus the stout Aryans
spread eastward through Northern India, pushed on from behind by later arrivals of their own stock, and driving before

them, or reducing to bondage, the earlier "black-skinned" races. They marched in whole communities from one river valley to another; each house-father a warrior, husbandman, and priest; with his wife, and his little ones, and his cattle.

These free-hearted tribes had a great trust in themselves and their gods. Like other conquering races, they believed that both themselves and their deities were altogether superior to the people of the land, and to their poor, rude objects of worship. Indeed, this noble self-confidence is a great aid to the success of a nation. Their divinities—*devas*, literally "the shining ones," from the Sanscrit root *div*, "to shine"—were the great powers of nature. They adored the Father-heaven,— *Dyaush-pitar* in Sanscrit, the *Dies piter* or *Jupiter* of Rome, the *Zeus* of Greece; and the Encompassing Sky—*Varuna* in Sanscrit, *Uranus* in Latin, *Ouranos* in Greek. *Indra*, or the Aqueous Vapor, that brings the precious rain on which plenty or famine still depends each autumn, received the largest number of hymns. By degrees, as the settlers realized more and more keenly the importance of the periodical rains to their new life as husbandmen, he became the chief of the Vedic gods. "The gods do not reach unto thee, O Indra, nor men; thou overcomest all creatures in strength." Agni, the God of Fire (Latin *ignis*), ranks perhaps next to Indra in the number of hymns addressed to him. He is "the Youngest of the Gods," "the Lord and Giver of Wealth." The Maruts are the Storm Gods, "who make the rock to tremble, who tear in pieces the forest." Ushas, "the High-born Dawn" (Greek *Eos*), "shines upon us like a young wife, rousing every living being to go forth to his work." The Asvins, the "Horsemen" or fleet outriders of the dawn, are the first rays of sunrise, "Lords of Lustre." The Solar Orb himself (Surya), the Wind (Vayu), the Sunshine or Friendly Day (Mitra), the intoxicating fermented juice of the Sacrificial Plant (Soma), and many other deities are invoked in the Veda—in all, about thirty-three gods, "who are eleven in heaven, eleven on earth, and eleven dwelling in glory in mid-air."

The Aryan settler lived on excellent terms with his bright gods. He asked for protection, with an assured conviction that it would be granted. At the same time, he was deeply stirred

by the glory and mystery of the earth and the heavens. Indeed, the majesty of nature so filled his mind, that when he
praises any one of his Shining Gods, he can think of none other
for the time being, and adores him as the supreme ruler.
Verses may be quoted declaring each of the greater deities to
be the One Supreme: "Neither gods nor men reach unto
thee, O Indra!" Another hymn speaks of Soma as "king of
heaven and earth, the conqueror of all." To Varuna also it is
said, "Thou art lord of all, of heaven and earth; thou art king
of all those who are gods, and of all those who are men." The
more spiritual of the Vedic singers, therefore, may be said to
have worshipped One God, though not One alone.

"In the beginning there arose the Golden Child. He was
the one born lord of all that is. He established the earth and
this sky. Who is the God to whom we shall offer our sacrifice?

"He who gives life, he who gives strength; whose command
all the Bright Gods revere; whose shadow is immortality, whose
shadow is death. Who is the God to whom we shall offer our
sacrifice?

"He who, through his power, is the one king of the breath-
ing and awakening world. He who governs all, man and beast.
Who is the God to whom we shall offer our sacrifice?

"He through whom the sky is bright and the earth firm;
he through whom the heaven was established, nay, the highest
heaven; he who measured out the light and the air. Who is
the God to whom we shall offer our sacrifice?

"He who by his might looked even over the water-clouds;
he who alone is God above all gods. Who is the God to whom
we shall offer our sacrifice?"

While the aboriginal races buried their dead in the earth or
under rude stone monuments, the Aryan—alike in India, in
Greece, and in Italy—made use of the funeral-pile. Several
exquisite Sanscrit hymns bid farewell to the dead:—"Depart
thou, depart thou by the ancient paths to the place whither our
fathers have departed. Meet with the Ancient Ones; meet
with the Lord of Death. Throwing off thine imperfections, go
to thy home. Become united with a body; clothe thyself in a
shining form." "Let him depart to those for whom flow the
rivers of nectar. Let him depart to those who, through medi-

tation, have obtained the victory; who, by fixing their thoughts on the unseen, have gone to heaven. Let him depart to the mighty in battle, to the heroes who have laid down their lives for others, to those who have bestowed their goods on the poor." The doctrine of transmigration was at first unknown. The circle round the funeral-pile sang with a firm assurance that their friend went direct to a state of blessedness and reunion with the loved ones who had gone before. "Do thou conduct us to heaven," says a hymn of the later Atharva-Veda; "let us be with our wives and children." "In heaven, where our friends dwell in bliss—having left behind the infirmities of the body, free from lameness, free from crookedness of limb—there let us behold our parents and our children." "May the water-shedding Spirits bear thee upward, cooling thee with their swift motion through the air, and sprinkling thee with dew." "Bear him, carry him; let him, with all his faculties complete, go to the world of the righteous. Crossing the dark valley which spreadeth boundless around him, let the unborn soul ascend to heaven. Wash the feet of him who is stained with sin; let him go upward with cleansed feet. Crossing the gloom, gazing with wonder in many directions, let the unborn soul go up to heaven."

By degrees the old collection of hymns, or the Rig-Veda, no longer sufficed. Three other collections or service-books were therefore added, making the Four Vedas. The word Veda is from the same root as the Latin *vid-ere*, to see: the early Greek *feid-enai*, infinitive of *oida*, I know: and the English *wisdom*, or I *wit*. The Brahmans taught that the Veda was divinely inspired, and that it was literally "the *wisdom* of God." There was, first, the Rig-Veda, or the hymns in their simplest form. Second, the Sama-Veda, made up of hymns of the Rig-Veda to be used at the Soma sacrifice. Third, the Yajur-Veda, consisting not only of Rig-Vedic hymns, but also of prose sentences, to be used at the great sacrifices; and divided into two editions, the Black and White Yajur. The fourth, or Atharva-Veda, was compiled from the least ancient hymns at the end of the Rig-Veda, very old religious spells, and later sources. Some of its spells have a similarity to the ancient German and Lithuanian charms, and appear to have come down from the most primitive times, before the Indian and European branches of the Aryan race struck out from their common home.

To each of the four Vedas were attached prose works, called Brahmanas, in order to explain the sacrifices and the duties of the priests. Like the Four Vedas, the Brahmanas were held to be the very word of God. The Vedas and the Brahmanas form the revealed Scriptures of the Hindus—the *sruti*, literally "Things *heard* from God." The Vedas supplied their divinely-inspired psalms, and the Brahmanas their divinely-inspired theology or body of doctrine. To them were afterward added the Sutras, literally "*Strings* of pithy sentences" regarding laws and ceremonies. Still later the Upanishads were composed, treating of God and the soul; the Aranyakas, or "Tracts for the forest recluse;" and, after a very long interval, the Puranas, or "Traditions from of old." All these ranked, however, not as divinely-inspired knowledge, or things "heard from God" (*sruti*), like the Vedas and Brahmanas, but only as sacred traditions—*smriti*, literally "The things *remembered*."

Meanwhile the Four Castes had been formed. In the old Aryan colonies among the Five Rivers of the Punjab, each house-father was a husbandman, warrior, and priest. But by degrees certain gifted families, who composed the Vedic hymns or learned them off by heart, were always chosen by the king to perform the great sacrifices. In this way probably the priestly caste sprang up. As the Aryans conquered more territory, fortunate soldiers received a larger share of the lands than others, and cultivated it not with their own hands, but by means of the vanquished non-Aryan tribes. In this way the Four Castes arose. First, the priests or Brahmans. Second, the warriors or fighting companions of the king, called Rajputs or Kchatryas, literally "of the *royal* stock." Third, the Aryan agricultural settlers, who kept the old name of Vaisyas, from the root *vis*, which in the primitive Vedic period had included the whole Aryan people. Fourth, the Sudras, or conquered non-Aryan tribes, who became serfs. The three first castes were of Aryan descent, and were honored by the name of the Twice-born Castes. They could all be present at the sacrifices, and they worshipped the same Bright Gods. The Sudras were "the slave-bands of black descent" of the Veda. They were distinguished from their "Twice-born" Aryan conquerors as being only "Once-born," and by many contemptuous epithets. They were not allowed to be present at the great national sacrifices, or at the feasts which followed them. They could never rise out of their servile condition; and to them was assigned the severest toil in the fields, and all the hard and dirty work of the village community.

The Brahmans or priests claimed the highest rank. But they seemed to have had a long struggle with the Kchatryas, or warrior caste, before they won their proud position at the head of the Indian people. They afterward secured themselves in that position by teaching that it had been given to them by God. At the beginning of the world, they said, the Brahman proceeded from the mouth of the Creator, the Kchatryas or Rajput from his arms, the Vaisya from his thighs or belly, and the Sudra from his feet. This legend is true so far that the Brahmans were really the brain power of the Indian people, the Kchatryas its armed hands, the Vaisyas the food-growers, and the Sudras the down-trodden serfs. When the Brahmans had established their power, they made a wise use of it. From the ancient Vedic times they recognized that if they were to exercise spiritual supremacy, they must renounce earthly pomp. In arrogating the priestly function, they gave up all claim to the royal office. They were divinely appointed to be the guides of nations and the counsellors of kings, but they could not be kings themselves. As the duty of the Sudra was to serve, of the Vaisya to till the ground and follow middle-class trades or crafts; so the business of the Kchatryas was to fight the public enemy, and of the Brahman to propitiate the national gods.

Each day brought to the Brahmans its routine of ceremonies, studies, and duties. Their whole life was mapped out into four clearly defined stages of discipline. For their existence, in its full religious significance, commenced not at birth, but on being invested at the close of childhood with the sacred thread of the Twice-born. Their youth and early manhood were to be entirely spent in learning the Veda by heart from an older Brahman, tending the sacred fire, and serving their preceptor. Having completed his long studies, the young Brahman entered on the second stage of his life, as a householder. He married, and commenced a course of family duties. When he had reared a family, and gained a practical knowledge of the world, he retired into the forest as a re·luse, for the third period of his life; feeding on roots or fruits, practising his religious duties with increased devotion. The fourth stage was that of the ascetic or religious mendicant, wholly withdrawn from earthly affairs, and striving to attain a condition of mind which, heedless of the joys, or pains, or wants of the body, is intent only on its final absorption into the deity. The Brahman, in this fourth stage of his life, ate nothing but what was given to him unasked, and abode not more than one day in any village, lest the vanities of the world should find entrance into his heart. This was the ideal life prescribed for a Brahman, and ancient Indian literature shows that it was to a large extent practically carried out. Throughout his whole existence the true Brahman practised a strict temperance; drinking no wine, using a simple diet, curbing the desires; shut off from the tumults of war, as his business was to pray, not to fight, and having his thoughts ever fixed on study and contemplation. "What is this world?" says a Brahman sage. "It is even as the bough of a tree, on which a bird rests for a night, and in the morning flies away."

The Brahmans, therefore, were a body of men who, in an early stage of this world's history, bound themselves by a rule of life the essential precepts of which were self-culture and self-restraint. The Brahmans of the present India are the result of 3000 years of hereditary education and temperance; and they have evolved a type of mankind quite distinct from the surrounding population. Even the passing traveller in India marks them out, alike from the bronze-cheeked, large-limbed, leisure-loving Rajput or Kchatryas, the warrior caste of Aryan descent; and from the dark-skinned, flat-nosed, thick-lipped low castes of non-Aryan origin, with their short bodies and bullet heads. The Brahman stands apart from both, tall and slim, with finely-modelled lips and nose, fair complexion, high forehead, and slightly cocoanut shaped skull—the man of self-centred refinement. He is an example of a class becoming the ruling power in a country, not by force of arms, but by the vigor of hereditary culture and temperance. One race has swept across India after another, dynasties have risen and fallen, religions have spread themselves over the land and disappeared. But since the dawn of history the Brahman has calmly ruled; swaying the minds and receiving the homage of the people, and accepted by foreign nations as the highest type of Indian mankind. The position which the Brahmans won resulted in no small measure from the benefits which they bestowed. For their own Aryan countrymen they developed a noble language and literature. The Brahmans were not only the priests and philosophers, but also the lawgivers, the men of science and the poets of their race. Their influence on the aboriginal peoples, the hill and forest races of India, was even more important. To these rude remnants of the flint and stone ages they brought in ancient times a knowledge of the metals and the gods.

As a social league, Hinduism arranged the people into the old division of the "Twice-born" Aryan castes, namely, the Brahmans, Kchatryas, Vaisyas; and the "Once-born" castes, consisting of the non-Aryan Sudras and the classes of mixed descent. This arrangement of the Indian races remains to the present day. The "Twice-born" castes still wear the sacred thread, and claim a joint, although an unequal, inheritance in the holy books of the Veda. The "Once-born" castes are still denied the sacred thread; and they were not allowed to study the holy books, until the English set up schools in India for all classes of the people. But while caste is thus founded on the distinctions of race, it has been influenced by two other systems of division, namely, the employments of the people, and the localities in which they live. Even in the oldest times, the castes had separate occupations assigned to them. They could be divided either into Brahmans, Kchatryas, Vaisyas, and Sudras; or into priests, warriors, husbandmen, and serfs. They are also divided according to the parts of India in which they live. Even the Brahmans have among themselves ten distinct classes, or rather nations. Five of these classes or Brahman nations live to the north of the Vindhya mountains; five of them live to the south. Each of the ten feels itself to be quite apart

from the rest; and they have among themselves no fewer than
1886 subdivisions or separate Brahmanical tribes. In like manner, the Kchatryas or Rajputs number 590 separate tribes in
different parts of India.

While, therefore, Indian caste seems at first a very simple
arrangement of the people into four classes, it is in reality a very
complex one. For it rests upon three distinct systems of division: namely, upon race, occupation, and geographical position.
It is very difficult even to guess at the number of the Indian
castes. But there are not fewer than 3,000 of them which have
separate names, and which regard themselves as separate
classes. The different castes cannot intermarry with each
other, and most of them cannot eat together. The ordinary
rule is that no Hindu of good caste can touch food cooked by a
man of inferior caste. By rights, too, each caste should keep
to its own occupation. Indeed, there has been a tendency to
erect every separate kind of employment or handicraft in each
separate province into a distinct caste. But, as a matter of
practice, the castes often change their occupation, and the lower
ones sometimes raise themselves in the social scale. Thus the
Vaisya caste were in ancient times the tillers of the soil. They
have in most provinces given up this toilsome occupation, and
the Vaisyas are now the great merchants and bankers of India.
Their fair skins, intelligent faces, and polite bearing must have
altered since the days when their forefathers ploughed, sowed,
and reaped under the hot sun. Such changes of employment
still occur on a smaller scale throughout India.

The system of caste exercises a great influence upon the
industries of the people. Each caste is, in the first place, a
trade-guild. It insures the proper training of the youth of its
own special craft; it makes rules for the conduct of the caste-
trade; it promotes good feeling by feasts or social gatherings.
The famous manufactures of mediæval India, its muslins, silks,
cloth of gold, inlaid weapons, and exquisite work in precious
stones—were brought to perfection under the care of the castes
or trade-guilds. Such guilds may still be found in full work in
many parts of India. Thus, in the northwestern districts of
Bombay all heads of artisan families are ranged under their
proper trade-guild. The trade-guild or caste prevents undue

competition among the members, and upholds the interest of its own body in any dispute arising with other craftsmen.

In 1873, for example, a number of the bricklayers in Ahmadabad could not find work. Men of this class sometimes added to their daily wages by rising very early in the morning, and working overtime. But when several families complained that they could not get employment, the bricklayers' guild met, and decided that as there was not enough work for all, no member should be allowed to work in extra hours. In the same city, the cloth dealers in 1872 tried to cut down the wages of the sizers or men who dress the cotton cloth. The sizers' guild refused to work at lower rates, and remained six weeks on strike. At length they arranged their dispute, and both the trade-guilds signed a stamped agreement fixing the rates for the future. Each of the higher castes or trade-guilds in Ahmadabad receives a fee from young men on entering their business. The revenue derived from these fees, and from fines upon members who break caste rules, is spent in feasts to the brethren of the guild, and in helping the poorer craftsmen or their orphans. A favorite plan of raising money in Surat is for the members of the trade to keep a certain day as a holiday, and to shut up all their shops except one. The right to keep open this one shop is put up to auction, and the amount bid is expended on a feast. The trade-guild or caste allows none of its members to starve. It thus acts as a mutual assurance society and takes the place of a poor-law in India. The severest social penalty which can be inflicted upon a Hindu is to be put out of his caste.

Hinduism is, however, not only a social league resting upon caste—it is also a religious alliance based upon worship. As the various race elements of the Indian people have been welded into caste, so the simple old beliefs of the Veda, the mild doctrines of Buddha, and the fierce rites of the non-Aryan tribes, have been thrown into the melting-pot, and poured out thence as a mixture of precious metal and dross, to be worked up into the complex worship of the Hindu gods.

FALL OF TROY

B.C. 1184

GEORGE GROTE

The siege of Troy is an event not to be reckoned as history, although Herodotus, the "Father of History," speaks of it as such, and it would be quite impossible to understand the history and character of the Greek people without a study of the *Iliad* and *Odyssey* poems attributed to " a blind bard of Scio's isle "—immortal Homer. The campaign of the Greek heroes in Asia is to be referred to a hazy point in the past when Europe was just beginning to have an Eastern Question. A vast circle of tales and poems has gathered round this mythical event, and the *Iliad*—Song of Ilium, or Troy—is still a poem of unfailing interest and fascination.

Ilium, or Troy, was a city of Asia Minor, a little south of the Hellespont. It was the centre of a powerful state, Grecian in race and language; and when Paris, son of King Priam, visited Sparta and carried off the beautiful wife of Menelaus, king of Sparta, all the heroes of Greece banded together and invaded Priam's dominions.

The twelve hundred ships that sailed for Troy transported one hundred thousand warriors to the valley of Simois and Scamander. Among them was Agamemnon, "king of men," brother of Menelaus. He was the leader, and in his train were Achilles, " swift of foot "; "god-like, wise " Ulysses, King of Ithaca, the two Ajaxes, and the aged Nestor. The narrative of their adventures is told in the Homeric poems with a power of musical expression, a charm of language, and a vividness of imagery unsurpassed in poetry.

For ten years the besiegers encircled the city of Priam. After many engagements and single combats on " the windy plain of Troy " the great hero of the Greeks, Achilles of Thessaly, is wronged by Agamemnon, who carries away Briseis, a fair captive girl allotted as the spoils of war to the " Swift-footed." The hero of Thessaly thenceforth refuses to join in the war, and sullenly shuts himself up in his tent. It is only when his dear friend Patroclus has been slain by the valiant Hector, eldest son of Priam, that he sallies forth, meets Hector in single combat, and finally slays him. Achilles then attaches the body of Hector to his chariot and insultingly trails it in the dust as he drives three times around the walls of Troy. The *Iliad* closes with the funeral rites celebrated over the corpse of Hector.

WE now arrive at the capital and culminating point of the
Grecian epic—the two sieges and captures of Troy,
with the destinies of the dispersed heroes, Trojan as well as
Grecian, after the second and most celebrated capture and destruction of the city.

It would require a large volume to convey any tolerable idea
of the vast extent and expansion of this interesting fable, first
handled by so many poets, epic, lyric, and tragic, with their
endless additions, transformations, and contradictions,—then
purged and recast by historical inquirers, who, under color of
setting aside the exaggerations of the poets, introduced a new
vein of prosaic invention,—lastly, moralized and allegorized by
philosophers. In the present brief outline of the general field
of Grecian legend, or of that which the Greeks believed to be
their antiquities, the Trojan war can be regarded as only one
among a large number of incidents upon which Hecatæus and
Herodotus looked back as constituting their fore-time. Taken
as a special legendary event, it is, indeed, of wider and larger
interest than any other, but it is a mistake to single it out from
the rest as if it rested upon a different and more trustworthy
basis. I must, therefore, confine myself to an abridged narrative of the current and leading facts; and amid the numerous
contradictory statements which are to be found respecting
every one of them, I know no better ground of preference than
comparative antiquity, though even the oldest tales which we
possess—those contained in the *Iliad*—evidently presuppose
others of prior date.

The primitive ancestor of the Trojan line of kings is Dardanus, son of Zeus, founder and eponymus of Dardania: in the
account of later authors, Dardanus was called the son of Zeus
by Electra, daughter of Atlas, and was further said to have
come from Samothrace, or from Arcadia, or from Italy; but of
this Homer mentions nothing. The first Dardanian town
founded by him was in a lofty position on the descent of Mount
Ida; for he was not yet strong enough to establish himself on
the plain. But his son Erichthonius, by the favor of Zeus, became the wealthiest of mankind. His flocks and herds having
multiplied, he had in his pastures three thousand mares, the
offspring of some of whom, by Boreas, produced horses of pre-

ternatural swiftness. Tros, the son of Erichthonius, and the eponym of the Trojans, had three sons—Ilus, Assaracus, and the beautiful Ganymedes, whom Zeus stole away to become his cup-bearer in Olympus, giving to his father Tros, as the price of the youth, a team of immortal horses.

From Ilus and Assaracus the Trojan and Dardanian lines diverge; the former passing from Ilus to Laomedon, Priam, and Hector; the latter from Assaracus to Capys, Anchises, and Æneas. Ilus founded in the plain of Troy the holy city of Ilium; Assaracus and his descendants remained sovereigns of Dardania.

It was under the proud Laomedon, son of Ilus, that Poseidon and Apollo underwent, by command of Zeus, a temporary servitude; the former building the walls of the town, the latter tending the flocks and herds. When their task was completed and the penal period had expired, they claimed the stipulated reward; but Laomedon angrily repudiated their demand, and even threatened to cut off their ears, to tie them hand and foot, and to sell them in some distant island as slaves. He was punished for this treachery by a sea-monster, whom Poseidon sent to ravage his fields and to destroy his subjects. Laomedon publicly offered the immortal horses given by Zeus to his father Tros, as a reward to any one who would destroy the monster. But an oracle declared that a virgin of noble blood must be surrendered to him, and the lot fell upon Hesione, daughter of Laomedon himself. Heracles, arriving at this critical moment, killed the monster by the aid of a fort built for him by Athene and the Trojans, so as to rescue both the exposed maiden and the people; but Laomedon, by a second act of perfidy, gave him mortal horses in place of the matchless animals which had been promised. Thus defrauded of his due, Heracles equipped six ships, attacked and captured Troy, and killed Laomedon, giving Hesione to his friend and auxiliary Telamon, to whom she bore the celebrated archer Teucros. A painful sense of this expedition was preserved among the inhabitants of the historical town of Ilium, who offered no worship to Heracles.

Among all the sons of Laomedon, Priam was the only one who had remonstrated against the refusal of the well-earned guerdon of Heracles; for which the hero recompensed him by placing him on the throne. Many and distinguished were his sons and daughters, as well by his wife Hecuba, daughter of Cisseus, as by other women. Among the sons were Hector, Paris, Deiphobus, Helenus, Troilus, Polites, Polydorus; among the daughters, Laodice, Creusa, Polyxena, and Cassandra.

The birth of Paris was preceded by formidable presage; for Hecuba dreamed that she was delivered of a firebrand, and Priam, on consulting the soothsayers, was informed that the son about to be born would prove fatal to him. Accordingly he directed the child to be exposed on Mount Ida; but the inauspicious kindness of the gods preserved him; and he grew up amid the flocks and herds, active and beautiful, fair of hair and symmetrical in person, and the special favorite of Aphrodite.

It was to this youth, in his solitary shepherd's walk on Mount Ida, that the three goddesses, Here, Athene, and Aphrodite, were conducted, in order that he might determine the dispute respecting their comparative beauty, which had arisen at the nuptials of Peleus and Thetis,—a dispute brought about in pursuance of the arrangement, and in accomplishment of the deep-laid designs of Zeus. For Zeus, remarking with pain the immoderate numbers of the then existing heroic race, pitied the earth for the overwhelming burden which she was compelled to bear, and determined to lighten it by exciting a destructive and long-continued war. Paris awarded the palm of beauty to Aphrodite, who promised him in recompense the possession of Helen, wife of the Spartan Menelaus, — the daughter of Zeus and the fairest of living women. At the instance of Aphrodite, ships were built for him, and he embarked on the enterprise so fraught with eventual disaster to his native city, in spite of the menacing prophecies of his brother Helenus, and the always neglected warnings of Cassandra.

Paris, on arriving at Sparta, was hospitably entertained by Menelaus as well as by Castor and Pollux, and was enabled to present the rich gifts which he had brought to Helen. Menelaus then departed to Crete, leaving Helen to entertain his Trojan guest—a favorable moment, which was employed by Aphrodite to bring about the intrigue aud the elopement. Paris carried away with him both Helen and a large sum of money belonging to Menelaus, made a prosperous voyage to Troy, and arrived there safely with his prize on the third day.

Menelaus, informed by Iris in Crete of the perfidious return made by Paris for his hospitality, hastened home in grief and indignation to consult with his brother Agamemnon, as well as with the venerable Nestor, on the means of avenging the outrage. They made known the event to the Greek chiefs around them, among whom they found universal sympathy; Nestor, Palamedes, and others went round to solicit aid in a contemplated attack of Troy, under the command of Agamemnon, to whom each chief promised both obedience and unwearied exertion until Helen should be recovered   Ten years were spent in equipping the expedition. The goddesses Here and Athene, incensed at the preference given by Paris to Aphrodite, and animated by steady attachment to Argos, Sparta, and Mycenæ, took an active part in the cause, and the horses of Here were fatigued with her repeated visits to the different parts of Greece.

By such efforts a force was at length assembled at Aulis in Bœotia, consisting of 1,186 ships and more than one hundred thousand men—a force outnumbering by more than ten to one anything that the Trojans themselves could oppose, and superior to the defenders of Troy even with all her allies included. It comprised heroes with their followers from the extreme points of Greece—from the northwestern portions of Thessaly under Mount Olympus, as well as the western islands of Dulichium and Ithaca, and the eastern islands of Crete and Rhodes. Agamemnon himself contributed 100 ships manned with the subjects of his kingdom Mycenæ, besides furnishing 60 ships to the Arcadians, who possessed none of their own. Menelaus brought with him 60 ships, Nestor from Pylus, 90, Idomeneus from Crete and Diomedes from Argos, 80 each. Forty ships were manned by the Elians, under four different chiefs; the like number under Meges from Dulichium and the Echinades, and under Thoas from Calydon and the other Ætolian towns. Odysseus from Ithaca, and Ajax from Salamis, brought 12 ships each. The Abantes from Eubœa, under Elphenor, filled 40 vessels; the Bœotians, under Peneleos and Leitus, 50; the inhabitants of Orchomenus and Aspledon, 30; the light-armed

Locrians, under Ajax son of Oileus, 40; the Phocians as many. The Athenians, under Menestheus, a chief distinguished for his skill in marshalling an army, mustered 50 ships; the Myrmidons from Phthia and Hellas, under Achilles, assembled in 50 ships; Protesilaus from Phylace and Pyrasus, and Eurypylus from Ormenium, each came with 40 ships; Machaon and Podaleirius, from Trikka, with 30; Eumelus, from Pheræ and the lake Bœbeis, with 11; and Philoctetes from Melibœa with 7; the Lapithæ, under Polypœtes, son of Peirithous, filled 40 vessels, the Ænianes and Perrhæbians, under Guneus, 22; and the Magnetes, under Prothous, 40; these last two were from the northernmost parts of Thessaly, near the mountains Pelion and Olympus. From Rhodes, under Tlepolemus, son of Heracles, appeared 9 ships; from Syme, under the comely but effeminate Nireus, 3; from Cos, Crapathus, and the neighboring islands, 30, under the orders of Pheidippus and Antiphus, sons of Thessalus and grandsons of Heracles.

Among this band of heroes were included the distinguished warriors Ajax and Diomedes, and the sagacious Nestor; while Agamemnon himself, scarcely inferior to either of them in prowess, brought with him a high reputation for prudence in command. But the most marked and conspicuous of all were Achilles and Odysseus; the former a beautiful youth born of a divine mother, swift in the race, of fierce temper and irresistible might; the latter not less efficient as an ally, from his eloquence, his untiring endurance, his inexhaustible resources under difficulty, and the mixture of daring courage with deep-laid cunning which never deserted him: the blood of the arch-deceiver Sisyphus, through an illicit connection with his mother Anticleia, was said to flow in his veins, and he was especially patronized and protected by the goddess Athene. Odysseus, unwilling at first to take part in the expedition, had even simulated insanity; but Palamedes, sent to Ithaca to invite him, tested the reality of his madness by placing in the furrow where Odysseus was ploughing his infant son Telemachus. Thus detected, Odysseus could not refuse to join the Achæan host, but the prophet Halitherses predicted to him that twenty years would elapse before he revisited his native land. To Achilles the gods had promised the full effulgence of heroic glory before the walls of Troy; nor could the place be taken without both his coöperation and that of his son after him. But they had forewarned him that this brilliant career would be rapidly brought to a close; and that if he desired a long life, he must remain tranquil and inglorious in his native land. In spite of the reluctance of his mother Thetis he preferred few years with bright renown, and joined the Achæan host. When Nestor and Odysseus came to Phthia to invite him, both he and his intimate friend Patroclus eagerly obeyed the call.

Agamemnon and his powerful host set sail from Aulis; but being ignorant of the locality and the direction, they landed by mistake in Teuthrania, a part of Mysia near the river Caicus, and began to ravage the country under the persuasion that it was the neighborhood of Troy. Telephus, the king of the country, opposed and repelled them, but was ultimately defeated and severely wounded by Achilles. The Greeks, now discovering their mistake, retired; but their fleet was dispersed by a storm and driven back to Greece. Achilles attacked and took Scyrus, and there married Deidamia, the daughter of Lycomedes. Telephus, suffering from his wounds, was directed by the oracle to come to Greece and present himself to Achilles to be healed, by applying the scrapings of the spear with which the wound had been given; thus restored, he became the guide of the Greeks when they were prepared to renew their expedition.

The armament was again assembled at Aulis, but the goddess Artemis, displeased with the boastful language of Agamemnon, prolonged the duration of adverse winds, and the offending chief was compelled to appease her by the well-known sacrifice of his daughter Iphigenia. They then proceeded to Tenedos, from whence Odysseus and Menelaus were dispatched as envoys to Troy, to redemand Helen and the stolen property. In spite of the prudent counsels of Antenor, who received the two Grecian chiefs with friendly hospitality, the Trojans rejected the demand, and the attack was resolved upon. It was foredoomed by the gods that the Greek who first landed should perish: Protesilaus was generous enough to put himself upon this forlorn hope, and accordingly fell by the hand of Hector.

Meanwhile, the Trojans had assembled a large body of

allies from various parts of Asia Minor and Thrace: Darda-
nians under Æneas, Lycians under Sarpedon, Mysians, Ca-
rians, Mæonians, Alizonians, Phrygians, Thracians, and Pæonians. But vain was the attempt to oppose the landing of the
Greeks: the Trojans were routed, and even the invulnerable
Cyncus, son of Poseidon, one of the great bulwarks of the de-
fense, was slain by Achilles. Having driven the Trojans within their walls, Achilles attacked and stormed Lyrnessus, Peda-
sus, Lesbos, and other places in the neighborhood, twelve towns
on the sea-coast, and eleven in the interior: he drove off the
oxen of Æneas and pursued the hero himself, who narrowly
escaped with his life: he surprised and killed the youthful Troilus, son of Priam, and captured several of the other sons,
whom he sold as prisoners into the islands of the Ægean. He
acquired as his captive the fair Briseis, while Chryseis was
awarded to Agamemnon; he was, moreover, eager to see the
divine Helen, the prize and stimulus of this memorable struggle; and Aphrodite and Thetis contrived to bring about an
interview between them.

At this period of the war the Grecian army was deprived of
Palamedes, one of its ablest chiefs. Odysseus had not forgiven
the artifice by which Palamedes had detected his simulated insanity, nor was he without jealousy of a rival clever and cunning in a degree equal, if not superior, to himself; one who had
enriched the Greeks with the invention of letters of dice for
amusement of night-watches as well as with other useful suggestions. According to the old Cyprian epic, Palamedes was
drowned while fishing by the hands of Odysseus and Diomedes.
Neither in the *Iliad* nor the *Odyssey* does the name of Palamedes
occur; the lofty position which Odysseus occupies in both those
poems—noticed with some degree of displeasure even by Pindar,
who described Palamedes as the wiser man of the two—is sufficient to explain the omission. But in the more advanced period
of the Greek mind, when intellectual superiority came to acquire
a higher place in the public esteem as compared with military
prowess, the character of Palamedes, combined with his unhappy fate, rendered him one of the most interesting personages in the Trojan legend. Æschylus, Sophocles, and Euripides each consecrated to him a special tragedy; but the mode

of his death as described in the old epic was not suitable to
Athenian ideas, and accordingly he was represented as having
been falsely accused of treason by Odysseus, who caused gold
to be buried in his tent, and persuaded Agamemnon and the
Grecian chiefs that Palamedes had received it from the Trojans.
He thus forfeited his life, a victim to the calumny of Odysseus
and to the delusion of the leading Greeks. The philosopher
Socrates, in the last speech made to his Athenian judges,
alludes with solemnity and fellow-feeling to the unjust condemnation of Palamedes as analogous to that which he himself was
about to suffer; and his companions seem to have dwelt with
satisfaction on the comparison. Palamedes passed for an instance of the slanderous enmity and misfortune which so often
wait upon superior genius.

In these expeditions the Grecian army consumed nine years,
during which the subdued Trojans dared not give battle without their walls for fear of Achilles. Ten years was the fixed
epical duration of the siege of Troy, just as five years was the
duration of the siege of Camicus by the Cretan armament
which came to avenge the death of Minos: ten years of preparation, ten years of siege, and ten years of wandering for Odysseus were periods suited to the rough chronological dashes of
the ancient epic, and suggesting no doubts nor difficulties with
the original hearers. But it was otherwise when the same
events came to be contemplated by the historicizing Greeks,
who could not be satisfied without either finding or inventing
satisfactory bonds of coherence between the separate events.
Thucydides tells us that the Greeks were less numerous than
the poets have represented, and that being, moreover, very
poor, they were unable to procure adequate and constant provisions: hence they were compelled to disperse their army, and
to employ a part of it in cultivating the Chersonese—a part in
marauding expeditions over the neighborhood. Could the
whole army have been employed against Troy at once (he
says), the siege would have been much more speedily and
easily concluded. If the great historian could permit himself
thus to amend the legend in so many points, we might have
imagined that a simpler course would have been to include the
duration of the siege among the list of poetical exaggerations,

and to affirm that the real siege had lasted only one year instead of ten. But it seems that the ten years' duration was so capital a feature in the ancient tale that no critic ventured to meddle with it.

A period of comparative intermission, however, was now at hand for the Trojans. The gods brought about the memorable fit of anger of Achilles, under the influence of which he refused to put on his armor, and kept his Myrmidons in camp. According to the *Cypria*, this was the behest of Zeus, who had compassion on the Trojans: according to the *Iliad*, Apollo was the originating cause, from anxiety to avenge the injury which his priest Chryses had endured from Agamemnon. For a considerable time, the combats of the Greeks against Troy were conducted without their best warrior, and severe, indeed, was the humiliation which they underwent in consequence. How the remaining Grecian chiefs vainly strove to make amends for his absence—how Hector and the Trojans defeated and drove them to their ships—how the actual blaze of the destroying flame, applied by Hector to the ship of Protesilaus, roused up the anxious and sympathizing Patroclus, and extorted a reluctant consent from Achilles to allow his friend and his followers to go forth and avert the last extremity of ruin—how Achilles, when Patroclus had been killed by Hector, forgetting his anger in grief for the death of his friend, reëntered the fight, drove the Trojans within their walls with immense slaughter, and satiated his revenge both upon the living and the dead Hector, —all these events have been chronicled, together with those divine dispensations on which most of them are made to depend, in the immortal verse of the *Iliad*.

Homer breaks off with the burial of Hector, whose body has just been ransomed by the disconsolate Priam; while the lost poem of Arctinus, entitled the *Æthiopis*, so far as we can judge from the argument still remaining of it, handled only the subsequent events of the siege. The poem of Quintus Smyrnæus, composed about the fourth century of the Christian era, seems in its first books to coincide with *Æthiopis*, in the subsequent books partly with the *Ilias Minor* of Lesches.

The Trojans, dismayed by the death of Hector, were again animated with hope by the appearance of the warlike and beautiful queen of the Amazons, Penthesilia, daughter of Ares, hitherto invincible in the field, who came to their assistance from Thrace at the head of a band of her country-women. She again led the besieged without the walls to encounter the Greeks in the open field; and under her auspices the latter were at first driven back, until she, too, was slain by the invincible arm of Achilles. The victor, on taking off the helmet of his fair enemy as she lay on the ground, was profoundly affected and captivated by her charms, for which he was scornfully taunted by Thersites: exasperated by this rash insult, he killed Thersites on the spot with a blow of his fist. A violent dispute among the Grecian chiefs was the result, for Diomedes, the kinsman of Thersites, warmly resented the proceeding; and Achilles was obliged to go to Lesbos, where he was purified from the act of homicide by Odysseus.

Next arrived Memnon, son of Tithonus and Eos, the most stately of living men, with a powerful band of black Ethiopians, to the assistance of Troy. Sallying forth against the Greeks, he made great havoc among them: the brave and popular Antilochus perished by his hand, a victim to filial devotion in defence of Nestor. Achilles at length attacked him, and for a long time the combat was doubtful between them: the prowess of Achilles and the supplication of Thetis with Zeus finally prevailed; while Eos obtained for her vanquished son the consoling gift of immortality. His tomb, however, was shown near the Propontis, within a few miles of the mouth of the river Æsopus, and was visited annually by the birds called Memnonides, who swept it and bedewed it with water from the stream. So the traveller Pausanias was told, even in the second century after the Christian era, by the Hellespontine Greeks.

But the fate of Achilles himself was now at hand. After routing the Trojans and chasing them into the town, he was slain near the Scæan gate by an arrow from the quiver of Paris, directed under the unerring auspices of Apollo. The greatest efforts were made by the Trojans to possess themselves of the body, which was, however, rescued and borne off to the Grecian camp by the valor of Ajax and Odysseus. Bitter was the grief of Thetis for the loss of her son; she came into the camp with the Muses and the Nereids to mourn over him; and when a magnificent funeral-pile had been prepared by the Greeks to burn him with every mark of honor, she stole away the body and conveyed it to a renewed and immortal life in the island of Leuce in the Euxine Sea. According to some accounts he was there blest with the nuptials and company of Helen.

Thetis celebrated splendid funeral games in honor of her son, and offered the unrivalled panoply which Hephæstus had forged and wrought for him as a prize to the most distinguished warrior in the Grecian army. Odysseus and Ajax became rivals for the distinction, when Athene, together with some Trojan prisoners, who were asked from which of the two their country had sustained greatest injury, decided in favor of the former. The gallant Ajax lost his senses with grief and humiliation: in a fit of frenzy he slew some sheep, mistaking them for the men who had wronged him, and then fell upon his own sword.

Odysseus now learned from Helenus, son of Priam, whom he had captured in an ambuscade, that Troy could not be taken unless both Philoctetes and Neoptolemus, son of Achilles, could be prevailed upon to join the besiegers. The former, having been stung in the foot by a serpent, and becoming insupportable to the Greeks from the stench of his wound, had been left at Lemnos in the commencement of the expedition, and had spent ten years in misery on that desolate island; but he still possessed the peerless bow and arrows of Heracles, which were said to be essential to the capture of Troy. Diomedes fetched Philoctetes from Lemnos to the Grecian camp, where he was healed by the skill of Machaon, and took an active part against the Trojans—engaging in single combat with Paris, and killing him with one of the Heracleian arrows. The Trojans were allowed to carry away for burial the body of this prince, the fatal cause of all their sufferings; but not until it had been mangled by the hand of Menelaus. Odysseus went to the island of Scyros to invite Neoptolemus to the army. The untried but impetuous youth, gladly obeying the call, received from Odysseus his father's armor; while, on the other hand, Eurypylus, son of Telephus, came from Mysia as auxiliary to the Trojans and rendered to them valuable service —turning the tide of fortune for a time against the Greeks, and killing some of their bravest chiefs, among whom were numbered Peneleos, and the unrivalled leech Machaon. The exploits of Neoptolemus were numerous, worthy of the glory of his race and the renown of his father. He encountered and slew Eurypylus, together with numbers of the Mysian warriors: he routed the Trojans and drove them within their walls, from whence they never again emerged to give battle: and he was not less distinguished for good sense and persuasive diction than for forward energy in the field.

Troy, however, was still impregnable so long as the Palladium, a statue given by Zeus himself to Dardanus, remained in the citadel; and great care had been taken by the Trojans not only to conceal this valuable present, but to construct other statues so like it as to mislead any intruding robber. Nevertheless, the enterprising Odysseus, having disguised his person with miserable clothing and self-inflicted injuries, found means to penetrate into the city and to convey the Palladium by stealth away. Helen alone recognized him; but she was now anxious to return to Greece, and even assisted Odysseus in concerting means for the capture of the town.

To accomplish this object, one final stratagem was resorted to. By the hands of Epeius of Panopeus, and at the suggestion of Athene, a capacious hollow wooden horse was constructed, capable of containing one hundred men. In the inside of this horse the élite of the Grecian heroes, Neoptolemus, Odysseus, Menelaus, and others, concealed themselves while the entire Grecian army sailed away to Tenedos, burning their tents and pretending to have abandoned the siege. The Trojans, overjoyed to find themselves free, issued from the city and contemplated with astonishment the fabric which their enemies had left behind. They long doubted what should be done with it; and the anxious heroes from within heard the surrounding consultations, as well as the voice of Helen when she pronounced their names and counterfeited the accents of their wives. Many of the Trojans were anxious to dedicate it to the gods in the city as a token of gratitude for their deliverance; but the more cautious spirits inculcated distrust of an enemy's legacy. Laocoon, the priest of Poseidon, manifested his aversion by striking the side of the horse with his spear.

The sound revealed that the horse was hollow, but the Trojans heeded not this warning of possible fraud. The unfortunate Laocoon, a victim to his own sagacity and patriotism, miserably perished before the eyes of his countrymen, together with one of his sons: two serpents being sent expressly by the gods out of the sea to destroy him. By this terrific spectacle, together with the perfidious counsels of Simon—a traitor whom the Greeks had left behind for the special purpose of giving false information—the Trojans were induced to make a breach in their own walls, and to drag the fatal fabric with triumph and exultation into their city.

The destruction of Troy, according to the decree of the gods, was now irrevocably sealed. While the Trojans indulged in a night of riotous festivity, Simon kindled the fire-signal to the Greeks at Tenedos, loosening the bolts of the wooden horse, from out of which the enclosed heroes descended. The city, assailed both from within and from without, was thoroughly sacked and destroyed, with the slaughter or captivity of the larger portion of its heroes as well as its people. The venerable Priam perished by the hand of Neoptolemus, having in vain sought shelter at the domestic altar of Zeus Herceius. But his son Deiphobus, who since the death of Paris had become the husband of Helen, defended his house desperately against Odysseus and Menelaus, and sold his life dearly. After he was slain, his body was fearfully mutilated by the latter.

Thus was Troy utterly destroyed—the city, the altars and temples, and the population. Æneas and Antenor were permitted to escape, with their families, having been always more favorably regarded by the Greeks than the remaining Trojans. According to one version of the story they had betrayed the city to the Greeks: a panther's skin had been hung over the door of Antenor's house as a signal for the victorious besiegers to spare it in general plunder. In the distribution of the principal captives, Astyanax, the infant son of Hector, was cast from the top of the wall and killed by Odysseus or Neoptolemus: Polyxena, the daughter of Priam, was immolated on the tomb of Achilles, in compliance with a requisition made by the shade of the deceased hero to his countrymen; while her sister Cassandra was presented as a prize to Agamemnon. She had sought sanctuary at the altar of Athene, where Ajax, the son of Oileus, making a guilty attempt to seize her, had drawn both upon himself and upon the army the serious wrath of the goddess, insomuch that the Greeks could hardly be restrained from stoning him to death. Andromache and Helenus were both given to Neoptolemus, who, according to the *Ilias Minor*, carried away also Æneas as his captive.

Helen gladly resumed her union with Menelaus; she accompanied him back to Sparta, and lived with him there many years in comfort and dignity, passing afterward to a happy immortality in the Elysian fields. She was worshipped as a goddess, with her brothers, the Dioscuri, and her husband, having her temple, statue, and altar at Therapnæ and elsewhere. Various examples of her miraculous intervention were cited among the Greeks. The lyric poet Stesichorus had ventured to denounce her, conjointly with her sister Clytemnestra, in a tone of rude and plain-spoken severity, resembling that of Euripides and Lycophron afterward, but strikingly opposite to the delicacy and respect with which she is always handled by Homer, who never admits reproaches against her except from her own lips. He was smitten with blindness, and made sensible of his impiety; but, having repented and composed a special poem formally retracting the calumny, was permitted to recover his sight. In his poem of recantation (the famous *Palinode* now unfortunately lost) he pointedly contradicted the Homeric narrative, affirming that Helen had never been at Troy at all, and that the Trojans had carried thither nothing but her image or *eidolon*. It is, probably, to the excited religious feelings of Stesichorus that we owe the first idea of this glaring deviation from the old legend, which could never have been recommended by any considerations of poetical interest.

Other versions were afterward started, forming a sort of compromise between Homer and Stesichorus, admitting that Helen had never really been at Troy, without altogether denying her elopement. Such is the story of her having been detained in Egypt during the whole term of the siege. Paris, on his departure from Sparta, had been driven thither by storms, and the Egyptian king Proteus, hearing of the grievous wrong which he had committed toward Menelaus, had sent him away

from the country with severe menaces, detaining Helen until
her lawful husband should come to seek her. When the
Greeks reclaimed Helen from Troy, the Trojans assured them
solemnly that she neither was nor ever had been in the town;
but the Greeks, treating this allegation as fraudulent, prosecuted the siege until their ultimate success confirmed the cor-
rectness of the statement. Menelaus did not recover Helen
until, on his return from Troy, he visited Egypt. Such was
the story told by the Egyptian priests to Herodotus, and it appeared satisfactory to his historicizing mind. "For if Helen
had really been at Troy," he argues, "she would certainly have
been given up, even had she been mistress of Priam himself instead of Paris: the Trojan king, with all his family and all his
subjects, would never knowingly have incurred utter and irre-
trievable destruction for the purpose of retaining her: their
misfortune was that, while they did not possess and therefore
could not restore her, they yet found it impossible to convince
the Greeks that such was the fact." Assuming the historical
character of the war of Troy, the remark of Herodotus admits
of no reply; nor can we greatly wonder that he acquiesced in
the tale of Helen's Egyptian detention, as a substitute for the
"incredible insanity" which the genuine legend imputes to
Priam and the Trojans. Pausanias, upon the same ground and
by the same mode of reasoning, pronounced that the Trojan
horse must have been, in point of fact, a battering-engine, because to admit the literal narrative would be to impute utter
childishness to the defenders of the city. And Mr. Payne
Knight rejects Helen altogether as the real cause of the Trojan
war, though she may have been the pretext of it; for he thinks
that neither the Greeks nor the Trojans could have been so
mad and silly as to endure calamities of such magnitude "for
one little woman." Mr. Knight suggests various political
causes as substitutes; these might deserve consideration, either
if any evidence could be produced to countenance them, or if
the subject on which they are brought to bear could be shown
to belong to the domain of history.

The return of the Grecian chiefs from Troy furnished matter to the ancient epic hardly less copious than the siege itself,
and the more susceptible of indefinite diversity, inasmuch as

those who had before acted in concert were now dispersed and isolated. Moreover, the stormy voyages and compulsory wanderings of the heroes exactly fell in with the common aspirations after an heroic founder, and enabled even the most remote Hellenic settlers to connect the origin of their town with this prominent event of their ante-historical and semi-divine world. And an absence of ten years afforded room for the supposition of many domestic changes in their native abode, and many family misfortunes and misdeeds during the interval. One of these historic "Returns," that of Odysseus, has been immortalized by the verse of Homer. The hero, after a series of long-protracted suffering and expatriation inflicted on him by the anger of Poseidon, at last reaches his native island, but finds his wife beset, his youthful son insulted, and his substance plundered by a troop of insolent suitors; he is forced to appear as a wretched beggar, and to endure in his own person their scornful treatment; but finally, by the interference of Athene coming in aid of his own courage and stratagem, he is enabled to overwhelm his enemies, to resume his family position, and to recover his property. The return of several other Grecian chiefs was the subject of an epic poem by Hagias which is now lost, but of which a brief abstract or argument still remains: there were in antiquity various other poems of similar title and analogous matter.

As usual with the ancient epic, the multiplied sufferings of this back voyage are traced to divine wrath, justly provoked by the sins of the Greeks, who, in the fierce exultation of a victory purchased by so many hardships, had neither respected nor even spared the altars of the gods in Troy. Athene, who had been their most zealous ally during the siege, was so incensed by their final recklessness, more especially by the outrage of Ajax, son of Oileus, that she actively harassed and embittered their return, in spite of every effort to appease her. The chiefs began to quarrel among themselves; their formal assembly became a scene of drunkenness; even Agamemnon and Menelaus lost their fraternal harmony, and each man acted on his own separate resolution. Nevertheless, according to the *Odyssey*, Nestor, Diomedes, Neoptolemus, Idomeneus, and Philoctetes reached home speedily and safely; Agamemnon also arrived in

Peloponnesus, to perish by the hand of a treacherous wife; but Menelaus was condemned to long wanderings and to the severest privations in Egypt, Cyprus, and elsewhere before he could set foot in his native land. The Locrian Ajax perished on the Gyræan rock. Though exposed to a terrible storm, he had already reached this place of safety, when he indulged in the rash boast of having escaped in defiance of the gods. No sooner did Poseidon hear this language than he struck with his trident the rock which Ajax was grasping and precipitated both into the sea. Calchas, the soothsayer, together with Leonteus and Polypœtes, proceeded by land from Troy to Colophon.

In respect, however, to these and other Grecian heroes, tales were told different from those in the *Odyssey*, assigning to them a long expatriation and a distant home. Nestor went to Italy, where he founded Metapontum, Pisa, and Heracleia: Philoctetes also went to Italy, founded Petilia and Crimisa, and sent settlers to Egesta in Sicily. Neoptolemus, under the advice of Thetis, marched by land across Thrace, met with Odysseus, who had come by sea, at Maroneia, and then pursued his journey to Epirus, where he became king of the Molossians. Idomeneus came to Italy, and founded Uria in the Salentine peninsula. Diomedes, after wandering far and wide, went along the Italian coast into the innermost Adriatic gulf, and finally settled in Daunia, founding the cities of Argyrippa, Beneventum, Atria, and Diomedeia: by the favor of Athene he became immortal, and was worshipped as a god in many different places. The Locrian followers of Ajax founded the Epizephyrian Locri on the southernmost corner of Italy, besides another settlement in Libya.

The previously exiled Teucros, besides founding the city of Salamis in Cyprus, is said to have established some settlements in the Iberian peninsula. Menestheus, the Athenian, did the like, and also founded both Elæa in Mysia and Scylletium in Italy. The Arcadian chief Agapenor founded Paphos in Cyprus. Epius, of Panopeus in Phocis, the constructor of the Trojan horse with the aid of the goddess Athene, settled at Lagaria, near Sybaris, on the coast of Italy; and the very tools which he had employed in that remarkable fabric were shown down to a late date in the temple of Athene at Metapontum.

Temples, altars, and towns were also pointed out in Asia Minor, in Samos, and in Crete, the foundation of Agamemnon or of his followers.   The inhabitants of the Grecian town of Scione, in the Thracian peninsula called Pallene or Pellene, accounted themselves the offspring of the Pellenians from Achæa in Peloponnesus, who had served under Agamemnon before Troy, and who on their return from the siege had been driven on the spot by a storm and there settled.   The Pamphylians, on the southern coast of Asia Minor, deduced their origin from the wanderings of Amphilochus and Calchas after the siege of Troy: the inhabitants of the Amphilochian Argos on the Gulf of Ambracia revered the same Amphilochus as their founder.   The Orchomenians under Iamenus, on quitting the conquered city, wandered or were driven to the eastern extremity of the Euxine Sea; and the barbarous Achæans under Mount Caucasus were supposed to have derived their first establishment from this source.   Meriones, with his Cretan followers, settled at Engyion in Sicily, along with the preceding Cretans who had remained there after the invasion of Minos.   The Elymians in Sicily also were composed of Trojans and Greeks separately driven to the spot, who, forgetting their previous differences, united in the joint settlements of Eryx and Egesta.   We hear of Podalerius both in Italy and on the coast of Caria; of Acamas, son of Theseus, at Amphipolus in Thrace, at Soli in Cyprus, and at Synnada in Phrygia; of Guneus, Prothous, and Eurypylus, in Crete as well as in Libya.   The obscure poem of Lycophron enumerates many of these dispersed and expatriated heroes, whose conquest of Troy was indeed a "Cadmean" victory (according to the proverbial phrase of the Greeks), wherein the sufferings of the victor were little inferior to those of the vanquished.   It was particularly among the Italian Greeks, where they were worshipped with very special solemnity, that their presence as wanderers from Troy was reported and believed.

I pass over the numerous other tales which circulated among the ancients, illustrating the ubiquity of the Grecian and Trojan heroes as well as that of the Argonauts—one of the most striking features in the Hellenic legendary world.   Among them all, the most interesting, individually, is Odysseus, whose romantic adventures in fabulous places and among fabulous persons have been made familiarly known by Homer. The goddesses Calypso and Circe; the semi-divine mariners of Phæacia, whose ships are endowed with consciousness and obey without a steersman; the one-eyed Cyclopes, the gigantic Læstrygones, and the wind-ruler Æolus; the Sirens, who ensnare by their song, as the Lotophagi fascinate by their food,— all these pictures formed integral and interesting portions of the old epic. Homer leaves Odysseus reëstablished in his house and family. But so marked a personage could never be permitted to remain in the tameness of domestic life; the epic poem called the *Telegonia* ascribed to him a subsequent series of adventures. Telegonus, his son by Circe, coming to Ithaca in search of his father, ravaged the island and killed Odysseus without knowing who he was. Bitter repentance overtook the son for his undesigned parricide: at his prayer and by the intervention of his mother Circe, both Penelope and Telemachus were made immortal: Telegonus married Penelope, and Telemachus married Circe.

We see by this poem that Odysseus was represented as the mythical ancestor of the Thesprotian kings, just as Neoptolemus was of the Molossian.

It has already been mentioned that Antenor and Æneas stand distinguished from the other Trojans by a dissatisfaction with Priam and a sympathy with the Greeks, which was by Sophocles and others construed as treacherous collusion,—a suspicion indirectly glanced at, though emphatically repelled, by the Æneas of Vergil. In the old epic of Arctinus, next in age to the *Iliad* and *Odyssey*, Æneas abandons Troy and retires to Mount Ida, in terror at the miraculous death of Laocoon, before the entry of the Greeks into the town and the last night-battle: yet Lesches, in another of the ancient epic poems, represented him as having been carried away captive by Neoptolemus. In a remarkable passage of the *Iliad*, Poseidon describes the family of Priam as having incurred the hatred of Zeus, and predicts that Æneas and his descendants shall reign over the Trojans: the race of Dardanus, beloved by Zeus more than all his other sons, would thus be preserved, since Æneas belonged to it. Accordingly, when Æneas is in imminent peril from the hands of Achilles, Poseidon specially interferes to rescue him, and even the implacable miso-Trojan goddess Here assents to the proceeding. These passages have been construed by various able critics to refer to a family of philo-Hellenic or semi-Hellenic Æneadæ, known even in the time of the early singers of the *Iliad* as masters of some territory in or near the Troad, and professing to be descended from, as well as worshipping, Æneas. In the town of Scepsis, situated in the mountainous range of Ida, about thirty miles eastward of Ilium, there existed two noble and priestly families who professed to be descended, the one from Hector, the other from Æneas. The Scepsian critic Demetrius (in whose time both these families were still to be found) informs us that Scamandrius, son of Hector, and Ascanius, son of Æneas, were the *archegets* or heroic founders of his native city, which had been originally situated on one of the highest ranges of Ida, and was subsequently transferred by them to the less lofty spot on which it stood in his time. In Arisbe and Gentinus there seem to have been families professing the same descent, since the same *archegets* were acknowledged. In Ophrynium, Hector had his consecrated edifice, while in Ilium both he and Æneas were worshipped as gods: and it was the remarkable statement of the Lesbian Menecrates that Æneas, "having been wronged by Paris and stripped of the sacred privileges which belonged to him, avenged himself by betraying the city, and then became one of the Greeks."

One tale thus among many respecting Æneas, and that, too, the most ancient of all, preserved among natives of the Troad, who worshipped him as their heroic ancestor, was that after the capture of Troy he continued in the country as king of the remaining Trojans, on friendly terms with the Greeks. But there were other tales respecting him, alike numerous and irreconcilable: the hand of destiny marked him as a wanderer (*fato profugus*) and his ubiquity is not exceeded even by that of Odysseus. We hear of him at Ænus in Thrace, in Pallene, at Æneia in the Thermaic Gulf, in Delos, at Orchomenus and Mantineia in Arcadia, in the islands of Cythera and Zacynthus, in Leucas and Ambracia, at Buthrotum in Epirus, on the Salentine peninsula and various other places in the southern region of Italy; at Drepana and Segesta in Sicily, at Carthage, at Cape Palinurus, Cumæ, Misenum, Caieta, and finally in Latium, where he lays the first humble foundation of the mighty Rome and her empire. And the reason why his wanderings were not continued still further was, that the oracles and the pronounced will of the gods directed him to settle in Latium. In each of these numerous places his visit was commemorated and certified by local monuments or special legends, particularly by temples and permanent ceremonies in honor of his mother Aphrodite, whose worship accompanied him everywhere: there were also many temples and many different tombs of Æneas himself. The vast ascendancy acquired by Rome, the ardor with which all the literary Romans espoused the idea of a Trojan origin, and the fact that the Julian family recognized Æneas as their gentile primary ancestor,—all contributed to give to the Roman version of this legend the preponderance over every other. The various other places in which monuments of Æneas were found came thus to be represented as places where he had halted for a time on his way from Troy to Latium. But though the legendary pretensions of these places were thus eclipsed in the eyes of those who constituted the literary public, the local belief was not extinguished; they claimed the hero as their permanent property, and his tomb was to them a proof that he had lived and died among them.

Antenor, who shares with Æneas the favorable sympathy of the Greeks, is said by Pindar to have gone from Troy along with Menelaus and Helen into the region of Cyrene in Libya. But according to the more current narrative, he placed himself at the head of a body of Eneti or Veneti from Paphlagonia, who had come as allies of Troy, and went by sea into the inner part of the Adriatic Gulf, where he conquered the neighboring barbarians and founded the town of Patavium (the modern Padua); the Veneti in this region were said to owe their origin to his immigration. We learn further from Strabo that Opsicellas, one of the companions of Antenor, had continued his wanderings even into Iberia, and that he had there established a settlement bearing his name. Thus endeth the Trojan war, together with its sequel, the dispersion of the heroes, victors as well as vanquished.

ACCESSION OF SOLOMON

BUILDING OF THE TEMPLE AT JERUSALEM

B.C. 1017

HENRY HART MILMAN

After many weary years of travail and fighting in the wilderness and the land of Canaan, the Jews had at last founded their kingdom, with Jerusalem as the capital. Saul was proclaimed the first king; afterward followed David, the "Lion of the tribe of Judah." During the many wars in which the Israelites had been engaged, the Ark of the Covenant was the one thing in which their faith was bound. No undertaking could fail while they retained possession of it.

In their wanderings the tabernacle enclosing the precious ark was first erected before the dwellings for the people. It had been captured by the Philistines, then restored to the Hebrews, and became of greater veneration than before. It will be remembered that, among other things, it contained the rod of Aaron which budded and was the cause of his selection as high-priest. It also contained the tables of stone which bore the Ten Commandments.

David desired to build a fitting shrine, a temple, in which to place the Ark of the Covenant; it should be a place wherein the people could worship; a centre of religion in which the ark should have paid it the distinction due it as the seat of tremendous majesty.

But David had been a man of war; this temple was a place of peace. Blood must not stain its walls; no shedder of gore could be its architect. Yet David collected stone, timber, and precious metals for its erection; and, not being allowed to erect the temple himself, was permitted to depute that office to his son and successor, "Solomon the Wise."

At this time all the enemies of Israel had been conquered, the country was at peace; the domain of the Hebrews was greater than at any other time, before or afterward. It was the fitting time for the erection of a great shrine to enclose the sacred ark. Nobly was this done, and no human work of ancient or modern times has so impressed mankind as the building of Solomon's Temple.

SOLOMON succeeded to the Hebrew kingdom at the age of twenty. He was environed by designing, bold, and dangerous enemies. The pretensions of Adonijah still commanded a powerful party: Abiathar swayed the priesthood; Joab the army. The singular connection in public opinion between the title to the crown and the possession of the deceased monarch's harem is well understood.[1] Adonijah, in making request for Abishag, a youthful concubine taken by David in his old age, was considered as insidiously renewing his claims to the sovereignty. Solomon saw at once the wisdom of his father's dying admonition: he seized the opportunity of crushing all future opposition and all danger of a civil war. He caused Adonijah to be put to death; suspended Abiathar from his office, and banished him from Jerusalem: and though Joab fled to the altar, he commanded him to be slain for the two murders of which he had been guilty, those of Abner and Amasa. Shimei, another dangerous man, was commanded to reside in Jerusalem, on pain of death if he should quit the city. Three years afterward he was detected in a suspicious journey to Gath, on the Philistine border; and having violated the compact, he suffered the penalty.

Thus secured by the policy of his father from internal enemies, by the terror of his victories from foreign invasion, Solomon commenced his peaceful reign, during which Judah and Israel dwelt safely, *Every man under his vine and under his fig-tree, from Dan to Beersheba.* This peace was broken only by a revolt of the Edomites. Hadad, of the royal race, after the exterminating war waged by David and by Joab, had fled to Egypt, where he married the sister of the king's wife. No sooner had he heard of the death of David and of Joab than he returned, and seems to have kept up a kind of predatory warfare during the reign of Solomon. Another adventurer, Rezon, a subject of Hadadezer, king of Zobah, seized on Damascus, and maintained a great part of Syria in hostility to Solomon.

Solomon's conquest of Hamath Zobah in a later part of his reign, after which he built Tadmor in the wilderness and raised a line of fortresses along his frontier to the Euphrates, is probably connected with these hostilities.[2] The justice of Solomon was proverbial. Among his first acts after his accession, it is related that when he had offered a costly sacrifice at Gibeon, the place where the Tabernacle remained, God had appeared

---

[1] I Kings, i.   [2] I Kings, xi., 23; I Chron., viii., 3.

to him in a dream, and offered him whatever gift he chose: the wise king requested an understanding heart to judge the people. God not merely assented to his prayer, but added the gift of honor and riches. His judicial wisdom was displayed in the memorable history of the two women who contested the right to a child. Solomon, in the wild spirit of Oriental justice, commanded the infant to be divided before their faces: the heart of the real mother was struck with terror and abhorrence, while the false one consented to the horrible partition, and by this appeal to nature the cause was instantaneously decided.

The internal government of his extensive dominions next demanded the attention of Solomon. Besides the local and municipal governors, he divided the kingdom into twelve districts: over each of these he appointed a purveyor for the collection of the royal tribute, which was received in kind; and thus the growing capital and the immense establishments of Solomon were abundantly furnished with provisions. Each purveyor supplied the court for a month. The daily consumption of his household was three hundred bushels of finer flour, six hundred of a coarser sort; ten fatted, twenty other oxen; one hundred sheep; besides poultry, and various kinds of venison. Provender was furnished for forty thousand horses, and a great number of dromedaries. Yet the population of the country did not, at first at least, feel these burdens: *Judah and Israel were many, as the sand which is by the sea in multitude, eating and drinking, and making merry.*

The foreign treaties of Solomon were as wisely directed to secure the profound peace of his dominions. He entered into a matrimonial alliance with the royal family of Egypt, whose daughter he received with great magnificence; and he renewed the important alliance with the king of Tyre.[1] The friendship of this monarch was of the highest value in contributing to the

---

[1] After inserting the correspondence between King Solomon and King Hiram of Tyre, according to I Kings, v., Josephus asserts that copies of these letters were not only preserved by his countrymen, but also in the archives of Tyre. I presume that Josephus adverts to the statement of Tyrian historians, not to an actual inspection of the archives, which he seems to assert as existing and accessible.

great royal and national work, the building of the Temple. The cedar timber could only be obtained from the forests of Lebanon: the Sidonian artisans, celebrated in the Homeric poems, were the most skilful workmen in every kind of manu-facture, particularly in the precious metals.

Solomon entered into a regular treaty, by which he bound himself to supply the Tyrians with large quantities of corn; re-ceiving in return their timber, which was floated down to Joppa, and a large body of artificers. The timber was cut by his own subjects, of whom he raised a body of thirty thousand; ten thousand employed at a time, and relieving each other every month; so that to one month of labor they had two of rest. He raised two other corps, one of seventy thousand porters of burdens, the other of eighty thousand hewers of stone, who were employed in the quarries among the mountains. All these labors were thrown, not on the Israelites, but on the strangers who, chiefly of Canaanitish descent, had been per-mitted to inhabit the country.

These preparations, in addition to those of King David, being completed, the work began. The eminence of Moriah, the Mount of Vision, *i.e.*, the height seen afar from the adjacent country, which tradition pointed out as the spot where Abra-ham had offered his son (where recently the plague had been stayed, by the altar built in the threshing-floor of Ornan or Araunah, the Jebusite), rose on the east side of the city. Its rugged top was levelled with immense labor; its sides, which to the east and south were precipitous, were faced with a wall of stone, built up perpendicular from the bottom of the valley, so as to appear to those who looked down of most terrific height; a work of prodigious skill and labor, as the immense stones were strongly mortised together and wedged into the rock. Around the whole area or esplanade, an irregular quad-rangle, was a solid wall of considerable height and strength: within this was an open court, into which the Gentiles were either from the first, or subsequently, admitted. A second wall encompassed another quadrangle, called the court of the Israelites. Along this wall, on the inside, ran a portico or cloister, over which were chambers for different sacred pur-poses. Within this again another, probably a lower, wall

separated the court of the priests from that of the Israelites.
To each court the ascent was by steps, so that the platform
of the inner court was on a higher level than that of the
outer.

The Temple itself was rather a monument of the wealth
than the architectural skill and science of the people. It was a
wonder of the world from the splendor of its materials, more
than the grace, boldness, or majesty of its height and dimensions. It had neither the colossal magnitude of the Egyptian,
the simple dignity and perfect proportional harmony of the
Grecian, nor perhaps the fantastic grace and lightness of later
Oriental architecture. Some writers, calling to their assistance
the visionary temple of Ezekiel, have erected a most superb
edifice; to which there is this fatal objection, that if the dimensions of the prophet are taken as they stand in the text, the
area of the Temple and its courts would not only have covered
the whole of Mount Moriah, but almost all Jerusalem. In fact
our accounts of the Temple of Solomon are altogether unsatisfactory. The details, as they now stand in the books of Kings
and Chronicles, the only safe authorities, are unscientific, and,
what is worse, contradictory.

Josephus has evidently blended together the three temples,
and attributed to the earlier all the subsequent additions and
alterations. The Temple, on the whole, was an enlargement
of the tabernacle, built of more costly and durable materials.
Like its model, it retained the ground-plan and disposition of
the Egyptian, or rather of almost all the sacred edifices of antiquity: even its measurements are singularly in unison with
some of the most ancient temples in Upper Egypt. It consisted of a propylæon, a temple, and a sanctuary; called respec-
tively the Porch, the Holy Place, and the Holy of Holies. Yet
in some respects, if the measurements are correct, the Temple
must rather have resembled the form of a simple Gothic
church.

In the front to the east stood the porch, a tall tower, rising
to the height of 210 feet. Either within, or, like the Egyptian
obelisks, before the porch, stood two pillars of brass; by one
account 27, by another above 60 feet high, the latter statement
probably including their capitals and bases. These were called

Jachin and Boaz (Durability and Strength).[1] The capitals of these were of the richest workmanship, with net-work, chain-work, and pomegranates. The porch was the same width with the Temple, 35 feet; its depth 17½. The length of the main building, including the Holy Place, 70 feet, and the Holy of Holies, 35, was in the whole 105 feet; the height 52½ feet.[2]

Josephus carries the whole building up to the height of the porch; but this is out of all credible proportion, making the height twice the length and six times the width. Along each side, and perhaps at the back of the main building, ran an aisle, divided into three stories of small chambers: the wall of the Temple being thicker at the bottom, left a rest to support the beams of these chambers, which were not let into the wall. These aisles, the chambers of which were appropriated as vestiaries, treasuries, and for other sacred purposes, seem to have reached about half way up the main wall of what we may call the nave and choir: the windows into the latter were probably above them; these were narrow, but widened inward.

If the dimensions of the Temple appear by no means imposing, it must be remembered that but a small part of the religious ceremonies took place within the walls. The Holy of Holies was entered only once a year, and that by the High-priest alone. It was the secret and unapproachable shrine of the Divinity. The Holy Place, the body of the Temple, admitted only the officiating priests. The courts, called in popular language the Temple, or rather the inner quadrangle,

[1] Ewald, following, he says, the Septuagint, makes these pillars not standing alone like obelisks before the porch, but as forming the front of the porch, with the capitals connected together, and supporting a kind of balcony, with ornamental work above it. The pillars measured 12 cubits (22 feet) round.

[2] Mr. Fergusson, estimating the cubit rather lower than in the text, makes the porch 30 by 15; the pronaos, or Holy Place, 60 by 30; the Holy of Holies, 30; the height 45 feet. Mr. Fergusson, following Josephus, supposes that the whole Temple had an upper story of wood, a talar, as appears in other Eastern edifices. I doubt the authority of Josephus as to the older Temple, though, as Mr. Fergusson observes, the discrepancies between the measurements in Kings and in Chronicles may be partially reconciled on this supposition. Mr. Fergusson makes the height of the eastern tower only 90 feet. The text followed 2 Chron., iii., 4, reckoning the cubit at 1 foot 9 inches.

were in fact the great place of divine worship. Here, under the open air, were celebrated the great public and national rites, the processions, the offerings, the sacrifices; here stood the great tank for ablution, and the high altar for burnt-offerings.

But the costliness of the materials, the richness and variety of the details, amply compensated for the moderate dimensions of the building. It was such a sacred edifice as a traveller might have expected to find in El Dorado. The walls were of hewn stone, faced within with cedar which was richly carved with knosps and flowers; the ceiling was of fir-tree. But in every part gold was lavished with the utmost profusion; within and without, the floor, the walls, the ceiling, in short, the whole house is described as overlaid with gold. The finest and purest —that of Parvaim, by some supposed to be Ceylon—was reserved for the sanctuary. Here the cherubim, which stood upon the covering of the Ark, with their wings touching each wall, were entirely covered with gold.

The sumptuous veil, of the richest materials and brightest colors, which divided the Holy of Holies from the Holy Place was suspended on chains of gold Cherubim, palm-trees, and flowers, the favorite ornaments, everywhere covered with gild-ing, were wrought in almost all parts. The altar within the Temple and the table of shewbread were likewise covered with the same precious metal. All the vessels, the ten candlesticks, five hundred basins, and all the rest of the sacrificial and other utensils, were of solid gold. Yet the Hebrew writers seem to dwell with the greatest astonishment and admiration on the works which were founded in brass by Huram, a man of Jewish extraction, who had learned his art at Tyre.

Besides the lofty pillars above mentioned, there was a great tank, called a sea, of molten brass, supported on twelve oxen, three turned each way; this was seventeen and one-half feet in diameter. There was also a great altar, and ten large vessels for the purpose of ablution, called lavers, standing on bases or pedestals, the rims of which were richly ornamented with a border, on which were wrought figures of lions, oxen, and cherubim. The bases below were formed of four wheels, like those of a chariot. All the works in brass were cast in a place near the Jordan, where the soil was of a stiff clay suited to the purpose.

For seven years and a half the fabric arose in silence. All the timbers, the stones, even of the most enormous size, measuring seventeen and eighteen feet, were hewn and fitted, so as to be put together without the sound of any tool whatever; as it has been expressed, with great poetical beauty:

" Like some tall palm the noiseless fabric grew."

At the end of this period, the Temple and its courts being completed, the solemn dedication took place, with the greatest magnificence which the king and the nation could display. All the chieftains of the different tribes, and all of every order who could be brought together, assembled.

David had already organized the priesthood and the Levites; and assigned to the thirty-eight thousand of the latter tribe each his particular office; twenty-four thousand were appointed for the common duties, six thousand as officers, four thousand as guards and porters, four thousand as singers and musicians. On this great occasion, the Dedication of the Temple, all the tribe of Levi, without regard to their courses, the whole priestly order of every class, attended. Around the great brazen altar, which rose in the court of the priests before the door of the Temple, stood in front the sacrificers, all around the whole choir, arrayed in white linen. One hundred and twenty of these were trumpeters, the rest had cymbals, harps, and psalteries. Solomon himself took his place on an elevated scaffold, or raised throne of brass. The whole assembled nation crowded the spacious courts beyond. The ceremony began with the preparation of burnt-offerings, so numerous that they could not be counted.

At an appointed signal commenced the more important part of the scene, the removal of the Ark, the installation of the God of Israel in his new and appropriate dwelling, to the sound of all the voices and all the instruments, chanting some of those splendid odes, the 47th, 97th, 98th, and 107th psalms. The Ark advanced, borne by the Levites, to the open portals of the Temple. It can scarcely be doubted that the 24th psalm, even if composed before, was adopted and used on this occasion.

The singers, as it drew near the gate, broke out in these words: —*Lift up your heads, O ye gates, and be ye lifted up, ye everlasting doors, and the King of Glory shall come in.* It was answered from the other part of the choir,—*Who is the King of Glory?*—the whole choir responded,—*The Lord of Hosts, he is the King of Glory.*

When the procession arrived at the Holy Place, the gates flew open; when it reached the Holy of Holies, the veil was drawn back. The Ark took its place under the extended wings of the cherubim, which might seem to fold over, and receive it under their protection. At that instant all the trumpeters and singers were at once *to make one sound to be heard in praising and thanking the Lord; and when they lifted up their voice, with the trumpets, and cymbals, and instruments of music, and praised the Lord, saying, For he is good, for his mercy endureth forever, the house was filled with a cloud, even the house of the Lord, so that the priests could not stand to minister by reason of the cloud; for the glory of the Lord had filled the house of God.* Thus the Divinity took possession of his sacred edifice.

The king then rose upon the brazen scaffold, knelt down, and spreading his hands toward heaven, uttered the prayer of consecration. The prayer was of unexampled sublimity: while it implored the perpetual presence of the Almighty, as the tutelar Deity and Sovereign of the Israelites, it recognized his spiritual and illimitable nature. *But will God in very deed dwell with men on the earth? behold heaven and the heaven of heavens cannot contain thee, how much less this house which I have built?* It then recapitulated the principles of the Hebrew theocracy, the dependence of the national prosperity and happiness on the national conformity to the civil and religious law. As the king concluded in these emphatic terms:—*Now, therefore, arise, O Lord God, into thy resting-place, thou and the ark of thy strength: let thy priests, O Lord God, be clothed with salvation, and thy saints rejoice in goodness. O Lord God, turn not away the face of thine anointed: remember the mercies of David thy servant,*—the cloud which had rested over the Holy of Holies grew brighter and more dazzling; fire broke out and consumed all the sacrifices; the priests stood without, awestruck by the insupportable splendor; the whole people fell on their faces, and worshipped and praised the Lord, *for he is good, for his mercy is forever.*

Which was the greater, the external magnificence, or the moral sublimity of this scene? Was it the Temple, situated on its commanding eminence, with all its courts, the dazzling splendor of its materials, the innumerable multitudes, the priesthood in their gorgeous attire, the king, with all the insignia of royalty, on his throne of burnished brass, the music, the radiant cloud filling the Temple, the sudden fire flashing upon the altar, the whole nation upon their knees? Was it not rather the religious grandeur of the hymns and of the prayer: the exalted and rational views of the Divine Nature, the union of a whole people in the adoration of the one Great, Incomprehensible, Almighty, Everlasting Creator?

This extraordinary festival, which took place at the time of that of Tabernacles, lasted for two weeks, twice the usual time: during this period twenty-two thousand oxen and one hundred and twenty thousand sheep were sacrificed,[1] every individual probably contributing to this great propitiatory rite; and the whole people feasting on those parts of the sacrifices which were not set apart for holy uses.

Though the chief magnificence of Solomon was lavished on the Temple of God, yet the sumptuous palaces which he erected for his own residence display an opulence and profusion which may vie with the older monarchs of Egypt or Assyria. The great palace stood in Jerusalem; it occupied thirteen years in building. A causeway bridged the deep ravine, and leading directly to the Temple, united the part either of Acra or Sion, on which the palace stood, with Mount Moriah.

---

[1] Gibbon, in one of his malicious notes, observes, " As the blood and smoke of so many hecatombs might be inconvenient, Lightfoot, the Christian Rabbi, removes them by a miracle. Le Clerc (*ad loc.*) is bold enough to suspect the fidelity of the numbers." To this I ventured to subjoin the following illustration: " According to the historian Kotobeddyn, quoted by Burckhardt, *Travels in Arabia*, p. 276, the Khalif Moktader sacrificed during his pilgrimage to Mecca, in the year of the Hegira 350, forty thousand camels and cows, and fifty thousand sheep. Barthema describes thirty thousand oxen slain, and their carcasses given to the poor. Tavernier speaks of one hundred thousand victims offered by the king of Tonquin." Gibbon, ch. xxiii., iv., p. 96, edit. Milman.

In this palace was a vast hall for public business, from its cedar
pillars called the House of the Forest of Lebanon. It was
175 feet long, half that measurement in width, above 50 feet
high; four rows of cedar columns supported a roof made of
beams of the same wood; there were three rows of windows on
each side facing each other. Besides this great hall, there
were two others, called porches, of smaller dimensions, in one
of which the throne of justice was placed. The harem, or
women's apartments, adjoined to these buildings; with other
piles of vast extent for different purposes, particularly, if we
may credit Josephus, a great banqueting hall.

The same author informs us that the whole was surrounded
with spacious and luxuriant gardens, and adds a less credible
fact, ornamented with sculptures and paintings. Another palace was built in a romantic part of the country in the valleys
at the foot of Lebanon for his wife, the daughter of the king of
Egypt; in the luxurious gardens of which we may lay the scene
of that poetical epithalamium,[1] or collection of Idyls, the Song
of Solomon.[2] The splendid works of Solomon were not confined to royal magnificence and display; they condescended to
usefulness. To Solomon are traced at least the first channels
and courses of the natural and artificial water supply which has
always enabled Jerusalem to maintain its thousands of worshippers at different periods, and to endure long and obstinate
sieges.[3]

The descriptions in the Greek writers of the Persian courts
in Susa and Ecbatana; the tales of the early travellers in the

[1] I here assume that the Song of Solomon was an epithalamium. I
enter not into the interminable controversy as to the literal or allegorical
or spiritual meaning of this poem, nor into that of its age. A very particular though succinct account of all these theories, ancient and modern,
may be found in a work by Dr. Ginsberg. I confess that Dr. Ginsberg's
theory, which is rather tinged with the virtuous sentimentality of the modern novel, seems to me singularly out of harmony with the Oriental and
ancient character of the poem. It is adopted, however, though modified,
by M. Rénan.

[2] According to Ewald, the ivory tower in this poem was raised in one
of these beautiful "pleasances," in the Anti-Libanus, looking toward
Hamath.

[3] Ewald: *Geschichte*, iii., pp. 62–68; a very remarkable and valuable
passage.

East about the kings of Samarcand or Cathay; and even the imagination of the Oriental romancers and poets, have scarcely conceived a more splendid pageant than Solomon, seated on his throne of ivory, receiving the homage of distant princes who came to admire his magnificence, and put to the test his noted wisdom.[1] This throne was of pure ivory, covered with gold; six steps led up to the seat, and on each side of the steps stood twelve lions.

All the vessels of his palace were of pure gold, silver was thought too mean: his armory was furnished with gold; two hundred targets and three hundred shields of beaten gold were suspended in the house of Lebanon. Josephus mentions a body of archers who escorted him from the city to his country palace, clad in dresses of Tyrian purple, and their hair powdered with gold dust. But enormous as this wealth appears, the statement of his expenditure on the Temple, and of his annual revenue, so passes all credibility, that any attempt at forming a calculation on the uncertain data we possess may at once be abandoned as a hopeless task. No better proof can be given of the uncertainty of our authorities, of our imperfect knowledge of the Hebrew weights of money, and, above all, of our total ignorance of the relative value which the precious metals bore to the commodities of life, than the estimate, made by Dr. Prideaux, of the treasures left by David, amounting to eight hundred millions, nearly the capital of our national debt.

Our inquiry into the sources of the vast wealth which Solomon undoubtedly possessed may lead to more satisfactory, though still imperfect, results. The treasures of David were accumulated rather by conquest than by traffic. Some of the nations he subdued, particularly the Edomites, were wealthy. All the tribes seem to have worn a great deal of gold and silver in their ornaments and their armor; their idols were often of gold, and the treasuries of their temples perhaps contained considerable wealth. But during the reign of Solomon almost the whole commerce of the world passed into his territories. The treaty with Tyre was of the utmost importance: nor is there any instance in which two neighboring nations so clearly

[1] Compare the great Mogul's throne, in Tavernier; that of the King of Persia, in Morier.

saw, and so steadily pursued, without jealousy or mistrust, their mutual and inseparable interests.[1]

On one occasion only, when Solomon presented to Hiram twenty inland cities which he had conquered, Hiram expressed great dissatisfaction, and called the territory by the opprobrious name of Cabul. The Tyrian had perhaps cast a wistful eye on the noble bay and harbor of Acco, or Ptolemais, which the prudent Hebrew either would not, or could not—since it was part of the promised land—dissever from his dominions. So strict was the confederacy, that Tyre may be considered the port of Palestine, Palestine the granary of Tyre. Tyre furnished the shipbuilders and mariners; the fruitful plains of Palestine victualled the fleets, and supplied the manufacturers and merchants of the Phœnician league with all the necessaries of life.[2]

[1] The very learned work of Movers, *Die Phönizier* (Bonn, 1841, Berlin, 1849) contains everything which true German industry and comprehensiveness can accumulate about this people. Movers, though in such an inquiry conjecture is inevitable, is neither so bold, so arbitrary, nor so dogmatic in his conjectures as many of his contemporaries. See on Hiram, ii. 326 *et seq.* Movers is disposed to appreciate as of high value the fragments preserved in Josephus of the Phœnician histories of Menander and Dios.

Mr. Kenrick's *Phœnicia* may also be consulted with advantage.

[2] To a late period Tyre and Sidon were mostly dependent on Palestine for their supply of grain. The inhabitants of these cities desired peace with Herod (Agrippa) because their country was nourished by the king's country (Acts xii., 20).

RISE AND FALL OF ASSYRIA

DESTRUCTION OF NINEVEH

B.C. 789

F. LENORMANT AND E. CHEVALLIER

Mesopotamia for many centuries was the field of battle for the opposing hosts of Babylonia and Assyria, each striving for mastery over the other. At first each city had its own prince, but at length one of these petty kingdoms absorbed the rest, and Nineveh became the capital of a united Assyria. Babylonia had her own kings, but they were little more than hereditary satraps receiving investiture from Nineveh.

From about B.C. 1060 to 1020 Babylon seems to have recovered the upper hand. Her victories put an end to what is known as the First Assyrian Empire. After a few generations a new family ascended the throne and ultimately founded the Second Assyrian Empire.

The first princes whose figured monuments have come down to us belonged to those days. The oldest of all was Assurnizirpal; the bas-reliefs with which his palace was decorated are now in the British Museum and the Louvre; most of them in the former. His son Shalmaneser III, and later Shalmaneser IV, made many campaigns against the neighboring peoples, and Assyria became rapidly a great and powerful nation. The effeminate Sardanapalus was the last of the dynasty.

The capital of Assyria was Nineveh, one of the most famous of cities. It was remarkable for extent, wealth, and architectural grandeur. Diodorus Siculus says its walls were sixty miles around and one hundred feet high. Three chariots could be driven abreast around the summit of its walls, which were defended by fifteen hundred bastions, each of them two hundred feet in height. These dimensions may be exaggerated, but the Hebrew scriptures and recent excavations at the ancient site leave no doubt as to the splendor of the Assyrian palaces and the greatness of the city of Nineveh in population, wealth, and power. In historical times it was destroyed by the Medes, under King Cyaxares, and by the Babylonians, under Nebuchadnezzar, about B.C. 607.

We are indebted to the monuments, tablets, and "books" recently discovered for the history of Assyria and other ancient oriental nations. Layard unearthed the greater portion, on the site of ancient Nineveh, of the Assyrian "books" (for so are named the tablets of clay, sometimes enamelled, at others only sun-dried or burnt). The writing on these "books" is the cuneiform, and was done by impressing the "style" on the clay while in a waxlike condition. Many of the tablets were broken when Layard and Rawlinson gave them over to the British Museum. The reconstruction of these tablets was undertaken by George Smith, an English Assyriologist of the British Museum, who displayed great skill and earnest application in the deciphering of the cuneiform text.

In each reign the history of the king and his acts was written by a poet or historian detailed to that office. The "books" were collected and kept in great libraries, the largest of these being made by Sardanapalus.

THE greater part of the expeditions of Shalmaneser IV, succeeding each other year after year, were directed, like those of his father, sometimes to the north, into Armenia and Pontus; sometimes to the east, into Media, never completely subdued; sometimes to the south, into Chaldæa, where revolts were of constant occurrence; and finally westward, toward Syria and the region of Amanus. In this direction he advanced farther than his predecessors, and came into contact with some personages mentioned in Bible history. The part of his annals relating to the campaigns that brought him into collision with the kings of Damascus and Israel possesses peculiar interest for us, much greater than that attaching to the narrative of any other wars.

The sixteenth campaign of Shalmaneser IV (B.C. 890) commenced a new series of wars; the King crossed the Zab, or Zabat, to make war on the mountain people of Upper Media, and afterward on the Scythian tribes around the Caspian Sea. He did not, however, abandon the western countries, where he soon found himself opposed by the new King whom the revolution arising from the influence of Elisha the prophet had placed on the throne of Damascus in the room of Benhidai.

"In my eighteenth campaign" (886), we read on the Nimrud obelisk, "I crossed the Euphrates for the sixteenth time. Hazael, king of Damascus, came toward me to give battle. I took from him eleven hundred and twenty-one chariots and four hundred and seventy horsemen, with his camp.

"In my nineteenth campaign (885) I crossed the Euphrates for the eighteenth time. I marched toward Mount Amanus, and there cut beams of cedar.

"In my twenty-first campaign (883) I crossed the Euphrates for the twenty-second time. I marched to the cities of Hazael of Damascus. I received tribute from Tyre, Sidon, and Byblus."

It evidently was at the end of this campaign that Jehu, king of Israel, whose territory Hazael had ravaged, appealed to Shalmaneser for help against his powerful enemy. The inscription on the obelisk says that the Assyrian King received tribute from Jehu, whom it names "son of Omri," for the great renown of the founder of Samaria had made the Assyrians consider all the kings of Israel as his descendants. One of the bas-reliefs of the same monument represents Jehu prostrating himself before Shalmaneser, as if acknowledging himself a vassal.

The annals of Shalmaneser say no more after this, either of the king of Damascus or of Israel. They record, as his twenty-seventh campaign, a great war in Armenia that brought about the submission of all the districts of that country that still resisted the Assyrian monarch. In the thirty-first campaign (873), the last mentioned on the obelisk, the King sent the general-in-chief of his armies, Tartan, again into Armenia, where he gave up to pillage fifty cities, among them Van; and during this time he himself went into Media, subjected part of the northern districts of that country, which were in a state of rebellion, chastised the people in the neighborhood of Mount Elwand, where in after-times Ecbatana was built, and finally made war on the Scythians of the Caspian Sea.

The official chronology of the Assyrians dates the termination of the reign of Shalmaneser IV in 870, the period of his death. But during the last two years his power was entirely lost, and he was reduced to the possession of two cities, Nineveh and Calah. His second son, Asshurdaninpal, in consequence of circumstances unknown to us, raised the standard of revolt against his father, assumed the royal title, and was supported by twenty-seven of the most important cities in the empire. One of the monuments has preserved a list of these cities, and among them we find Arrapkha, capital of the province of Arrapachitis, Amida (now Diarbekr), Arbela, Ellasar, and all the towns of the banks of the Tigris. War broke out between the father and his rebellious son; the army embraced the cause of the latter; he was recognized by all the provinces,

and kept Shalmaneser until his death shut up and closely block-
aded in his capital.

Shalmaneser died in B.C. 870; his son, Shamash-Bin, continued the legitimate line. He succeeded in repressing the
revolt of his brother Asshurdaninpal and in depriving him of
the authority he had usurped. The monument recording the
exploits of his first years gives no details, however, of the civil
war; it merely records, after enumerating the cities that had
joined the revolt of Asshurdaninpal, " With the aid of the great
gods, my masters, I subjected them to my sceptre."

The usurpation of the second son of Shalmaneser and a
civil war of five years had introduced many disorders into the
empire and shaken the fidelity of many provinces. The early
years of Shamash-Bin were occupied in reducing the whole to
order. In the narrative which has been preserved, extending
only to his fourth year, we find that the King overran and chastised with terrible severity Osrhoene or Aramæan Mesopotamia, where the people had been in rebellion, and reduced to
obedience the mountainous districts, where are the sources of
the Tigris and Euphrates, and finally Armenia proper. In his
fourth year he marched against Mardukbalatirib, king of Babylon, who had taken advantage of the disorders in Assyria to assert his independence, and who was supported by the Susianians or Elamites. He completely defeated him and compelled
him to fly to the desert, killed very many of his army in the
battle, took two hundred war chariots, and made seven thousand prisoners, of whom five thousand were put to death on the
field of battle as an example. Unfortunately our information
ceases at that period and we know absolutely nothing of the
greater part of the reign of Shamash-Bin, or of the expeditions
to the west of Asia, Syria, and Palestine, that must have been
made after the termination of the campaigns by which the royal
authority was reëstablished in all the ancient provinces of the
empire. This King remained on the throne until 857. In 859
and 858 he had to repress a great revolt in Babylon and Chaldæa.

Binlikhish [or Binnirari] III, the next king, reigned twenty-
nine years, from 857 to 828. An inscription of his, engraved
in the first years of his reign, describing the extent of the em-

pire, says that he governed on one side "From the land of Si-
luna, toward the rising sun, the countries of Elam, Albania (at
the foot of Caucasus), Kharkhar, Araziash, Misu, Media, Gi-
ratbunda (a portion of Atropatene, frequently mentioned in
the cuneiform inscriptions), the lands of Munna, Parsua (Par-
thia), Allabria (Hyrcania), Abdadana (Hecatompyla), Namri
(the Caspian Scythians), even to all the tribes of the Andiu
(a Turanian or Scythian people, whose country is far off), the
whole of the mountainous country as far as the sea of the rising
sun, the Caspian Sea; on the other side from the Euphrates,
Syria, all Phœnicia, the land of Tyre, of Sidon, the land of Omri
(Samaria), Edom, the Philistines, as far as the sea of the setting sun (the Mediterranean)"; on all these countries he says
that "he imposed tribute."

"I marched," he says again, "against the land of Syria,
and I took Marih, king of Syria, in Damascus, the city of his
kingdom. The great dread of Asshur, my master, persuaded
him; he embraced my knees and made submission."

Binlikhish III was a warlike prince; every year of his reign
was marked by an expedition. We have a summary of these
in a chronological tablet in the British Museum, containing a
fragment—from the end of the reign of Shamash-Bin to that of
Tiglath-pileser II—of a canon of eponymes mentioning the principal events year by year. They nearly all occurred in Southern Armenia and in the land of Van, where obedience was only
maintained by incessant military demonstrations, and subsequently in the countries to the north of Media as far as the
Caspian Sea. Other expeditions were also made as far as Par-
thia, toward Ariana and the various countries that, to the Assyrians, were the extreme East. We do not, however, know
what that region was called by them, as it is always designated
by a group of ideographic characters of unknown pronunciation. By the defeat of Marih, king of Damascus, the submission of the western provinces was secured for the remainder of
this reign, for there is no record of any other campaign there.

The year 849 was marked by a great plague in Assyria; 834
by a religious festival, of which unfortunately no particulars are
known; and, lastly, 833 by the solemn inauguration of a new
temple to the god Nebo, in the capital.

But the most interesting monument of the reign of Binlik-hish III is the statue of Nebo, one of the great gods of Babylon, discovered by Mr. Loftus and now in the British Museum; the inscription on the base of the statue mentions the wife of the King, and calls her "the queen Sammuramat"; this is the only historical Semiramis, the one mentioned by Herodotus. He places her correctly about a century and a half before Nitocris, the wife of Nabopolassar, king of Babylon. "Semiramis," says the father of history, "raised magnificent embankments to restrain the river (Euphrates), which till then used to overflow and flood the whole country round Babylon." But why did Herodotus, and the Babylonian tradition he has so faithfully reported, attribute these useful works to the queen and not to her husband, Binlikhish? It was once supposed, as a solution of this problem, that Sammuramat had governed alone for some time, as queen regnant, after the death of her husband. But this conjecture is absolutely contradicted by the table of eponymes in the British Museum, where it can be seen that Sammuramat never reigned alone. In our opinion the only possible explanation will be found in regarding Binlikhish and Sammuramat as the Ferdinand and Isabella of Mesopotamia. The restless desire of Babylonia and Chaldæa to form a state separate from Assyria grew more decided as time went on; in the time of Binlikhish it had already gained great strength, and the day was not far distant when the separation was definitely to take place, and to occasion the utter ruin of Nineveh. In this position of affairs it was natural for a king of Assyria to seek to strengthen his authority in Chaldæa by a marriage with a daughter of the royal line of that country, who were his vassals, and thus, in the opinion of the people of Babylon, acquire a legitimate right to the possession of the country by means of his wife, as well as the advantages to be derived from the attachment of the people to their own legitimate sovereign. We shall therefore consider Sammuramat as a Babylonian princess married by Binlikhish, and as reigning nominally at Babylon while her husband occupied the throne at Nineveh, and as being the only sovereign registered by the Babylonians in their national annals. In fact, her position must have been a peculiar one; she must have been considered

the rightful queen in one part of the empire, to have been
named as queen, and in the same rank as the king, in such an
official document as the inscription on the statue of the god
Nebo. She is the only princess mentioned in any of the Assyrian texts, as we might naturally suppose; for unless under
such very exceptional circumstances as we imagine in the case
of Sammuramat, there can have been no queens, but only favorite concubines, under the organization of harem life, such as it
was under the Assyrian kings, and as it still is in our days.

The exaggerated development of the Assyrian empire was
quite unnatural; the kings of Nineveh had never succeeded in
welding into one nation the numerous tribes whom they subdued by force of arms, or in checking in them the spirit of independence; they had not even attempted to do so. The
empire was absolutely without cohesion; the administrative system was so imperfect, the bond attaching the various provinces
to each other, and to the centre of the monarchy, so weak that
at the commencement of almost every reign a revolt broke out,
sometimes at one point, sometimes at another.

It was therefore easy to foresee that, so soon as the reins of
government were no longer in a really strong hand—so soon as
the king of Assyria should cease to be an active and warlike
king, always in the field, always at the head of his troops—the
great edifice laboriously built up by his predecessors of the
tenth and ninth centuries would collapse, and the immense
fabric of empire would vanish like smoke with such rapidity as
to astonish the world. And this is exactly what occurred after
the death of Binlikhish III.

The tablet in the British Museum allows us to follow year
by year the events and the progress of the dissolution of the
empire. Under Shalmaneser V, who reigned from B.C. 828 to
818, some foreign expeditions were still made, as, for instance,
to Damascus in B.C. 819; but the forces of the empire were
especially engaged during many following years in attempting
to hold countries already subdued, such as Armenia, then in a
chronic state of revolt; the wars in one and the same province
were constant, and occupied some six successive campaigns—
the Armenian war was from B.C. 827 to 822—proving that no
decisive results were obtained.

Under Asshur-edil-ilani II, who reigned from B.C. 818 to 800, we do not see any new conquests; insurrections constantly broke out, and were no longer confined to the extremities of the empire; they encroached on the heart of the country, and gradually approached nearer to Nineveh. The revolutionary spirit increased in the provinces, a great insurrection became imminent, and was ready to break out on the slightest excuse. At this period, B.C. 804, it is that the British Museum tablet registers, as a memorable fact in the column of events, "Peace in the land." Two great plagues are also mentioned under this reign, in 811 and 805, and on the 13th of June, B.C. 809—30 Sivan in the eponymos of Bur-el-salkhi—an almost total eclipse of the sun, visible at Nineveh.

The revolution was not long in coming. Asshurlikhish [Assurbanipal] ascended the throne in B.C. 800, and fixed his residence at Nineveh, instead of Ellasar, where his predecessor had lived after quitting Nineveh; he is the Sardanapalus of the Greeks, the ever-famous prototype of the voluptuous and effeminate prince. The tablet in the British Museum only mentions two expeditions in his reign, both of small importance, in 795 and 794; to all the other years the only notice is "in the country," proving that nothing was done and that all thought of war was abandoned.

Sardanapalus had entirely given himself up to the orgies of his harem, and never left his palace walls, entirely renouncing all manly and warlike habits of life. He had reigned thus for seven years, and discontent continued to increase; the desire for independence was spreading in the subject provinces; the bond of their obedience each year relaxed still more, and was nearer breaking, when Arbaces, who commanded the Median contingent of the army and was himself a Mede, chanced to see in the palace at Nineveh the King, in a female dress, spindle in hand, hiding in the retirement of the harem his slothful cowardice and voluptuous life.

He considered that it would be easy to deal with a prince so degraded, who would be unable to renew the valorous traditions of his ancestors. The time seemed to him to have come when the provinces, held only by force of arms, might finally throw off the weighty Assyrian yoke. Arbaces communicated his ideas and projects to the prince then intrusted with the government of Babylon, the Chaldæan Phul (Palia?), surnamed Balazu (the Terrible), a name the Greeks have made into Belesis; he entered into the plot with the willingness to be expected from a Babylonian, one of a nation so frequently rising in revolt.

Arbaces and Balazu consulted with other chiefs, who commanded contingents of foreign troops, and with the vassal kings of those countries that aspired to independence; and they all formed the resolution of overthrowing Sardanapalus. Arbaces engaged to raise the Medes and Persians, while Balazu set on foot the insurrection in Babylon and Chaldæa. At the end of a year the chiefs assembled their soldiers, to the number of forty thousand, in Assyria, under the pretext of relieving, according to custom, the troops who had served the former year.

When once there, the soldiers broke into open rebellion. The tablet in the British Museum tells us that the insurrection commenced at Calah in B.C. 792. Immediately after this the confusion became so great that from this year there was no nomination of an eponyme.

Sardanapalus, rudely interrupted in his debaucheries by a danger he had not been able to foresee, showed himself suddenly inspired with activity and courage; he put himself at the head of the native Assyrian troops who remained faithful to him, met the rebels, and gained three complete victories over them.

The confederates already began to despair of success, when Phul, calling in the aid of superstition to a cause that seemed lost, declared to them that if they would hold together for five days more, the gods, whose will he had ascertained by consulting the stars, would undoubtedly give them the victory.

In fact, some days afterward a large body of troops, whom the King had summoned to his assistance from the provinces near the Caspian Sea, went over, on their arrival, to the side of the insurgents and gained them a victory. Sardanapalus then shut himself up in Nineveh, and determined to defend himself to the last. The siege continued two years, for the walls of the city were too strong for the battering machines of

the enemy, who were compelled to trust to reducing it by famine. Sardanapalus was under no apprehension, confiding in an
oracle declaring that Nineveh should never be taken until the
river became its enemy.

But, in the third year, rain fell in such abundance that the
waters of the Tigris inundated part of the city and overturned
one of its walls for a distance of twenty *stades*. Then the King,
convinced that the oracle was accomplished and despairing of
any means of escape, to avoid falling alive into the enemy's
hands constructed in his palace an immense funeral pyre,
placed on it his gold and silver and his royal robes, and then,
shutting himself up with his wives and eunuchs in a chamber
formed in the midst of the pile, disappeared in the flames.

Nineveh opened its gates to the besiegers, but this tardy
submission did not save the proud city. It was pillaged and
burned, and then razed to the ground so completely as to evidence the implacable hatred enkindled in the minds of subject
nations by the fierce and cruel Assyrian government. The
Medes and Babylonians did not leave one stone upon another
in the ramparts, palaces, temples, or houses of the city that for
two centuries had been dominant over all Western Asia.

So complete was the destruction that the excavations of
modern explorers on the site of Nineveh have not yet found
one single wall slab earlier than the capture of the city by Arbaces and Balazu. All we possess of the first Nineveh is one
broken statue. History has no other example of so complete a
destruction.

The Assyrian empire was, like the capital, overthrown, and
the people who had taken part in the revolt formed independent
states—the Medes under Arbaces, the Babylonians under Phul
or Balazu, and the Susianians under Shutruk-Nakhunta. Assyria, reduced to the enslaved state in which she had so long
held other countries, remained for some time a dependency of
Babylon.

This great event occurred in the year B.C. 789.

[When the noble sculptures and vast palaces of Nimrud had
been first uncovered, it was natural to suppose that they marked
the real site of ancient Nineveh; a passage of Strabo, and another of Ptolemy, lent confirmation to this theory. Shortly

afterward a rival claimant started up in the region farther to the north.

"After a while an attempt was made to reconcile the rival claims by a theory the grandeur of which gained it acceptance, despite its improbability. It was suggested that the various ruins, which had hitherto disputed the name, were in fact all included within the circuit of the ancient Nineveh, which was described as a rectangle, or oblong square, eighteen miles long and twelve broad. The remains at Khorsabad, Koyunjik, Nimrud, and Keremles marked the four corners of this vast quadrangle, which contained an area of two hundred and sixteen square miles—about ten times that of London!

"In confirmation of this view was urged, first, the description in Diodorus, derived probably from Ctesias, which corresponded (it was said) both with the proportions and with the actual distances; and, next, the statements contained in the Book of Jonah, which, it was argued, implied a city of some such dimensions. The parallel of Babylon, according to the description given by Herodotus, might fairly have been cited as a further argument; since it might have seemed reasonable to suppose that there was no great difference of size between the chief cities of the two kindred empires."—*Rawlinson.*]

THE FOUNDATION OF ROME

B.C. 753

BARTHOLD GEORG NIEBUHR

Rome occupies a unique position in the history of the world. The whole Mediterranean basin was at one time merely a Roman lake, and the adjacent countries were Roman in letters, law, religion and the practice of war. Roman roads crossed the continents east and west and penetrated to the depths of Asia and Africa. Roman garrisons were stationed in every important city of the provinces, and when the great city on the banks of the Tiber at last fell before successive irruptions of northeasterly barbarians and Roman power was at its extreme ebb, the spirit of Roman institutions still survived in the civilization of Spain, France, Italy, Britain, even in Greece and Asia. Roman law had become the code of the world. Iberian, Gaul, and Italian had modified in varying degree their native dialects in conformity with the more copious and logical idiom of Latium.

A group of legends gathers round the birthplace of the Eternal City. It is Æneas who escapes from Troy and brings into the land of Italian Latinus his native gods. His son Ascanius conquers and slays Mezentius in a battle between Latins and Etruscans, and eleven kings of Alba, all surnamed Silvius, succeeded him on the throne. The last king of Alba Longa is Procas, whose usurping son Amulius drives his eldest brother Numitor from the throne. Numitor's daughter, Silvia, becomes the mother of the immortal twins Romulus and Remus, by Mamers, the god of war; the children are exposed by cruel Amulius, suckled by a wolf, and become founders of Rome.

Such is the outline of the poem, or rather tissue of poetry in which the founding of Rome is embalmed.

The critical acumen of Niebuhr may have dispelled some of the clouds and contradictions in which early historians and poets have wrapped the record of this great event. But no critic can ever destroy the beauty and charm of the old Latin chronicles or diminish the glory of the day that saw the first walls rise about the seven hills of the most important of ancient European cities.

I BELIEVE that few persons, when Alba is mentioned, can get rid of the idea, to which I too adhered for a long time, that the history of Alba is lost to such an extent, that we can speak of it only in reference to the Trojan time and the preceding period, as if all the statements made concerning it by the Romans were based upon fancy and error; and that accordingly it must be effaced from the pages of history altogether. It is true that what we read concerning the foundation of Alba by Ascanius, and the wonderful signs accompanying it, as well as the whole series of the Alban kings, with the years of their reigns, the story of Numitor and Amulius and the story of the destruction of the city, do not belong to history; but the historical existence of Alba is not at all doubtful on that account, nor have the ancients ever doubted it. The *Sacra Albana* and the *Albani tumuli atque luci*, which existed as late as the time of Cicero, are proofs of its early existence; ruins indeed no longer exist, but the situation of the city in the valley of Grotta Ferrata may still be recognized. Between the lake and the long chain of hills near the monastery of Palazzuolo one still sees the rock cut steep down toward the lake, evidently the work of man, which rendered it impossible to attack the city on that side; the summit on the other side formed the arx. That the Albans were in possession of the sovereignty of Latium is a tradition which we may believe to be founded on good authority, as it is traced to Cincius. Afterward the Latins became the masters of the district and temple of Jupiter. Further, the statement that Alba shared the flesh of the victim on the Alban mount with the thirty towns, and that after the fall of Alba the Latins chose their own magistrates, are glimpses of real history. The ancient tunnel made for discharging the water of the Alban Lake still exists, and through its vault a canal was made called *Fossa Cluilia:* this vault, which is still visible, is a work of earlier construction than any Roman one. But all that can be said of Alba and the Latins at that time is, that Alba was the capital, exercising the sovereignty over Latium; that its temple of Jupiter was the rallying point of the people who were governed by it; and that the gens Silvia was the ruling clan.

It cannot be doubted that the number of Latin towns was actually thirty, just that of the Albensian demi; this number afterward occurs again in the later thirty Latin towns and in the thirty Roman tribes, and it is moreover indicated by the story of the foundation of Lavinium by thirty families, in which we may recognize the union of the two tribes. The statement

that Lavinium was a Trojan colony and was afterward abandoned, but restored by Alba, and further that the sanctuary
could not be transferred from it to Alba, is only an accommo-
dation to the Trojan and native tradition, however much it may
bear the appearance of antiquity. For Lavinium is nothing
else than a general name for Latium, just as Panionium is for
Ionia, *Latinus, Lavinus*, and *Lavicus* being one and the same
name, as is recognized even by Servius. Lavinium was the
central point of the Prisci Latini, and there is no doubt that in
the early period before Alba ruled over Lavinium, worship was
offered mutually at Alba and at Lavinium, as was afterward the
case at Rome in the temple of Diana on the Aventine, and at
the festivals of the Romans and Latins on the Alban mount.

The personages of the Trojan legend therefore present
themselves to us in the following light. Turnus is nothing else
but Turinus, in Dionysius Τυῤῥηνός; Lavinia, the fair maiden, is
the name of the Latin people, which may perhaps be so distinguished that the inhabitants of the coast were called Tyrrhenians, and those further inland Latins. Since, after the battle
of Lake Regillus, the Latins are mentioned in the treaty with
Rome as forming thirty towns, there can be no doubt that the
towns, over which Alba had the supremacy in the earliest
times, were likewise thirty in number; but the confederacy did
not at all times contain the same towns, as some may afterward
have perished and others may have been added. In such political developments there is at work an instinctive tendency to
fill up that which has become vacant; and this instinct acts as
long as people proceed unconsciously according to the ancient
forms and not in accordance with actual wants. Such also was
the case in the twelve Achæan towns and in the seven Frisian
maritime communities; for as soon as one disappeared, another,
dividing itself into two, supplied its place. Wherever there is
a fixed number, it is kept up, even when one part dies away,
and it ever continues to be renewed. We may add that the
state of the Latins lost in the West, but gained in the East.
We must therefore, I repeat it, conceive on the one hand Alba
with its thirty *demi*, and on the other the thirty Latin towns,
the latter at first forming a state allied with Alba, and at a later
time under its supremacy.

According to an important statement of Cato preserved in Dionysius, the ancient towns of the Aborigines were small places scattered over the mountains. One town of this kind was situated on the Palatine hill, and bore the name of Roma, which is most certainly Greek. Not far from it there occur several other places with Greek names, such as Pyrgi and Alsium; for the people inhabiting those districts were closely akin to the Greeks; and it is by no means an erroneous conjecture, that Terracina was formerly called Τραχεινή, or the "rough place on a rock"; Formiæ must be connected with ὅρμος, "a roadstead" or "place for casting anchor." As certain as Pyrgi signifies "towers," so certainly does *Roma* signify "strength," and I believe that those are quite right who consider that the name Roma in this sense is not accidental. This Roma is described as a Pelasgian place in which Evander, the introducer of scientific culture, resided. According to tradition, the first foundation of civilization was laid by Saturn, in the golden age of mankind. The tradition in Vergil, who was extremely learned in matters of antiquity, that the first men were created out of trees, must be taken quite literally; for as in Greece the μύρμηκες were metamorphosed into the Myrmidons, and the stones thrown by Deucalion and Pyrrha into men and women, so in Italy trees, by some divine power, were changed into human beings. These beings, at first only half human, gradually acquired a civilization which they owed to Saturn; but the real intellectual culture was traced to Evander, who must not be regarded as a person who had come from Arcadia, but as *the good man*, as the teacher of the alphabet and of mental culture, which man gradually works out for himself.

The Romans clung to the conviction that Romulus, the founder of Rome, was the son of a virgin by a god, that his life was marvellously preserved, that he was saved from the floods of the river and was reared by a she-wolf. That this poetry is very ancient cannot be doubted; but did the legend at all times describe Romulus as the son of Rea Silvia or Ilia? Perizonius was the first who remarked against Ryccius that Rea Ilia never occurs together, and that Rea Silvia was a daughter of Numitor, while Ilia is called a daughter of Æneas. He is perfectly right: Nævius and Ennius called Romulus a son of Ilia, the daughter of Æneas, as is attested by Servius on Vergil and Porphyrio on Horace; but it cannot be hence inferred that this was the national opinion of the Romans themselves, for the poets who were familiar with the Greeks might accommodate their stories to Greek poems. The ancient Romans, on the other hand, could not possibly look upon the mother of the founder of their city as a daughter of Æneas, who was believed to have lived three hundred and thirty-three or three hundred and sixty years earlier. Dionysius says that his account, which is that of Fabius, occurred in the sacred songs, and it is in itself perfectly consistent. Fabius cannot have taken it, as Plutarch asserts, from Diocles, a miserable unknown Greek author; the statue of the she-wolf was erected in the year A.U. 457, long before Diocles wrote, and at least a hundred years before Fabius. This tradition therefore is certainly the more ancient Roman one; and it puts Rome in connection with Alba. A monument has lately been discovered at Bovillæ: it is an altar which the *Gentiles Julii* erected *lege Albana*, and therefore expresses a religious relation of a Roman gens to Alba. The connection of the two towns continues down to the founder of Rome; and the well-known tradition, with its ancient poetical details, many of which Livy and Dionysius omitted from their histories lest they should seem to deal too much in the marvellous, runs as follows:

Numitor and Amulius were contending for the throne of Alba. Amulius took possession of the throne, and made Rea Silvia, the daughter of Numitor, a vestal virgin, in order that the Silvian house might become extinct. This part of the story was composed without any insight into political laws, for a daughter could not have transmitted any gentilician rights. The name Rea Silvia is ancient, but Rea is only a surname: *rea femmina* often occurs in Boccaccio, and is used to this day in Tuscany to designate a woman whose reputation is blighted; a priestess Rea is described by Vergil as having been overpowered by Hercules. While Rea was fetching water in a grove for a sacrifice the sun became eclipsed, and she took refuge from a wolf in a cave, where she was overpowered by Mars. When she was delivered, the sun was again eclipsed and the statue of Vesta covered its eyes. Livy has here abandoned the marvellous. The tyrant threw Rea with her infants into the river Anio: she lost her life in the waves, but the god of the river took her soul and changed it into an immortal goddess, whom he married. This story has been softened down into the tale of her imprisonment, which is unpoetical enough to be a later invention. The river Anio carried the cradle, like a boat, into the Tiber, and the latter conveyed it to the foot of the Palatine, the water having overflowed the country, and the cradle was upset at the root of a fig-tree. A she-wolf carried the babies away and suckled them; Mars sent a woodpecker which provided the children with food, and the bird *parra* which protected them from insects. These statements are gathered from various quarters; for the historians got rid of the marvellous as much as possible. Faustulus, the legend continues, found the boys feeding on the milk of the huge wild beast; he brought them up with his twelve sons, and they became the staunchest of all. Being at the head of the shepherds on Mount Palatine, they became involved in a quarrel with the shepherds of Numitor on the Aventine—the Palatine and the Aventine are always hostile to each other. Remus being taken prisoner was led to Alba, but Romulus rescued him, and their descent from Numitor being discovered, the latter was restored to the throne, and the two young men obtained permission to form a settlement at the foot of Mount Palatine where they had been saved.

Out of this beautiful poem the falsifiers endeavored to make some credible story: even the unprejudiced and poetical Livy tried to avoid the most marvellous points as much as he could, but the falsifiers went a step farther. In the days when men had altogether ceased to believe in the ancient gods, attempts were made to find something intelligible in the old legends, and thus a history was made up, which Plutarch fondly embraced and Dionysius did not reject, though he also relates the ancient tradition in a mutilated form. He says that many people believe in demons, and that such a demon might have been the father of Romulus; but he himself is very far from believing it, and rather thinks that Amulius himself, in disguise, violated Rea Silvia amid thunder and lightning produced by artifice. This he is said to have done in order to have a pretext for getting rid of her, but being entreated by his daughter not to drown her, he imprisoned her for life. The children were saved by the shepherd who was commissioned to expose them, at the request of Numitor, and two other boys were put in their place. Numitor's grandsons were taken to a friend at Gabii, who caused them to be educated according to their rank, and to be instructed in Greek literature. Attempts have actually been made to introduce this stupid forgery into history, and some portions of it have been adopted in the narrative of our historians; for example, that the ancient Alban nobility migrated with the two brothers to Rome; but if this had been the case there would have been no need of opening an asylum, nor would it have been necessary to obtain by force the *connubium* with other nations.

But of more historical importance is the difference of opinion between the two brothers respecting the building of the city and its site. According to the ancient tradition, both were kings and the equal heads of the colony; Romulus is universally said to have wished to build on the Palatine, while Remus, according to some, preferred the Aventine; according to others, the hill Remuria. Plutarch states that the latter is a hill three miles south of Rome, and cannot have been any other than the hill nearly opposite St. Paul, which is the more credible, since this hill, though situated in an otherwise unhealthy district, has an extremely fine air: a very important point in investigations respecting the ancient Latin towns, for it may be taken for certain that where the air is now healthy it was so in those times also, and that where it is now decidedly unhealthy, it was anciently no better. The legend now goes on to say that a dispute arose between Romulus and Remus as to which of them should give the name to the town, and also as to where it was to be built. A town Remuria therefore undoubtedly existed on that hill, though subsequently we find the name transferred to the Aventine, as is the case so frequently. According to the common tradition, the auguries were to decide between the brothers: Romulus took his stand on the Palatine, Remus on the Aventine. The latter observed the whole night, but saw nothing until about sunrise, when he saw six vultures flying from north to south, and sent word of it to Romulus; but at that very time the latter, annoyed at not having seen any sign, fraudulently sent a messenger to say that he had seen twelve vultures, and at the very moment the messenger arrived there did appear twelve vultures, to which Romulus appealed. This account is impossible; for the Palatine and Aventine are so near each other that, as every Roman well knew, whatever a person on one of the two hills saw high in the air, could not escape the observation of any one who was watching on the other. This part of the story therefore cannot be ancient, and can be saved only by substituting the Remuria for the Aventine. As the Palatine was the seat of the noblest patrician tribe, and the Aventine the special town of the plebeians, there existed between the two a perpetual feud, and thus it came to pass that in after times the story relating to the Remuria, which was far away from the city, was transferred to the Aventine. According to Ennius, Romulus made his observations on the Aventine; in this case Remus must certainly have been on the Remuria, and it is said that when Romulus obtained the augury he threw his spear toward the Palatine. This is the ancient legend which was neglected by the later writers. Romulus took possession of the Palatine. The spear taking root and becoming a tree, which existed down to the time of Nero, is a symbol of the eternity of the new city, and of the protection of the gods. The statement that Romulus tried to deceive his brother is a later addition; and the beautiful poem of Ennius, quoted by Cicero, knows nothing of this circumstance. The conclusion which must be drawn from all this is, that in the earliest times there were two towns, Roma and Remuria, the latter being far distant from the city and from the Palatine.

Romulus now fixed the boundary of his town, but Remus scornfully leaped across the ditch, for which he was slain by Celer, a hint that no one should cross the fortifications of Rome with impunity. But Romulus fell into a state of melancholy occasioned by the death of Remus; he instituted festivals to honor him, and ordered an empty throne to be put up by the side of his own. Thus we have a double kingdom, which ends with the defeat of Remuria.

The question now is, What were these two towns of Roma and Remuria? They were evidently Pelasgian places: the ancient tradition states that Sicelus migrated from Rome southward to the Pelasgians, that is, the Tyrrhenian Pelasgians were pushed forward to the Morgetes, a kindred nation in Lucania and in Sicily. Among the Greeks it was, as Dionysius states, a general opinion that Rome was a Pelasgian, that is, a Tyrrhenian city, but the authorities from whom he learned this are no longer extant. There is, however, a fragment in which it is stated that Rome was a sister city of Antium and Ardea; here too we must apply the statement from the chronicle of Cumæ, that Evander, who, as an Arcadian, was likewise a Pelasgian, had his *palatium* on the Palatine. To us he appears of less importance than in the legend, for in the latter he is one of the benefactors of nations, and introduced among the Pelasgians in Italy the use of the alphabet and other arts, just as Damaratus did among the Tyrrhenians in Etruria. In this sense, therefore, Rome was certainly a Latin town, and had not a mixed but a purely Tyrrheno-Pelasgian population. The subsequent vicissitudes of this settlement may be gathered from the allegories.

Romulus now found the number of his fellow-settlers too small; the number of three thousand foot and three hundred horse, which Livy gives from the commentaries of the pontiffs, is worth nothing; for it is only an outline of the later military arrangement transferred to the earliest times. According to the ancient tradition, Romulus's band was too small, and he opened an asylum on the Capitoline hill. This asylum, the old description states, contained only a very small space, a proof how little these things were understood historically. All manner of people, thieves, murderers, and vagabonds of every kind, flocked thither. This is the simple view taken of the origin of the clients. In the bitterness with which the estates subsequently looked upon one another, it was made a matter of reproach to the Patricians that their earliest ancestors had been vagabonds; though it was a common opinion that the Patricians were descended from the free companions of Romulus, and that those who took refuge in the asylum placed themselves as clients under the protection of the real free citizens. But now they wanted women, and attempts were made to obtain the *connubium* with neighboring towns, especially perhaps

The Sabine women—now mothers—suing for peace between the combatants (their Roman husbands and their Sabine relations)

Painting by Jacques L. David

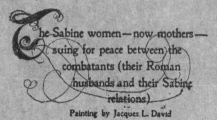

The Sabine women—now mothers—
suing for peace between the
combatants (their Roman
husbands and their Sabine
relations)

Painting by Jacques L. David

with Antemnæ, which was only four miles distant from Rome, with the Sabines and others. This being refused Romulus had recourse to a stratagem, proclaiming that he had discovered the altar of Consus, the god of counsels, an allegory of his cunning in general. In the midst of the solemnities, the Sabine maidens, thirty in number, were carried off, from whom the *curiæ* received their names: this is the genuine ancient legend, and it proves how small ancient Rome was conceived to have been. In later times the number was thought too small; it was supposed that these thirty had been chosen by lot for the purpose of naming the *curiæ* after them; and Valerius Antias fixed the number of the women who had been carried off at five hundred and twenty-seven. The rape is placed in the fourth month of the city, because the *consualia* fall in August, and the festival commemorating the foundation of the city in April; later writers, as Cn. Gellius, extended this period to four years, and Dionysius found this of course far more credible. From this rape there arose wars, first with the neighboring towns, which were defeated one after another, and at last with the Sabines. The ancient legend contains not a trace of this war having been of long continuance; but in later times it was necessarily supposed to have lasted for a considerable time, since matters were then measured by a different standard. Lucumo and Cælius came to the assistance of Romulus, an allusion to the expedition of Cæles Vibenna, which however belongs to a much later period. The Sabine king, Tatius, was induced by treachery to settle on the hill which is called the Tarpeian *arx.* Between the Palatine and the Tarpeian rock a battle was fought, in which neither party gained a decisive victory, until the Sabine women threw themselves between the combatants, who agreed that henceforth the sovereignty should be divided between the Romans and the Sabines. According to the annals, this happened in the fourth year of Rome.

But this arrangement lasted only a short time; Tatius was slain during a sacrifice at Lavinium, and his vacant throne was not filled up. During their common reign, each king had a senate of one hundred members, and the two senates, after consulting separately, used to meet, and this was called *comitium.* Romulus during the remainder of his life ruled alone; the ancient legend knows nothing of his having been a tyrant: according to Ennius he continued, on the contrary, to be a mild and benevolent king, while Tatius was a tyrant. The ancient tradition contained nothing beyond the beginning and the end of the reign of Romulus; all that lies between these points, the war with the Veientines, Fidenates, and so on, is a foolish invention of later annalists. The poem itself is beautiful, but this inserted narrative is highly absurd, as for example the statement that Romulus slew ten thousand Veientines with his own hand. The ancient poem passed on at once to the time when Romulus had completed his earthly career, and Jupiter fulfilled his promise to Mars, that Romulus was the only man whom he would introduce among the gods. According to this ancient legend, the king was reviewing his army near the marsh of Capræ, when, as at the moment of his conception, there occurred an eclipse of the sun and at the same time a hurricane, during which Mars descended in a fiery chariot and took his son up to heaven. Out of this beautiful poem the most wretched stories have been manufactured: Romulus, it is said, while in the midst of his senators was knocked down, cut into pieces, and thus carried away by them under their togas. This stupid story was generally adopted, and that a cause for so horrible a deed might not be wanting, it was related that in his latter years Romulus had become a tyrant, and that the senators took revenge by murdering him.

After the death of Romulus, the Romans and the people of Tatius quarrelled for a long time with each other, the Sabines wishing that one of their nation should be raised to the throne, while the Romans claimed that the new king should be chosen from among them. At length they agreed, it is said, that the one nation should choose a king from the other.

We have now reached the point at which it is necessary to speak of the relation between the two nations, such as it actually existed.

All the nations of antiquity lived in fixed forms, and their civil relations were always marked by various divisions and subdivisions. When cities raise themselves to the rank of nations, we always find a division at first into tribes; Herodotus mentions such tribes in the colonization of Cyrene, and the same was afterward the case at the foundation of Thurii; but when a place existed anywhere as a distinct township, its nature was characterized by the fact of its citizens being at a certain time divided into *gentes* (γένη), each of which had a common chapel and a common hero. These *gentes* were united in definite numerical proportions into *curiæ* (φράτραι). The *gentes* are not families, but free corporations, sometimes close and sometimes open; in certain cases the whole body of the state might assign to them new associates; the great council at Venice was a close body, and no one could be admitted whose ancestors had not been in it, and such also was the case in many oligarchical states of antiquity.

All civil communities had a council and an assembly of burghers, that is, a small and a great council; the burghers consisted of the guilds or *gentes*, and these again were united, as it were, in parishes; all the Latin towns had a council of one hundred members, who were divided into ten *curiæ;* this division gave rise to the name of *decuriones,* which remained in use as a title of civic magistrates down to the latest times, and through the *lex Julia* was transferred to the constitution of the Italian *municipia.* That this council consisted of one hundred persons has been proved by Savigny, in the first volume of his history of the Roman law. This constitution continued to exist till a late period of the middle ages, but perished when the institution of guilds took the place of municipal constitutions. Giovanni Villani says, that previously to the revolution in the twelfth century there were at Florence one hundred *buoni nomini,* who had the administration of the city. There is nothing in the German cities which answers to this constitution. We must not conceive those hundred to have been nobles; they were an assembly of burghers and country people, as was the case in our small imperial cities, or as in the small cantons of Switzerland. Each of them represented a *gens;* and they are those whom Propertius calls *patres pelliti.* The *curia* of Rome, a cottage covered with straw, was a faithful memorial of the times when Rome stood buried in the night of history, as a small country town surrounded by its little domain.

The most ancient occurrence which we can discover from the form of the allegory, by a comparison of what happened in other parts of Italy, is a result of the great and continued commotion among the nations of Italy. It did not terminate when the Oscans had been pressed forward from Lake Fucinus to the lake of Alba, but continued much longer. The Sabines may have rested for a time, but they advanced far beyond the districts about which we have any traditions. These Sabines began as a very small tribe, but afterward became one of the greatest nations of Italy, for the Marrucinians, Caudines, Vestinians, Marsians, Pelignians, and in short all the Samnite tribes, the Lucanians, the Oscan part of the Bruttians, the Picentians, and several others were all descended from the Sabine stock, and yet there are no traditions about their settlements except in a few cases. At the time to which we must refer the foundation of Rome, the Sabines were widely diffused. It is said that, guided by a bull, they penetrated into Opica, and thus occupied the country of the Samnites. It was perhaps at an earlier time that they migrated down the Tiber, whence we there find Sabine towns mixed with Latin ones; some of their places also existed on the Anio. The country afterward inhabited by the Sabines was probably not occupied by them till a later period, for Falerii is a Tuscan town, and its population was certainly at one time thoroughly Tyrrhenian.

As the Sabines advanced, some Latin towns maintained their independence, others were subdued; Fidenæ belonged to the former, but north of it all the country was Sabine. Now by the side of the ancient Roma we find a Sabine town on the Quirinal and Capitoline close to the Latin town; but its existence is all that we know about it. A tradition states that there previously existed on the Capitoline a Siculian town of the name of Saturnia, which, in this case, must have been conquered by the Sabines. But whatever we may think of this, as well as of the existence of another ancient town on the Janiculum, it is certain that there were a number of small towns in that district. The two towns could exist perfectly well side by side, as there was a deep marsh between them.

The town on the Palatine may for a long time have been in a state of dependence on the Sabine conqueror whom tradition calls Titus Tatius; hence he was slain during the Laurentine sacrifice, and hence also his memory was hateful. The exist-

ence of a Sabine town on the Quirinal is attested by the undoubted occurrence there of a number of Sabine chapels, which
were known as late as the time of Varro, and from which he
proved that the Sabine ritual was adopted by the Romans.
This Sabine element in the worship of the Romans has almost
always been overlooked, in consequence of the prevailing desire
to look upon everything as Etruscan; but, I repeat, there is no
doubt of the Sabine settlement, and that it was the result of a
great commotion among the tribes of middle Italy.

The tradition that the Sabine women were carried off because there existed no *connubium*, and that the rape was followed by a war, is undoubtedly a symbolical representation of
the relation between the two towns, previous to the establishment of the right of intermarriage; the Sabines had the ascendancy and refused that right, but the Romans gained it by force
of arms. There can be no doubt that the Sabines were originally the ruling people, but that in some insurrection of the
Romans various Sabine places, such as Antemnæ, Fidenæ,
and others, were subdued, and thus these Sabines were separated from their kinsmen. The Romans, therefore, reëstablished their independence by a war, the result of which may
have been such as we read it in the tradition—Romulus being,
of course, set aside—namely, that both places as two closely
united towns formed a kind of confederacy, each with a senate
of one hundred members, a king, an offensive and defensive
alliance, and on the understanding that in common deliberations the burghers of each should meet together in the space
between the two towns which was afterward called the *comitium*.
In this manner they formed a united state in regard to foreign
nations.

The idea of a double state was not unknown to the ancient
writers themselves, although the indications of it are preserved
only in scattered passages, especially in the scholiasts. The
head of Janus, which in the earliest times was represented on
the Roman *as*, is the symbol of it, as has been correctly observed by writers on Roman antiquities. The vacant throne
by the side of the *curule* chair of Romulus points to the time
when there was only one king, and represents the equal but
quiescent right of the other people.

That concord was not of long duration is an historical fact likewise; nor can it be doubted that the Roman king assumed the supremacy over the Sabines, and that in consequence the two councils were united so as to form one senate under one king, it being agreed that the king should be alternately a Roman and a Sabine, and that each time he should be chosen by the other people: the king, however, if displeasing to the non-electing people, was not to be forced upon them, but was to be invested with the *imperium* only on condition of the auguries being favorable to him, and of his being sanctioned by the whole nation. The non-electing tribe accordingly had the right of either sanctioning or rejecting his election. In the case of Numa this is related as a fact, but it is only a disguisement of the right derived from the ritual books. In this manner the strange double election, which is otherwise so mysterious and was formerly completely misunderstood, becomes quite intelligible. One portion of the nation elected and the other sanctioned; it being intended that, for example, the Romans should not elect from among the Sabines a king devoted exclusively to their own interests, but one who was at the same time acceptable to the Sabines.

When, perhaps after several generations of a separate existence, the two states became united, the towns ceased to be towns, and the collective body of the burghers of each became tribes, so that the nation consisted of two tribes. The form of addressing the Roman people was from the earliest times *Populus Romanus Quirites*, which, when its origin was forgotten, was changed into *Populus Romanus Quiritium*, just as *lis vindiciæ* was afterward changed into *lis vindiciarum*. This change is more ancient than Livy; the correct expression still continued to be used, but was to a great extent supplanted by the false one. The ancient tradition relates that after the union of the two tribes the name *Quirites* was adopted as the common designation for the whole people; but this is erroneous, for the name was not used in this sense till a very late period. This designation remained in use and was transferred to the plebeians at a time when the distinction between Romans and Sabines, between these two and the Luceres, nay, when even that between patricians and plebeians had almost ceased to be noticed. Thus the two towns stood side by side as tribes forming one state, and it is merely a recognition of the ancient tradition when we call the Latins *Ramnes*, and the Sabines *Tities;* that the derivation of these appellations from Romulus and T. Tatius is incorrect is no argument against the view here taken.

Dionysius, who had good materials and made use of a great many, must, as far as the consular period is concerned, have had more than he gives; there is in particular one important change in the constitution, concerning which he has only a few words, either because he did not see clearly or because he was careless. But as regards the kingly period, he was well acquainted with his subject; he says that there was a dispute between the two tribes respecting the senates, and that Numa settled it by not depriving the Ramnes, as the first tribe, of anything, and by conferring honors on the Tities. This is perfectly clear. The senate, which had at first consisted of one hundred and now two hundred members, was divided into ten *decuries*, each being headed by one, who was its leader; these are the *decem primi*, and they were taken from the Ramnes. They formed the college, which, when there was no king, undertook the government, one after another, each for five days, but in such a manner that they always succeeded one another in the same order, as we must believe with Livy, for Dionysius here introduces his Greek notions of the Attic *prytanes*, and Plutarch misunderstands the matter altogether.

After the example of the senate the number of the augurs and pontiffs also was doubled, so that each college consisted of four members, two being taken from the Ramnes and two from the Tities. Although it is not possible to fix these changes chronologically, as Dionysius and Cicero do, yet they are as historically certain as if we actually knew the kings who introduced them.

Such was Rome in the second stage of its development. This period of equalization is one of peace, and is described as the reign of Numa, about whom the traditions are simple and brief. It is the picture of a peaceful condition with a holy man at the head of affairs, like Nicolas von der Flue in Switzerland. Numa was supposed to have been inspired by the goddess

Egeria, to whom he was married in the grove of the Camenæ, and who introduced him into the choir of her sisters; she melted away in tears at his death, and thus gave her name to the spring which arose out of her tears. Such a peace of forty years, during which no nation rose against Rome, because Numa's piety was communicated to the surrounding nations, is a beautiful idea, but historically impossible in those times, and manifestly a poetical fiction.

The death of Numa forms the conclusion of the first *sæculum,* and an entirely new period follows, just as in the Theogony of Hesiod the age of heroes is followed by the iron age; there is evidently a change, and an entirely new order of things is conceived to have arisen. Up to this point we have had nothing except poetry, but with Tullus Hostilius a kind of history begins, that is, events are related which must be taken in general as historical, though in the light in which they are presented to us they are not historical. Thus, for example, the destruction of Alba is historical, and so in all probability is the reception of the Albans at Rome. The conquests of Ancus Martius are quite credible; and they appear like an oasis of real history in the midst of fables. A similar case occurs once in the chronicle of Cologne. In the Abyssinian annals, we find in the thirteenth century a very minute account of one particular event, in which we recognize a piece of contemporaneous history, though we meet with nothing historical either before or after.

The history which then follows is like a picture viewed from the wrong side, like phantasmata; the names of the kings are perfectly fictitious; no man can tell how long the Roman kings reigned, as we do not know how many there were, since it is only for the sake of the number that seven were supposed to have ruled, seven being a number which appears in many relations, especially in important astronomical ones. Hence the chronological statements are utterly worthless. We must conceive as a succession of centuries the period from the origin of Rome down to the times wherein were constructed the enormous works, such as the great drains, the wall of Servius, and others, which were actually executed under the kings and rival the great architectural works of the Egyptians. Romulus and

Numa must be entirely set aside; but a long period follows, in which the nations gradually unite and develop themselves until the kingly government disappears and makes way for republican institutions.

But it is nevertheless necessary to relate the history, such as it has been handed down, because much depends upon it. There was not the slightest connection between Rome and Alba, nor is it even mentioned by the historians, though they suppose that Rome received its first inhabitants from Alba; but in the reign of Tullus Hostilius the two cities on a sudden appear as enemies: each of the two nations seeks war, and tries to allure fortune by representing itself as the injured party, each wishing to declare war. Both sent ambassadors to demand reparation for robberies which had been committed. The form of procedure was this: the ambassadors, that is the Fetiales, related the grievances of their city to every person they met, they then proclaimed them in the market-place of the other city, and if, after the expiration of thrice ten days no reparation was made, they said, "We have done enough and now return," whereupon the elders at home held counsel as to how they should obtain redress. In this formula accordingly the *res*, that is, the surrender of the guilty and the restoration of the stolen property, must have been demanded. Now it is related that the two nations sent such ambassadors quite simultaneously, but that Tullus Hostilius retained the Alban ambassadors, until he was certain that the Romans at Alba had not obtained the justice due to them, and had therefore declared war. After this he admitted the ambassadors into the senate, and the reply made to their complaint was, that they themselves had not satisfied the demands of the Romans. Livy then continues: *bellum in trigesimum diem dixerant*. But the real formula is, *post trigesimum diem*, and we may ask, Why did Livy or the annalist whom he followed make this alteration? For an obvious reason: a person may ride from Rome to Alba in a couple of hours, so that the detention of the Alban ambassadors at Rome for thirty days, without their hearing what was going on in the mean time at Alba, was a matter of impossibility. Livy saw this, and therefore altered the formula. But the ancient poet was not concerned about such things, and without hesitation increased the distance in his imagination, and represented Rome and Alba as great states.

The whole description of the circumstances under which the fate of Alba was decided is just as manifestly poetical, but we shall dwell upon it for a while in order to show how a semblance of history may arise. Between Rome and Alba there was a ditch, *Fossa Cluilia* or *Cloelia*, and there must have been a tradition that the Albans had been encamped there; Livy and Dionysius mention that Cluilius, a general of the Albans, had given the ditch its name, having perished there. It was necessary to mention the latter circumstance, in order to explain the fact that afterward their general was a different person, Mettius Fuffetius, and yet to be able to connect the name of that ditch with the Albans. The two states committed the decision of their dispute to champions, and Dionysius says that tradition did not agree as to whether the name of the Roman champions was Horatii or Curiatii, although he himself, as well as Livy, assumes that it was Horatii, probably because it was thus stated by the majority of the annalists. Who would suspect any uncertainty here if it were not for this passage of Dionysius? The contest of the three brothers on each side is a symbolical indication that each of the two states was then divided into three tribes. Attempts have indeed been made to deny that the three men were brothers of the same birth, and thus to remove the improbability; but the legend went even further, representing the three brothers on each side as the sons of two sisters, and as born on the same day. This contains the suggestion of a perfect equality between Rome and Alba. The contest ended in the complete submission of Alba; it did not remain faithful, however, and in the ensuing struggle with the Etruscans, Mettius Fuffetius acted the part of a traitor toward Rome, but not being able to carry his design into effect, he afterward fell upon the fugitive Etruscans. Tullus ordered him to be torn to pieces and Alba to be razed to the ground, the noblest Alban families being transplanted to Rome. The death of Tullus is no less poetical. Like Numa he undertook to call down lightning from heaven, but he thereby destroyed himself and his house.

If we endeavor to discover the historical substance of these legends, we at once find ourselves in a period when Rome no longer stood alone, but had colonies with Roman settlers, possessing a third of the territory and exercising sovereign power over the original inhabitants. This was the case in a small number of towns, for the most part of ancient Siculian origin. It is an undoubted fact that Alba was destroyed, and that after this event the towns of the *Prisci Latini* formed an independent and compact confederacy; but whether Alba fell in the manner described, whether it was ever compelled to recognize the supremacy of Rome, and whether it was destroyed by the Romans and Latins conjointly, or by the Romans or Latins alone, are questions which no human ingenuity can solve. It is, however, most probable that the destruction of Alba was the work of the Latins, who rose against her supremacy: whether in this case the Romans received the Albans among themselves, and thus became their benefactors instead of destroyers, must ever remain a matter of uncertainty. That Alban families were transplanted to Rome cannot be doubted, any more than that the *Prisci Latini* from that time constituted a compact state; if we consider that Alba was situated in the midst of the Latin districts, that the Alban mount was their common sanctuary, and that the grove of Ferentina was the place of assembly for all the Latins, it must appear more probable that Rome did not destroy Alba, but that it perished in an insurrection of the Latin towns, and that the Romans strengthened themselves by receiving the Albans into their city.

Whether the Albans were the first that settled on the Cælian hill, or whether it was previously occupied, cannot be decided. The account which places the foundation of the town on the Cælius in the reign of Romulus suggests that a town existed there before the reception of the Albans; but what is the authenticity of this account? A third tradition represents it as an Etruscan settlement of Cæles Vibenna. This much is certain, that the destruction of Alba greatly contributed to increase the power of Rome. There can be no doubt that a third town, which seems to have been very populous, now existed on the Cælius and on a portion of the Esquiliæ: such a settlement close to other towns was made for the sake of mutual protection. Between the two more ancient towns there continued to be a marsh or swamp, and Rome was protected on the south by stagnant water; but between Rome and the third town there was a dry plain. Rome also had a considerable suburb toward the Aventine, protected by a wall and a ditch, as is implied in the story of Remus. He is a personification of the *plebs*, leaping across the ditch from the side of the Aventine, though we ought to be very cautious in regard to allegory.

The most ancient town on the Palatine was Rome; the Sabine town also must have had a name, and I have no doubt that, according to common analogy, it was Quirium, the name of its citizens being Quirites. This I look upon as certain. I have almost as little doubt that the town on the Cælian was called Lucerum, because when it was united with Rome, its citizens were called, *Lucertes* (*Luceres*). The ancients derive this name from Lucumo, king of the Tuscans, or from Lucerus, king of Ardea; the latter derivation probably meaning that the race was Tyrrheno-Latin, because Ardea was the capital of that race. Rome was thus enlarged by a third element, which, however, did not stand on a footing of equality with the two others, but was in a state of dependence similar to that of Ireland relatively to Great Britain down to the year 1782. But although the Luceres were obliged to recognize the supremacy of the two older tribes, they were considered as an integral part of the whole state, that is, as a third tribe with an administration of its own, but inferior rights. What throws light upon our way here is a passage of Festus, who is a great authority on matters of Roman antiquity, because he made his excerpts from Verrius Flaccus; it is only in a few points that, in my opinion, either of them was mistaken; all the rest of the mistakes in Festus may be accounted for by the imperfection of the abridgment, Festus not always understanding Verrius Flaccus. The statement of Festus to which I here allude is that Tarquinius Superbus increased the number of the Vestals in order that each tribe might have two. With this we must connect a passage from the tenth book of Livy, where he says that the augurs were to represent the three tribes. The numbers in the Roman colleges of priests were always multiples either of two or of three; the latter was the case with the Vestal Virgins and the great Flamines, and the former with the Augurs, Pontiffs, and

Fetiales, who represented only the first two tribes. Previously to the passing of the Ogulnian law the number of augurs was four, and when subsequently five plebeians were added, the basis of this increase was different, it is true, but the ancient rule of the number being a multiple of three was preserved. The number of pontiffs, which was then four, was increased only by four: this might seem to contradict what has just been stated, but it has been overlooked that Cicero speaks of *five* new ones having been added, for he included the Pontifex Maximus, which Livy does not. In like manner there were twenty Fetiales, ten for each tribe. To the Salii on the Palatine Numa added another brotherhood on the Quirinal; thus we everywhere see a manifest distinction between the first two tribes and the third, the latter being treated as inferior.

The third tribe, then, consisted of free citizens, but they had not the same rights as the members of the first two; yet its members considered themselves superior to all other people; and their relation to the other two tribes was the same as that existing between the Venetian citizens of the mainland and the *nobili*. A Venetian nobleman treated those citizens with far more condescension than he displayed toward others, provided they did not presume to exercise any authority in political matters. Whoever belonged to the Luceres called himself a Roman, and if the very dictator of Tusculum had come to Rome, a man of the third tribe there would have looked upon him as an inferior person, though he himself had no influence whatever.

Tullus was succeeded by Ancus. Tullus appears as one of the Ramnes, and as descended from Hostus Hostilius, one of the companions of Romulus; but Ancus was a Sabine, a grandson of Numa. The accounts about him are to some extent historical, and there is no trace of poetry in them. In his reign, the development of the state again made a step in advance. According to the ancient tradition, Rome was at war with the Latin towns, and carried it on successfully. How many of the particular events which are recorded may be historical I am unable to say; but that there was a war is credible enough. Ancus, it is said, carried away after this war many thousands of Latins, and gave them settlements on the Aventine. The ancients express various opinions about him; sometimes he is described as a *captator auræ popularis ;* sometimes he is called *bonus Ancus.* Like the first three kings, he is said to have been a legislator, a fact which is not mentioned in reference to the later kings. He is moreover stated to have established the colony of Ostia, and thus his kingdom must have extended as far as the mouth of the Tiber.

Ancus and Tullus seem to me to be historical personages; but we can scarcely suppose that the latter was succeeded by the former, and that the events assigned to their reigns actually occurred in them. These events must be conceived in the following manner: Toward the end of the fourth reign, when, after a feud which lasted many years, the Romans came to an understanding with the Latins about the renewal of the long-neglected alliance, Rome gave up its claims to the supremacy which it could not maintain, and indemnified itself by extending its dominion in another and safer direction. The eastern colonies joined the Latin towns which still existed: this is evident, though it is nowhere expressly mentioned; and a portion of the Latin country was ceded to Rome, with which the rest of the Latins formed a connection of friendship, perhaps of isopolity. Rome here acted as wisely as England did when she recognized the independence of North America.

In this manner Rome obtained a territory. The many thousand settlers whom Ancus is said to have led to the Aventine were the population of the Latin towns which became subject to Rome, and they were far more numerous than the two ancient tribes, even after the latter had been increased by their union with the third tribe. In these country districts lay the power of Rome, and from them she raised the armies with which she carried on her wars. It would have been natural to admit this population as a fourth tribe, but such a measure was not agreeable to the Romans: the constitution of the state was completed and was looked upon as a sacred trust in which no change ought to be introduced. It was with the Greeks and Romans as it was with our own ancestors, whose separate tribes clung to their hereditary laws, and differed from one another in this respect as much as they did from the Gauls in the color of their eyes and hair. They knew well enough that it was in their power to alter the laws, but they considered them as something which ought not to be altered. Thus when the emperor Otho was doubtful on a point of the law of inheritance, he caused the case to be decided by an ordeal or judgment of God. In Sicily, one city had Chalcidian, another Doric laws, although their populations, as well as their dialects, were greatly mixed; but the leaders of those colonies had been Chalcidians in the one case and Dorians in the others. The Chalcidians, moreover, were divided into four, the Dorians into three tribes, and their differences in these respects were manifested even in their weights and measures. The division into three tribes was a genuine Latin institution; and there are reasons which render it probable that the Sabines had a division of their states into four tribes. The transportation of the Latins to Rome must be regarded as the origin of the *plebs*

PRINCE JIMMU FOUNDS JAPAN'S CAPITAL

B.C. 660

SIR EDWARD REED   THE "NEHONGI"

Prince Jimmu is the founder of the Empire of Japan, according to Japanese tradition. The whole of his history is overlaid with myth and legend. But it points to the immigration of western Asiatics by way of Corea into the Japanese islands of Izumo and Kyushu.

The historical records of the Japanese relate that Jimmu, accompanied by an elder brother, Prince Itsuse, started from their grandfather's palace on Mount Takaclicho. They marched with a large number of followers, a horde of men, women, and children, as well as a band of armed men. On landing in Japan, after many years wandering by sea and land, they had serious conflicts with the native tribes. They eventually succeeded in overcoming all opposition and in conquering the country, so that Prince Jimmu was enabled to build a palace and set up a capital, Kashiha-bara, in Yamato. This prince is regarded by Japanese historians as the founder of the Japanese Empire. He is said to have reigned seventy-five years after his accession, and to have died at the age of one hundred and twenty-seven years, and his burial place is pointed out on the northern side of Mount Unebi, in the province of Yamato.

Prince Jimmu, or whoever was the foreign ruler who conquered and founded an empire in Japan, must have been a bold, enterprising, and sagacious man. The islands he subdued were barbarous, and he civilized them; the inhabitants were warlike and cruel, and he kept them in peace. He founded a dynasty which extended its dominion over Nagato, Izumo, and Owari, and still has representatives in rulers whose people are by far the most progressive dwellers in the East.

That part of the following historical matter, which is translated from the old Japanese chronicle, the *Nehongi*, is marked by local color and by Oriental characteristics, whereby it curiously contrasts with the plain recitals of modern and Western history.

SIR EDWARD REED

THERE are endless varying legends about this god-period of Japan. All that we need now say in the way of reciting the legends of the gods has relation to the descent of the mikados of Japan from the deities.

It was the misconduct of Susanoo that drove the sun-goddess into the cave and for this misconduct he was banished. Some say that, instead of proceeding to his place of banishment, he descended, with his son Idakiso no Mikoto, upon Shiraga (in Corea), but not liking the place went back by a vessel to the bank of the Hinokawa River, in Idzumo, Japan.

At the time of their descent, Idakiso had many plants or seeds of trees with him, but he planted none in Shiraga, but took them across with him, and scattered them from Kuishiu all over Japan, so that the whole country became green with trees. It is said that Idakiso is respected as the god of merit, and is worshipped in Kinokuni. His two sisters also took care of the plantation. One of the gods who reigned over the country in the prehistoric period was Ohonamuchi, who is said by some to be the son of Susanoo, and by others to be one of his later descendants; "And which is right, it is more than we can say," remarked one of my scholarly friends.

However, during his reign he was anxious about the people, and, consulting with Sukuna no Mikoto, applied "his whole heart," we are told, to their good government, and they all became loyal to him. One time he said to his friend just named, "Do you think we are governing the people well?" And his friend answered: "In some respects well, and in some not," so that they were frank and honest with each other in those days.

When Sukunahikona went away, Ohonamuchi said: "It is I who should govern this country. Is there any who will assist me?" Then there appeared over the sea a divine light, and there came a god floating and floating, and said: "You cannot govern the country without me." And this proved to be the god Ohomiwa no Kami, who built a palace at Mimuro, in Yamato, and dwelt therein. He affords a direct link with the Mikado family, for his daughter became the empress of the first historic emperor Jimmu. Her name was Humetatara Izudsu-hime.

All the descendants of her father are named, like him, Ohomiwa no Kami, and it is said that the present empress of Japan is probably a descendant of this god. As regards the descent of the Emperor Jimmu himself we already know that

Ninigi no Mikoto, "the sovran grandchild" of the sun-goddess, was sent down with the sacred symbols of empire given to him in the sun by the sun-goddess herself before he started for the earth. Now Ninigi married (reader, forgive me for quoting the lady's name and her father's) Konohaneno-sakuya-hime, the daughter of Ohoyamazumino-Kami, and the pair had three sons, of whom the last named Howori no Mikoto succeeded to the throne. He is sometimes called by the following simple—and possibly endearing—name: Amatsuhitakahi Koho-ho-demi no Mikoto.

He married Toyatama-hime, the daughter of the sea-god, and they had a son, Ugaya-fuki-ayedsu no Mikoto, born, it is said, under an unfinished roof of cormorants' wings, who succeeded the father, and who married Tamayori-hime, also a daughter of the sea-god. This illustrious couple had four sons, of whom the last succeeded to the throne in the year B.C. 660. He was named Kamuyamatoi warehiko no Mikoto, but posterity has fortunately simplified his designation to the now familiar Jimmu-Tenno, the first historic Emperor of Japan, and the ancestor of the present emperor.

The histories of Japan, prepared under the sanction of the present Japanese government, date the commencement of the historic period from the first year of the reign of the first emperor, Jimmu-Tenno, who is said to have ruled for seventy-six years, viz., from B.C. 660 to 585. Some persons consider that this reign, and a few reigns that succeeded it, probably or possibly belong to the legendary period, because while, on the one hand, the Emperor Jimmu is described as the founder of the present empire and the ancestor of the present emperor, on the other, he is described as the fourth son of Ukay Fukiaezu no Mikoto, who was fifth in direct descent from the beautiful sun-goddess, Tensho-Daijin. But as no such thing as writing existed in Japan in those days, or for many centuries afterward, it would not be surprising if a real monarch should have a mythical origin assigned to him; and as I have quite lately heard the guns firing at Nagasaki an imperial salute in honor of his coronation, and have seen the flags waving over the capital city, Tokio, in honor of the birthday, the Emperor Jimmu is quite historical enough for my present purpose.

The commencement of his reign shall fix for us, as it does for others, the Japanese year 1, which was 660 years prior to our year 1, so that any date of the Christian era can be converted into one of the Japanese era by the addition of 660 years, and *vice-versa*. Some of the emperors will be found to have lived very long lives, no doubt; but as I have said elsewhere, none of them lived nearly so long as our Adam, Methuselah, and others, in whose longevity so many of us profess to believe; and besides, it is impossible for me to attempt to correct a chronology which Japanese scholars, and Englishmen versed in the Japanese language, have thus far left without specific correction. Deferring for after consideration the incidents of the successive imperial reigns, except in so far as they bear directly upon the descent of the crown, let us, then, first glance at the succession of emperors and empresses who have ruled in the Morning Land.

After the death of the Emperor Jimmu there appears to have been an interregnum for three years—although it is seldom taken account of—the second Emperor Suisei, who was the fifth son of the first emperor, having ascended the throne B.C. 581 and reigned till 549. The cause of the interregnum appears to have been the extreme grief which Suisei felt at the death of his father, in consequence of which he committed the administration of the empire, for a time, to one of his relatives —an unworthy fellow, as he proved, named Tagishi Mimi no Mikoto, who tried to assassinate his master and seize the throne for himself, and who was put to death by Suisei for his pains. The fifth son of the Emperor Jimmu was nominated by him as the successor, and it is probable that older sons were living and passed over, and that the throne was inherited in part by nomination even in this its first transfer.

Some writers on Japanese history profess to see in the pantheon of Japan, pictured in the Kojiki and Nihonki, nothing more than a collection of distinguished personages who lived and labored and contended in the country before the historic period, thus bringing deified men and women down to earth again. Such persons accept the records of Jimmu-Tenno's origin as essentially accurate in so far as they state what is human and reasonable, rejecting them only when they set forth what is supernatural, and, to them, unbelievable.

Others, on the contrary, consider, or profess to consider, the supernatural portions of those narratives as perfectly trust-worthy, and discredit only those statements concerning the first of the sacred emperors which would seem in any way to detract from his divinity. I should be sorry to have to argue the case with either of these parties, but I must take the liberty of accepting as sufficiently accurate as much of the recorded lives of Jimmu and his successors as the modern prosaic his-tories in Japan are content to put forth, and no more.

Proceeding upon this basis, there is not much to be said of the reigns of the mikados who ruled before the Christian era, beyond what has been already stated. As regards the first emperor, his ancestor Ninigi no Mikoto—whether a god or not, or whether he came down from the sun by means of "the bridge of heaven" or not—appears to have established his residence at the ancient Himuka, now Hiuga; there it was that Jimmu-Tenno first resided, and thence it was that he started on his historic and memorable career. The central parts of Japan were militarily occupied by rebels (whose names are preserved), and it was to subdue them that he pro-ceeded eastward. He stopped for three years at Taka Shima, constructing the necessary vessels for crossing the waters, and then, in the course of years, making his way victoriously as far as Nanieva, the modern Osaka, encountered his foes at Kawa-chi, and defeated them, the chief general being left dead on the battle-field.

Jimmu was now sole master of Japan, as then known, and in the following year he mounted the throne. The eastern and northern parts of the country were, however, still, and long afterwards, peopled by the Aino race, who were at a later period treated as troublesome savages, and conquered by a famous prince, Yamato-Dake, by help of the sacred sword. The spot selected by the Emperor Jimmu for his capital was Kashiwabara, in the province of Yamato, not far from the present western capital of Kioto. He there did honor to the gods, married, built himself a palace, and deposited in the throne-room the sacred mirror, sword, and ball, the insignia of the imperial power handed down from the sun-goddess. He organized two imperial guards, one as a body-guard to protect the interior of the palace, and the other to act as sentinels around the palace.

THE "NEHONGI"

The Emperor Kami Yamato Iharebiko's personal name was Hikohoho-demi. He was the fourth child of Hiko-nagisa-take-ugaya-fuki-ahezu no Mikoto. His mother's name was Tama-yori-hime, daughter of the sea-god. From his birth this emperor was of clear intelligence and resolute will. At the age of fifteen he was made heir to the throne. When he grew up he married Ahira-tsu-hime, of the district of Ata in the province of Hiuga, and made her his consort. By her he had Tagishi-mimi no Mikoto and Kisu-mimi no Mikoto.

When he reached the age of forty-five, he addressed his elder brothers and his children, saying: "Of old, our heavenly deities Taka-mi-Musubi no Mikoto, and Oho-hiru-me no Mikoto, pointing to this land of fair rice-ears of the fertile reed-plain, gave it to our heavenly ancestor, Hiko-ho no Ninigi no Mikoto. Thereupon Hiko-ho no Ninigi no Mikoto, throwing open the barrier of heaven and clearing a cloud-path, urged on his super-human course until he came to rest. At this time the world was given over to widespread desolation. It was an age of darkness and disorder. In this gloom, therefore, he fostered justice, and so governed this western border.

"Our imperial ancestors and imperial parent, like gods, like sages, accumulated happiness and amassed glory. Many years elapsed from the date when our heavenly ancestor descended until now it is over 1,792,470 years. But the remote regions do not yet enjoy the blessings of imperial rule. Every town has always been allowed to have its lord, and every village its chief, who, each one for himself, makes division of territory and practises mutual aggression and conflict.

"Now I have heard from the Ancient of the Sea, that in the East there is a fair land encircled on all sides by blue mountains. Moreover, there is there one who flew down riding in a heavenly rock-boat. I think that this land will undoubtedly be suitable for the extension of the heavenly task, so that its

glory should fill the universe. It is doubtless the centre of
the world. The person who flew down was, I believe, Nigi-
haya-hi. Why should we not proceed thither, and make it the
capital?"

All the imperial princes answered, and said: "The truth of
this is manifest. This thought is constantly present to our
minds also. Let us go thither quickly." This was the year
Kinoye Tora (51st) of the Great Year.

In that year, in winter, on the Kanoto Tori day (the 5th)
of the 10th month, the new moon of which was on the day
Hinoto Mi, the emperor in person led the imperial princes and
a naval force on an expedition against the East. When he
arrived at the Haya-suhi gate, there was there a fisherman who
came riding in a boat. The emperor summoned him and then
inquired of him, saying: "Who art thou?" He answered and
said: "Thy servant is a country-god, and his name is Utsuhiko.
I angle for fish in the bays of ocean. Hearing that the son of
the heavenly deity was coming, therefore I forthwith came to
receive him." Again he inquired of him, saying: "Canst thou
act as my guide?" He answered and said: "I will do so."
The emperor ordered the end of a pole of Shihi wood to be
given to the fisher, and caused him to be taken and pulled into
the imperial vessel, of which he was made pilot.

A name was especially granted him, and he was called
Shihi-ne-tsu-hiko. He was the first ancestor of the Yamato
no Atahe.

Proceeding on their voyage, they arrived at Usa in the land
of Tsukushi. At this time there appeared the ancestors of the
Kuni-tsu-ko of Usa, named Usa-tsu-hiko and Usa-tsu-hime.
They built a palace raised on one pillar on the banks of the
River Usa, and offered them a banquet. Then, by imperial
command, Usa-tsu-hime was given in marriage to the emperor's
attendant minister Ama notane no Mikoto. Now, Ama notane no Mikoto was the remote ancestor of the Nakatomi Uji.

Eleventh month, 9th day. The emperor arrived at the harbor of Oka in the Land of Tsukushi.

Twelfth month, 27th day. He arrived at the province of
Aki, where he dwelt in the palace of Ye.

The year Kinoto U, Spring, 3d month, 6th day. Going

onward, he entered the land of Kibi, and built a temporary palace in which he dwelt. It was called the palace of Taka-shima. Three years passed, during which time he set in order the helms of his ships, and prepared a store of provisions. It was his desire by a single effort to subdue the empire.

The year Tsuchinoye Muma, Spring, 2d month, 11th day. The imperial forces at length proceeded eastward, the prow of one ship touching the stern of another. Just when they reached Cape Naniho they encountered a current of great swiftness. Whereupon that place was called Nami-haya (wave-swift) or Nami-hana (wave-flower). It is now called Naniha, which is a corruption of this.

Third month, 10th day. Proceeding upwards against the stream, they went straight on, and arrived at the port of Awo-Kumo no Shira-date, in the township of Kusaka, in the province of Kafuchi.

Summer, 4th month, 9th day. The imperial forces in martial array marched on to Tatsuta. The road was narrow and precipitous, and the men were unable to march abreast, so they returned and again endeavored to go eastward, crossing over Mount Ikoma. In this way they entered the inner country.

Now when Naga-sune-hiko heard this, he said: "The object of the children of the heavenly deity in coming hither is assuredly to rob me of my country." So he straightway levied all the forces under his dominion, and intercepted them at the Hill of Kusaka. A battle was engaged, and Itsuse no Mikoto was hit by a random arrow on the elbow. The imperial forces were unable to advance against the enemy. The emperor was vexed, and revolved in his inmost heart a divine plan, saying: "I am the descendant of the sun-goddess, and if I proceed against the sun to attack the enemy, I shall act contrary to the way of heaven. Better to retreat and make a show of weakness. Then, sacrificing to the gods of heaven and earth, and bringing on our backs the might of the sun goddess, let us follow her rays and trample them down. If we do so, the enemy will assuredly be routed of themselves, and we shall not stain our swords with blood."

They all said: "It is good." Thereupon he gave orders to the army, saying: "Wait a while and advance no further."

So he withdrew his forces, and the enemy also did not dare to attack him.   He then retired to the port of Kusaka, where he set up shields, and made a warlike show.   Therefore the name of this port was changed to Tatetsu, which is now corrupted into Tadetsu.

Before this, at the battle of Kusaka, there was a man who hid in a great tree, and by so doing escaped danger.   So pointing to this tree, he said: "I am grateful to it, as to my mother." Therefore the people of the day called that place Omo no ki no Mura.

Fifth month, 8th day.   The army arrived at the port of Yamaki in Chinu (also called Port Yama no wi).   Now Itsuse no Mikoto's arrow wound was extremely painful.   He grasped his sword, and striking a martial attitude, said: "How exasperating it is that a man should die of a wound received at the hands of slaves, and should not avenge it!"   The people of that day therefore called the place Wo no Minoto.

Proceeding onward, they reached Mount Kama in the Land of Kii, where Itsuse no Mikoto died in the army, and was therefore buried at Mount Kama.

Sixth month, 23d day.   The army arrived at the village of Nagusa, where they put to death the Tohe of Nagusa.   Finally they crossed the moor of Sano, and arrived at the village of Kami in Kumano.   Here he embarked in the rock-boat of heaven, and leading his army, proceeded onward by slow degrees.   In the midst of the sea, they suddenly met with a violent wind, and the imperial vessel was tossed about.   Then Ina-ihi no Mikoto exclaimed and said: "Alas! my ancestors were heavenly deities, and my mother was a goddess of the sea.   Why do they harass me by land, and why, moreover, do they harass me by sea?"   When he had said this, he drew his sword and plunged into the sea, where he became changed into the god Sabi-Mochi.

Miki In no no Mikoto, also indignant at this, said: "My mother and my aunt are both sea-goddesses; why do they raise great billows to overwhelm us?"   So, treading upon the waves, he went to the Eternal Land.   The emperor was now alone with the imperial prince, Tagishi-Mimi no Mikoto.   Leading his army forward, he arrived at Port Arazaka in Kumano (also called Nishiki Bay), where he put to death the Tohe of Nishiki. At this time the gods belched up a poisonous vapor, from which every one suffered. For this reason the imperial army was again unable to exert itself. Then there was there a man by name Kumano no Takakuraji, who unexpectedly had a dream, in which Ama-terasu no Ohokami spoke to Take-mika-tsuchi no Kami, saying: "I still hear a sound of disturbance from the central land of reed-plains. Do thou again go and chastise it."

Take-mika-tsuchi no Kami answered and said: "Even if I go not I can send down my sword, with which I subdued the land, upon which the country will of its own accord become peaceful." To this Ama-terasu no Kami assented. Thereupon Take-mika-tsuchi no Kami addressed Taka Kuraji, saying: "My sword, which is called Futsu no Mitama, I will now place in the storehouse. Do thou take it and present it to the heavenly grandchild." Taka Kuraji said, "Yes," and thereupon awoke. The next morning, as instructed in his dream, he opened the storehouse, and on looking in, there was indeed there a sword which had fallen down (from heaven) and was standing upside down on the plank floor of the storehouse. So he took it and offered it to the emperor. At this time the emperor happened to be asleep. He awoke suddenly, and said: "What a long time I have slept."

On inquiry he found that the troops who had been affected by the poison had all recovered their senses and were afoot. The emperor then endeavored to advance into the interior, but among the mountains it was so precipitous that there was no road by which they could travel. And they wandered about not knowing whither to direct their march.

Then Ama-terasu no Oho-Kami instructed the emperor in a dream of the night saying: "I will now send the Yata-garasu, make it thy guide through the land." Then there did indeed appear the Yata-garasu flying down from the void.

The emperor said: "The coming of this crow is in due accordance with my auspicous dream. How grand! How splendid! My imperial ancestor Ama-terasu no Oho-Kami, desires therewith to assist me in creating the hereditary institution."

At this time Hi no Omi no Mikoto, ancestor of the Oho-
tomo House, taking with him Oho-kume as commander of the
main body, guided by the direction taken by the crow, looked
up to it and followed after, until at length they arrived at the
district of Lower Uda.   Therefore they named the place which
they reached the village of Ukechi in Uda.   At this time by
an imperial order he commended Hi no Omi no Mikoto, saying:
"Thou art faithful and brave, and art moreover a successful
guide.   Therefore will I give thee a new name, and will call
thee Michi no Omi!"

Autumn, 8th month, 2d day.   The emperor sent to summon Ukeshi the elder and Ukeshi the younger.   These two
were chiefs of the district of Uda.   Now Ukeshi the elder did
not come.   But Ukeshi the younger came, and making obei-
sance at the gate of the camp, declared as follows: "Thy servant's elder brother, Ukeshi the elder, shows signs of resistance.
Hearing that the descendant of heaven was about to arrive, he
forthwith raised an army with which to make an attack.   But
having seen from afar the might of the imperial army, he was
afraid, and did not dare to oppose it.   Therefore he has
secretly placed his troops in ambush, and has built for the occasion a new palace, in the hall of which he has prepared engines.
It is his intention to invite the emperor to a banquet there, and
then to do him a mischief.   I pray that this treachery be noted,
and that good care be taken to make preparation against it."

The emperor straightway sent Michi no Omi no Mikoto to
observe the signs of his opposition.   Michi no Omi no Mikoto
clearly ascertained his hostile intentions, and being greatly
enraged, shouted at him in a blustering manner: "Wretch!
thou shalt thyself dwell in the house which thou hast made."
So grasping his sword and drawing his bow, he urged him and
drove him within it.   Ukeshi the elder being guilty before
heaven, and the matter not admitting of excuse, of his own
accord trod upon the engine and was crushed to death.   His
body was then brought out and decapitated, and the blood
which flowed from it reached above the ankle.   Therefore that
place was called Udan no chi-hara.   After this Ukeshi the
younger prepared a great feast of beef and *sake*, with which he
entertained the imperial army.   The emperor distributed this

flesh and *sake* to the common soldiers, upon which they sang
the following verses:

"In the high $\left\{ \begin{array}{c} \text{castle} \\ \text{tree} \end{array} \right\}$ of Uda
 I set a snare for woodcock,
 And waited,
 But no woodcock came to it;
 A valiant whale came to it."

This is called a Kume song. At the present time, when the
department of music performs this song, there is still the measurement of great and small by the hand, as well as a distinction
of coarse and fine in the notes of the voice. This is by a rule
handed down from antiquity. After this the emperor wished
to respect the Land of Yoshino, so, taking personal command
of the light troops, he made a progress round by way of Ukechi
Mura in Uda. When he came to Yoshino, there was a man
who came out of a well. He shone and had a tail. The
emperor inquired of him, saying: "What man art thou?" He
answered and said: "Thy servant is a local deity, and his name
is Wihikari." He it is who was the first ancestor of the
Yoshino no Obito.

Proceeding a little further, there was another man with a
tail, who burst open a rock and came forth from it. The
emperor inquired of him, saying: "What man art thou?" He
answered and said: "Thy servant is the child of Iha-oshiwake."
It is he who was the first ancestor of the Kuzu of Yoshino.
Then, skirting the river, he proceded westward, when there
appeared another man, who had made a fishtrap and was catch-
ing fish. On the emperor making inquiry of him, he answered
and said: "Thy servant is the son of Nihe-molsu." He it is
who was the first ancestor of the U-kahi of Ata.

Ninth month, 5th day. The emperor ascended to the peak
of Mount Takakura in Uda, whence he had a prospect over all
the land. On Kuni-mi Hill there were descried eighty bandits.
Moreover at the acclivity of the Me-Zaka there was posted
an army of women, and at the acclivity of Wo-Zaka there was
stationed a force of men. At the acclivity of Sumi-Zaka was

placed burning charcoal. This was the origin of the names
Me-Zaka, Wo-Zaka and Sumi-Zaka.

Again there was the army of Ye-Shiki, which covered all
the village of Ihare. All the places occupied by the enemy
were strong positions, and therefore the roads were cut off and
obstructed, so that there was no room for passage. The emperor, indignant at this, made prayer on that night in person,
and then fell asleep. The heavenly deity appeared to him in
a dream, and instructed him, saying: "Take earth from within
the shrine of the heavenly mount Kagu, and of it make eighty
heavenly platters. Also make sacred jars and therewith sacrifice to the gods of heaven and earth. Moreover pronounce a
solemn imprecation. If thou doest so, the enemy will render
submission of their own accord."

The emperor received with reverence the directions given
in his dream, and proceeded to carry them into execution.
Now Ukeshi the younger again addressed the emperor, saying:
"There are in the province of Yamato, in the village of Shiki,
eighty Shiki bandits. Moreover in the village of Taka-wohari
(some say Katsuraki) there are eighty Akagane bandits.

"All these tribes intend to give battle to the emperor, and
thy servant is anxious in his own mind on his account. It were
now good to take clay from the heavenly mount Kagu and
therewith to make heavenly platters with which to sacrifice to
the gods of the heavenly shrines and of the earthly shrines.
If after doing so thou dost attack the enemy, they may be
easily driven off."

The emperor, who had already taken the words of his dream
for a good omen, when he now heard the words of Ukeshi the
younger, was still more pleased in his heart. He caused Shihi-
netsu-hiko to put on ragged garments and a grass hat and to
disguise himself as an old man. He also caused Ukeshi the
younger to cover himself with a winnowing tray, so as to
assume the appearance of an old woman, and then addressed
them, saying: "Do ye two proceed to the heavenly mount
Kagu, and secretly take earth from its summit. Having done
so, return hither. By means of you I shall then divine whether
my undertaking will be successful or not. Do your utmost
and be watchful." Now the enemy's army filled the road,

and made all passage impossible.   Then Shihi-netsu-hiko
prayed, and said: "If it will be possible for our emperor to
conquer this land, let the road by which we must travel become
open.   But if not, let the brigands surely oppose our passage."

Having thus spoken they set forth and went straight
onward.   Now the hostile band, seeing the two men, laughed
loudly, and said: "What an uncouth old man and old woman!"
So with one accord they left the road, and allowed the two
men to pass and proceed to the mountain, where they took the
clay and returned with it.   Hereupon the emperor was greatly
pleased, and with this clay he made eighty platters, eighty
heavenly small jars and sacred jars, with which he went to the
upper waters of the River Nifu and sacrificed to the gods of
heaven and earth.   Immediately, on the Asahara plain by the
river of Uda, it became as it were like foam on the water,
the result of the curse cleaving to them.   Moreover the emperor went on to utter a vow, saying: "I will now make *Ame* in
the eighty platters without using water.   If the *Ame* is formed,
then shall I assuredly without effort and without recourse to
the might of arms reduce the empire to peace."   So he made
Ame, which forthwith became formed of itself.   Again he
made a vow, saying: "I will now take the sacred jars and sink
them in the River Nifu.   If the fishes, whether great or small,
become every one drunken and are carried down the stream,
like as it were to floating *maki* leaves, then shall I assuredly
succeed in establishing this land.   But if this be not so, there
will never be any results."

Thereupon he sank the jars in the river with their mouths
downward.   After a while the fish all came to the surface gap-
ing, gasping as they floated down the stream.   Then Shihi-
netsu–hiko, seeing this, represented it to the emperor, who was
greatly rejoiced, and plucking up a five-hundred-branched
masakaki tree of the upper waters of the River Nifu, he did
worship therewith to all the gods.   It was with this that the
custom began of selling sacred jars.

At this time he commanded Michi no Omi no Mikoto, saying: "We are now in person about to celebrate a public festival to Taka-mi-Musubi no Mikoto, and I appoint thee ruler of
the festival, and I grant thee the title of Idzu-hime.   The

earthen jars which are set up shall be called the Idzube or sacred jars, the fire shall be called Idzu no Kagu-tsuchi or sacred-fire-elder, the water shall be called Idzu no Midzu-ha no me or sacred-water-female, the food shall be called Idzuuka no me, or sacred-food-female, the firewood shall be called Idzu no Yama-tsuchi or sacred-mountain-elder, and the grass shall be called Idzu no no-tsuchi or sacred-moor-elder."

Winter, 10th month, 1st day. The emperor tasted the food of the Idzube, and arraying his troops set forth upon his march. He first of all attacked the eighty bandits at Mount Kunimi, routed and slew them. It was in this campaign that the emperor, fully resolved on victory, made these verses, saying:

> "Like the Shitadami
> Which creep round
> The great rock
> Of the Sea of Ise,
> Where blows the divine wind—
> Like the Shitadami,
> My boys! My boys!
> We will creep around
> And smite them utterly,
> And smite them utterly."

In this poem, by the "great rock" is intended the Hill of Kunimi.

After this the band which remained was still numerous, and their disposition could not be fathomed. So the emperor privately commanded Michi no Omi no Mikoto, saying: "Do thou take with thee the Oho Kume, and make a great *muro* at the village of Osaka. Prepare a copious banquet, invite the enemy to it, and then capture them." Michi no Omi no Mikoto thereupon, in obedience to the emperor's sacred behest, dug a *muro* at Osaka, and having selected his bravest soldiers, stayed therein mingled with the enemy. He secretly arranged with them, saying: "When they have got tipsy with *sake*, I will strike up a song. Do you when you hear the sound of my song, all at the same time stab the enemy."

Having made this arrangement they took their seats, and the drinking bout proceeded. The enemy, unaware that there was any plot, abandoned themselves to their feelings, and

promptly became intoxicated.   Then Michi no Omi no Mikoto
struck up the following song:

> " At Osaka
> In the great Muro-house,
> Though men in plenty
> Enter and stay,
> We the glorious
> Sons of warriors,
> Wielding our mallet-heads,
> Wielding our stone-mallets,
> Will smite them utterly."

Now when our troops heard this song, they all drew at the
same time their mallet-headed swords, and simultaneously slew
the enemy, so that there were no eaters left.   The imperial
army were greatly delighted; they looked up to heaven and
laughed.   Therefore he made a song saying:

> "Though folk say
> That one Yemishi
> Is a match for one hundred men,
> They do not so much as resist."

The practice according to which, at the present time, the
Kume sing this and then laugh loud, had this origin.   Again
he sang, saying:

> " Ho! now is the time!
> Ho! now is the time!
> Ha! Ha! Psha!
> Even now
> My boys!
> Even now,
> My boys!"

All these songs were sung in accordance with the secret
behest of the emperor.   He had not presumed to compose
them with his own motion.

Then the emperor said: "It is the part of a good general
when victorious to avoid arrogance.   The chief brigands have
now been destroyed, but there are ten bands of villains of a
similar stamp, who are disputatious.

"Their disposition cannot be ascertained.   Why should we

remain for a long time in one place? By so doing we could not
have control over emergencies!" So he removed his camp to
another place.

Eleventh month, 7th day. The imperial army proceeded
in great force to attack the Hiko of Shiki. First of all the
emperor sent a messenger to summon Shiki the elder, but he
refused to obey. Again the Yata-garasu was sent to bring
him. When the crow reached his camp it cried to him, saying:
"The child of the heavenly deity sends for thee. Haste!
haste!" Shiki the elder was enraged at this and said: "Just
when I heard that the conquering deity of heaven was coming
I was indignant at this; why shouldst thou, a bird of the crow
tribe, utter such an abominable cry?" So he drew his bow
and aimed at it. The crow forthwith fled away, and next proceeded to the house of Shiki the younger, where it cried, saying: "The child of the heavenly deity summons thee. Haste!
haste!" Then Shiki the younger was afraid, and changing
countenance, said: "Thy servant, hearing of the approach of
the conquering deity of heaven, is full of dread morning and
evening. Well hast thou cried to me, O crow!"

He straightway made eight leaf-platters, on which he disposed food, and entertained the crow. Accordingly, in obedience to the crow, he proceeded to the emperor and informed
him, saying: "My elder brother, Shiki the elder, hearing of
the approach of the child of the heavenly deity, forthwith
assembled eighty bandits and provided arms, with which he
is about to do battle with thee. It will be well to take measures against him without delay." The emperor accordingly
assembled his generals and inquired of them, saying: "It
appears that Shiki the elder has now rebellious intentions. I
summoned him, but again he will not come. What is to be
done?" The generals said: "Shiki the elder is a crafty knave.
It will be well, first of all, to send Shiki the younger to make
matters clear to him, and at the same time to make explanations to Kuraji the elder and Kuraji the younger. If after
that they still refuse submission, it will not be too late to take
warlike measures against them."

Shiki the younger was accordingly sent to explain to them
their interests. But Shiki the elder and the others adhered

to their foolish design, and would not consent to submit. Then
Shiki-netsu-hiko advised as follows: "Let us first send out our
feebler troops by the Osaka road. When the enemy sees them
he will assuredly proceed thither with all his best troops. We
should then straightway urge forward our robust troops, and
make straight for Sumi-Zaka.

"Then with the water of the River Uda we should sprinkle
the burning charcoal, and suddenly take them unawares;
when they cannot fail to be routed." The emperor approved
this plan, and sent out the feebler troops toward the enemy,
who, thinking that a powerful force was approaching, awaited
them with all their power. Now up to this time, whenever the
imperial army attacked, they invariably captured, and when
they fought they were invariably victorious, so that the fighting men were all wearied out. Therefore the emperor, to comfort the hearts of his leaders and men, struck off this verse:

> " As we fight
> Going forth and watching
> From between the trees
> Of Mount Inasa,
> We are famished.
> Ye keepers of cormorants
> (Birds of the island)
> Come now to our aid."

In the end he crossed Sumi-Zaka with the stronger troops,
and, going round by the rear, attacked them from two sides
and put them to the rout, killing their chieftains, Shiki the
elder, and the others.

Third month, 7th day. The emperor made an order, saying: "During the six years that our expedition against the
East has lasted, owing to my reliance on the majesty of Imperial Heaven, the wicked bands have met death. It is true that
the frontier lands are still unpurified, and that a remnant of
evil is still refractory. But in the region of the Central Land
there is no more wind and dust. Truly we should make a vast
and spacious capital and plan it great and strong.

"At present things are in a crude and obscure condition, and
the people's minds are unsophisticated. They roost in nests
or dwell in caves. Their manners are simply what is custom-

ary. Now if a great man were to establish laws, justice could not fail to flourish. And even if some gain should accrue to the people, in what way would this interfere with the sage's action? Moreover it will be well to open up and clear the mountains and forests, and to construct a palace. Then I may reverently assume the precious dignity, and so give peace to my good subjects. Above, I should then respond to the kindness of the heavenly powers in granting me the kingdom; and below, I should extend the line of the imperial descendants and foster rightmindedness. Thereafter the capital may be extended so as to embrace all the six cardinal points (*sic*), and the eight cords may be covered so as to form a roof. Will this not be well? When I observe the Kashiha-bara plain, which lies southwest of Mount Unebi, it seems the centre of the land. I must set it in order." Accordingly, he, in this month, commanded officers to set about the construction of an imperial residence.

Year Kanoye Saru, Autumn, 8th month, 16th day. The emperor, intending to appoint a wife, sought afresh children of noble families. Now there was a man who made representation to him, saying: "There is a child who was born to Koto-Shiro-Nushi no Kami by his union with Tama-Kushi-hime, daughter of Mizo-kuhi-ni no Kami of Mishima. Her name is Hime-tatara-i-suzu-hime no Mikoto. She is a woman of remarkable beauty." The emperor was rejoiced. And on the 24th day of the 9th month he received Hime-tatara-i-suzu-hime no Mikoto and made her his wife.

Year Kanoto Tori, Spring, 1st month, 1st day. The emperor assumed the imperial dignity in the palace of Kashiha-bara. This year is reckoned the first year of his reign. He honored his wife by making her empress. The children born to him by her were Kami-ya-wi-Mimi no Mikoto and Kami-Nunagaha-Mimi no Mikoto. Therefore there is an ancient saying in praise of this, as follows: "In Kashiha-bara in Unebi, he mightily established his palace-pillars on the foundation of the bottom rock, and reared aloft the cross roof-timbers to the plain of high heaven. The name of the emperor who thus began to rule the empire was Kami Yamato Ihare-biko Hohodemi."

Fourth year, Spring, 2d month, 23d day. The emperor issued the following decree: "The spirits of our imperial ancestors, reflecting their radiance down from heaven, illuminate and assist us. All our enemies have now been subdued, and there is peace within the seas. We ought to take advantage of this to perform sacrifice to the heavenly deities, and therewith develop filial duty."

He accordingly established spirit-terraces among the Tomi hills, which were called Kami-tsu-wono no Kaki-hara and Shimo tsu-wono no Kaki-hara. There he worshipped his imperial ancestors, the heavenly deities.

Seventy-sixth year, Spring, 3d month, 11th day. The emperor died in the palace of Kashiha-bara. His age was then 127. The following year, Autumn, the 12th day of the 9th month, he was buried in the Misasigi, northeast of Mount Unebi.

THE FOUNDATION OF BUDDHISM

B.C. 623

THOMAS WILLIAM RHYS-DAVIDS

Not so many years ago, at the time when Buddhism first became known in Europe through philosophic writings of about six centuries after Buddha, then newly translated, it caused amazement that a religion which had brought three hundred millions of people under its sway should acknowledge no god. But the religion of Buddha, during a thousand years of practice by the Hindus, is entirely different from the representations given us in these translations. As shown by the bas-reliefs covering the ancient monuments of India, this religion, changed by modern scientists into a belief in atheism, is, in fact, of all religions the most polytheistic.

In the first Buddhist monuments, dating back eighteen to twenty centuries, the reformer simply figures as an emblem. The imprint of his feet, the figure of the "Bo tree" under which he entered the state of supreme wisdom, are worshipped; and though he disdained all gods, and only sought to teach a new code of morals, we shortly see Buddha himself depicted as a god. In the early stages he is generally represented as alone, but gradually appears in the company of the Brahman gods. He is finally lost in a crowd of gods, and becomes nothing more than an incarnation of one of the Brahman deities. From that time Buddhism has been practically extinct in India.

This transformation took a thousand years to bring about. During part of this great interval Buddha was being worshipped as an all-powerful god. Legends are told of his appearance to his disciples, and of favors he granted them.

It has been said that Buddha tried to set aside the laws of caste. This is an error. Neither did he attempt to break the Brahmanic Pantheon.

Buddhism, which to-day is the religion of three hundred million people, about one-fifth of the world's inhabitants, toward the seventh or eighth century of our era almost entirely disappeared from its birthplace, India, whence it had spread over the rest of Asia, China, Russian Tartary, Burmah, etc. Only the two extreme frontiers of India, Nepal, in the north, and Ceylon, in the south, now practise the Buddhist cult.

Gautama Buddha left behind him no written works. The Buddhists believe that he composed works which his immediate disciples learned

160

by heart, and which were committed to writing long afterward.   This is
not impossible, as the *Vedas*[1] were handed down in this manner for many
hundreds of years.

There was certainly an historical basis for the Buddhist legend.   In
fact, the legends group themselves round a number of very distinct
occurrences.

At the end of the sixth century B.C. those Aryan tribes sprung from
the same stem as our own ancestors, who have preserved for us in their
Vedic songs so precious a relic of ancient thought and life, had pushed
on beyond the five rivers of the Punjab, and were settled far down into
the valley of the Ganges.   They had given up their nomadic habits,
dwelling in villages and towns, their wealth being in land, produce, and
cattle.

From democratic beginnings the whole nation had gradually become
bound by an iron system of caste.   The country was split up into little
sections, each governed by some petty despot, and harassed by interne-
cine feuds.   Religion had become a debasing ritualism, with charms and
incantations, fear of the influence of the stars, and belief in dreams and
omens.   The idea of the existence of a soul was supplemented by the
doctrine of transmigration.

The priests were well-meaning, ignorant, and possessed of a sincere
belief in their own divinity.   The religious use of the *Vedas* and the
right to sacrifice were strictly confined to the Brahmans.   There were
travelling logicians, anchorites, ascetics, and solitary hermits.   Although
the ranks of the priesthood were closed against intruders, still a man of
lower caste might become a religious teacher and reformer.   Such were
the conditions which welcomed Gautama Buddha.

ONE hundred miles northeast of Benares, at Kapilavastu,
on the banks of the river Rohini, the modern Kohana,
there lived about five hundred years before Christ a tribe
called Sakyas.   The peaks of the mighty Himalayas could
be seen in the distance.   The Sakyas frequently quarrelled
with the Koliyans, a neighboring tribe, over their water supplies from the river.   Just now the two clans were at peace,
and two daughters of the rajah of the Koliyans were wives of
Suddhodana, the rajah of the Sakyas.   Both were childless.
This was deemed a very great misfortune among the Aryans,
who thought that the star of a man's existence after death
depended upon ceremonies to be performed by his heir.   There

[1] *Vedas:* The sacred books of the Hindus, in Sanscrit; probably
written about six or seven centuries before Christ.   *Veda* means knowledge.   The books comprise hymns, prayers, and liturgical forms.

was great rejoicing, therefore, when, in about the forty-fifth year of her age, the elder sister promised her husband a son. In due time she started with the intention of being confined at her parents' house, but it was on the way, under the shade of some lofty satin trees in a pleasant grove called Lumbini, that her son, the future Buddha, was unexpectedly born. The mother and child were carried back to Suddhodana's house, and there, seven days afterward, the mother died; but the boy found a careful nurse in his mother's sister, his father's other wife.

Many marvellous stories have been told about the miraculous birth and precocious wisdom and power of Gautama. The name Siddhartha is said to have been given him as a child, Gautama being the family name. Numerous were his later titles, such as Sakyasinha, the lion of the tribe of Sakya; Sakya-muni, the Sakya sage; Sugata, the happy one; Sattha, the teacher; Jina, the conqueror; Bhagava, the blessed one, and many others.

In his twentieth year he was married to his cousin, Yasodhara, daughter of the rajah of Koli. Devoting himself to home pleasures, he was accused by his relations of neglecting those manly exercises necessary for one who might at any time have to lead his people in war. Gautama heard of this, and appointed a day for a general tournament, at which he distinguished himself by being easily the first at all the trials of skill and prowess, thus winning the good opinions of all the clansmen. This is the solitary record of his youth.

Nothing more is heard of him until, in his twenty-ninth year, Gautama suddenly abandoned his home to devote himself entirely to the study of religion and philosophy. It is said that an angel appeared to him in four visions: a man broken down by age, a sick man, a decaying corpse, and lastly, a dignified hermit. Each time Channa, his charioteer, told him that decay and death were the fate of all living beings. The charioteer also explained to him the character and aims of the ascetics, exemplified by the hermit.

Thoughts of the calm life of the hermit strongly stirred him. One day, the occasion of the last vision, as he was entering his chariot to return home, news was brought to him that his wife

Yasodhara had given birth to a son, his only child, who was called Rahula. This was about ten years after his marriage. The idea that this new tie might become too strong for him to break seems to have been the immediate cause of his flight. He returned home thoughtful and sad.

But the people of Kapilavastu were greatly delighted at the birth of the young heir, their rajah's only grandson. Gautama's return became an ovation, and he entered the town amid a general celebration of the happy event. Amid the singers was a young girl, his cousin, whose song contained the words, "Happy the father, happy the mother, happy the wife of such a son and husband." In the word "Happy" there was a double meaning: it meant also "freed" from the chains of sin and of existence, saved. In gratitude to one who at such a time reminded him of his higher duties, Gautama took off his necklace of pearls and sent it to her. She imagined that she had won the love of young Siddhartha, but he took no further notice of her.

That night the dancing girls came, but he paid them no attention, and gradually fell into an uneasy slumber. At midnight he awoke, and sent Channa for his horse. While waiting for the steed Gautama gently opened the door of the room where Yasodhara was sleeping, surrounded by flowers, with one hand on the head of her child. After one loving, fond glance he tore himself away. Accompanied only by Channa he left his home and wealth and power, his wife and only child behind him, to become a penniless wanderer. This was the Great Renunciation.

There follows a story of a vision. Mara, the great tempter, the spirit of evil, appears in the sky, urging Gautama to stop. He promises him a universal kingdom over the four great continents if he will but give up his enterprise. The tempter does not prevail, but from that time he followed Gautama as a shadow, hoping to seduce him from that right way.

All night Gautama rode, and at the dawn, when beyond the confines of his father's domain, dismounts. He cuts off his long hair with his sword, and sends back all his ornaments and his horse by the faithful charioteer.

Seven days he spends alone beneath the shade of a mango

grove, and then fares onward to Rajogriha, the capital of
Magadha. This town was the seat of Bimbasara, one of the
most powerful princes in the eastern valley of the Ganges.
In the hillside caves near at hand were several hermits. To
one of these Brahman teachers, Alara, Gautama attached himself, and later to another named Udraka. From these he
learned all that Hindu philosophy could teach.

Still unsatisfied, Gautama next retired to the jungle of
Uruvela, on the most northerly spur of the Viadhya range of
mountains, near the present temple of Buddha Gaya. Here
for six years he gave himself up to the severest penance until
he was wasted away to a shadow by fasting and self-mortifica-
tion. Such self-control spread his fame "like the sound of a
great bell hung in the skies." But the more he fasted and
denied himself, the more he felt himself a prey to a mental
torture worse than any bodily suffering.

At last one day when walking slowly up and down, lost in
thought, through extreme weakness he staggered and fell to
the ground. His disciples thought he was dead, but he recovered. Despairing of further profit from such rigorous penance,
he began to take regular food and gave up his self-mortifica-
tion. At this his disciples forsook him and went away to
Benares. In their opinion mental conquest lay only through
bodily suppression.

There now ensued a second crisis in Gautama's career which
culminated in his withstanding the renewed attacks of the
tempter after violent struggles.

Soon after, if not on the very day when his disciples had left
him, he wandered out toward the banks of the Nairaujara,
receiving his morning meal from the hands of Sujuta, the
daughter of a neighboring villager, and sat down to eat it under
the shade of a large tree (*ficus religiosa*), called from that day
the sacred "Bo tree," or tree of wisdom. He remained there
all day long, pondering what next to do. All the attractions
of the luxurious home he had abandoned rose up before him
most alluringly. But as the day ended his lofty spirit had won
the victory. All doubts had lifted as mists before the morning
sun. He had become Buddha, that is, enlightened. He had
grasped the solution of the great mystery of sorrow. He

thought, having solved its causes and its cure, he had gained the haven of peace, and believed that in the power over the human heart of inward culture and of love to others he had discovered a foundation which could never be shaken.

From this time Gautama claimed no merit for penances. A feeling of great loneliness possessed him as he arrived at his psychological and ethical conclusions. He almost despaired of winning his fellow-men to his system of salvation, salvation merely by self-control and ove, without any of the rites, ceremonies, charms, or incantations of the Hindu religion.

The thought of mankind, otherwise, as he imagined, utterly doomed and lost, made Gautama resolve, at whatever hazard, to proclaim his doctrine to the world. It is certain that he had a most intense belief in himself and his mission.

He had intended first to proclaim his new doctrine to his old teachers, Alara and Udraka, but finding that they were dead, he proceeded to the deer forest near Benares where his former disciples were then living. In the cool of the evening he enters the deer-park near the city, but his former disciples resolve not to recognize him as a master. He tells them that they are still in the way of death, whereas he has found the way of salvation and can lead them to it, having become a Buddha. And as they reply with objections to his claims, he explains the fundamental truths of his system and principles of his new gospel, which the aged Kondanya was the first to accept from his master's lips. This exposition is preserved in the Dhammacakkappavattana Sutta, the Sutra of the Foundations of the Kingdom of Righteousness.

Gautama Buddha taught that everything corporeal is material and therefore impermanent. Man in his bodily existence is liable to sorrow, decay, and death. The reign of unholy desires in his heart produces unsatisfactory longings, useless weariness, and care. Attempted purification by oppressing the body is only wasted effort. It is the moral evil of the heart which keeps a man chained down in the degraded state of bodily life, which binds him in a union with the material world. Virtue and goodness will only insure him for a time, and, in another birth, a higher form of material life. From the chains of existence only the complete eradication of all evil will set him free.

But these ideas must not be confused with Christian beliefs, for Buddhism teaches nothing of any immaterial existence. The foundations of its creed have been summed up in the Four Great Truths, which are as follows:

1. That misery always accompanies existence;
2. That all modes of existence of men or animals, in death or heaven, result from passion or desire (tanha);
3. That there is no escape from existence except by destruction of desire;
4. That this may be accomplished by following the fourfold way to Nirvana.

The four stages are called the Paths, the first being an awakening of the heart. The first enemy which the believer has to fight against is sensuality and the last is unkindliness. Above everything is universal charity. Till he has gained that the believer is still bound, his mind is still dark. True enlightenment, true freedom, are complete only in love. The last great reward is " Nirvana," eternal rest or extinction.

For forty-five years Gautama taught in the valley of the Ganges. In the twentieth year his cousin Ananda became a mendicant and attended on Gautama. Another cousin, however, stirred up some persecution of the great teacher, and the oppositions of the Brahmans had to be faced.

There are clear accounts of the last few days of Gautama's life. On a journey toward Kusi-nagara he had rested in a grove at Pawa, presented to the society by a goldsmith of that place named Chunda. After a midday meal of rice and pork, prepared by Chunda, the Master started for Kusi-nagara, but stopped to rest at the river Kukusta. Feeling that he was dying, he left a message for Chunda, promising him a great reward in some future existence. He died at the river Kukusta, near Kusi-nagara, teaching to the last.

Gautama's power arose from his practical philanthropy. His philosophy and ethics attracted the masses. He did not seek to found a new religion, but thought that all men would accept his form of the ancient creed. It was his society, the Sangha, or Buddhist order, rather than his doctrine, which gave to his religion its practical vitality.

The following lines, filled with the poetic beauty of the Orient, are taken from the last spoken words of the great founder of Buddhism and the *Book of the Great Decease*. They give a clew to the cult of that religion and breathe the spirit of Nirvana in every scintillating sentence. As nearly as may be the translation is a literal one, done by Rhys-Davids, the world's greatest living authority on this subject:

Now the Blessed One addressed the venerable Ananda, and said: "It may be, Ananda, that in some of you the thought may arise, ' The word of the Master is ended, we have no teacher more!' But it is not thus, Ananda, that you should regard it. The truths and the rules of the order which I have set forth and laid down for you all, let them, after I am gone, be the Teacher to you.

"Ananda! when I am gone address not one another in the way in which the brethren have heretofore addressed each other —with the epithet, that is, of 'Avuso' (Friend). A younger brother may be addressed by an elder with his name, or his family name, or the title ' Friend.' But an elder should be addressed by a younger brother as ' Lord ' or as ' Venerable Sir.'

"When I am gone, Ananda, let the order, if it should so wish, abolish all the lesser and minor precepts.

"When I am gone, Ananda, let the higher penalty be imposed on brother Khanna."

"But what, Lord, is the higher penalty?"

"Let Khanna say whatever he may like, Ananda; the brethren should neither speak to him, nor exhort him, nor admonish him."

Then the Blessed One addressed the brethren, and said: "It may be, brethren, that there may be doubt or misgiving in the mind of some brother as to the Buddha, or the truth, or the path, or the way. Inquire, brethren, freely. Do not have to reproach yourselves afterward with the thought, ' Our teacher was face to face with us, and we could not bring our- selves to inquire of the Blessed One when we were face to face with him.' "

And when he had thus spoken the brethren were silent.

And again the second and the third time the Blessed One

addressed the brethren, and said: "It may be, brethren, that there may be doubt or misgiving in the mind of some brother as to the Buddha, or the truth, or the path, or the way. Inquire, brethren, freely. Do not have to reproach yourselves afterward with the thought, ' Our teacher was face to face with us, and we could not bring ourselves to inquire of the Blessed One when we were face to face with him.' "

And even the third time the brethren were silent.

Then the Blessed One addressed the brethren, and said: "It may be, brethren, that you put no questions out of reverence for the teacher. Let one friend communicate to another."

And when he had thus spoken the brethren were silent.

And the venerable Ananda said to the Blessed One: "How wonderful a thing is it, Lord, and how marvellous! Verily, I believe that in this whole assembly of the brethren there is not one brother who has any doubt or misgiving as to the Buddha, or the truth, or the path, or the way!"

"It is out of the fulness of faith that thou hast spoken, Ananda! But, Ananda, the Tathagata knows for certain that in this whole assembly of the brethren there is not one brother who has any doubt or misgiving as to the Buddha, or the truth, or the path, or the way! For even the most backward, Ananda, of all these five hundred brethren has become converted, and is no longer liable to be born in a state of suffering, and is assured of final salvation."

Then the Blessed One addressed the brethren, and said: "Behold now, brethren, I exhort you, saying, ' Decay is inherent in all component things! Work out your salvation with diligence!' "

This was the last word of the Tathagata!

Then the Blessed One entered into the first stage of deep meditation. And rising out of the first stage he passed into the second. And rising out of the second he passed into the third. And rising out of the third stage he passed into the fourth. And rising out of the fourth stage of deep meditation he entered into the state of mind to which the infinity of space is alone present. And passing out of the mere consciousness of the infinity of space he entered into the state of mind to which nothing at all was specially present. And passing out

)f the consciousness of no special object he fell into a state
between consciousness and unconsciousness. And passing out
of the state between consciousness and unconsciousness he fell
into a state in which the consciousness both of sensations and
of ideas had wholly passed away.

Then the venerable Ananda said to the venerable Anuruddha: "O my Lord, O Anuruddha, the Blessed One is dead!"

"Nay! brother Ananda, the Blessed One is not dead. He
has entered into that state in which both sensations and ideas
have ceased to be!"

Then the Blessed One passing out of the state in which
both sensations and ideas have ceased to be, entered into the
state between consciousness and unconsciousness. And passing out of the state between consciousness and unconsciousness he entered into the state of mind to which nothing at all
is specially present. And passing out of the consciousness of
no special object he entered into the state of mind to which the
infinity of thought is alone present. And passing out of the
mere consciousness of the infinity of thought he entered into
the state of mind to which the infinity of space is alone present. And passing out of the mere consciousness of the infinity of space he entered into the fourth stage of deep meditation.
And passing out of the fourth stage he entered into the third.
And passing out of the third stage he entered into the second.
And passing out of the second he entered into the first. And
passing out of the first stage of deep meditation he entered the
second. And passing out of the second stage he entered into
the third. And passing out of the third stage he entered into
the fourth stage of deep meditation. And passing out of the
last stage of deep meditation he immediately expired.

When the Blessed One died there arose, at the moment of
his passing out of existence, a mighty earthquake, terrible and
awe-inspiring: and the thunders of heaven burst forth.

When the Blessed One died, Brahma Sahampati, at the
moment of his passing away from existence, uttered this stanza:

> "They all, all beings that have life, shall lay
> Aside their complex form—that aggregation
> Of mental and material qualities,
> That gives them, or in heaven or on earth,

Their fleeting individuality !
E'en as the teacher—being such a one,
Unequalled among all the men that are,
Successor of the prophets of old time,
Mighty by wisdom, and in insight clear—
        Hath died !"

When the Blessed One died, Sakka, the king of the gods, at the moment of his passing away from existence, uttered this stanza:

" They're transient all, each being's parts and powers,
Growth is their nature, and decay.
They are produced, they are dissolved again,
And then is best, when they have sunk to rest!"

When the Blessed One died, the venerable Anuruddha, at the moment of his passing away from existence, uttered these stanzas:

" When he who from all craving want was free,
Who to Nirvana's tranquil state had reached,
When the great sage finished his span of life,
No gasping struggle vexed that steadfast heart!
All resolute, and with unshaken mind,
He calmly triumphed o'er the pain of death.
E'en as a bright flame dies away, so was
His last deliverance from the bonds of life !"

When the Blessed One died, the venerable Ananda, at the moment of his passing away from existence, uttered this stanza:

" Then was there terror !
Then stood the hair on end !
When he endowed with every grace—
The supreme Buddha—died !"

When the Blessed One died, of those of the brethren who were not free from the passions, some stretched out their arms and wept, and some fell headlong to the ground, rolling to and fro in anguish at the thought: "Too soon has the Blessed One died! Too soon has the Happy One passed away from existence! Too soon has the Light gone out in the world!" But those of the brethren who were free from the passions (the Arahats) bore their grief collected and composed at the thought: "Impermanent are all component things! How is it possible that [they should not be dissolved]?"

Then the venerable Anuruddha exhorted the brethren, and said: "Enough, my brethren! Weep not, neither lament! Has not the Blessed One formerly declared this to us, that it is in the very nature of all things near and dear unto us, that we must divide ourselves from them, leave them, sever ourselves from them? How, then, brethren, can this be possible—that whereas anything whatever born, brought into being, and organized, contains within itself the inherent necessity of dissolution—how then can this be possible that such a being should not be dissolved? No such condition can exist! Even the spirits, brethren, will reproach us."

"But of what kind of spirits is the Lord, the venerable Anuruddha, thinking?"

"There are spirits, brother Ananda, in the sky, but of worldly mind, who dishevel their hair and weep, and stretch forth their arms and weep, fall prostrate on the ground, and roll to and fro in anguish at the thought: ' Too soon has the Blessed One died! Too soon has the Happy One passed away! Too soon has the Light gone out in the world!'

"There are spirits, too, Ananda, on the earth, and of worldly mind, who tear their hair and weep, and stretch forth their arms and weep, fall prostrate on the ground, and roll to and fro in anguish at the thought: ' Too soon has the Blessed One died! Too soon has the Happy One passed away! Too soon has the Light gone out in the world!'

"But the spirits who are free from passion hear it, calm and self-possessed, mindful of the saying which begins, ' Impermanent indeed are all component things. How then is it possible [that such a being should not be dissolved]?'"

Now the venerable Anuruddha and the venerable Ananda spent the rest of that night in religious discourse. Then the venerable Anuruddha said to the venerable Ananda: "Go now, brother Ananda, into Kusinara and inform the Mallas of Kusinara, saying, 'The Blessed One, O Vasetthas, is dead: do, then, whatever seemeth to you fit!'"

"Even so, Lord!" said the venerable Ananda, in assent to the venerable Anuruddha. And having robed himself early in the morning, he took his bowl, and went into Kusinara with one of the brethren as an attendant.

Now at that time the Mallas of Kusinara were assembled in the council hall concerning that very matter.

And the venerable Ananda went to the council hall of the Mallas of Kusinara; and when he had arrived there, he informed them, saying, "The Blessed One, O Vasetthas, is dead; do, then, whatever seemeth to you fit!"

And when they had heard this saying of the venerable Ananda, the Mallas, with their young men and their maidens and their wives, were grieved, and sad, and afflicted at heart. And some of them wept, dishevelling their hair, and some stretched forth their arms and wept, and some fell prostrate on the ground, and some reeled to and fro in anguish at the thought: "Too soon has the Blessed One died! Too soon has the Happy One passed away! Too soon has the Light gone out in the world!"

Then the Mallas of Kusinara gave orders to their attendants, saying, "Gather together perfumes and garlands, and all the music in Kusinara!"

And the Mallas of Kusinara took the perfumes and garlands, and all the musical instruments, and five hundred suits of apparel, and went to the Upavattana, to the Sala Grove of the Mallas, where the body of the Blessed One lay. There they passed the day in paying honor, reverence, respect, and homage to the remains of the Blessed One with dancing, and hymns, and music, and with garlands and perfumes; and in making canopies of their garments, and preparing decoration wreaths to hang thereon.

Then the Mallas of Kusinara thought: "It is much too late to burn the body of the Blessed One to-day. Let us now perform the cremation to-morrow." And in paying honor, reverence, respect, and homage to the remains of the Blessed One with dancing, and hymns, and music, and with garlands and perfumes; and in making canopies of their garments, and preparing decoration wreaths to hang thereon, they passed the second day too, and then the third day, and the fourth, and the fifth, and the sixth day also.

Then on the seventh day the Mallas of Kusinara thought:

"Let us carry the body of the Blessed One, by the south and outside, to a spot on the south, and outside of the city,—paying it honor, and reverence, and respect, and homage, with dance and song and music, with garlands and perfumes,—and there, to the south of the city, let us perform the cremation ceremony!"

And thereupon eight chieftains among the Mallas bathed their heads, and clad themselves in new garments with the intention of bearing the body of the Blessed One. But, behold, they could not lift it up!

Then the Mallas of Kusinara said to the venerable Anuruddha: "What, Lord, can be the reason, what can be the cause that eight chieftains of the Mallas who have bathed their heads, and clad themselves in new garments with the intention of bearing the body of the Blessed One, are unable to lift it up?"

"It is because you, O Vasetthas, have one purpose and the spirits have another purpose."

"But what, Lord, is the purpose of the spirits?"

"Your purpose, O Vasetthas, is this: 'Let us carry the body of the Blessed One, by the south and outside, to a spot on the south, and outside of the city,—paying it honor, and reverence, and respect, and homage, with dance and song and music, with garlands and perfumes,—and there, to the south of the city, let us perform the cremation ceremony.' But the purpose of the spirits, Vasetthas, is this: 'Let us carry the body of the Blessed One by the north to the north of the city, and entering the city by the north gate, let us bring it through the midst of the city into the midst thereof. And going out again by the eastern gate,—paying honor, and reverence, and respect, and homage to the body of the Blessed One, with heavenly dance, and song, and music, and garlands, and perfumes,—let us carry it to the shrine of the Mallas called Makuta-bandhana, to the east of the city, and there let us perform the cremation ceremony.'"

"Even according to the purpose of the spirits, so, Lord, let it be!"

Then immediately all Kusinara down even to the dust-bins and rubbish heaps became strewn knee-deep with Mandarava flowers from heaven! and while both the spirits from the skies, and the Mallas of Kusinara upon earth, paid honor, and reverence, and respect, and homage to the body of the Blessed One, with dance and song and music, with garlands and with perfumes, they carried the body by the north to the north of the city; and entering the city by the north gate they carried it through the midst of the city into the midst thereof; and going out again by the eastern gate they carried it to the shrine of the Mallas, called Makuta-bandhana; and there, to the east of the city, they laid down the body of the Blessed One.

Then the Mallas of Kusinara said to the venerable Ananda: "What should be done, Lord, with the remains of the Tathagata?"

"As men treat the remains of a king of kings, so, Vasetthas, should they treat the remains of a Tathagata."

"And how, Lord, do they treat the remains of a king of kings?"

"They wrap the body of a king of kings, Vasetthas, in a new cloth. When that is done they wrap it in cotton wool. When that is done they wrap it in a new cloth,—and so on till they have wrapped the body in five hundred successive layers of both kinds. Then they place the body in an oil vessel of iron, and cover that close up with another oil vessel of iron. They then build a funeral pile of all kinds of perfumes, and burn the body of the king of kings. And then at the four cross roads they erect a dagaba to the king of kings. This, Vasetthas, is the way in which they treat the remains of a king of kings. And as they treat the remains of a king of kings, so, Vasetthas, should they treat the remains of the Tathagata. At the four cross roads a dagaba should be erected to the Tathagata. And whosoever shall there place garlands or perfumes or paint, or make salutation there, or become in its presence calm in heart—that shall long be to them for a profit and a joy."

Therefore the Mallas gave orders to their attendants, saying, "Gather together all the carded cotton wool of the Mallas!"

Then the Mallas of Kusinara wrapped the body of the Blessed One in a new cloth. And when that was done they wrapped it in cotton wool. And when that was done, they wrapped it in a new cloth,—and so on till they had wrapped the body of the Blessed One in five hundred layers of both kinds. And then they placed the body in an oil vessel of iron, and covered that close up with another vessel of iron. And then they built a funeral pile of all kinds of perfumes, and upon it they placed the body of the Blessed One.

Now at that time the venerable Maha Kassapa was journeying along the high road from Pava to Kusinara with a great company of the brethren, with about five hundred of the brethren. And the venerable Maha Kassapa left the high road, and sat himself down at the foot of a certain tree.

Just at that time a certain naked ascetic who had picked up a Mandarava flower in Kusinara was coming along the high road to Pava. And the venerable Maha Kassapa saw the naked ascetic coming in the distance; and when he had seen him he said to the naked ascetic: "O friend! surely thou knowest our Master?"

"Yea, friend! I know him. This day the Samana Gautama has been dead a week! That is how I obtained this Mandarava flower."

And immediately of those of the brethren who were not yet free from the passions, some stretched out their arms and wept, and some fell headlong on the ground, and some reeled to and fro in anguish at the thought: "Too soon has the Blessed One died! Too soon has the Happy One passed away from existence! Too soon has the Light gone out in the world!"

But those of the brethren who were free from the passions (the Arahats) bore their grief collected and composed at the thought: "Impermanent are all component things! How is it possible that they should not be dissolved?"

Now at that time a brother named Subhadda, who had been received into the order in his old age, was seated there in their company. And Subhadda the old addressed the brethren and said: "Enough, brethren! Weep not, neither lament! We are well rid of the great Samana. We used to be annoyed by being told, 'This beseems you, this beseems you not.' But now we shall be able to do whatever we like; and what we do not like that we shall not have to do!"

But the venerable Maha Kassapa addressed the brethren,

and said: "Enough, my brethren! Weep not, neither lament! Has not the Blessed One formerly declared this to us, that it is in the very nature of all things near and dear unto us that we must divide ourselves from them, leave them, sever ourselves from them? How then, brethren, can this be possible— that whereas anything whatever born, brought into being, and organized contains within itself the inherent necessity of dissolution—how then can this be possible that such a being should not be dissolved? No such condition can exist!"

Now just at that time four chieftains of the Mallas had bathed their heads and clad themselves in new garments with the intention of setting on fire the funeral pile of the Blessed One. But, behold, they were unable to set it alight! Then the Mallas of Kusinara said to the venerable Anuruddha: "What, Lord, can be the reason, and what the cause, that four chieftains of the Mallas who have bathed their heads, and clad themselves in new garments, with the intention of setting on fire the funeral pile of the Blessed One, are unable to set it on fire?"

"It is because you, O Vasetthas, have one purpose, and the spirits have another purpose."

"But what, Lord, is the purpose of the spirits?"

"The purpose of the spirits, O Vasetthas, is this: 'That venerable brother Maha Kassapa is now journeying along the high road from Pava to Kusinara with a great company of the brethren, with five hundred of the brethren. The funeral pile of the Blessed One shall not catch fire, until the venerable Maha Kassapa shall have been able reverently to salute the sacred feet of the Blessed One.'"

"Even according to the purpose of the spirits, so, Lord, let it be!"

Then the venerable Maha Kassapa went on to Makuta-bandhana of Kusinara, to the shrine of the Mallas, to the place where the funeral pile of the Blessed One was. And when he had come up to it, he arranged his robe on one shoulder; and bowing down with clasped hands he thrice walked reverently round the pile; and then, uncovering the feet, he bowed down in reverence at the feet of the Blessed One. And those five hundred brethren arranged their robes on one shoulder; and bowing down with clasped hands, they thrice walked reverently round the pile, and then bowed down in reverence at the feet of the Blessed One.

And when the homage of the venerable Maha Kassapa and of those five hundred brethren was ended, the funeral pile of the Blessed One caught fire of itself. Now as the body of the Blessed One burned itself away, from the skin and the integument, and the flesh, and the nerves, and the fluid of the joints, neither soot nor ash was seen: and only the bones remained behind.

Just as one sees no soot nor ash when glue or oil is burned, so, as the body of the Blessed One burned itself away, from the skin and the integument, and the flesh, and the nerves, and the fluid of the joints, neither soot nor ash was seen: and only the bones remained behind. And of those five hundred pieces of raiment the very innermost and outermost were both consumed. And when the body of the Blessed One had been burned up, there came down streams of water from the sky and extinguished the funeral pile of the Blessed One; and there burst forth streams of water from the storehouse of the waters (beneath the earth), and extinguished the funeral pile of the Blessed One. The Mallas of Kusinara also brought water scented with all kinds of perfumes, and extinguished the funeral pile of the Blessed One.

Then the Mallas of Kusinara surrounded the bones of the Blessed One in their council hall with a lattice work of spears, and with a rampart of bows; and there for seven days they paid honor and reverence and respect and homage to them with dance and song and music, and with garlands and perfumes.

Now the king of Magadha, Agatasattu, the son of the queen of the Videha clan, heard the news that the Blessed One had died at Kusinara. Then the king of Magadha, Agatasattu, the son of the queen of the Videha clan, sent a messenger to the Mallas, saying, "The Blessed One belonged to the soldier caste, and I too am of the soldier caste. I am worthy to receive a portion of the relics of the Blessed One. Over the remains of the Blessed One will I put up a sacred cairn, and in honor thereof will I celebrate a feast!"

And the Likkhavis of Vesali heard the news that the

Blessed One had died at Kusinara. And the Likkhavis of Vesali sent a messenger to the Mallas, saying, "The Blessed One belonged to the soldier caste, and we too are of the soldier caste. We are worthy to receive a portion of the relics of the Blessed One. Over the remains of the Blessed One will we put up a sacred cairn, and in honor thereof will we celebrate a feast!"

And the Sakiyas of Kapila-vatthu heard the news that the Blessed One had died at Kusinara. And the Sakiyas of Kapila-vatthu sent a messenger to the Mallas, saying "The Blessed One was the pride of our race. We are worthy to receive a portion of the relics of the Blessed One. Over the remains of the Blessed One will we put up a sacred cairn, and in honor thereof will we celebrate a feast!"

And the Bulis of Allakappa heard the news that the Blessed One had died at Kusinara. And the Bulis of Allakappa sent a messenger to the Mallas, saying, "The Blessed One belonged to the soldier caste, and we too are of the soldier caste. We are worthy to receive a portion of the relics of the Blessed One. Over the remains of the Blessed One will we put up a sacred cairn, and in honor thereof will we celebrate a feast!"

And the Brahman of Vethadipa heard the news that the Blessed One had died at Kusinara. And the Brahman of Vethadipa sent a messenger to the Mallas, saying, "The Blessed One belonged to the soldier caste, and I am a Brahman. I am worthy to receive a portion of the relics of the Blessed One. Over the remains of the Blessed One will I put up a sacred cairn, and in honor thereof will I celebrate a feast!"

And the Mallas of Pava heard the news that the Blessed One had died at Kusinara. Then the Mallas of Pava sent a messenger to the Mallas, saying, "The Blessed One belonged to the soldier caste, and we too are of the soldier caste. We are worthy to receive a portion of the relics of the Blessed One. Over the remains of the Blessed One will we put up a sacred cairn, and in honor thereof will we celebrate a feast!"

When they heard these things the Mallas of Kusinara spoke to the assembled brethren, saying, "The Blessed One died in our village domain. We will not give away any part of the remains of the Blessed One!" When they had thus spoken,

Dona the Brahman addressed the assembled brethren, and said:

> "Hear, reverend sir, one single word from me.
> Forbearance was our Buddha wont to teach.
> Unseemly is it that over the division
> Of the remains of him who was the best of beings
> Strife should arise, and wounds, and war!
> Let us all, sirs, with one accord unite
> In friendly harmony to make eight portions.
> Wide spread let Thupas rise in every land
> That in the Enlightened One mankind may trust!"

"Do thou then, O Brahman, thyself divide the remains of the Blessed One equally into eight parts with fair division."

"Be it so, sir!" said Dona, in assent, to the assembled brethren. And he divided the remains of the Blessed One equally into eight parts, with fair division. And he said to them: "Give me, sirs, this vessel, and I will set up over it a sacred cairn, and in its honor will I establish a feast." And they gave the vessel to Dona the Brahman.

And the Moriyas of Pipphalivana heard the news that the Blessed One had died at Kusinara. Then the Moriyas of Pipphalivana sent a messenger to the Mallas, saying, "The Blessed One belonged to the soldier caste, and we too are of the soldier caste. We are worthy to receive a portion of the relics of the Blessed One. Over the remains of the Blessed One will we put up a sacred cairn, and in honor thereof will we celebrate a feast!" And when they heard the answer, saying, "There is no portion of the remains of the Blessed One left over. The remains of the Blessed One are all distributed," then they took away the embers.

Then the king of Magadha, Agatasattu, the son of the queen of the Videha clan, made a mound in Ragagaha over the remains of the Blessed One, and held a feast. And the Likkhavis of Vesali made a mound in Vesali over the remains of the Blessed One, and held a feast. And the Bulis of Allakappa made a mound in Allakappa over the remains of the Blessed One, and held a feast. And the Koliyas of Ramagama made a mound in Ramagama over the remains of the Blessed One, and held a feast. And Vethadipaka the Brahman made a mound in Vethadipa over the remains of the Blessed One, and held a feast. And the Mallas of Pava made a mound in Pava over the remains of the Blessed One, and held a feast. And the Mallas of Kusinara made a mound in Kusinara over the remains of the Blessed One, and held a feast. And Dona the Brahman made a mound over the vessel in which the body had been burned, and held a feast. And the Moriyas of Pipphalivana made a mound over the embers, and held a feast.

Thus were there eight mounds [Thupas] for the remains, and one for the vessel, and one for the embers. This was how it used to be. Eight measures of relics there were of him of the far-seeing eye, of the best of the best of men. In India seven are worshipped, and one measure in Ramagama, by the kings of the serpent race. One tooth, too, is honored in heaven, and one in Gandhara's city, one in the Kalinga realm, and one more by the Naga race. Through their glory the bountiful earth is made bright with offerings painless, for with such are the Great Teacher's relics best honored by those who are honored, by gods and by Nagas and kings, yea, thus by the noblest of monarchs—bow down with clasped hands! Hard, hard is a Buddha to meet with through hundreds of ages!

End of the *Book of the Great Decease*

PYTHIAN GAMES AT DELPHI

B.C. 585

GEORGE GROTE

Among the leading features of Greek life, especially those belonging to its religious customs and observances none are more characteristic, and none possess a more attractive interest for the modern reader and student than the peculiar festivals which it was their practice to hold. The four great national festivals or games were: The Olympic, held every four years, in honor of Zeus, on the banks of the Alpheus, in Elis; the Pythian, celebrated once in four years, in honor of Apollo, at Delphi; the Isthmian, held every two years, at the isthmian sanctuary in the Isthmus of Corinth, in honor of Poseidon (Neptune); and the Nemean, celebrated at Nemea, in the second and fourth years of each Olympiad, in honor of the Nemean Juno.

With regard to the influence of these games or festivals upon the political and social life of Greece, much has been written by historians and special students of the Grecian states. While the celebrations do not appear to have accomplished much for the political union of Greece, they are to be credited with marked beneficial effects in the promotion of a pan-Hellenic spirit which, if it failed to produce such a union of the Greek race, nevertheless quickened and strengthened the common feeling of family relationship. Thus a sense of their identical origin and racial traits was kept alive, and the tendencies of Greek development and culture preserved their essential character and distinction. By means of these periodical gatherings, representing all parts of the Greek world, not only was friendly competition in every field of talent and performance secured, but even trade and commerce found through them new channels of activity. So in various ways the national games proved a source of fresh energy and broader enterprise among the various branches of the Grecian people. The particular character and significance of the Pythian games at Delphi, and their relation to the other national festivals, form an interesting subject for study in connection with the general history of Greece.

WHAT are called the Olympic, Pythian, Nemean, and Isthmian games (the four most conspicuous amid many others analogous) were in reality great religious festivals—for the gods then gave their special sanction, name, and presence to

recreative meetings—the closest association then prevailed between the feelings of common worship and the sympathy in
common amusement.   Though this association is now no
longer recognized, it is nevertheless essential that we should
keep it fully before us if we desire to understand the life and
proceedings of the Greek.   To Herodotus and his contemporaries these great festivals, then frequented by crowds from
every part of Greece, were of overwhelming importance and
interest; yet they had once been purely local, attracting no
visitors except from a very narrow neighborhood.   In the Homeric poems much is said about the common gods, and about
special places consecrated to and occupied by several of them;
the chiefs celebrate funeral games in honor of a deceased
father, which are visited by competitors from different parts of
Greece, but nothing appears to manifest public or town festivals open to Grecian visitors generally.   And though the
rocky Pytho with its temple stands out in the *Iliad* as a
place both venerated and rich—the Pythian games, under
the superintendence of the Amphictyons, with continuous
enrollment of victors and a pan-Hellenic reputation, do not
begin until after the Sacred War, in the 48th Olympiad, or
B.C. 586.

The Olympic games, more conspicuous than the Pythian as
well as considerably older, are also remarkable on another
ground, inasmuch as they supplied historical computers with the
oldest backward record of continuous time.   It was in the year
B.C. 776 that the Eleans inscribed the name of their countryman Corœbus as victor in the competition of runners, and that
they began the practice of inscribing in like manner, in each
Olympic or fifth recurring year, the name of the runner who
won the prize.   Even for a long time after this, however, the
Olympic games seem to have remained a local festival; the
prize being uniformly carried off, at the first twelve Olympiads,
by some competitor either of Elis or its immediate neighborhood.   The Nemean and Isthmian games did not become notorious or frequented until later even than the Pythian.   Solon
in his legislation proclaimed the large reward of 500 drams for
every Athenian who gained an Olympic prize, and the lower
sum of 100 drams for an Isthmiac prize.   He counts the former

as pan-Hellenic rank and renown, an ornament even to the city of which the victor was a member—the latter as partial and confined to the neighborhood.

Of the beginnings of these great solemnities we cannot presume to speak, except in mythical language; we know them only in their comparative maturity. But the habit of common sacrifice, on a small scale and between near neighbors, is a part of the earliest habits of Greece. The sentiment of fraternity, between two tribes or villages, first manifested itself by sending a sacred legation or Theoria to offer sacrifices to each other's festivals and to partake in the recreations which followed; thus establishing a truce with solemn guarantee, and bringing themselves into direct connexion each with the god of the other under his appropriate local surname. The pacific communion so fostered, and the increased asssurance of intercourse, as Greece gradually emerged from the turbulence and pugnacity of the heroic age, operated especially in extending the range of this ancient habit: the village festivals became town festivals, largely frequented by the citizens of other towns, and sometimes with special invitations sent round to attract Theors from every Hellenic community—and thus these once humble assemblages gradually swelled into the pomp and immense confluence of the Olympic and Pythian games. The city administering such holy ceremonies enjoyed inviolability of territory during the month of their occurrence, being itself under obligation at that time to refrain from all aggression, as well as to notify by heralds the commencement of the truce to all other cities not in avowed hostility with it   Elis imposed heavy fines upon other towns—even on the powerful Lacedæmon—for violation of the Olympic truce, on pain of exclusion from the festival in case of non-payment.

Sometimes this tendency to religious fraternity took a form called an *Amphictyony*, different from the common festival. A certain number of towns entered into an exclusive religious partnership for the celebration of sacrifices periodically to the god of a particular temple, which was supposed to be the common property and under the common protection of all, though one of the number was often named as permanent administrator; while all other Greeks were excluded. That there were

many religious partnerships of this sort, which have never acquired a place in history, among the early Grecian villages, we
may perhaps gather from the etymology of the word *Amphictyons*—designating residents around, or neighbors, considered in the point of view of fellow-religionists—as well as from
the indications preserved to us in reference to various parts of
the country. Thus there was an Amphictyony of seven cities
at the holy island of Caluria, close to the harbor of Trœzen.
Hermione, Epidaurus, Ægina, Athens, Prasiæ, Nauplia, and
Orchomenus, jointly maintained the temple and sanctuary of
Poseidon in that island—with which it would seem that the city
of Trœzen, though close at hand, had no connection—meeting
there at stated periods, to offer formal sacrifices. These seven
cities indeed were not immediate neighbors, but the speciality
and exclusiveness of their interest in the temple is seen from
the fact that when the Argians took Nauplia, they adopted
and fulfilled these religious obligations on behalf of the prior
inhabitants: so also did the Lacedæmonians when they had
captured Prasiæ. Again, in Triphylia, situated between the
Pisatid and Messenia in the western part of Peloponnesus,
there was a similar religious meeting and partnership of the
Triphylians on Cape Samicon, at the temple of the Samian
Poseidon. Here the inhabitants of Maciston were intrusted
with the details of superintendence, as well as with the duty
of notifying beforehand the exact time of meeting (a precaution essential amidst the diversities and irregularities of the
Greek calendar) and also of proclaiming what was called the
Samian truce—a temporary abstinence from hostilities which
bound all Triphylians during the holy period. This latter custom discloses the salutary influence of such institutions in
presenting to men's minds a common object of reverence, common duties, and common enjoyments; thus generating sympathies and feelings of mutual obligation amid petty communities not less fierce than suspicious. So, too, the twelve chief
Ionic cities in and near Asia Minor had their pan-Ionic Amphictyony peculiar to themselves: the six Doric cities, in and
near the southern corner of that peninsula, combined for the
like purpose at the temple of the Triopian Apollo, and the
feeling of special partnership is here particularly illustrated by

the fact that Halicarnassus, one of the six, was formally ex-
truded by the remaining five in consequence of a violation of
the rules.   There was also an Amphictyonic union at Onches-
tus in Bœotia, in the venerated grove and temple at Poseidon:
of whom it consisted we are not informed.   There are some
specimens of the sort of special religious conventions and assemblies which seem to have been frequent throughout Greece.
Nor ought we to omit those religious meetings and sacrifices
which were common to all the members of one Hellenic subdi-
vision, such as the pan-Bœotia to all the Bœotians, celebrated
at the temple of the Ionian Athene near Coroneia; the common observances, rendered to the temple of Apollo Pythæus
at Argos, by all those neighboring towns which had once been
attached by this religious thread to the Argian; the similar
periodical ceremonies, frequented by all who bore the Achæan
or Ætolian name; and the splendid and exhilarating festivals,
so favorable to the diffusion of the early Grecian poetry, which
brought all Ionians at stated intervals to the sacred island of
Delos.   This later class of festivals agreed with the Amphictyony in being of a special and exclusive character, not open to
all Greeks.

But there was one among these many Amphictyonies,
which, though starting from the smallest beginnings, gradually
expanded into so comprehensive a character, had acquired so
marked a predominance over the rest, as to be called the "Amphictyonic assembly," and even to have been mistaken by some
authors for a sort of federal Hellenic diet.   Twelve sub-races,
out of the number which made up entire Hellas, belonged to
this ancient Amphictyony, the meetings of which were held
twice in every year: in spring at the temple of Apollo at Delphi; in autumn at Thermopylæ, in the sacred precinct of Demeter Amphictyonis.   Sacred deputies, including a chief called
the *Hieromnemon* and subordinates called the *Pylagoræ*, attended at these meetings from each of the twelve races: a
crowd of volunteers seem to have accompanied them, for purposes of sacrifice, trade, or enjoyment.   Their special, and
most important, function consisted in watching over the Delphian temple, in which all the twelve sub-races had a joint interest, and it was the immense wealth and national ascendency

of this temple which enhanced to so great a pitch the dignity of its acknowledged administrators.

The twelve constituent members were as follows: Thessalians, Bœotians, Dorians, Ionians, Perrhæbians, Magnetes, Locrians, Œtæans, Achæans, Phocians, Dolopes, and Malians. All are counted as *races* (if we treat the Hellenes as a race, we must call these *sub-races*), no mention being made of cities: all count equally in respect to voting, two votes being given by the deputies from each of the twelve: moreover, we are told that in determining the deputies to be sent or the manner in which the votes of each race should be given, the powerful Athens, Sparta, and Thebes had no more influence than the humblest Ionian, Dorian, or Bœotian city. This latter fact is distinctly stated by Æschines, himself a Pylagore sent to Delphi by Athens. And so, doubtless, the theory of the case stood: the votes of the Ionic races counted for neither more nor less than two, whether given by deputies from Athens, or from the small towns of Erythræ and Priene; and in like manner the Dorian votes were as good in the division, when given by deputies from Bœon and Cytinion in the little territory of Doris, as if the men delivering them had been Spartans. But there can be as little question that in practice the little Ionic cities and the little Doric cities pretended to no share in the Amphictyonic deliberations. As the Ionic vote came to be substantially the vote of Athens, so, if Sparta was ever obstructed in the management of the Doric vote, it must have been by powerful Doric cities like Argos or Corinth, not by the insignificant towns of Doris. But the theory of Amphictyonic suffrage as laid down by Æschines, however little realized in practice during his day, is important inasmuch as it shows in full evidence the primitive and original constitution. The first establishment of the Amphictyonic convocation dates from a time when all the twelve members were on a footing of equal independence, and when there were no overwhelming cities—such as Sparta and Athens—to cast in the shade the humbler members; when Sparta was only one Doric city, and Athens only one Ionic city, among various others of consideration not much inferior.

There are also other proofs which show the high antiquity

of this Amphictyonic convocation. Æschines gives us an extract from the oath which had been taken by the sacred deputies who attended on behalf of their respective races, ever since its first establishment, and which still apparently continued to be taken in his day. The antique simplicity of this oath, and of the conditions to which the members bind themselves, betrays the early age in which it originated, as well as the humble resources of those towns to which it was applied. "We will not destroy any Amphictyonic town—we will not cut off any Amphictyonic town from running water"—such are the two prominent obligations which Æschines specifies out of the old oath. The second of the two carries us back to the simplest state of society, and to towns of the smallest size, when the maidens went out with their basins to fetch water from the spring, like the daughters of Celeos at Eleusis, or those of Athens from the fountain Callirrhoe. We may even conceive that the special mention of this detail, in the covenant between the twelve races, is borrowed literally from agreements still earlier, among the villages or little towns in which the members of each race were distributed. At any rate, it proves satisfactorily the very ancient date to which the commencement of the Amphictyonic convocations must be referred. The belief of Æschines (perhaps also the belief general in his time) was, that it commenced simultaneously with the first foundation of the Delphian temple—an event of which we have no historical knowledge; but there seems reason to suppose that its original establishment is connected with Thermopylæ and Demeter Amphictyonia, rather than with Delphi and Apollo. The special surname by which Demeter and her temple at Thermopylæ was known—the temple of the hero Amphictyon which stood at its side—the word *Pylæa*, which obtained footing in the language to designate the half-yearly meeting of the deputies both at Thermopylæ and at Delphi—these indications point to Thermopylæ (the real central point for all the twelve) as the primary place of meeting, and to the Delphian half-year as something secondary and superadded. On such a matter, however, we cannot go beyond a conjecture.

The hero Amphictyon, whose temple stood at Thermopylæ, passed in mythical genealogy for the brother of Hellen. And

it may be affirmed, with truth, that the habit of forming Amphictyonic unions, and of frequenting each other's religious
festivals, was the great means of creating and fostering the
primitive feeling of brotherhood among the children of Hellen,
in those early times when rudeness, insecurity, and pugnacity
did so much to isolate them. A certain number of salutary
habits and sentiments, such as that which the Amphictyonic
oath embodies, in regard to abstinence from injury as well as
to mutual protection, gradually found their way into men's
minds: the obligations thus brought into play acquired a substantive efficacy of their own, and the religious feeling which
always remained connected with them, came afterward to be
only one out of many complex agencies by which the later historical Greek was moved. Athens and Sparta in the days of
their might, and the inferior cities in relation to them, played
each their own political game, in which religious considerations
will be found to bear only a subordinate part.

The special function of the Amphictyonic council, so far as
we know it, consisted in watching over the safety, the interests, and the treasures of the Delphian temple. "If any one
shall plunder the property of the god, or shall be cognizant
thereof, or shall take treacherous counsel against the things in
the temple, we will punish him with foot, and hand, and voice,
and by every means in our power." So ran the old Amphictyonic oath, with an energetic imprecation attached to it. And
there are some examples in which the council constitutes its
functions so largely as to receive and adjudicate upon complaints against entire cities, for offences against the religious
and patriotic sentiment of the Greeks generally. But for the
most part its interference relates directly to the Delphian temple. The earliest case in which it is brought to our view is the
Sacred War against Cirrha, in the 46th Olympiad or B.C. 595,
conducted by Eurolychus the Thessalian, and Clisthenes of
Sicyon, and proposed by Solon of Athens: we find the Amphictyons also about half a century afterward undertaking the
duty of collecting subscriptions throughout the Hellenic world,
and making the contract with the Alcmæonids for rebuilding
the temple after a conflagration. But the influence of this
council is essentially of a fluctuating and intermittent charac-

ter. Sometimes it appears forward to decide, and its decisions command respect; but such occasions are rare, taking
the general course of known Grecian history; while there are
other occasions, and those too especially affecting the Delphian
temple, on which we are surprised to find nothing said about
it. In the long and perturbed period which Thucydides describes, he never once mentions the Amphictyons, though the
temple and the safety of its treasures form the repeated subject as well of dispute as of express stipulation between Athens and Sparta. Moreover, among the twelve constituent
members of the council, we find three—the Perrhæbians, the
Magnetes, and the Achæans of Phthia—who were not even independent, but subject to the Thessalians; so that its meetings, when they were not matters of mere form, probably expressed only the feelings of the three or four leading members. When one or more of these great powers had a party
purpose to accomplish against others—when Philip of Macedon
wished to extrude one of the members in order to procure admission for himself—it became convenient to turn this ancient
form into a serious reality; and we shall see the Athenian Æschines providing a pretext for Philip to meddle in favor of the
minor Bœotian cities against Thebes, by alleging that these
cities were under the protection of the old Amphictyonic oath.

It is thus that we have to consider the council as an element in Grecian affairs—an ancient institution, one among
many instances of the primitive habit of religious fraterniza-
tion, but wider and more comprehensive than the rest; at first
purely religious, then religious and political at once, lastly
more the latter than the former; highly valuable in the infancy,
but unsuited to the maturity of Greece, and called into real
working only on rare occasions, when its efficiency happened
to fall in with the views of Athens, Thebes, or the king of
Macedon. In such special moments it shines with a transient
light which affords a partial pretense for the imposing title
bestowed on it by Cicero—*commune Græciæ concilium;* but we
should completely misinterpret Grecian history if we regarded
it as a federal council habitually directed or habitually obeyed.
Had there existed any such " commune concilium " of tolerable
wisdom and patriotism, and had the tendencies of the Hellenic

mind been capable of adapting themselves to it, the whole course of later Grecian history would probably have been altered; the Macedonian kings would have remained only as respectable neighbors, borrowing civilization from Greece and expending their military energies upon Thracians and Illyrians; while united Hellas might even have maintained her own territory against the conquering legions of Rome.

The twelve constituent Amphictyonic races remained unchanged until the Sacred War against the Phocians (B.C. 355), after which, though the number twelve was continued, the Phocians were disfranchised, and their votes transferred to Philip of Macedon. It has been already mentioned that these twelve did not exhaust the whole of Hellas. Arcadians, Eleans, Pisans, Minyæ, Dryopes, Ætolians, all genuine Hellenes, are not comprehended in it; but all of them had a right to make use of the temple of Delphi, and to contend in the Pythian and Olympic games. The Pythian games, celebrated near Delphi, were under the superintendence of the Amphictyons, or of some acting magistrate chosen by and presumed to represent them. Like the Olympic games, they came round every four years (the interval between one celebration and another being four complete years, which the Greeks called a *Pentæteris*): the Isthmian and Nemean games recurred every two years. In its first humble form a competition among bards to sing a hymn in praise of Apollo, this festival was doubtless of immemorial antiquity; but the first extension of it into panHellenic notoriety (as I have already remarked), the first multiplication of the subjects of competition, and the first introduction of a continuous record of the conquerors, date only from the time when it came under the presidency of the Amphictyon, at the close of the Sacred War against Cirrha. What is called the first Pythian contest coincides with the third year of the 48th Olympiad, or B.C. 585. From that period forward the games become crowded and celebrated: but the date just named, nearly two centuries after the first Olympiad, is a proof that the habit of periodical frequentation of festivals, by numbers and from distant parts, grew up but slowly in the Grecian world.

The foundation of the temple of Delphi itself reaches far

beyond all historical knowledge, forming one of the aboriginal institutions of Hellas. It is a sanctified and wealthy place even in the *Iliad;* the legislation of Lycurgus at Sparta is introduced under its auspices, and the earliest Grecian colonies, those of Sicily and Italy in the eighth century B.C., are established in consonance with its mandate. Delphi and Dodona appear, in the most ancient circumstances of Greece, as universally venerated oracles and sanctuaries: and Delphi not only receives honors and donations, but also answers questions from Lydians, Phrygians, Etruscans, Romans, etc.: it is not exclusively Hellenic. One of the valuable services which a Greek looked for from this and other great religious establishments was, that it should resolve his doubts in cases of perplexity; that it should advise him whether to begin a new, or to persist in an old project; that it should foretell what would be his fate under given circumstances, and inform him, if suffering under distress, on what conditions the gods would grant him relief.

The three priestesses of Dodona with their venerable oak, and the priestess of Delphi sitting on her tripod under the influence of a certain gas or vapor exhaling from the rock, were alike competent to determine these difficult points: and we shall have constant occasion to notice in this history with what complete faith both the question was put and the answer treasured up—what serious influence it often exercised both upon public and private proceeding. The hexameter verses in which the Pythian priestess delivered herself were indeed often so equivocal or unintelligible, that the most serious believer, with all anxiety to interpret and obey them, often found himself ruined by the result. Yet the general faith in the oracle was no way shaken by such painful experience. For as the unfortunate issue always admitted of being explained upon two hypotheses—either that the god had spoken falsely, or that his meaning had not been correctly understood—no man of genuine piety ever hesitated to adopt the latter. There were many other oracles throughout Greece besides Delphi and Dodona; Apollo was open to the inquiries of the faithful at Ptoon in Bœotia, at Abæ in Phocis, at Branchidæ near Miletus, at Patara in Lycia, and other places: in like manner, Zeus gave

answers at Olympia, Poseidon at Tænarus, Amphiaraus at
Thebes, Amphilochus at Mallus, etc.   And this habit of consulting the oracle formed part of the still more general tendency of the Greek mind to undertake no enterprise without
having first ascertained how the gods viewed it, and what measures they were likely to take.   Sacrifices were offered, and the
interior of the victim carefully examined, with the same intent:
omens, prodigies, unlooked-for coincidences, casual expressions, etc., were all construed as significant of the divine will.
To sacrifice with a view to this or that undertaking, or to consult the oracle with the same view, are familiar expressions
embodied in the language.   Nor could any man set about a
scheme with comfort until he had satisfied himself in some
manner or other that the gods were favorable to it.

The disposition here adverted to is one of these mental
analogies pervading the whole Hellenic nation, which Herodotus indicates.   And the common habit among all Greeks of
respectfully listening to the oracle of Delphi will be found on
many occasions useful in maintaining unanimity among men
not accustomed to obey the same political superior.   In the
numerous colonies especially, founded by mixed multitudes
from distant parts of Greece, the minds of the emigrants were
greatly determined toward cordial coöperation by their knowledge that the expedition had been directed, the œcist indicated, and the spot either chosen or approved by Apollo of
Delphi.   Such in most cases was the fact: that god, according
to the conception of the Greeks, "takes delight always in the
foundation of new cities, and himself in person lays the first
stone."

These are the elements of union with which the historical
Hellenes take their start: community of blood, language, religious point of view, legends, sacrifices, festivals, and also (with
certain allowances) of manners and character.   The analogy
of manners and character between the rude inhabitants of the
Arcadian Cynætha and the polite Athens, was, indeed, accompanied with wide differences; yet if we compare the two with
foreign contemporaries, we shall find certain negative characteristics of much importance common to both.   In no city of
historical Greece did there prevail either human sacrifices or

deliberate mutilation, such as cutting off the nose, ears, hands, feet, etc.; or castration; or selling of children into slavery; or polygamy; or the feeling of unlimited obedience toward one man: all customs which might be pointed out as existing among the contemporary Carthaginians, Egyptians, Persians, Thracians, etc. The habit of running, wrestling, boxing, etc., in gymnastic contests, with the body perfectly naked, was common to all Greeks, having been first adopted as a Lacedæmonian fashion in the fourteenth Olympiad: Thucydides and Herodotus remark that it was not only not practised, but even regarded as unseemly, among non-Hellenes. Of such customs, indeed, at once common to all the Greeks, and peculiar to them as distinguished from others, we cannot specify a great number, but we may see enough to convince ourselves that there did really exist, in spite of local differences, a general Hellenic sentiment and character, which counted among the cementing causes of a union apparently so little assured.

During the two centuries succeeding B.C. 776, the festival of the Olympic Zeus in the Pisatid gradually passed from a local to a national character, and acquired an attractive force capable of bringing together into temporary union the dispersed fragments of Hellas, from Marseilles to Trebizond. In this important function it did not long stand alone. During the sixth century B.C., three other festivals, at first local, became successively nationalized—the Pythia near Delphi, the Isthmia near Corinth, the Nemea near Cleone, between Sicyon and Argos.

In regard to the Pythian festival, we find a short notice of the particular incidents and individuals by whom its reconstitution and enlargement were brought about—a notice the more interesting inasmuch as these very incidents are themselves a manifestation of something like pan-Hellenic patriotism, standing almost alone in an age which presents little else in operation except distinct city interests. At the time when the Homeric Hymn to the Delphinian Apollo was composed (probably in the seventh century B.C), the Pythian festival had as yet acquired little eminence. The rich and holy temple of Apollo was then purely oracular, established for the purpose of com-

municating to pious inquirers "the counsels of the Immortals."
Multitudes of visitors came to consult it, as well as to sacrifice
victims and to deposit costly offerings; but while the god delighted in the sound of the harp as an accompaniment to the
singing of pæans, he was by no means anxious to encourage
horse-races and chariot-races in the neighborhood.   Nay, this
psalmist considers that the noise of horses would be "a nui-
sance," the drinking of mules a desecration to the sacred
fountains, and the ostentation of fine-built chariots objection-
able, as tending to divert the attention of spectators away from
the great temple and its wealth.   From such inconveniences
the god was protected by placing his sanctuary "in the rocky
Pytho"—a rugged and uneven recess, of no great dimensions,
embosomed in the southern declivity of Parnassus, and about
two thousand feet above the level of the sea, while the topmost
Parnassian summits reach a height of near eight thousand
feet.   The situation was extremely imposing, but unsuited by
nature for the congregation of any considerable number of
spectators; altogether impracticable for chariot-races; and
only rendered practicable by later art and outlay for the theatre
as well as for the stadium.   Such a site furnished little means
of subsistence, but the sacrifices and presents of visitors enabled the ministers of the temple to live in abundance, and gathered together by degrees a village around it.

Near the sanctuary of Pytho, and about the same altitude,
was situated the ancient Phocian town of Crissa, on a projecting spur of Parnassus—overhung above by the line of rocky
precipice called the Phædriades, and itself overhanging below
the deep ravine through which flows the river Peistus.   On the
other side of this river rises the steep mountain Cirphis, which
projects southward into the Corinthian gulf—the river reaching that gulf through the broad Crissœan plain, which stretches
westward nearly to the Locrian town of Amphissa; a plain for
the most part fertile and productive, though least so in its eastern part immediately under the Cirphis, where the seaport Cirrha was placed.   The temple, the oracle, and the wealth of
Pytho, belong to the very earliest periods of Grecian antiquity.
But the octennial solemnity in honor of the god included at
first no other competition except that of bards, who sang each

a pæan with the harp. The Amphictyonic assembly held one of its half-yearly meetings near the temple of Pytho, the other at Thermopylæ.

In those early times when the Homeric Hymn to Apollo was composed, the town of Crissa appears to have been great and powerful, possessing all the broad plain between Parnassus, Cirphis, and the gulf, to which latter it gave its name— and possessing also, what was a property not less valuable, the adjoining sanctuary of Pytho itself, which the Hymn identifies with Crissa, not indicating Delphi as a separate place. The Crissæans doubtless derived great profits from the number of visitors who came to visit Delphi, both by land and by sea, and Cirrha was originally only the name for their seaport. Gradually, however, the port appears to have grown in importance at the expense of the town, just as Apollonia and Ptolemais came to equal Cyrene and Barca, and as Plymouth Dock has swelled into Devonport; while at the same time the sanctuary of Pytho with its administrators expanded into the town of Delphi, and came to claim an independent existence of its own. The original relations between Crissa, Cirrha, and Delphi, were in this manner at length subverted, the first declining and the two latter rising. The Crissæans found themselves dispossessed of the management of the temple, which passed to the Delphians; as well as of the profits arising from the visitors, whose disbursements went to enrich the inhabitants of Cirrha. Crissa was a primitive city of the Phocian name, and could boast of a place as such in the Homeric Catalogue, so that her loss of importance was not likely to be quietly endured. Moreover, in addition to the above facts, already sufficient in themselves as seeds of quarrel, we are told that the Cirrhæans abused their position as masters of the avenue to the temple by sea, and levied exorbitant tolls on the visitors who landed there—a number constantly increasing from the multiplication of the transmarine colonies, and from the prosperity of those in Italy and Sicily. Besides such offence against the general Grecian public, they had also incurred the enmity of their Phocian neighbors by outrages upon women, Phocian as well as Argian, who were returning from the temple.

Thus stood the case, apparently, about B.C. 595, when the

Amphictyonic meeting interfered—either prompted by the Phocians, or perhaps on their own spontaneous impulse, out of regard to the temple—to punish the Cirrhæans. After a war of ten years, the first sacred war in Greece, this object was completely accomplished by a joint force of Thessalians under Eurolychus, Sicyonians under Clisthenes, and Athenians under Alcmæon; the Athenian Solon being the person who originated and enforced in the Amphictyonic council the proposition of interference. Cirrha appears to have made a strenuous resistance until its supplies from the sea were intercepted by the naval force of the Sicyonian Clisthenes. Even after the town was taken, its inhabitants defended themselves for some time on the heights of Cirphis. At length, however, they were thoroughly subdued. Their town was destroyed or left to subsist merely as a landing-place; while the whole adjoining plain was consecrated to the Delphian god, whose domains thus touched the sea. Under this sentence, pronounced by the religious feeling of Greece, and sanctified by a solemn oath publicly sworn and inscribed at Delphi, the land was condemned to remain untilled and unplanted, without any species of human care, and serving only for the pasturage of cattle. The latter circumstance was convenient to the temple, inasmuch as it furnished abundance of victims for the pilgrims who landed and came to sacrifice—for without preliminary sacrifice no man could consult the oracle; while the entire prohibition of tillage was the only means of obviating the growth of another troublesome neighbor on the seaboard. The ruin of Cirrha in this war is certain: though the necessity of a harbor for visitors arriving by sea, led to the gradual revival of the town upon a humbler scale of pretension. But the fate of Crissa is not so clear, nor do we know whether it was destroyed, or left subsisting in a position of inferiority with regard to Delphi. From this time forward, however, the Delphian community appear as substantive and autonomous, exercising in their own right the management of the temple; though we shall find, on more than one occasion, that the Phocians contest this right, and lay claim to the management of it for themselves—a remnant of that early period when the oracle stood in the domain of the Phocian Crissa. There seems, moreover, to have been a standing antipathy between the Delphians and the Phocians.

The Sacred War emanating from a solemn Amphictyonic decree, carried on jointly by troops of different states whom we do not know to have ever before coöperated, and directed exclusively toward an object of common interest—is in itself a fact of high importance, as manifesting a decided growth of pan-Hellenic feeling. Sparta is not named as interfering—a circumstance which seems remarkable when we consider both her power, even as it then stood, and her intimate connection with the Delphian oracle—while the Athenians appear as the chief movers, through the greatest and best of their citizens. The credit of a large-minded patriotism rests prominently upon them.

But if this sacred war itself is a proof that the pan-Hellenic spirit was growing stronger, the positive result in which it ended reinforced that spirit still farther. The spoils of Cirrha were employed by the victorious allies in founding the Pythian games. The octennial festival hitherto celebrated at Delphi in honor of the god, including no other competition except in the harp and the pæan, was expanded into comprehensive games on the model of the Olympic, with matches not only of music, but also of gymnastics and chariots—celebrated, not at Delphi itself, but on the maritime plain near the ruined Cirrha—and under the direct superintendence of the Amphictyons themselves. I have already mentioned that Solon provided large rewards for such Athenians as gained victories in the Olympic and Isthmian games, thereby indicating his sense of the great value of the national games as a means of promoting Hellenic intercommunion. It was the same feeling which instigated the foundation of the new games on the Cirrhæan plain, in commemoration of the vindicated honor of Apollo, and in the territory newly made over to him. They were celebrated in the autumn, or first half of every third Olympic year; the Amphictyons being the ostensible *Agonothets* or administrators, and appointing persons to discharge the duty in their names. At the first Pythian ceremony (in B.C. 586), valuable rewards were given to the different victors; at the second (B.C. 582), nothing was conferred but wreaths of laurel—the rapidly attained celebrity of the games being such as to render any further recompense superfluous. The Sicyonian despot, Clisthenes himself, once the leader in the conquest of Cirrha, gained the prize at the chariot-race of the second Pythia. We find other great personages in Greece frequently mentioned as competitors, and the games long maintained a dignity second only to the Olympic, over which indeed they had some advantages; first, that they were not abused for the purpose of promoting petty jealousies and antipathies of any administering state, as the Olympic games were perverted by the Eleans on more than one occasion; next, that they comprised music and poetry as well as bodily display. From the circumstances attending their foundation, the Pythian games deserved, even more than the Olympic, the title bestowed on them by Demosthenes—"the common *Agon* of the Greeks."

The Olympic and Pythian games continued always to be the most venerated solemnities in Greece. Yet the Nemea and Isthmia acquired a celebrity not much inferior; the Olympic prize counting for the highest of all. Both the Nemea and Isthmia were distinguished from the other two festivals by occurring not once in four years, but once in two years; the former in the second and fourth years of each Olympiad, the latter in the first and third years. To both is assigned, according to Greek custom, an origin connected with the interesting persons and circumstances of legendary antiquity; but our historical knowledge of both begins with the sixth century B.C. The first historical Nemead is presented as belonging to Olympiad B.C. 52 or 53 (572–568), a few years subsequent to the Sacred War above mentioned and to the origin of the Pythia. The festival was celebrated in honor of the Nemean Zeus, in the valley of Nemea between Philus and Cleonæ. The Cleonæans themselves were originally its presidents, until, some period after B.C. 460, the Argians deprived them of that honor and assumed the honors of administration to themselves. The Nemean games had their Hellanodicæ to superintend, to keep order, and to distribute the prizes, as well as the Olympic.

Respecting the Isthmian festival, our first historical information is a little earlier, for it has already been stated that

Solon conferred a premium upon every Athenian citizen who
gained a prize at that festival as well as at the Olympian—in
or after B.C. 594. It was celebrated by the Corinthians at
their isthmus, in honor of Poseidon, and if we may draw any
inference from the legends respecting its foundation, which is
ascribed sometimes to Theseus, the Athenians appear to have
identified it with the antiquities of their own state.

We thus perceive that the interval between B.C. 600–560,
exhibits the first historical manifestation of the Pythia, Isthmia, and Nemea—the first expansion of all the three from
local into pan-Hellenic festivals. To the Olympic games, for
some time the only great centre of union among all the widely
dispersed Greeks, are now added three other sacred *Agones* of
the like public, open, national character; constituting visible
marks, as well as tutelary bonds, of collective Hellenism, and
insuring to every Greek who went to compete in the matches,
a safe and inviolate transit even through hostile Hellenic
states. These four, all in or near Peloponnesus, and one of
which occurred in each year, formed the period or cycle of sacred games, and those who had gained prizes at all the four
received the enviable designation of Periodonices. The honors paid to Olympic victors, on their return to their native city,
were prodigious even in the sixth century B.C., and became
even more extravagant afterward. We may remark that in
the Olympic games alone, the oldest as well as the most illustrious of the four, the musical and intellectual element was
wanting. All the three more recent *Agones* included crowns
for exercises of music and poetry, along with gymnastics, chariots, and horses.

It was not only in the distinguishing national stamp set
upon these four great festivals, that the gradual increase of
Hellenic family feeling exhibited itself, during the course of
this earliest period of Grecian history. Pursuant to the same
tendencies, religious festivals in all the considerable towns
gradually became more and more open and accessible, attracting guests as well as competitors from beyond the border.
The comparative dignity of the city, as well as the honor rendered to the presiding god, were measured by the numbers, admiration, and envy, of the frequenting visitors. There is no

positive evidence indeed of such expansion in the Attic festivals earlier than the reign of Pisistratus, who first added the quadrennial or greater Panathenæ to the ancient annual or lesser Panathenæa. Nor can we trace the steps of progress in regard to Thebes, Orchomenus, Thespiæ, Megara, Sicyon, Pellene, Ægina, Argos, etc., but we find full reason for believing that such was the general reality. Of the Olympic or Isthmian victors whom Pindar and Simonides celebrated, many derived a portion of their renown from previous victories acquired at several of these local contests—victories sometimes so numerous as to prove how wide-spread the habit of reciprocal frequentation had become: though we find, even in the third century B.C., treaties of alliance between different cities in which it is thought necessary to confer such mutual right by express stipulation. Temptation was offered, to the distinguished gymnastic or musical competitors, by prizes of great value. Timæus even asserted, as a proof of the over-weening pride of Croton and Sybaris, that these cities tried to supplant the preëminence of the Olympic games by instituting games of their own with the richest prizes to be celebrated at the same time—a statement in itself not worthy of credit, yet nevertheless illustrating the animated rivalry known to prevail among the Grecian cities in procuring for themselves splendid and crowded games. At the time when the Homeric hymn to Demeter was composed, the worship of that goddess seems to have been purely local at Eleusis. But before the Persian war, the festival celebrated by the Athenians every year, in honor of the Eleusinian Demeter, admitted Greeks of all cities to be initiated, and was attended by vast crowds of them.

It was thus that the simplicity and strict local application of the primitive religious festival among the greater states in Greece gradually expanded, on certain great occasions periodically recurring, into an elaborate and regulated series of exhibitions not merely admitting, but soliciting, the fraternal presence of all Hellenic spectators. In this respect Sparta seems to have formed an exception to the remaining states. Her festivals were for herself alone, and her general rudeness toward other Greeks was not materially softened even at the Carneia and Hyacinthia, or Gymnopædiæ. On the other hand, the Attic Dionysia were gradually exalted, from their original rude spontaneous outburst of village feeling in thankfulness to the god, followed by song, dance and revelry of various kinds, into costly and diversified performances, first by a trained chorus, next by actors superadded to it.

And the dramatic compositions thus produced, as they embodied the perfection of Grecian art, so they were eminently calculated to invite a pan-Hellenic audience and to encourage the sentiment of Hellenic unity. The dramatic literature of Athens however belongs properly to a later period. Previous to the year B.C 560, we see only those commencements of innovation which drew upon Thespis the rebuke of Solon; who however himself contributed to impart to the Panathenaic festival a more solemn and attractive character by checking the license of the rhapsodes and insuring to those present a full orderly recital of the *Iliad*.

The sacred games and festivals took hold of the Greek mind by so great a variety of feelings as to counterbalance in a high degree the political disseverance, and to keep alive among their widespread cities, in the midst of constant jealousy and frequent quarrel, a feeling of brotherhood and congenial sentiment such as must otherwise have died away. The Theors, or sacred envoys who came to Olympia or Delphi from so many different points, all sacrificed to the same god and at the same altar, witnessed the same sports, and contributed by their donatives to enrich or adorn one respective scene. Moreover the festival afforded opportunity for a sort of fair, including much traffic amid so large a mass of spectators; and besides the exhibitions of the games themselves, there were recitations and lectures in a spacious council-room for those who chose to listen to them, by poets, rhapsodes, philosophers and historians —among which last the history of Herodotus is said to have been publicly read by its author. Of the wealthy and great men in the various cities, many contended simply for the chariot-victories and horse-victories. But there were others whose ambition was of a character more strictly personal, and who stripped naked as runners, wrestlers, boxers, or pancratiasts, having gone through the extreme fatigue of a complete previous training. Cylon, whose unfortunate attempt to usurp the

scepter at Athens has been recounted, had gained the prize in
the Olympic stadium; Alexander son of Amyntas, the prince
of Macedon, had run for it; the great family of the Diagoridæ
at Rhodes, who furnished magistrates and generals to their native city, supplied a still greater number of successful boxers
and pancratiasts at Olympia, while other instances also occur
of generals named by various cities from the list of successful
Olympic gymnasts; and the odes of Pindar, always dearly
purchased, attest how many of the great and wealthy were
found in that list. The perfect popularity and equality of persons at these great games, is a feature not less remarkable
than the exact adherence to predetermined rule, and the self-
imposed submission of the immense crowd to a handful of servants armed with sticks, who executed the orders of the Elean
Hellanodice. The ground upon which the ceremony took
place, and even the territory of the administering state, was
protected by a " Truce of God " during the month of the festival, the commencement of which was formally announced by
heralds sent round to the different states. Treaties of peace
between different cities were often formally commemorated by
pillars there erected, and the general impression of the scene
suggested nothing but ideas of peace and brotherhood among
Greeks. And I may remark that the impression of the games
as belonging to all Greeks, and to none but Greeks, was
stronger and clearer during the interval between B.C. 600–300
than it came to be afterward. For the Macedonian conquests
had the effect of diluting and corrupting Hellenism, by spreading an exterior varnish of Hellenic tastes and manners over a
wide area of incongruous foreigners who were incapable of the
real elevation of the Hellenic character; so that although in
later times the games continued undiminished both in attraction and in number of visitors, the spirit of pan-Hellenic
communion which had once animated the scene was gone
forever.

SOLON'S EARLY GREEK LEGISLATION

B.C. 594

GEORGE GROTE

Lycurgus, the reputed Spartan lawgiver, is credited with the construction, about B.C. 800, of the earliest Grecian commonwealth founded upon a specific code of laws. These laws had mainly a military basis, and through obedience to them the Spartans became a people of great hardiness, accustomed to self-discipline, famous for their prowess and endurance in war, and for sternness of individual and social virtues.

In Athens there were no written laws until the time of Draco, B.C. 621, the government before that period having been long in the hands of an oligarchy. In the year above named Draco was archon, and to him was intrusted the work of framing a legal code, conditions under the oligarchic rule having become intolerable to the people at large. The chief features of Draco's legislation had reference to the punishment of crime, and so extreme were the severities of the system and so cruel the penalties it prescribed that in later times it was declared to have been written in blood.

The Draconian laws remained in force until superseded by the great system of Solon, whose advent as the new lawgiver was brought about mainly through the conspiracy of Cylon, twelve years after the legislation of Draco. Affairs in Athens were in a deplorable state of confusion and violence, the revolt of the poor against the power and privilege of the rich leading to dangerous dissensions and collisions. Solon, who enjoyed a universal reputation for wisdom and uprightness, was called upon by the oligarchy, which again held rule, to assume what was, in fact, almost absolute power. The character of his legislation and its influence upon the course of Greek history have been set forth by many authors, and the following account is perhaps the best that has appeared in modern literature.

SOLON, son of Execestides, was a Eupatrid of middling fortune, but of the purest heroic blood, belonging to the *gens* or family of the Codrids and Neleids, and tracing his origin to the god Poseidon. His father is said to have diminished his substance by prodigality, which compelled Solon in his earlier years to have recourse to trade, and in this pursuit he visited many parts of Greece and Asia. He was thus enabled to enlarge the sphere of his observation, and to provide material for thought as well as for composition. His poetical talents displayed themselves at a very early age, first on light, afterward on serious subjects. It will be recollected that there was at that time no Greek prose writing, and that the acquisitions as well as the effusions of an intellectual man, even in their simplest form, adjusted themselves not to the limitations of the period and the semicolon, but to those of the hexameter and pentameter. Nor, in point of fact, do the verses of Solon aspire to any higher effect than we are accustomed to associate with an earnest, touching, and admonitory prose composition. The advice and appeals which he frequently addressed to his countrymen were delivered in this easy metre, doubtless far less difficult than the elaborate prose of subsequent writers or speakers, such as Thucydides, Isocrates, or Demosthenes. His poetry and his reputation became known throughout many parts of Greece, so that he was classed along with Thales of Miletus, Bias of Priene, Pittacus of Mitylene, Periander of Corinth, Cleobulus of Lindus, Cheilon of Lacedæmon—altogether forming the constellation afterward renowned as the seven wise men.

The first particular event in respect to which Solon appears as an active politician, is the possession of the island of Salamis, then disputed between Megara and Athens. Megara was at that time able to contest with Athens, and for some time to contest with success, the occupation of this important island— a remarkable fact, which perhaps may be explained by supposing that the inhabitants of Athens and its neighborhood carried on the struggle with only partial aid from the rest of Attica. However this may be, it appears that the Megarians had actually established themselves in Salamis, at the time when Solon began his political career, and that the Athenians had experienced so much loss in the struggle as to have formally prohibited any citizen from ever submitting a proposition for its reconquest. Stung with this dishonorable abnegation, Solon counterfeited a state of ecstatic excitement, rushed into the agora, and there on the stone usually occupied by the official herald, pronounced to the surrounding crowd a short elegiac poem which he had previously composed on the subject of

Salamis. Enforcing upon them the disgrace of abandoning the island, he wrought so powerfully upon their feelings that they rescinded the prohibitory law. "Rather (he exclaimed) would I forfeit my native city and become a citizen of Pholegandrus, than be still named an Athenian, branded with the shame of surrendered Salamis!" The Athenians again entered into the war, and conferred upon him the command of it—partly, as we are told, at the instigation of Pisistratus, though the latter must have been at this time (B.C. 600–594) a very young man, or rather a boy.

The stories in Plutarch, as to the way in which Salamis was recovered, are contradictory as well as apocryphal, ascribing to Solon various stratagems to deceive the Megarian occupiers. Unfortunately no authority is given for any of them. According to that which seems the most plausible, he was directed by the Delphian god first to propitiate the local heroes of the island; and he accordingly crossed over to it by night, for the purpose of sacrificing to the heroes Periphemus and Cychreus on the Salaminian shore. Five hundred Athenian volunteers were then levied for the attack of the island, under the stipulation that if they were victorious they should hold it in property and citizenship. They were safely landed on an outlying promontory, while Solon, having been fortunate enough to seize a ship which the Megarians had sent to watch the proceedings, manned it with Athenians and sailed straight toward the city of Salamis, to which the Athenians who had landed also directed their march. The Megarians marched out from the city to repel the latter, and during the heat of the engagement Solon, with his Megarian ship and Athenian crew, sailed directly to the city. The Megarians, interpreting this as the return of their own crew, permitted the ship to approach without resistance, and the city was thus taken by surprise. Permission having been given to the Megarians to quit the island, Solon took possession of it for the Athenians, erecting a temple to Enyalius, the god of war, on Cape Sciradium, near the city of Salamis.

The citizens of Megara, however, made various efforts for the recovery of so valuable a possession, so that a war ensued long as well as disastrous to both parties. At last it was agreed between them to refer the dispute to the arbitration of Sparta, and five Spartans were appointed to decide it—Critolaidas, Amompharetus, Hypsechidas, Anaxilas, and Cleomenes. The verdict in favor of Athens was founded on evidence which it is somewhat curious to trace. Both parties attempted to show that the dead bodies buried in the island conformed to their own peculiar mode of interment, and both parties are said to have cited verses from the catalogue of the *Iliad*—each accusing the other of error or interpolation. But the Athenians had the advantage on two points: first, there were oracles from Delphi, wherein Salamis was mentioned with the epithet Ionian; next Philæus and Eurysaces, sons of the Telamonian Ajax, the great hero of the island, had accepted the citizenship of Athens, made over Salamis to the Athenians, and transferred their own residences to Brauron and Melite in Attica, where the *deme*, or *gens*, Philaidæ still worshipped Philæus as its eponymous ancestor. Such a title was held sufficient, and Salamis was adjudged by the five Spartans to Attica, with which it ever afterward remained incorporated until the days of Macedonian supremacy. Two centuries and a half later, when the orator Æschines argued the Athenian right to Amphipolis against Philip of Macedon, the legendary elements of the title were indeed put forward, but more in the way of preface or introduction to the substantial political grounds. But in the year 600 B.C. the authority of the legend was more deep-seated and operative, and adequate by itself to determine a favorable verdict.

In addition to the conquest of Salamis, Solon increased his reputation by espousing the cause of the Delphian temple against the extortionate proceedings of the inhabitants of Cirrha, and the favor of the oracle was probably not without its effect in procuring for him that encouraging prophecy with which his legislative career opened.

It is on the occasion of Solon's legislation that we obtain our first glimpse—unfortunately but a glimpse—of the actual state of Attica and its inhabitants. It is a sad and repulsive picture, presenting to us political discord and private suffering combined.

Violent dissensions prevailed among the inhabitants of Attica, who were separated into three factions—the Pedieis, or

men of the plain, comprising Athens, Eleusis, and the neighboring territory, among whom the greatest number of rich families were included; the mountaineers in the east and north of
Attica, called Diacrii, who were, on the whole, the poorest
party; and the Paralii in the southern portion of Attica from
sea to sea, whose means and social position were intermediate
between the two. Upon what particular points these intestine
disputes turned we are not distinctly informed. They were
not, however, peculiar to the period immediately preceding the
archonship of Solon. They had prevailed before, and they reap-
pear afterward prior to the despotism of Pisistratus; the latter
standing forward as the leader of the Diacrii, and as champion,
real or pretended, of the poorer population.

But in the time of Solon these intestine quarrels were aggravated by something much more difficult to deal with—a
general mutiny of the poorer population against the rich, result-
ing from misery combined with oppression. The Thetes, whose
condition we have already contemplated in the poems of Homer
and Hesiod, are now presented to us as forming the bulk of
the population of Attica—the cultivating tenants, metayers,
and small proprietors of the country. They are exhibited as
weighed down by debts and dependence, and driven in large
numbers out of a state of freedom into slavery—the whole mass
of them (we are told) being in debt to the rich, who were proprietors of the greater part of the soil. They had either borrowed money for their own necessities, or they tilled the lands
of the rich as dependent tenants, paying a stipulated portion of
the produce, and in this capacity they were largely in arrear.

All the calamitous effects were here seen of the old harsh
law of debtor and creditor—once prevalent in Greece, Italy,
Asia, and a large portion of the world—combined with the recognition of slavery as a legitimate status, and of the right of
one man to sell himself as well as that of another man to buy
him. Every debtor unable to fulfil his contract was liable to
be adjudged as the slave of his creditor, until he could find
means either of paying it or working it out; and not only he
himself, but his minor sons and unmarried daughters and sisters
also, whom the law gave him the power of selling. The poor
man thus borrowed upon the security of his body (to translate

literally the Greek phrase) and upon that of the persons in his family. So severely had these oppressive contracts been enforced, that many debtors had been reduced from freedom to slavery in Attica itself, many others had been sold for exportation, and some had only hitherto preserved their own freedom by selling their children. Moreover, a great number of the smaller properties in Attica were under mortgage, signified—according to the formality usual in the Attic law, and continued down throughout the historical times—by a stone pillar erected on the land, inscribed with the name of the lender and the amount of the loan. The proprietors of these mortgaged lands, in case of an unfavorable turn of events, had no other prospect except that of irremediable slavery for themselves and their families, either in their own native country robbed of all its delights, or in some barbarian region where the Attic accent would never meet their ears. Some had fled the country to escape legal adjudication of their persons, and earned a miserable subsistence in foreign parts by degrading occupations. Upon several, too, this deplorable lot had fallen by unjust condemnation and corrupt judges; the conduct of the rich, in regard to money sacred and profane, in regard to matters public as well as private, being thoroughly unprincipled and rapacious.

The manifold and long-continued suffering of the poor under this system, plunged into a state of debasement not more tolerable than that of the Gallic *plebs*—and the injustices of the rich, in whom all political power was then vested—are facts well attested by the poems of Solon himself, even in the short fragments preserved to us. It appears that immediately preceding the time of his archonship the evils had ripened to such a point, and the determination of the mass of sufferers to extort for themselves some mode of relief had become so pronounced, that the existing laws could no longer be enforced. According to the profound remark of Aristotle—that seditions are generated by great causes but out of small incidents—we may conceive that some recent events had occurred as immediate stimulants to the outbreak of the debtors, like those which lent so striking an interest to the early Roman annals, as the inflaming sparks of violent popular movements for which the train had long before been laid. Condemnations by the archons of insolvent debtors may have been unusually numerous; or the maltreatment of some particular debtor, once a respected freeman, in his condition of slavery, may have been brought to act vividly upon the public sympathies; like the case of the old plebeian centurion at Rome—first impoverished by the plunder of the enemy, then reduced to borrow, and lastly adjudged to his creditor as an insolvent—who claimed the protection of the people in the forum, rousing their feelings to the highest pitch by the marks of the slave-whip visible on his person. Some such incidents had probably happened, though we have no historians to recount them. Moreover, it is not unreasonable to imagine that that public mental affliction which the purifier Epimenides had been invoked to appease, as it sprung in part from pestilence, so it had its cause partly in years of sterility, which must of course have aggravated the distress of the small cultivators. However this may be, such was the condition of things in B.C. 594 through mutiny of the poor freemen and *Thetes*, and uneasiness of the middling citizens, that the governing oligarchy, unable either to enforce their private debts or to maintain their political power, were obliged to invoke the well-known wisdom and integrity of Solon. Though his vigorous protest—which doubtless rendered him acceptable to the mass of the people—against the iniquity of the existing system had already been proclaimed in his poems, they still hoped that he would serve as an auxiliary to help them over their difficulties. They therefore chose him, nominally as archon along with Philombrotus, but with power in substance dictatorial.

It had happened in several Grecian states that the governing oligarchies, either by quarrels among their own members or by the general bad condition of the people under their government, were deprived of that hold upon the public mind which was essential to their power. Sometimes—as in the case of Pittacus of Mitylene anterior to the archonship of Solon, and often in the factions of the Italian republics in the middle ages—the collision of opposing forces had rendered society intolerable, and driven all parties to acquiesce in the choice of some reforming dictator. Usually, however, in the early Greek oligarchies, this ultimate crisis was anticipated by some ambitious individual, who availed himself of the public discontent to overthrow the oligarchy and usurp the powers of a despot. And so probably it might have happened in Athens, had not the recent failure of Cylon, with all its miserable consequences, operated as a deterring motive. It is curious to read, in the words of Solon himself, the temper in which his appointment was construed by a large portion of the community, but more especially by his own friends: bearing in mind that at this early day, so far as our knowledge goes, democratical government was a thing unknown in Greece—all Grecian governments were either oligarchical or despotic—the mass of the freemen having not yet tasted of constitutional privilege. His own friends and supporters were the first to urge him, while redressing the prevalent discontents, to multiply partisans for himself personally, and seize the supreme power. They even "chid him as a madman, for declining to haul up the net when the fish were already enmeshed." The mass of the people, in despair with their lot, would gladly have seconded him in such an attempt; while many even among the oligarchy might have acquiesced in his personal government, from the mere apprehension of something worse if they resisted it. That Solon might easily have made himself despot admits of little doubt. And though the position of a Greek despot was always perilous, he would have had greater facility for maintaining himself in it than Pisistratus possessed after him; so that nothing but the combination of prudence and virtue, which marks his lofty character, restricted him within the trust specially confided to him. To the surprise of every one—to the dissatisfaction of his own friends—under the complaints alike (as he says) of various extreme and dissentient parties, who required him to adopt measures fatal to the peace of society—he set himself honestly to solve the very difficult and critical problem submitted to him.

Of all grievances, the most urgent was the condition of the poorer class of debtors. To their relief Solon's first measure, the memorable *Seisachtheia*, or shaking off of burdens, was directed. The relief which it afforded was complete and immediate. It cancelled at once all those contracts in which the debtor had borrowed on the security either of his person or of his land: it forbade all future loans or contracts in which the person of the debtor was pledged as security: it deprived the creditor in future of all power to imprison, or enslave, or extort work, from his debtor, and confined him to an effective judgment at law authorizing the seizure of the property of the latter. It swept off all the numerous mortgage pillars from the landed properties in Attica, leaving the land free from all past claims. It liberated and restored to their full rights all debtors actually in slavery under previous legal adjudication; and it even provided the means (we do not know how) of repurchasing in foreign lands, and bringing back to a renewed life of liberty in Attica, many insolvents who had been sold for exportation. And while Solon forbade every Athenian to pledge or sell his own person into slavery, he took a step farther in the same direction by forbidding him to pledge or sell his son, his daughter, or an unmarried sister under his tutelage—excepting only the case in which either of the latter might be detected in unchastity. Whether this last ordinance was contemporaneous with the Seisachtheia, or followed as one of his subsequent reforms, seems doubtful.

By this extensive measure the poor debtors—the Thetes, small tenants, and proprietors—together with their families, were rescued from suffering and peril. But these were not the only debtors in the state: the creditors and landlords of the exonerated Thetes were doubtless in their turn debtors to others, and were less able to discharge their obligations in consequence of the loss inflicted upon them by the Seisachtheia. It was to assist these wealthier debtors, whose bodies were in no danger—yet without exonerating them entirely—that Solon resorted to the additional expedient of debasing the money standard. He lowered the standard of the drachma in a proportion of something more than 25 per cent., so that 100 drachmas of the new standard contained no more silver than 73 of the old, or 100 of the old were equivalent to 138 of the new. By this change the creditors of these more substantial debtors were obliged to submit to a loss, while the debtors acquired an exemption to the extent of about 27 per cent.

Lastly, Solon decreed that all those who had been condemned by the archons to *atimy* (civil disfranchisement) should be restored to their full privileges of citizens—excepting, however, from this indulgence those who had been condemned by the Ephetæ, or by the Areopagus, or by the Phylo-Basileis (the four kings of the tribes), after trial in the Prytaneum, on charges either of murder or treason. So wholesale a measure of amnesty affords strong grounds for believing that the previous judgments of the archons had been intolerably harsh; and it is to be recollected that the Draconian ordinances were then in force.

Such were the measures of relief with which Solon met the dangerous discontent then prevalent. That the wealthy men and leaders of the people—whose insolence and iniquity he has himself severely denounced in his poems, and whose views in nominating him he had greatly disappointed—should have detested propositions which robbed them without compensation of many legal rights, it is easy to imagine. But the statement of Plutarch that the poor emancipated debtors were also dissatisfied, from having expected that Solon would not only remit their debts, but also redivide the soil of Attica, seems utterly incredible; nor is it confirmed by any passage now remaining of the Solonian poems. Plutarch conceives the poor debtors as having in their minds the comparison with Lycurgus and the equality of property at Sparta, which, in my opinion, is clearly a matter of fiction; and even had it been true as a matter of history long past and antiquated, would not have been likely to work upon the minds of the multitude of Attica in the forcible way that the biographer supposes. The Seisachtheia must have exasperated the feelings and diminished the fortunes of many persons; but it gave to the large body of Thetes and small proprietors all that they could possibly have hoped. We are told that after a short interval it became eminently acceptable in the general public mind, and procured for Solon a great increase of popularity—all ranks concurring in a common sacrifice of thanksgiving and harmony. One incident there was which occasioned an outcry of indignation. Three rich friends of Solon, all men of great family in the state, and bearing names which appear in history as borne by their descendants—namely: Conon, Cleinias, and Hipponicus—having obtained from Solon some previous hint of his designs, profited by it, first to borrow money, and next to make purchases of lands; and this selfish breach of confidence would have disgraced Solon himself, had it not been found that he was personally a great loser, having lent money to the extent of five talents.

In regard to the whole measure of the Seisachtheia, indeed, though the poems of Solon were open to every one, ancient authors gave different statements both of its purport and of its extent. Most of them construed it as having cancelled indiscriminately all money contracts; while Androtion and others thought that it did nothing more than lower the rate of interest and depreciate the currency to the extent of 27 per cent., leaving the letter of the contracts unchanged. How Androtion came to maintain such an opinion we cannot easily understand. For the fragments now remaining from Solon seem distinctly to refute it, though, on the other hand, they do not go so far as to substantiate the full extent of the opposite view entertained by many writers—that all money contracts indiscriminately were rescinded—against which there is also a further reason, that if the fact had been so, Solon could have had no motive to debase the money standard. Such debasement supposes that there must have been *some* debtors at least whose contracts remained valid, and whom nevertheless he desired partially to assist. His poems distinctly mention three things: 1. The removal of the mortgage-pillars. 2. The enfranchisement of the land. 3. The protection, liberation, and restoration of the persons of endangered or enslaved debtors. All these expressions point distinctly to the Thetes and small proprietors, whose sufferings and peril were the most urgent, and whose case required a remedy immediate as well as complete. We find that his repudiation of debts was carried far enough to exonerate them, but no farther.

It seems to have been the respect entertained for the character of Solon which partly occasioned these various misconceptions of his ordinances for the relief of debtors. Androtion in ancient, and some eminent critics in modern times are anxious to make out that he gave relief without loss or injustice to any one. But this opinion seems inadmissible. The loss to creditors by the wholesale abrogation of numerous preëxisting contracts, and by the partial depreciation of the coin, is a fact not to be disguised. The Seisachtheia of Solon, unjust so far as it rescinded previous agreements, but highly salutary in its consequences, is to be vindicated by showing that in no other way could the bonds of government have been held together, or the misery of the multitude alleviated. We are to consider, first, the great personal cruelty of these preëxisting contracts, which condemned the body of the free debtor and his family to slavery; next, the profound detestation created by such a system in the large mass of the poor, against both the judges and the creditors by whom it had been enforced, which rendered their feelings unmanageable so soon as they came together under the sentiment of a common danger and with the determination to insure to each other mutual protection. Moreover, the law which vests a creditor with power over the person of his debtor so as to convert him into a slave, is likely to give rise to a class of loans which inspire nothing but abhorrence—money lent with the foreknowledge that the borrower will be unable to repay it, but also in the conviction that the value of his person as a slave will make good the loss; thus reducing him to a condition of extreme misery, for the purpose sometimes of aggrandizing, sometimes of enriching, the lender. Now the foundation on which the respect for contracts rests, under a good law of debtor and creditor, is the very reverse of this. It rests on the firm conviction that such contracts are advantageous to both parties as a class, and that to break up the confidence essential to their existence would produce extensive mischief throughout all society. The man whose reverence for the obligation of a contract is now the most profound, would have entertained a very different sentiment if he had witnessed the dealings of lender and borrower at Athens under the old ante-Solonian law. The oligarchy had tried their best to enforce this law of debtor and creditor with its disastrous series of contracts, and the only reason why they consented to invoke the aid of Solon was because they had lost the power of enforcing it any longer, in consequence of the newly awakened courage and combination of the people. That which they could not do for themselves, Solon could not have done for them, even had he been willing. Nor had he in his position the means either of exempting or compensating those creditors who, separately taken, were open to no reproach; indeed, in

following his proceedings, we see plainly that he thought compensation due, not to the creditors, but to the past sufferings
of the enslaved debtor, since he redeemed several of them from
foreign captivity, and brought them back to their homes. It is
certain that no measure simply and exclusively prospective
would have sufficed for the emergency. There was an absolute
necessity for overruling all that class of preëxisting rights
which had produced so violent a social fever. While, therefore,
to this extent, the Seisachtheia cannot be acquitted of injustice,
we may confidently affirm that the injustice inflicted was an
indispensable price paid for the maintenance of the peace of
society, and for the final abrogation of a disastrous system as
regarded insolvents. And the feeling as well as the legislation
universal in the modern European world, by interdicting beforehand all contracts for selling a man's person or that of his children into slavery, goes far to sanction practically the Solonian
repudiation.

One thing is never to be forgotten in regard to this measure, combined with the concurrent amendments introduced by
Solon in the law—it settled finally the question to which it referred. Never again do we hear of the law of debtor and creditor as disturbing Athenian tranquillity. The general sentiment
which grew up at Athens, under the Solonian money-law and
under the democratical government, was one of high respect for
the sanctity of contracts. Not only was there never any demand in the Athenian democracy for new tables or a depreciation of the money standard, but a formal abnegation of any
such projects was inserted in the solemn oath taken annually
by the numerous Dicasts, who formed the popular judicial body
called Heliæa or the Heliastic jurors: the same oath which
pledged them to uphold the democratical constitution, also
bound them to repudiate all proposals either for an abrogation
of debts or for a redivision of the lands. There can be little
doubt that under the Solonian law, which enabled the creditor
to seize the property of his debtor, but gave him no power over
the person, the system of money-lending assumed a more beneficial character. The old noxious contracts, mere snares for
the liberty of a poor freeman and his children, disappeared, and
loans of money took their place, founded on the property and

prospective earnings of the debtor, which were in the main use-ful to both parties, and therefore maintained their place in the moral sentiment of the public. And though Solon had found himself compelled to rescind all the mortgages on land subsisting in his time, we see money freely lent upon this same security throughout the historical times of Athens, and the evidentiary mortgage-pillars remaining ever after undisturbed.

In the sentiment of an early society, as in the old Roman law, a distinction is commonly made between the principal and the interest of a loan, though the creditors have sought to blend them indissolubly together. If the borrower cannot fulfil his promise to repay the principal, the public will regard him as having committed a wrong which he must make good by his person. But there is not the same unanimity as to his promise to pay interest: on the contrary, the very exaction of interest will be regarded by many in the same light in which the English law considers usurious interest, as tainting the whole transaction. But in the modern mind, principal, and interest within a limited rate, have so grown together, that we hardly understand how it can ever have been pronounced unworthy of an honorable citizen to lend money on interest. Yet such is the declared opinion of Aristotle and other superior men of antiquity; while at Rome, Cato the censor went so far as to denounce the practice as a heinous crime. It was comprehended by them among the worst of the tricks of trade—and they held that all trade, or profit derived from interchange, was unnatural, as being made by one man at the expense of another: such pursuits therefore could not be commended, though they might be tolerated to a certain extent as a matter of necessity, but they belonged essentially to an inferior order of citizens. What is remarkable in Greece is, that the antipathy of a very early state of society against traders and money-lenders lasted longer among the philosophers than among the mass of the people—it harmonized more with the social *idéal* of the former, than with the practical instincts of the latter.

In a rude condition such as that of the ancient Germans described by Tacitus, loans on interest are unknown. Habitually careless of the future, the Germans were gratified both in giving and receiving presents, but without any idea that they thereby either imposed or contracted an obligation. To a people in this state of feeling, a loan on interest presents the repulsive idea of making profit out of the distress of the borrower. Moreover, it is worthy of remark that the first borrowers must have been for the most part men driven to this necessity by the pressure of want, and contracting debt as a desperate resource, without any fair prospect of ability to repay: debt and famine run together in the mind of the poet Hesiod. The borrower is, in this unhappy state, rather a distressed man soliciting aid than a solvent man capable of making and fulfilling a contract. If he cannot find a friend to make him a free gift in the former character, he will not, under the latter character, obtain a loan from a stranger, except by the promise of exorbitant interest, and by the fullest eventual power over his person which he is in a condition to grant. In process of time a new class of borrowers arise who demand money for temporary convenience or profit, but with full prospect of repayment—a relation of lender and borrower quite different from that of the earlier period, when it presented itself in the repulsive form of misery on the one side, set against the prospect of very large profit on the other. If the Germans of the time of Tacitus looked to the condition of the poor debtors in Gaul, reduced to servitude under a rich creditor, and swelling by hundreds the crowd of his attendants, they would not be disposed to regret their own ignorance of the practice of money-lending. How much the interest of money was then regarded as an undue profit extorted from distress is powerfully illustrated by the old Jewish law; the Jew being permitted to take interest from foreigners—whom the lawgiver did not think himself obliged to protect—but not from his own countrymen. The *Koran* follows out this point of view consistently, and prohibits the taking of interest altogether. In most other nations laws have been made to limit the rate of interest, and at Rome especially the legal rate was successively lowered—though it seems, as might have been expected, that the restrictive ordinances were constantly eluded. All such restrictions have been intended for the protection of debtors; an effect which large experience proves them never to produce, unless it be called protection to render the obtaining of money on loan impracticable for the most distressed borrow-

ers. But there was another effect which they *did* tend to produce—they softened down the primitive antipathy against the
practice generally, and confined the odious name of usury to
loans lent above the fixed legal rate.

In this way alone could they operate beneficially, and their
tendency to counterwork the previous feeling was at that time
not unimportant, coinciding as it did with other tendencies arising out of the industrial progress of society, which gradually
exhibited the relation of lender and borrower in a light more
reciprocal, beneficial, and less repugnant to the sympathies of
the bystander.

At Athens the more favorable point of view prevailed
throughout all the historical times. The march of industry and
commerce, under the mitigated law which prevailed subsequently to Solon, had been sufficient to bring it about at a very
early period and to suppress all public antipathy against lenders
at interest. We may remark, too, that this more equitable tone
of opinion grew up spontaneously, without any legal restriction
on the rate of interest—no such restriction having ever been
imposed and the rate being expressly declared free by a law
ascribed to Solon himself. The same may probably be said of
the communities of Greece generally—at least there is no information to make us suppose the contrary. But the feeling
against lending money at interest remained in the bosoms of
the philosophical men long after it had ceased to form a part of
the practical morality of the citizens, and long after it had
ceased to be justified by the appearances of the case as at first
it really had been. Plato, Aristotle, Cicero, and Plutarch, treat
the practice as a branch of the commercial and money-getting
spirit which they are anxious to discourage; and one consequence of this was that they were less disposed to contend
strenuously for the inviolability of existing money-contracts.
The conservative feeling on this point was stronger among the
mass than among the philosophers. Plato even complains of it
as inconveniently preponderant, and as arresting the legislator
in all comprehensive projects of reform. For the most part, indeed, schemes of cancelling debts and redividing lands were
never thought of except by men of desperate and selfish ambition, who made them stepping-stones to despotic power. Such

men were denounced alike by the practical sense of the community and by the speculative thinkers: but when we turn to the case of the Spartan king, Agis III, who proposed a complete extinction of debts and an equal redivision of the landed property of the state, not with any selfish or personal views, but upon pure ideas of patriotism, well or ill understood, and for the purpose of renovating the lost ascendancy of Sparta— we find Plutarch expressing the most unqualified admiration of this young king and his projects, and treating the opposition made to him as originating in no better feelings than meanness and cupidity. The philosophical thinkers on politics conceived —and to a great degree justly, as I shall show hereafter—that the conditions of security, in the ancient world, imposed upon the citizens generally the absolute necessity of keeping up a military spirit and willingness to brave at all times personal hardship and discomfort: so that increase of wealth, on account of the habits of self-indulgence which it commonly introduces, was regarded by them with more or less of disfavor. If in their estimation any Grecian community had become corrupt, they were willing to sanction great interference with preëxisting rights for the purpose of bringing it back nearer to their ideal standard. And the real security for the maintenance of these rights lay in the conservative feelings of the citizens generally, much more than in the opinions which superior minds imbibed from the philosophers.

Such conservative feelings were in the subsequent Athenian democracy peculiarly deep-rooted. The mass of the Athenian people identified inseparably the maintenance of property in all its various shapes with that of their laws and constitution. And it is a remarkable fact, that though the admiration entertained at Athens for Solon was universal, the principle of his Seisachtheia and of his money-depreciation was not only never imitated, but found the strongest tacit reprobation; whereas at Rome, as well as in most of the kingdoms of modern Europe, we know that one debasement of the coin succeeded another. The temptation of thus partially eluding the pressure of financial embarrassments proved, after one successful trial, too strong to be resisted, and brought down the coin by successive depreciations from the full pound of twelve ounces to the standard of one half ounce. It is of some importance to take notice of this fact, when we reflect how much "Grecian faith" has been degraded by the Roman writers into a byword for duplicity in pecuniary dealings. The democracy of Athens —and indeed the cities of Greece generally, both oligarchies and democracies—stands far above the senate of Rome, and far above the modern kingdoms of France and England until comparatively recent times, in respect of honest dealing with the coinage. Moreover, while there occurred at Rome several political changes which brought about new tables, or at least a partial depreciation of contracts, no phenomenon of the same kind ever happened at Athens, during the three centuries between Solon and the end of the free working of the democracy. Doubtless there were fraudulent debtors at Athens; while the administration of private law, though not in any way conniving at their proceedings, was far too imperfect to repress them as effectually as might have been wished. But the public sentiment on the point was just and decided. It may be asserted with confidence that a loan of money at Athens was quite as secure as it ever was at any time or place of the ancient world —in spite of the great and important superiority of Rome with respect to the accumulation of a body of authoritative legal precedent, the source of what was ultimately shaped into the Roman jurisprudence. Among the various causes of sedition or mischief in the Grecian communities, we hear little of the pressure of private debt.

By the measures of relief above described, Solon had accomplished results surpassing his own best hopes. He had healed the prevailing discontents; and such was the confidence and gratitude which he had inspired, that he was now called upon to draw up a constitution and laws for the better working of the government in future. His constitutional changes were great and valuable: respecting his laws, what we hear is rather curious than important.

It has been already stated that, down to the time of Solon, the classification received in Attica was that of the four Ionic tribes, comprising in one scale the Phratries and Gentes, and in another scale the three Trittyes and forty-eight Naucraries— while the Eupatridæ, seemingly a few specially respected gentes, and perhaps a few distinguished families in all the gentes, had in their hands all the powers of government. Solon introduced a new principle of classification—called in Greek the "timocratic principle." He distributed all the citizens of the tribes, without any reference to their gentes or phratries, into four classes, according to the amount of their property, which he caused to be assessed and entered in a public schedule. Those whose annual income was equal to five hundred medimni of corn (about seven hundred imperial bushels) and upward—one medimnus being considered equivalent to one drachma in money—he placed in the highest class; those who received between three hundred and five hundred medimni or drachmas formed the second class; and those between two hundred and three hundred, the third. The fourth and most numerous class comprised all those who did not possess land yielding a produce equal to two hundred medimni. The first class, called Pentacosiomedimni, were alone eligible to the archonship and to all commands: the second were called the knights or horsemen of the state, as possessing enough to enable them to keep a horse and perform military service in that capacity: the third class, called the Zeugitæ, formed the heavy-armed infantry, and were bound to serve, each with his full panoply. Each of these three classes was entered in the public schedule as possessed of a taxable capital calculated with a certain reference to his annual income, but in a proportion diminishing according to the scale of that income—and a man paid taxes to the state according to the sum for which he stood rated in the schedule; so that this direct taxation acted really like a graduated income-tax. The ratable property of the citizen belonging to the richest class (the Pentacosiomedimnus) was calculated and entered on the state schedule at a sum of capital equal to twelve times his annual income; that of the Hippeus, horseman or knight, at a sum equal to ten times his annual income: that of the Zeugite, at a sum equal to five times his annual income. Thus a Pentacosiomedimnus, whose income was exactly 500 drachmas (the minimum qualification of his class), stood rated in the schedule for a taxable property of 6,000 drachmas or one talent, being twelve times his income —if his annual income were 1,000 drachmas, he would stand

rated for 12,000 drachmas or two talents, being the same proportion of income to ratable capital. But when we pass to the
second class, horsemen or knights, the proportion of the two is
changed. The horseman possessing an income of just 300
drachmas (or 300 medimni) would stand rated for 3,000 drachmas, or ten times his real income, and so in the same proportion for any income above 300 and below 500. Again, in the
third class, or below 300, the proportion is a second time altered
—the Zeugite possessing exactly 200 drachmas of income was
rated upon a still lower calculation, at 1,000 drachmas, or a sum
equal to five times his income; and all incomes of this class
(between 200 and 300 drachmas) would in like manner be multiplied by five in order to obtain the amount of ratable capital.
Upon these respective sums of schedule capital all direct taxation was levied. If the state required 1 per cent. of direct
tax, the poorest Pentacosiomedimnus would pay (upon 6,000
drachmas) 60 drachmas; the poorest Hippeus would pay (upon
3,000 drachmas) 30; the poorest Zeugite would pay (upon
1,000 drachmas) 10 drachmas. And thus this mode of assess-
ment would operate like a *graduated* income-tax, looking at it
in reference to the three different classes—but as an *equal* income tax, looking at it in reference to the different individuals
comprised in one and the same class.

All persons in the state whose annual income amounted to
less than two hundred medimni or drachmas were placed in the
fourth class, and they must have constituted the large majority
of the community. They were not liable to any direct taxation,
and perhaps were not at first even entered upon the taxable
schedule, more especially as we do not know that any taxes
were actually levied upon this schedule during the Solonian
times. It is said that they were all called Thetes, but this ap-
pellation is not well sustained, and cannot be admitted: the
fourth compartment in the descending scale was indeed termed
the Thetic census, because it contained all the Thetes, and because most of its members were of that humble description;
but it is not conceivable that a proprietor whose land yielded
to him a clear annual return of 100, 120, 140, or 180 drachmas,
could ever have been designated by that name.

Such were the divisions in the political scale established by

Solon, called by Aristotle a *timocracy*, in which the rights, honors, functions, and liabilities of the citizens were measured out according to the assessed property of each. The highest honors of the state—that is, the places of the nine archons annually chosen, as well as those in the senate of Areopagus, into which the past archons always entered (perhaps also the posts of Prytanes of the Naukrari) were reserved for the first class: the poor Eupatrids became ineligible, while rich men, not Eupatrids, were admitted. Other posts of inferior distinction were filled by the second and third classes, who were, moreover, bound to military service—the one on horseback, the other as heavy-armed soldiers on foot. Moreover, the *liturgies* of the state, as they were called—unpaid functions such as the trierarchy, choregy, gymnasiarchy, etc., which entailed expense and trouble on the holder of them—were distributed in some way or other between the members of the three classes, though we do not know how the distribution was made in these early times. On the other hand, the members of the fourth or lowest class were disqualified from holding any individual office of dignity. They performed no liturgies, served in case of war only as light-armed or with a panoply provided by the state, and paid nothing to the direct property-tax or Eisphora. It would be incorrect to say that they paid *no* taxes, for indirect taxes, such as duties on imports, fell upon them in common with the rest; and we must recollect that these latter were, throughout a long period of Athenian history, in steady operation, while the direct taxes were only levied on rare occasions.

But though this fourth class, constituting the great numerical majority of the free people, were shut out from individual office, their collective importance was in another way greatly increased. They were invested with the right of choosing the annual archons, out of the class of Pentacosiomedimni; and what was of more importance still, the archons and the magistrates generally, after their year of office, instead of being accountable to the senate of Areopagus, were made formally accountable to the public assembly sitting in judgment upon their past conduct. They might be impeached and called upon to defend themselves, punished in case of misbehavior, and debarred from the usual honor of a seat in the senate of Areopagus.

Had the public assembly been called upon to act alone without aid or guidance, this accountability would have proved only nominal. But Solon converted it into a reality by another new institution, which will hereafter be found of great moment in the working out of the Athenian democracy. He created the pro-bouleutic, or pre-considering senate, with intimate and especial reference to the public assembly—to prepare matters for its discussion, to convoke and superintend its meetings, and to insure the execution of its decrees. The senate, as first constituted by Solon, comprised four hundred members, taken in equal proportions from the four tribes; not chosen by lot, as they will be found to be in the more advanced stage of the democracy, but elected by the people, in the same way as the archons then were—persons of the fourth, or poorest class of the census, though contributing to elect, not being themselves eligible.

But while Solon thus created the new pre-considering senate, identified with and subsidiary to the popular assembly, he manifested no jealousy of the preëxisting Areopagitic senate. On the contrary, he enlarged its powers, gave to it an ample supervision over the execution of the laws generally, and imposed upon it the censorial duty of inspecting the lives and occupation of the citizens, as well as of punishing men of idle and dissolute habits. He was himself, as past archon, a member of this ancient senate, and he is said to have contemplated that by means of the two senates the state would be held fast, as it were with a double anchor, against all shocks and storms.

Such are the only new political institutions (apart from the laws to be noticed presently) which there are grounds for ascribing to Solon, when we take proper care to discriminate what really belongs to Solon and his age from the Athenian constitution as afterward remodelled. It has been a practice common with many able expositors of Grecian affairs, and followed partly even by Dr. Thirlwall, to connect the name of Solon with the whole political and judicial state of Athens as it stood between the age of Pericles and that of Demosthenes—the regulations of the senate of five hundred, the numerous public dicasts or jurors taken by lot from the people—as well as the body annually selected for law-revision, and called *nomothets*—and the open prosecution (called the *graphe paranomon*) to be instituted against the proposer of any measure illegal, unconstitutional, or dangerous. There is indeed some countenance for this confusion between Solonian and post-Solonian Athens, in the usage of the orators themselves. For Demosthenes and Æschines employ the name of Solon in a very loose manner, and treat him as the author of institutions belonging evidently to a later age—for example: the striking and characteristic oath of the Heliastic jurors, which Demosthenes ascribes to Solon, proclaims itself in many ways as belonging to the age after Clisthenes, especially by the mention of the senate of five hundred, and not of four hundred. Among the citizens who served as jurors or dicasts, Solon was venerated generally as the author of the Athenian laws. An orator, therefore, might well employ his name for the purpose of emphasis, without provoking any critical inquiry whether the particular institution, which he happened to be then impressing upon his audience, belonged really to Solon himself or to the subsequent periods. Many of those institutions, which Dr. Thirlwall mentions in conjunction with the name of Solon, are among the last refinements and elaborations of the democratical mind of Athens—gradually prepared, doubtless, during the interval between Clisthenes and Pericles, but not brought into full operation until the period of the latter (B.C. 460–429). For it is hardly possible to conceive these numerous dicasteries and assemblies in regular, frequent, and long-standing operation, without an assured payment to the dicasts who composed them. Now such payment first began to be made about the time of Pericles, if not by his actual proposition; and Demosthenes had good reason for contending that if it were suspended, the judicial as well as the administrative system of Athens would at once fall to pieces. It would be a marvel, such as nothing short of strong direct evidence would justify us in believing, that in an age when even partial democracy was yet untried, Solon should conceive the idea of such institutions; it would be a marvel still greater, that the half-emancipated Thetes and small proprietors, for whom he legislated—yet trembling under the rod of the Eupatrid archons, and utterly inexperienced in collective business—should have been found suddenly competent to fulfil these ascendant functions, such as the citizens of conquering Athens in the days of Pericles, full of the sentiment of force and actively identifying themselves with the dignity of their community, became gradually competent, and not more than competent, to exercise with effect. To suppose that Solon contemplated and provided for the periodical revision of his laws by establishing a nomothetic jury or dicastery, such as that which we find in operation during the time of Demosthenes, would be at variance (in my judgment) with any reasonable estimate either of the man or of the age. Herodotus says that Solon, having exacted from the Athenians solemn oaths that *they* would not rescind any of his laws for ten years, quitted Athens for that period, in order that he might not be compelled to rescind them himself. Plutarch informs us that he gave to his laws force for a century. Solon himself, and Draco before him, had been lawgivers evoked and empowered by the special emergency of the times: the idea of a frequent revision of laws, by a body of lot-selected dicasts, belongs to a far more advanced age, and could not well have been present to the minds of either. The wooden rollers of Solon, like the tables of the Roman decemvirs, were doubtless intended as a permanent "*fons omnis publici privatique juris.*"

If we examine the facts of the case, we shall see that nothing more than the bare foundation of the democracy of Athens as it stood in the time of Pericles can reasonably be ascribed to Solon. "I gave to the people (Solon says in one of his short remaining fragments) as much strength as sufficed for their needs, without either enlarging or diminishing their dignity: for those too, who possessed power and were noted for wealth, I took care that no unworthy treatment should be reserved. I stood with the strong shield cast over both parties so as not to allow an unjust triumph to either." Again, Aristotle tells us that Solon bestowed upon the people as much power as was indispensable, but no more: the power to elect their magistrates and hold them to accountability: if the people had had less than this, they could not have been expected to remain tranquil—they would have been in slavery and hostile to the constitution. Not less distinctly does Herodotus speak, when he describes the revolution subsequently operated by Clisthenes—the latter (he tells us) found "the Athenian people excluded from everything." These passages seem positively to contradict the supposition, in itself sufficiently improbable, that Solon is the author of the peculiar democratical institutions of Athens, such as the constant and numerous dicasts for judicial trials and revision of laws. The genuine and forward democratical movement of Athens begins only with Clisthenes, from the moment when that distinguished Alcmæonid, either spontaneously, or from finding himself worsted in his party strife with Isagoras, purchased by large popular concessions the hearty coöperation of the multitude under very dangerous circumstances. While Solon, in his own statement as well as in that of Aristotle, gave to the people as much power as was strictly needful—but no more—Clisthenes (to use the significant phrase of Herodotus), "being vanquished in the party contest with his rival, *took the people into partnership.*" It was, thus, to the interests of the weaker section, in a strife of contending nobles, that the Athenian people owed their first admission to political ascendancy—in part, at least, to this cause, though the proceedings of Clisthenes indicate a hearty and spontaneous popular sentiment. But such constitutional admission of the people would not have been so astonishingly fruitful in positive results, if the course of public events for the half century after Clisthenes had not been such as to stimulate most powerfully their energy, their self-reliance, their mutual sympathies, and their ambition. I shall recount in a future chapter these historical causes, which, acting upon the Athenian character, gave such efficiency and expansion to the great democratical impulse communicated by Clisthenes: at present it is enough to remark that that impulse commences properly with Clisthenes, and not with Solon.

But the Solonian constitution, though only the foundation, was yet the indispensable foundation, of the subsequent democracy. And if the discontents of the miserable Athenian population, instead of experiencing his disinterested and healing management, had fallen at once into the hands of selfish power-seekers like Cylon or Pisistratus—the memorable expansion of the Athenian mind during the ensuing century would never have taken place, and the whole subsequent history of Greece would probably have taken a different course. Solon left the essential powers of the state still in the hands of the oligarchy. The party combats between Pisistratus, Lycurgus, and Megacles, thirty years after his legislation, which ended in the despotism of Pisistratus, will appear to be of the same purely oligarchical character as they had been before Solon was appointed archon. But the oligarchy which he established was very different from the unmitigated oligarchy which he found, so teeming with oppression and so destitute of redress, as his own poems testify.

It was he who first gave both to the citizens of middling property and to the general mass a *locus standi* against the Eupatrids. He enabled the people partially to protect themselves, and familiarized them with the idea of protecting themselves, by the peaceful exercise of a constitutional franchise. The new force, through which this protection was carried into effect, was the public assembly called *Heliæa*, regularized and armed with enlarged prerogatives and further strengthened by its indispensable ally—the pro-bouleutic, or pre-considering, senate. Under the Solonian constitution, this force was merely secondary and defensive, but after the renovation of Clisthenes it became paramount and sovereign. It branched out gradually into those numerous popular dicasteries which so powerfully modified both public and private Athenian life, drew to itself the undivided reverence and submission of the people, and by degrees rendered the single magistracies essentially subordinate functions. The popular assembly, as constituted by Solon, appearing in modified efficiency and trained to the office of reviewing and judging the general conduct of a past magistrate—forms the intermediate stage between the passive Homeric agora and those omnipotent assemblies and dicasteries which listened to Pericles or Demosthenes. Compared with these last, it has in it but a faint streak of democracy—and so it naturally appeared to Aristotle, who wrote with a practical experience of Athens in the time of the orators; but compared with the first, or with the ante-Solonian constitution of Attica, it must doubtless have appeared a concession eminently democratical. To impose upon the Eupatrid archon the necessity of being elected, or put upon his trial of after-accountability, by the *rabble* of freemen (such would be the phrase in Eupatrid society), would be a bitter humiliation to those among whom it was first introduced; for we must recollect that this was the most extensive scheme of constitutional reform yet propounded in Greece, and that despots and oligarchies shared between them at that time the whole Grecian world. As it appears that Solon, while constituting the popular assembly with its pro-bouleutic senate, had no jealousy of the senate of Areopagus, and indeed, even enlarged its powers, we may infer that his grand object was, not to weaken the oligarchy generally, but to improve the administration and to repress the misconduct and irregularities of the individual archons; and that, too, not by diminishing their powers, but by making some degree of popularity the condition both of their entry into office, and of their safety or honor after it.

It is, in my judgment, a mistake to suppose that Solon transferred the judicial power of the archons to a popular dicastery. These magistrates still continued self-acting judges, deciding and condemning without appeal—not mere presidents of an assembled jury, as they afterward came to be during the next century. For the general exercise of such power they were accountable after their year of office. Such accountability was the security against abuse—a very insufficient security, yet not wholly inoperative. It will be seen, however, presently that these archons, though strong to coerce, and perhaps to oppress, small and poor men, had no means of keeping down rebellious nobles of their own rank, such as Pisistratus, Lycurgus, and Megacles, each with his armed followers. When we compare the drawn swords of these ambitious competitors, ending in the despotism of one of them, with the vehement parliamentary strife between Themistocles and Aristides afterward, peaceably decided by the vote of the sovereign people and never disturbing the public tranquillity—we shall see that the democracy of the ensuing century fulfilled the conditions of order, as well as of progress, better than the Solonian constitution.

To distinguish this Solonian constitution from the democracy which followed it, is essential to a due comprehension of the progress of the Greek mind, and especially of Athenian affairs. That democracy was achieved by gradual steps. Demosthenes and Æschines lived under it as a system consummated and in full activity, when the stages of its previous growth were no longer matter of exact memory; and the dicasts then assembled in judgment were pleased to hear their constitution associated with the names either of Solon or of Theseus. Their inquisitive contemporary Aristotle was not thus misled: but even commonplace Athenians of the century preceding would have escaped the same delusion. For during the whole course of the democratical movement, from the Persian invasion down to the Peloponnesian war, and especially during the changes proposed by Pericles and Ephialtes, there was always a strenuous party of resistance, who would not suffer the people to forget that they had already forsaken, and were on the point of forsaking still more, the orbit marked out by Solon. The illustrious Pericles underwent innumerable attacks both from the orators in the assembly and from the comic writers in the theatre. And among these sarcasms on the political tendencies of the day we are probably to number the complaint, breathed by the poet Cratinus, of the desuetude into which both Solon and Draco had fallen—"I swear (said he in a fragment of one of his comedies) by Solon and Draco, whose wooden tablets (of laws) are now employed by people to roast their barley." The laws of Solon respecting penal offences, respecting inheritance and adoption, respecting the private relations generally, etc., remained for the most part in force: his quadripartite census also continued, at least for financial purposes, until the archonship of Nausinicus in B.C. 377—so that Cicero and others might be warranted in affirming that his laws still prevailed at Athens: but his political and judicial arrangements had undergone a revolution not less complete and memorable than the character and spirit of the Athenian people generally. The choice, by way of lot, of archons and other magistrates—and the distribution by lot of the general body of dicasts or jurors into panels for judicial business—may be decidedly considered as not belonging to Solon, but adopted after the revolution of Clisthenes; probably the choice of senators by lot also. The lot was a symptom of pronounced democratical spirit, such as we must not seek in the Solonian institutions.

It is not easy to make out distinctly what was the political position of the ancient gentes and phratries, as Solon left them.

The four tribes consisted altogether of gentes and phratries, insomuch that no one could be included in any one of the tribes who was not also a member of some gens and phratry. Now the new pro-bouleutic, or pre-considering, senate consisted of four hundred members,—one hundred from each of the tribes: persons not included in any gens or phratry could therefore have had no access to it. The conditions of eligibility were similar, according to ancient custom, for the nine archons—of course, also, for the senate of Areopagus. So that there remained only the public assembly, in which an Athenian not a member of these tribes could take part: yet he was a citizen, since he could give his vote for archons and senators, and could take part in the annual decision of their accountability, besides being entitled to claim redress for wrong from the archons in his own person—while the alien could only do so through the intervention of an avouching citizen or Prostates. It seems, therefore, that all persons not included in the four tribes, whatever their grade of fortune might be, were on the same level in respect to political privilege as the fourth and poorest class of the Solonian census. It has already been remarked, that even before the time of Solon the number of Athenians not included in the gentes or phratries was probably considerable: it tended to become greater and greater, since these bodies were close and unexpansive, while the policy of the new lawgiver tended to invite industrious settlers from other parts of Greece and Athens. Such great and increasing inequality of political privilege helps to explain the weakness of the government in repelling the aggressions of Pisistratus, and exhibits the importance of the revolution afterward wrought by Clisthenes, when he abolished (for all political purposes) the four old tribes, and created ten new comprehensive tribes in place of them.

In regard to the regulations of the senate and the assembly of the people, as constituted by Solon, we are altogether without information: nor is it safe to transfer to the Solonian constitution the information, comparatively ample, which we possess respecting these bodies under the later democracy.

The laws of Solon were inscribed on wooden rollers and triangular tablets, in the species of writing called *Boustrophedon* (lines alternating first from left to right, and next from right to left, like the course of the ploughman—and preserved first in the Acropolis, subsequently in the Prytaneum. On the tablets, called *Cyrbis,* were chiefly commemorated the laws respecting sacred rites and sacrifices; on the pillars or rollers, of which there were at least sixteen, were placed the regulations respecting matters profane. So small are the fragments which have come down to us, and so much has been ascribed to Solon by the orators which belongs really to the subsequent times, that it is hardly possible to form any critical judgment respecting the legislation as a whole, or to discover by what general principles or purposes he was guided.

He left unchanged all the previous laws and practices respecting the crime of homicide, connected as they were intimately with the religious feelings of the people. The laws of Draco on this subject, therefore, remained, but on other subjects, according to Plutarch, they were altogether abrogated: there is, however, room for supposing that the repeal cannot have been so sweeping as this biographer represents.

The Solonian laws seem to have borne more or less upon all the great departments of human interest and duty. We find regulations political and religious, public and private, civil and criminal, commercial, agricultural, sumptuary, and disciplinarian. Solon provides punishment for crimes, restricts the profession and status of the citizen, prescribes detailed rules for marriage as well as for burial, for the common use of springs and wells, and for the mutual interest of conterminous farmers in planting or hedging their properties. As far as we can judge from the imperfect manner in which his laws come before us, there does not seem to have been any attempt at a systematic order or classification. Some of them are mere general and vague directions, while others again run into the extreme of specialty.

By far the most important of all was the amendment of the law of debtor and creditor which has already been adverted to, and the abolition of the power of fathers and brothers to sell their daughters and sisters into slavery. The prohibition of all contracts on the security of the body was itself sufficient to produce a vast improvement in the character and condition of the poorer population,—a result which seems to have been so sensibly obtained from the legislation of Solon, that Boeckh and some other eminent authors suppose him to have abolished villeinage and conferred upon the poor tenants a property in their lands, annulling the seigniorial rights of the landlord. But this opinion rests upon no positive evidence, nor are we warranted in ascribing to him any stronger measure in reference to the land than the annulment of the previous mortgages.

The first pillar of his laws contained a regulation respecting exportable produce. He forbade the exportation of all produce of the Attic soil, except olive oil alone. And the sanction employed to enforce observance of this law deserves notice, as an illustration of the ideas of the time: the archon was bound, on pain of forfeiting one hundred drachmas, to pronounce solemn curses against every offender. We are probably to take this prohibition in conjunction with other objects said to have been contemplated by Solon, especially the encouragement of artisans and manufacturers at Athens. Observing (we are told) that many new immigrants were just then flocking into Attica to seek an establishment, in consequence of its greater security, he was anxious to turn them rather to manufacturing industry than to the cultivation of a soil naturally poor. He forbade the granting of citizenship to any immigrants, except to such as had quitted irrevocably their former abodes and come to Athens for the purpose of carrying on some industrial profession; and in order to prevent idleness, he directed the senate of Areopagus to keep watch over the lives of the citizens generally, and punish every one who had no course of regular labor to support him. If a father had not taught his son some art or profession, Solon relieved the son from all obligation to maintain him in his old age. And it was to encourage the multiplication of these artisans that he insured, or sought to insure, to the residents in Attica, the exclusive right of buying and consuming all its landed produce except olive oil, which was raised in abundance, more than sufficient for their wants. It was his wish that the trade with foreigners should be carried on by exporting the produce of artisan labor, instead of the produce of land.

This commercial prohibition is founded on principles substantially similar to those which were acted upon in the early history of England, with reference both to corn and to wool, and

in other European countries also. In so far as it was at all operative it tended to lessen the total quantity of produce raised upon
the soil of Attica, and thus to keep the price of it from rising.
But the law of Solon must have been altogether inoperative, in
reference to the great articles of human subsistence; for Attica
imported, both largely and constantly, grain and salt provisions,
probably also wool and flax for the spinning and weaving of
the women, and certainly timber for building. Whether the
law was ever enforced with reference to figs and honey may
well be doubted; at least these productions of Attica were in
after times trafficked in, and generally consumed throughout
Greece. Probably also in the time of Solon the silver mines
of Laurium had hardly begun to be worked: these afterward
became highly productive, and furnished to Athens a commod-
ity for foreign payments no less convenient than lucrative.

It is interesting to notice the anxiety, both of Solon and of
Draco, to enforce among their fellow-citizens industrious and
self-maintaining habits; and we shall find the same sentiment
proclaimed by Pericles, at the time when Athenian power was
at its maximum. Nor ought we to pass over this early manifestation in Attica of an opinion equitable and tolerant toward
sedentary industry, which in most other parts of Greece was
regarded as comparatively dishonorable. The general tone of
Grecian sentiment recognized no occupations as perfectly worthy of a free citizen except arms, agriculture, and athletic and
musical exercises; and the proceedings of the Spartans, who
kept aloof even from agriculture and left it to their helots,
were admired, though they could not be copied, throughout
most of the Hellenic world. Even minds like Plato, Aristotle,
and Xenophon concurred to a considerable extent in this feeling, which they justified on the ground that the sedentary life
and unceasing house-work of the artisan were inconsistent with
military aptitude. The town-occupations are usually described
by a word which carries with it contemptuous ideas, and though
recognized as indispensable to the existence of the city, are
held suitable only for an inferior and semi-privileged order of
citizens. This, the received sentiment among Greeks, as well
as foreigners, found a strong and growing opposition at
Athens, as I have already said—corroborated also by a similar

feeling at Corinth. The trade of Corinth, as well as of Chalcis in Eubœa, was extensive, at a time when that of Athens had scarce any existence. But while the despotism of Periander can hardly have failed to operate as a discouragement to industry at Corinth, the contemporaneous legislation of Solon provided for traders and artisans a new home at Athens, giving the first encouragement to that numerous town-population both in the city and in the Piræus, which we find actually residing there in the succeeding century. The multiplication of such town residents, both citizens and *metics* (*i.e.*, resident persons, not citizens, but enjoying an assured position and civil rights), was a capital fact in the onward march of Athens, since it determined not merely the extension of her trade, but also the preëminence of her naval forces—and thus, as a further consequence, lent extraordinary vigor to her democratical government. It seems, moreover, to have been a departure from the primitive temper of Atticism, which tended both to cantonal residence and rural occupation. We have, therefore, the greater interest in noting the first mention of it as a consequence of the Solonian legislation.

To Solon is first owing the admission of a power of testamentary bequest at Athens in all cases in which a man had no legitimate children. According to the preëxisting custom, we may rather presume that if a deceased person left neither children nor blood relations, his property descended (as at Rome) to his gens and phratry. Throughout most rude states of society the power of willing is unknown, as among the ancient Germans—among the Romans prior to the twelve tables—in the old laws of the Hindus, etc. Society limits a man's interest or power of enjoyment to his life, and considers his relatives as having joint reversionary claims to his property, which take effect, in certain determinate proportions, after his death. Such a law was the more likely to prevail at Athens, since the perpetuity of the family sacred rites, in which the children and near relatives partook of right, was considered by the Athenians as a matter of public as well as of private concern. Solon gave permission to every man dying without children to bequeath his property by will as he should think fit; and the testament was maintained unless it could be shown to have been procured by some compulsion or improper seduction. Speaking generally, this continued to be the law throughout the historical times of Athens. Sons, wherever there were sons, succeeded to the property of their father in equal shares, with the obligation of giving out their sisters in marriage along with a certain dowry. If there were no sons, then the daughters succeeded, though the father might by will, within certain limits, determine the person to whom they should be married, with their rights of succession attached to them; or might, with the consent of his daughters, make by will certain other arrangements about his property. A person who had no children or direct lineal descendants might bequeath his property at pleasure: if he died without a will, first his father, then his brother or brother's children, next his sister or sister's children succeeded: if none such existed, then the cousins by the father's side, next the cousins by the mother's side,—the male line of descent having preference over the female.

Such was the principle of the Solonian laws of succession, though the particulars are in several ways obscure and doubtful. Solon, it appears, was the first who gave power of superseding by testament the rights of agnates and gentiles to succession,—a proceeding in consonance with his plan of encouraging both industrious occupation and the consequent multiplication of individual acquisitions.

It has been already mentioned that Solon forbade the sale of daughters or sisters into slavery by fathers or brothers; a prohibition which shows how much females had before been looked upon as articles of property. And it would seem that before his time the violation of a free woman must have been punished at the discretion of the magistrates; for we are told that he was the first who enacted a penalty of one hundred drachmas against the offender, and twenty drachmas against the seducer of a free woman. Moreover, it is said that he forbade a bride when given in marriage to carry with her any personal ornaments and appurtenances, except to the extent of three robes and certain matters of furniture not very valuable. Solon further imposed upon women several restraints in regard to proceeding at the obsequies of deceased relatives. He forbade profuse demonstrations of sorrow, singing of composed dirges, and costly sacrifices and contributions. He limited strictly the quantity of meat and drink admissible for the funeral banquet, and prohibited nocturnal exit, except in a car and with a light. It appears that both in Greece and Rome, the feelings of duty and affection on the part of surviving relaties prompted them to ruinous expense in a funeral, as well as to unmeasured effusions both of grief and conviviality; and the general necessity experienced for legal restriction is attested by the remark of Plutarch, that similar prohibitions to those enacted by Solon were likewise in force at his native town of Chæronea.

Other penal enactments of Solon are yet to be mentioned. He forbade absolutely evil speaking with respect to the dead. He forbade it likewise with respect to the living, either in a temple or before judges or archons, or at any public festival— on pain of a forfeit of three drachmas to the person aggrieved, and two more to the public treasury. How mild the general character of his punishments was, may be judged by this law against foul language, not less than by the law before mentioned against rape. Both the one and the other of these offences were much more severely dealt with under the subsequent law of democratical Athens. The peremptory edict against speaking ill of a deceased person, though doubtless springing in a great degree from disinterested repugnance, is traceable also in part to that fear of the wrath of the departed which strongly possessed the early Greek mind.

It seems generally that Solon determined by law the outlay for the public sacrifices, though we do not know what were his particular directions. We are told that he reckoned a sheep and a medimnus (of wheat or barley?) as equivalent, either of them, to a drachma, and that he also prescribed the prices to be paid for first-rate oxen intended for solemn occasions. But it astonishes us to see the large recompense which he awarded out of the public treasury to a victor at the Olympic or Isthmian games: to the former, five hundred drachmas, equal to one year's income of the highest of the four classes on the census; to the latter one hundred drachmas. The magnitude of these rewards strikes us the more when we compare them with the fines on rape and evil speaking. We cannot be surprised that the philosopher Xenophanes noticed, with some degree of severity, the extravagant estimate of this species of excellence, current among the Grecian cities. At the same time, we must remember both that these Pan-Hellenic games presented the chief visible evidence of peace and sympathy among the numerous communities of Greece, and that in the time of Solon, factitious reward was still needful to encourage them. In respect to land and agriculture Solon proclaimed a public reward of five drachmas for every wolf brought in, and one drachma for every wolf's cub; the extent of wild land has at all times been considerable in Attica. He also provided rules respecting the use of wells between neighbors, and respecting the planting in conterminous olive grounds. Whether any of these regulations continued in operation during the better-known period of Athenian history cannot be safely affirmed.

In respect to theft, we find it stated that Solon repealed the punishment of death which Draco had annexed to that crime, and enacted, as a penalty, compensation to an amount double the value of the property stolen. The simplicity of this law perhaps affords ground for presuming that it really does belong to Solon. But the law which prevailed during the time of the orators respecting theft must have been introduced at some later period, since it enters into distinctions and mentions both places and forms of procedure, which we cannot reasonably refer to the forty-sixth Olympiad. The public dinners at the Prytaneum, of which the archons and a select few partook in common, were also either first established, or perhaps only more strictly regulated, by Solon. He ordered barley cakes for their ordinary meals, and wheaten loaves for festival days, prescribing how often each person should dine at the table. The honor of dining at the table of the Prytaneum was maintained throughout as a valuable reward at the disposal of the government.

Among the various laws of Solon, there are few which have attracted more notice than that which pronounces the man who in a sedition stood aloof, and took part with neither side, to be dishonored and disfranchised. Strictly speaking, this seems more in the nature of an emphatic moral denunciation, or a religious curse, than a legal sanction capable of being for-

mally applied in an individual case and after judicial trial,—
though the sentence of *atimy*, under the more elaborated Attic
procedure, was both definite in its penal consequences and also
judicially delivered. We may, however, follow the course of
ideas under which Solon was induced to write this sentence
on his tables, and we may trace the influence of similar ideas
in later Attic institutions. It is obvious that his denunciation
is confined to that special case in which a sedition has already
broken out: we must suppose that Cylon has seized the Acropolis, or that Pisistratus, Megacles, and Lycurgus are in arms
at the head of their partisans. Assuming these leaders to be
wealthy and powerful men, which would in all probability be
the fact, the constituted authority—such as Solon saw before
him in Attica, even after his own organic amendments—was
not strong enough to maintain the peace; it became, in fact,
itself one of the contending parties. Under such given circumstances, the sooner every citizen publicly declared his adherence to some of them, the earlier this suspension of legal
authority was likely to terminate. Nothing was so mischiev-
ous as the indifference of the mass, or their disposition to let
the combatants fight out the matter among themselves, and
then to submit to the victor. Nothing was more likely to encourage aggression on the part of an ambitious malcontent,
than the conviction that if he could once overpower the small
amount of physical force which surrounded the archons, and
exhibit himself in armed possession of the Prytaneum or the
Acropolis, he might immediately count upon passive submission on the part of all the freemen without. Under the state
of feeling which Solon inculcates, the insurgent leader would
have to calculate that every man who was not actively in his
favor would be actively against him, and this would render his
enterprise much more dangerous. Indeed, he could then never
hope to succeed, except on the double supposition of extraordinary popularity in his own person and widespread detestation of the existing government. He would thus be placed
under the influence of powerful deterring motives; so that ambition would be less likely to seduce him into a course which
threatened nothing but ruin, unless under such encourage-
ments from the preëxisting public opinion as to make his suc-

cess a result desirable for the community. Among the small political societies of Greece—especially in the age of Solon, when the number of despots in other parts of Greece seems to have been at its maximum—every government, whatever might be its form, was sufficiently weak to make its overthrow a matter of comparative facility. Unless upon the supposition of a band of foreign mercenaries—which would render the government a system of naked force, and which the Athenian lawgiver would of course never contemplate—there was no other stay for it except a positive and pronounced feeling of attachment on the part of the mass of citizens. Indifference on their part would render them a prey to every daring man of wealth who chose to become a conspirator. That they should be ready to come forward, not only with voice but with arms—and that they should be known beforehand to be so— was essential to the maintenance of every good Grecian government. It was salutary in preventing mere personal attempts at revolution; and pacific in its tendency, even where the revolution had actually broken out, because in the greater number of cases the proportion of partisans would probably be very unequal, and the inferior party would be compelled to renounce their hopes.

It will be observed that, in this enactment of Solon, the existing government is ranked merely as one of the contending parties. The virtuous citizen is enjoined, not to come forward in its support, but to come forward at all events, either for it or against it. Positive and early action is all which is prescribed to him as matter of duty. In the age of Solon there was no political idea or system yet current which could be assumed as an unquestionable datum—no conspicuous standard to which the citizens could be pledged under all circumstances to attach themselves. The option lay only between a mitigated oligarchy in possession, and a despot in possibility; a contest wherein the affections of the people could rarely be counted upon in favor of the established government. But this neutrality in respect to the constitution was at an end after the revolution of Clisthenes, when the idea of the sovereign people and the democratical institutions became both familiar and precious to every individual citizen. We shall hereafter find the Athenians binding themselves by the most sincere and solemn oaths to uphold their democracy against all attempts to subvert it; we shall discover in them a sentiment not less positive and uncompromising in its direction, than energetic in its inspirations. But while we notice this very important change in their character, we shall at the same time perceive that the wise precautionary recommendation of Solon, to obviate sedition by an early declaration of the impartial public between two contending leaders, was not lost upon them. Such, in point of fact, was the purpose of that salutary and protective institution which is called the *Ostracism*. When two party leaders, in the early stages of the Athenian democracy, each powerful in adherents and influence, had become passionately embarked in bitter and prolonged opposition to each other, such opposition was likely to conduct one or other to violent measures. Over and above the hopes of party triumph, each might well fear that, if he himself continued within the bounds of legality, he might fall a victim to aggressive proceedings on the part of his antagonists. To ward off this formidable danger, a public vote was called for, to determine which of the two should go into temporary banishment, retaining his property and unvisited by any disgrace. A number of citizens, not less than six thousand, voting secretly, and therefore independently, were required to take part, pronouncing upon one or other of these eminent rivals a sentence of exile for ten years. The one who remained became, of course, more powerful, yet less in a situation to be driven into anti-constitutional courses than he was before. Tragedy and comedy were now beginning to be grafted on the lyric and choric song. First, one actor was provided to relieve the chorus; next, two actors were introduced to sustain fictitious characters and carry on a dialogue in such manner that the songs of the chorus and the interlocution of the actors formed a continuous piece. Solon, after having heard Thespis acting (as all the early composers did, both tragic and comic) in his own comedy, asked him afterward if he was not ashamed to pronounce such falsehoods before so large an audience. And when Thespis answered that there was no harm in saying and doing such things merely for amusement, Solon indignantly exclaimed, striking the ground with his stick, "If once we come to praise and esteem such amusement as this, we shall quickly find the effects of it in our daily transactions." For the authenticity of this anecdote it would be rash to vouch, but we may at least treat it as the protest of some early philosopher against the deceptions of the drama: and it is interesting as marking the incipient struggles of that literature in which Athens afterward attained such unrivaled excellence.

It would appear that all the laws of Solon were proclaimed, inscribed, and accepted without either discussion or resistance. He is said to have described them, not as the best laws which he could himself have imagined, but as the best which he could have induced the people to accept. He gave them validity for the space of ten years, during which period both the senate collectively and the archons individually swore to observe them with fidelity; under penalty, in case of nonobservance, of a golden statue as large as life to be erected at Delphi. But though the acceptance of the laws was accomplished without difficulty, it was not found so easy either for the people to understand and obey, or for the framer to explain them. Every day persons came to Solon either with praise, or criticism, or suggestions of various improvements, or questions as to the construction of particular enactments; until at last he became tired of this endless process of reply and vindication, which was seldom successful either in removing obscurity or in satisfying complainants. Foreseeing that if he remained he would be compelled to make changes, he obtained leave of absence from his countrymen for ten years, trusting that before the expiration of that period they would have become accustomed to his laws. He quitted his native city in the full certainty that his laws would remain unrepealed until his return; for (says Herodotus) "the Athenians *could not* repeal them, since they were bound by solemn oaths to observe them for ten years." The unqualified manner in which the historian here speaks of an oath, as if it created a sort of physical necessity and shut out all possibility of a contrary result, deserves notice as illustrating Grecian sentiment.

On departing from Athens, Solon first visited Egypt, where he communicated largely with Psenophis of Heliopolis and Sonchis of Sais, Egyptian priests who had much to tell respecting their ancient history, and from whom he learned matters, real or pretended, far transcending in alleged antiquity the oldest Grecian genealogies—especially the history of the vast submerged island of Atlantis, and the war which the ancestors of the Athenians had successfully carried on against it, nine thousand years before. Solon is said to have commenced an epic poem upon this subject, but he did not live to finish it, and nothing of it now remains. From Egypt he went to Cyprus, where he visited the small town of Æpia, said to have been originally founded by Demophon, son of Theseus, and ruled at this period by the prince Philocyprus—each town in Cyprus having its own petty prince. It was situated near the river Clarius in a position precipitous and secure, but inconvenient and ill-supplied. Solon persuaded Philocyprus to quit the old site and establish a new town down in the fertile plain beneath. He himself stayed and became *œcist* of the new establishment, making all the regulations requisite for its safe and prosperous march, which was indeed so decisively manifested that many new settlers flocked into the new plantation, called by Philocyprus *Soli*, in honor of Solon. To our deep regret, we are not permitted to know what these regulations were; but the general fact is attested by the poems of Solon himself, and the lines in which he bade farewell to Philocyprus on quitting the island are yet before us. On the dispositions of this prince his poem bestowed unqualified commendation.

Besides his visit to Egypt and Cyprus, a story was also current of his having conversed with the Lydian king Crœsus at Sardis. The communication said to have taken place between them has been woven by Herodotus into a sort of moral tale which forms one of the most beautiful episodes in his whole history. Though this tale has been told and retold as if it were genuine history, yet as it now stands it is irreconcilable with chronology—although very possibly Solon may at some time or other have visited Sardis, and seen Crœsus as hereditary prince.

But even if no chronological objections existed, the moral purpose of the tale is so prominent, and pervades it so systematically from beginning to end, that these internal grounds are of themselves sufficiently strong to impeach its credibility as a matter of fact, unless such doubts happen to be outweighed—which in this case they are not—by good contemporary testimony. The narrative of Solon and Crœsus can be taken for nothing else but an illustrative fiction, borrowed by Herodotus from some philosopher, and clothed in his own peculiar beauty of expression, which on this occasion is more decidedly poetical than is habitual with him. I cannot transcribe, and I hardly dare to abridge it. The vainglorious Crœsus, at the summit of his conquests and his riches, endeavors to win from his visitor Solon an opinion that he is the happiest of mankind. The latter, after having twice preferred to him modest and meritorious Grecian citizens, at length reminds him that his vast wealth and power are of a tenure too precarious to serve as an evidence of happiness; that the gods are jealous and meddlesome, and often make the show of happiness a mere prelude to extreme disaster; and that no man's life can be called happy until the whole of it has been played out, so that it may be seen to be out of the reach of reverses. Crœsus treats this opinion as absurd, but "a great judgment from God fell upon him, after Solon was departed—probably (observes Herodotus) because he fancied himself the happiest of all men." First he lost his favorite son Atys, a brave and intelligent youth (his only other son being dumb). For the Mysians of Olympus being ruined by a destructive and formidable wild boar, which they were unable to subdue, applied for aid to Crœsus, who sent to the spot a chosen hunting force, and permitted—though with great reluctance, in consequence of an alarming dream—that his favorite son should accompany them. The young prince was unintentionally slain by the Phrygian exile Adrastus, whom Crœsus had sheltered and protected. Hardly had the latter recovered from the anguish of this misfortune, when the rapid growth of Cyrus and the Persian power induced him to go to war with them, against the advice of his wisest counsellors. After a struggle of about three years he was completely defeated, his capital Sardis taken by storm, and himself made prisoner. Cyrus ordered a large pile to be prepared, and placed upon it Crœsus in fetters, together with fourteen young Lydians, in the intention of burning them alive either as a religious offering, or in fulfilment of a vow, "or perhaps (says Herodotus) to see whether some of the gods would not interfere to rescue a man so preëmiently pious as the king of Lydia." In this sad extremity, Crœsus bethought him of the warning which he had before despised, and thrice pronounced, with a deep groan, the name of Solon. Cyrus desired the interpreters to inquire whom he was invoking, and learnt in reply the anecdote of the Athenian lawgiver, together with the solemn memento which he had offered to Crœsus during more prosperous days, attesting the frail tenure of all human greatness. The remark sunk deep into the Persian monarch as a token of what might happen to himself: he repented of his purpose, and directed that the pile, which had already been kindled, should be immediately extinguished. But the orders came too late. In spite of the most zealous efforts of the bystanders, the flame was found unquenchable, and Crœsus would still have been burned, had he not implored with prayers and tears the succor of Apollo, to whose Delphian and Theban temples he had given such munificent presents. His prayers were heard, the fair sky was immediately overcast and a profuse rain descended, sufficient to extinguish the flames. The life of Crœsus was thus saved, and he became afterward the confidential friend and adviser of his conqueror.

Such is the brief outline of a narrative which Herodotus has given with full development and with impressive effect. It would have served as a show-lecture to the youth of Athens not less admirably than the well-known fable of the Choice of Heracles, which the philosopher Prodicus, a junior contemporary of Herodotus, delivered with so much popularity. It illustrates forcibly the religious and ethical ideas of antiquity; the deep sense of the jealousy of the gods, who would not endure pride in any one except themselves; the impossibility, for any man, of realizing to himself more than a very moderate share of happiness; the danger from a reactionary Nemesis, if at any time he had overpassed such limit; and the necessity of calculations taking in the whole of life, as a basis for rational comparison of different individuals. And it embodies, as a practical consequence from these feelings, the often-repeated

protest of moralists against vehement impulses and unrestrained aspirations. The more valuable this narrative appears,
in its illustrative character, the less can we presume to treat it
as a history.

It is much to be regretted that we have no information respecting events in Attica immediately after the Solonian
laws and constitution, which were promulgated in B.C. 594, so
as to understand better the practical effect of these changes.
What we next hear respecting Solon in Attica refers to a period immediately preceding the first usurpation of Pisistratus
in B.C. 560, and after the return of Solon from his long absence. We are here again introduced to the same oligarchical
dissensions as are reported to have prevailed before the Solonian legislation: the Pediis, or opulent proprietors of the plain
round Athens, under Lycurgus; the Parali of the south of Attica, under Megacles; and the Diacrii or mountaineers of the
eastern cantons, the poorest of the three classes, under Pisistratus, are in a state of violent intestine dispute. The account
of Plutarch represents Solon as returning to Athens during the
height of this sedition. He was treated with respect by all
parties, but his recommendations were no longer obeyed, and
he was disqualified by age from acting with effect in public.
He employed his best efforts to mitigate party animosities,
and applied himself particularly to restrain the ambition of
Pisistratus, whose ulterior projects he quickly detected.

The future greatness of Pisistratus is said to have been first
portended by a miracle which happened, even before his birth,
to his father Hippocrates at the Olympic games. It was realized, partly by his bravery and conduct, which had been displayed in the capture of Nisæa from the Megarians—partly
by his popularity of speech and manners, his championship of
the poor, and his ostentatious disavowal of all selfish pretensions—partly by an artful mixture of stratagem and force. Solon, after having addressed fruitless remonstrances to Pisistratus himself, publicly denounced his designs in verses addressed to the people. The deception, whereby Pisistratus
finally accomplished his design, is memorable in Grecian tradition. He appeared one day in the agora of Athens in his chariot with a pair of mules: he had intentionally wounded both his

person and the mules, and in this condition he threw himself
upon the compassion and defence of the people, pretending
that his political enemies had violently attacked him. He
implored the people to grant him a guard, and at the moment
when their sympathies were freshly aroused both in his favor
and against his supposed assassins, Aristo proposed formally
to the ecclesia (the pro-bouleutic senate, being composed of
friends of Pisistratus, had previously authorized the proposition) that a company of fifty club-men should be assigned as a
permanent body-guard for the defence of Pisistratus. To
this motion Solon opposed a strenuous resistance, but found
himself overborne, and even treated as if he had lost his senses.
The poor were earnest in favor of it, while the rich were afraid
to express their dissent; and he could only comfort himself
after the fatal vote had been passed, by exclaiming that he was
wiser than the former and more determined than the latter.
Such was one of the first known instances in which this memorable stratagem was played off against the liberty of a Grecian
community.

The unbounded popular favor which had procured the passing of this grant was still further manifested by the absence
of all precautions to prevent the limits of the grant from being
exceeded. The number of the body-guard was not long confined to fifty, and probably their clubs were soon exchanged
for sharper weapons. Pisistratus thus found himself strong
enough to throw off the mask and seize the Acropolis. His
leading opponents, Megacles and the Alcinæonids, immediately
fled the city, and it was left to the venerable age and undaunted
patriotism of Solon to stand forward almost alone in a vain
attempt to resist the usurpation. He publicly presented himself in the market-place, employing encouragement, remonstrance and reproach, in order to rouse the spirit of the people.
To prevent this despotism from coming (he told them) would
have been easy; to shake it off now was more difficult, yet at
the same time more glorious. But he spoke in vain, for all who
were not actually favorable to Pisistratus listened only to their
fears, and remained passive; nor did any one join Solon, when,
as a last appeal, he put on his armor and planted himself in
military posture before the door of his house. "I have done

my duty (he exclaimed at length); I have sustained to the best of my power my country and the laws"; and he then renounced all further hope of opposition—though resisting the instances of his friends that he should flee, and returning for answer, when they asked him on what he relied for protection, "On my old age." Nor did he even think it necessary to repress the inspirations of his Muse. Some verses yet remain, composed seemingly at a moment when the strong hand of the new despot had begun to make itself sorely felt, in which he tells his countrymen—"If ye have endured sorrow from your own baseness of soul, impute not the fault of this to the gods. Ye have yourselves put force and dominion into the hands of these men, and have thus drawn upon yourselves wretched slavery."

It is gratifying to learn that Pisistratus, whose conduct throughout his despotism was comparatively mild, left Solon untouched. How long this distinguished man survived the practical subversion of his own constitution, we cannot certainly determine; but according to the most probable statement he died during the very next year, at the advanced age of eighty.

We have only to regret that we are deprived of the means of following more in detail his noble and exemplary character. He represents the best tendencies of his age, combined with much that is personally excellent: the improved ethical sensibility; the thirst for enlarged knowledge and observation, not less potent in old age than in youth; the conception of regularized popular institutions, departing sensibly from the type and spirit of the governments around him, and calculated to found a new character in the Athenian people; a genuine and reflecting sympathy with the mass of the poor, anxious not merely to rescue them from the oppressions of the rich, but also to create in them habits of self-relying industry; lastly, during his temporary possession of a power altogether arbitrary, not merely an absence of all selfish ambition, but a rare discretion in seizing the mean between conflicting exigencies. In reading his poems we must always recollect that what now appears commonplace was once new, so that to his comparatively unlettered age the social pictures which he draws were still fresh, and his exhortations calculated to live in the memory. The poems composed on moral subjects generally inculcate a spirit of gentleness toward others and moderation in personal objects. They represent the gods as irresistible, retributive, favoring the good and punishing the bad, though sometimes very tardily. But his compositions on special and present occasions are usually conceived in a more vigorous spirit; denouncing the oppressions of the rich at one time, and the timid submission to Pisistratus at another—and expressing in emphatic language his own proud consciousness of having stood forward as champion of the mass of the people. Of his early poems hardly anything is preserved. The few lines remaining seem to manifest a jovial temperament which we may well conceive to have been overlaid by such political difficulties as he had to encounter—difficulties arising successively out of the Megarian war, the Cylonian sacrilege, the public despondency healed by Epimenides, and the task of arbiter between a rapacious oligarchy and a suffering people. In one of his elegies addressed to Mimnermus, he marked out the sixtieth year as the longest desirable period of life, in preference to the eightieth year, which that poet had expressed a wish to attain. But his own life, as far as we can judge, seems to have reached the longer of the two periods; and not the least honorable part of it (the resistance to Pisistratus) occurs immediately before his death.

There prevailed a story that his ashes were collected and scattered around the island of Salamis, which Plutarch treats as absurd—though he tells us at the same time that it was believed both by Aristotle and by many other considerable men. It is at least as ancient as the poet Cratinus, who alluded to it in one of his comedies, and I do not feel inclined to reject it. The inscription on the statue of Solon at Athens described him as a Salaminian; he had been the great means of acquiring the island for his country, and it seems highly probable that among the new Athenian citizens, who went to settle there, he may have received a lot of land and become enrolled among the Salaminian *demots*. The dispersion of his ashes connecting him with the island as its *œcist*, may be construed, if not as the expression of a public vote, at least as a piece of affectionate vanity on the part of his surviving friends.

CONQUESTS OF CYRUS THE GREAT

B.C. 538

GEORGE GROTE

On the destruction of Nineveh three great Powers still stood on the stage of history, being bound together by the strong ties of a mutually supporting alliance. These were Media, Lydia, and Babylon. The capital of Lydia was Sardis. According to Herodotus, the first king of Lydia was Manes. In the semi-mythic period of Lydian history rose the great dynasty of the Heraclidæ, which reigned for 505 years, numbering twenty-two kings—B.C. 1229 to B.C. 745. The Lydians are said by Herodotus to have colonized Tyrrhenia, in the Italic peninsula, and to have extended their conquests into Syria, where they founded Ascalon in the territory later known as Palestine.

In the reign of Gyges, B.C. 724, they began to attack the Greek cities of Asia Minor: Miletus, Smyrna, and Priene. The glory of the Lydian Empire culminated in the reign of Crœsus, the fifth and last historic king, B.C. 568. The well-known story of Solon's warning to Crœsus was full of ominous import with regard to the ultimate downfall of the Lydian Empire: "For thyself, O Crœsus," said the Greek sage in answer to the question, Who is the happiest man? "I see that thou art wonderfully rich, and art the lord of many nations; but in respect to that whereon thou questionest me, I have no answer to give until I hear that thou hast closed thy life happily."

The Median Empire occupied a territory indefinitely extending over a region south of the Caspian, between the Kurdish Mountains and the modern Khorassan. The Median monarchy, according to Herodotus, commenced B.C. 708. The Medes, which were racially akin to the Persians, had been for fifty years subject to the Assyrian monarchy when they revolted, setting up an independent empire. Putting aside the dates given by the Greek historians, we shall perhaps be correct in considering that the great Median kingdom was established by Cyaxares, B.C. 633; and that in B.C. 610 a great struggle of six years between Media and Lydia was amicably ended, under the terror occasioned by an eclipse, by the establishment of a treaty and alliance between the contending powers. With the death of Cyaxares, B.C. 597, the glory of the great Median Empire passed away, for under his,son, Astyages, the country was conquered by Cyrus.

The rise of the Babylonian Empire seems to have originated B.C. 2234, when the Cushite inhabitants of southern Babylonia raised a native dynasty to the throne, liberated themselves from the yoke of the Zoroastrian Medes, and instituted an empire with several large capitals, where they built mighty temples and introduced the worship of the heavenly bodies in contradistinction to the elemental worship of the Magian Medes. The record of Babylonian kings is full of obscurity, even in the light of recent archæological discoveries. We can trace, however, a gradual expansion of Babylonian dominion, even to the borders of Egypt. Nabo Polassar, B.C. 625 to B.C. 604, was a great warrior, and at Carchemish defeated even the almost invincible Egyptians, B.C. 604.

His successor, Nebuchadnezzar, B.C. 604, immediately set about the fortification of his capital. A space of more than 130 square miles was enclosed within walls 80 feet in breadth and 300 or 400 in height, if we may believe the record. Meanwhile, with the assistance of Cyaxares, King of Media, he captured Tyre, in Phœnicia, and Jerusalem, in Syria; but fifteen years after Crœsus had been taken prisoner and the Persian Empire extended to the shores of the Ægean, the Empire of Babylon fell before the conquering armies of Cyrus, the Persian.

THE Ionic and Æolic Greeks on the Asiatic coast had been conquered and made tributary by the Lydian king Crœsus: "Down to that time (says Herodotus) all Greeks had been free." Their conqueror, Crœsus, who ascended the throne in 560 B.C., appeared to be at the summit of human prosperity and power in his unassailable capital, and with his countless treasures at Sardis. His dominions comprised nearly the whole of Asia Minor, as far as the river Halys to the east; on the other side of that river began the Median monarchy under his brother-in-law Astyages, extending eastward to some boundary which we cannot define, but comprising, in a south-eastern direction, Persis proper or Farsistan, and separated from the Kissians and Assyrians on the east by the line of Mount Zagros (the present boundary-line between Persia and Turkey). Babylonia, with its wondrous city, between the Uphrates and the Tigris, was occupied by the Assyrians or Chaldæans, under their king Labynetus: a territory populous and fertile, partly by nature, partly by prodigies of labor, to a degree which makes us mistrust even an honest eye-witness who describes it afterward in its decline—but which was then in its most flourishing condition. The Chaldean dominion under Labynetus reached to the borders of Egypt, including as dependent territories both Judæa and Phenicia. In Egypt reigned the native king Amasis, powerful and affluent, sustained in his throne by a large body of Grecian mercenaries and himself favorably disposed to Grecian commerce and settlement. Both with Labynetus and with Amasis, Crœsus was on terms of alliance; and as Astyages was his brother-in-law, the four kings might well be deemed out of the reach of calamity. Yet within the space of thirty years, or a little more, the whole of their territories had become embodied in one vast empire, under the son of an adventurer as yet not known even by name.

The rise and fall of oriental dynasties have been in all times distinguished by the same general features. A brave and adventurous prince, at the head of a population at once poor, warlike, and greedy, acquires dominion; while his successors, abandoning themselves to sensuality and sloth, probably also to oppressive and irascible dispositions, become in process of time victims to those same qualities in a stranger which had enabled their own father to seize the throne. Cyrus, the great founder of the Persian empire, first the subject and afterward the dethroner of the Median Astyages, corresponds to their general description, as far, at least, as we can pretend to know his history. For in truth even the conquests of Cyrus, after he became ruler of Media, are very imperfectly known, while the facts which preceded his rise up to that sovereignty cannot be said to be known at all: we have to choose between different accounts at variance with each other, and of which the most complete and detailed is stamped with all the character of romance. The Cyropædia of Xenophon is memorable and interesting, considered with reference to the Greek mind, and as a philosophical novel. That it should have been quoted so largely as authority on matters of history, is only one proof among many how easily authors have been satisfied as to the essentials of historical evidence. The narrative given by Herodotus of the relations between Cyrus and Astyages, agreeing with Xenophon in little more than the fact that it makes Cyrus son of Cambyses and Mandane and grandson of Astyages, goes even beyond the story of Romulus and Remus in respect to tragical incident and contrast. Astyages, alarmed by a dream, condemns the newborn infant of his daughter Mandane to be exposed: Harpagus, to whom the order is given, delivers the child to one of the royal herdsmen, who exposes it in the mountains, where it is miraculously suckled by a bitch. Thus preserved, and afterward brought up as the herdsman's child, Cyrus manifests great superiority, both physical and mental; is chosen king in play by the boys of the village, and in this capacity severely chastises the son of one of the courtiers; for which offense he is carried before Astyages, who recognizes him for his grandson, but is assured by the Magi that the dream is out and that he has no further danger to apprehend from the boy—and therefore permits him to live. With Harpagus, however, Astyages is extremely incensed, for not having executed his orders: he causes the son of Harpagus to be slain, and served up to be eaten by his unconscious father at a regal banquet. The father, apprised afterward of the fact, dissembles his feelings, but meditates a deadly vengeance against Astyages for this Thyestean meal. He persuades Cyrus, who has been sent back to his father and mother in Persia, to head a revolt of the Persians against the Medes; whilst Astyages—to fill up the Grecian conception of madness as a precursor to ruin—sends an army against the revolters, commanded by Harpagus himself. Of course the army is defeated—Astyages, after a vain resistance, is dethroned—Cyrus becomes king in his place—and Harpagus repays the outrage which he has undergone by the bitterest insults.

Such are the heads of a beautiful narrative which is given at some length in Herodotus. It will probably appear to the reader sufficiently romantic; though the historian intimates that he had heard three other narratives different from it, and that all were more full of marvels, as well as in wider circulation, than his own, which he had borrowed from some unusually sober-minded Persian informants. In what points the other three stories departed from it we do not hear.

To the historian of Halicarnassus we have to oppose Ctesias—the physician of the neighboring town of Cnidus—who contradicted Herodotus, not without strong terms of censure, on many points, and especially upon that which is the very foundation of the early narrative respecting Cyrus; for he affirmed that Cyrus was no way related to Astyages. However indignant we may be with Ctesias for the disparaging epithets which he presumed to apply to an historian whose work is to us inestimable—we must nevertheless admit that, as surgeon in actual attendance on king Artaxerxes Mnemon, and healer of the wound inflicted on that prince at Cunaxa by his brother Cyrus the younger, he had better opportunities even than Herodotus of conversing with sober-minded Persians, and that the discrepancies between the two statements are to be taken as a proof of the prevalence of discordant, yet equally accredited, stories. Herodotus himself was in fact compelled to choose one out of four. So rare and late a plant is historical authenticity.

That Cyrus was the first Persian conqueror, and that the space which he overran covered no less than fifty degrees of longitude, from the coast of Asia Minor to the Oxus and the Indus, are facts quite indisputable; but of the steps by which this was achieved, we know very little. The native Persians, whom he conducted to an empire so immense, were an aggregate of seven agricultural, and four nomadic tribes—all of them rude, hardy, and brave—dwelling in a mountainous region, clothed in skins, ignorant of wine, or fruit, or any of the commonest luxuries of life, and despising the very idea of purchase or sale. Their tribes were very unequal in point of dignity, probably also in respect to numbers and powers, among one another. First in estimation among them stood the Pasargadæ; and the first phratry or clan among the Pasargadæ were the Achæmenidæ, to whom Cyrus himself belonged. Whether his relationship to the Median king whom he dethroned was a matter of fact, or a politic fiction, we cannot well determine. But Xenophon, in noticing the spacious deserted cities, Larissa and Mespila, which he saw in his march with the ten thousand Greeks on the eastern side of the Tigris, gives us to understand that the conquest of Media by the Persians was reported to him as having been an obstinate and protracted struggle. However this may be, the preponderance of the Persians was at last complete: though the Medes always continued to be the second nation in the empire, after the Persians, properly so called; and by early Greek writers the great enemy in the East is often called "the Mede" as well as "the Persian." The Median Ekbatana too remained as one of the capital cities, and the usual summer residence, of the kings of Persia; Susa on the Choaspes, on the Kissian plain farther southward, and east of the Tigris, being their winter abode.

The vast space of country comprised between the Indus on the east, the Oxus and Caspian Sea to the north, the Persian Gulf and Indian Ocean to the south, and the line of Mount Zagros to the west, appears to have been occupied in these times by a great variety of different tribes and people, yet all or most of them belonging to the religion of Zoroaster, and speaking dialects of the Zend language. It was known amongst its inhabitants by the common name of Iran or Aria: it is, in its central parts at least, a high, cold plateau, totally destitute of wood, and scantily supplied with water; much of it indeed is a salt and sandy desert, unsusceptible of culture. Parts of it are eminently fertile, where water can be procured and irrigation applied. Scattered masses of tolerably dense population thus grew up; but continuity of cultivation is not practicable, and in ancient times, as at present, a large proportion of the population of Iran seems to have consisted of wandering or nomadic tribes with their tents and cattle. The rich pastures, and the freshness of the summer climate, in the region of mountain and valley near Ekbatana, are extolled by modern travellers, just as they attracted the Great King in ancient times during the hot months. The more southerly province called Persis proper (Faristan) consists also in part of mountain land interspersed with valley and plain, abundantly watered, and ample in pasture, sloping gradually down to low grounds on the sea-coast which are hot and dry: the care bestowed both by Medes and Persians on the breeding of their horses was remarkable. There were doubtless material differences between different parts of the population of this vast plateau of Iran. Yet it seems that, along with their common language and religion, they had also something of a common character, which contrasted with the Indian population east of the Indus, the Assyrians west of Mount Zagros, and the Massagetæ and other Nomads of the Caspian and the Sea of Aral —less brutish, restless and blood-thirsty than the latter—more fierce, contemptuous and extortionate, and less capable of sustained industry, than the two former. There can be little doubt, at the time of which we are now speaking, when the wealth and cultivation of Assyria were at their maximum, that Iran also was far better peopled than ever it has been since European observers have been able to survey it—especially the north-eastern portion, Bactria and Sogdiana—so that the invasions of the Nomads from Turkestan and Tartary, which have been so destructive at various intervals since the Mohammedan conquest, were before that period successfully kept back.

The general analogy among the population of Iran probably enabled the Persian conqueror with comparative ease to extend his empire to the east, after the conquest of Ekbatana, and to become the full heir of the Median kings. If we may believe Ctesias, even the distant province of Bactria had been before subject to those kings. At first it resisted Cyrus, but finding that he had become son-in-law of Astyages, as well as master of his person, it speedily acknowledged his authority.

According to the representation of Herodotus, the war between Cyrus and Crœsus of Lydia began shortly after the capture of Astyages, and before the conquest of Bactria. Crœsus was the assailant, wishing to avenge his brother-in-law, to arrest the growth of the Persian conqueror, and to increase his own dominions. His more prudent counsellors in vain represented to him that he had little to gain, and much to lose, by war with a nation alike hardy and poor. He is represented as just at that time recovering from the affliction arising out of the death of his son.

To ask advice of the oracle, before he took any final decision, was a step which no pious king would omit. But in the present perilous question, Crœsus did more—he took a precaution so extreme, that if his piety had not been placed beyond all doubt by his extraordinary munificence to the temples, he might have drawn upon himself the suspicion of a guilty scepticism. Before he would send to ask advice respecting the project itself, he resolved to test the credit of some of the chief surrounding oracles—Delphi, Dodona, Branchidæ near Miletus, Amphiaraus at Thebes, Trophonius at Labadeia, and Ammon in Libya. His envoys started from Sardis on the same day, and were all directed on the hundredth day afterward to ask at the respective oracles how Crœsus was at that precise moment employed. This was a severe trial: of the manner in which it was met by four out of the six oracles consulted we have no information, and it rather appears that their answers were unsatisfactory. But Amphiaraus maintained his credit undiminished, while Apollo at Delphi, more omniscient than Apollo at Branchidæ, solved the question with such unerring precision, as to afford a strong additional argument against persons who might be disposed to scoff at divination. No sooner had the envoys put the question to the Delphian priestess, on the day named, "What is Crœsus now doing?" than she exclaimed in the accustomed hexameter verse, "I know the number of grains of sand, and the measures of the sea: I understand the dumb, and I hear the man who speaks not. The smell reaches me of a hard-skinned tortoise boiled in a copper with lamb's flesh—copper above and copper below." Crœsus was awe-struck on receiving this reply. It described with the utmost detail that which he had been really doing, so that he accounted the Delphian oracle and that of Amphiaraus the only trustworthy oracles on earth—following up these feelings with a holocaust of the most munificent character, in order to win the favor of the Delphian god. Three thousand cattle were offered up, and upon a vast sacrificial pile were placed the most splendid purple robes and tunics, together with couches and censers of gold and silver; besides which he sent to Delphi itself the richest presents in gold and silver— ingots, statues, bowls, jugs, etc., the size and weight of which we read with astonishment; the more so as Herodotus himself saw them a century afterwards at Delphi. Nor was Crœsus altogether unmindful of Amphiaraus, whose answer had been creditable, though less triumphant than that of the Pythian priestess. He sent to Amphiaraus a spear and shield of pure gold, which were afterward seen at Thebes by Herodotus: this large donative may help the reader to conceive the immensity of those which he sent to Delphi.

The envoys who conveyed these gifts were instructed to ask at the same time, whether Crœsus should undertake an expedition against the Persians—and if so, whether he should solicit any allies to assist him. In regard to the second question, the answer both of Apollo and of Amphiaraus was decisive, recommending him to invite the alliance of the most powerful Greeks. In regard to the first and most momentous question, their answer was as remarkable for circumspection as it had been before for detective sagacity: they told Crœsus that if he invaded the Persians, he would subvert a mighty monarchy. The blindness of Crœsus interpreted this declaration into an unqualified promise of success: he sent further presents to the oracle, and again inquired whether his kingdom would be durable. "When a mule shall become king of the Medes (replied the priestess) then must thou run away— be not ashamed."

More assured than ever by such an answer, Crœsus sent to Sparta, under the kings Anaxandrides and Aristo, to tender presents and solicit their alliance. His propositions were favorably entertained—the more so, as he had before gratuitously furnished some gold to the Lacedæmonians for a statue to Apollo. The alliance now formed was altogether general— no express effort being as yet demanded from them, though it soon came to be. But the incident is to be noted, as marking the first plunge of the leading Grecian state into Asiatic politics; and that too without any of the generous Hellenic sympathy which afterward induced Athens to send her citizens across the Ægean. At this time Crœsus was the master and tribute-exactor of the Asiatic Greeks, whose contingents seem to have formed part of his army for the expedition now contemplated; an army consisting principally, not of native Lydians, but of foreigners.

The river Halys formed the boundary at this time between the Median and Lydian empires: and Crœsus, marching across that river into the territory of the Syrians or Assyrians of Cappadocia, took the city of Pteria, with many of its surrounding dependencies, inflicting damage and destruction upon these distant subjects of Ekbatana. Cyrus lost no time in bringing an army to their defence considerably larger than that of Crœsus; trying at the same time, though unsuccessfully, to prevail on the Ionians to revolt from him. A bloody battle took place between the two armies, but with indecisive result: after which Crœsus, seeing that he could not hope to accomplish more with his forces as they stood, thought it wise to return to his capital, and collect a larger army for the next campaign. Immediately on reaching Sardis he despatched envoys to Labynetus king of Babylon; to Amasis, king of Egypt; to the Lacedæmonians, and to other allies; calling upon all of them to send auxiliaries to Sardis during the course of the fifth month. In the mean time he dismissed all the foreign troops who had followed him into Cappadocia.

Had these allies appeared, the war might perhaps have been prosecuted with success. And on the part of the Lacedæmonians, at least, there was no tardiness; for their ships were ready and their troops almost on board, when the unexpected news reached them that Crœsus was already ruined. Cyrus had foresen and forestalled the defensive plan of his enemy. Pushing on with his army to Sardis without delay, he obliged the Lydian prince to give battle with his own unassisted subjects. The open and spacious plain before that town was highly favorable to Lydian cavalry, which at that time (Herodotus tells us) was superior to the Persian. But Cyrus, employing a strategem whereby this cavalry was rendered unavailable, placed in front of his line the baggage camels, which the Lydian horses could not endure either to smell or to behold. The horsemen of Crœsus were thus obliged to dismount; nevertheless they fought bravely on foot, and were not driven into the town till after a sanguinary combat.

Though confined within the walls of his capital, Crœsus had still good reason for hoping to hold out until the arrival of his allies, to whom he sent pressing envoys of acceleration. For Sardis was considered impregnable—and one assault had already been repulsed, and the Persians would have been reduced to the slow process of blockade. But on the fourteenth day of the siege, accident did for the besiegers that which they could not have accomplished either by skill or force. Sardis was situated on an outlying peak of the northern side of Tmolus; it was well fortified everywhere except toward the mountain; and on that side the rock was so precipitous and inaccessible, that fortifications were thought unnecessary, nor did the inhabitants believe assault to be possible in that quarter. But Hyrœades, a Persian soldier, having accidentally seen one of the garrison descending this precipitous rock to pick up his helmet which had rolled down, watched his opportunity, tried to climb up, and found it not impracticable; others followed his example, the stronghold was thus seized first, and the whole city speedily taken by storm.

Cyrus had given especial orders to spare the life of Crœsus, who was accordingly made prisoner. But preparations were made for a solemn and terrible spectacle; the captive king was destined to be burned in chains, together with fourteen Lydian youths, on a vast pile of wood. We are even told that the pile was already kindled and the victim beyond the reach of human aid, when Apollo sent a miraculous rain to preserve him. As to the general fact of supernatural interposition, in one way or another, Herodotus and Ctesias both agree, though they described differently the particular miracles wrought. It is certain that Crœsus, after some time, was released and well treated by his conqueror, and lived to become the confidential adviser of the latter as well as of his son Cambyses: Ctesias also acquaints us that a considerable town and territory near Ekbatana, called Barene, was assigned to him, according to a practice which we shall find not infrequent with the Persian kings.

The prudent counsel and remarks as to the relations between Persians and Lydians, whereby Crœsus is said by Herodotus to have first earned this favorable treatment, are hardly worth repeating; but the indignant remonstrance sent by Crœsus to the Delphian god is too characteristic to be passed over. He obtained permission from Cyrus to lay upon the holy pavement of the Delphian temple the chains with which he had at first been bound. The Lydian envoys were instructed, after exhibiting to the god these humiliating memorials, to ask whether it was his custom to deceive his benefactors, and whether he was not ashamed to have encouraged the king of Lydia in an enterprise so disastrous? The god, condescending to justify himself by the lips of the priestess, replied: "Not even a god can escape his destiny. Crœsus has suffered for the sin of his fifth ancestor (Gyges), who, conspiring with a woman, slew his master and wrongfully seized the sceptre. Apollo employed all his influence with the Mœræ (Fates) to obtain that this sin might be expiated by the children of Crœsus, and not by Crœsus himself; but the Mœræ would grant nothing more than a postponement of the judgment for three years. Let Crœsus know that Apollo has thus procured for him a reign three years longer than his original destiny, after having tried in vain to rescue him altogether. Moreover he sent that rain which at the critical moment extinguished the burning pile. Nor has Crœsus any right to complain of the prophecy by which he was encouraged to enter on the war; for when the god told him that he would subvert *a great empire*, it was his duty to have again inquired which empire the god meant; and if he neither understood the meaning, nor chose to ask for information, he has himself to blame for the result. Besides, Crœsus neglected the warning given to him about the acquisition of the Median kingdom by a mule: Cyrus was that mule —son of a Median mother of royal breed, by a Persian father at once of different race and of lower position."

This triumphant justification extorted even from Crœsus himself a full confession that the sin lay with him, and not with the god. It certainly illustrates in a remarkable manner the theological ideas of the time. It shows us how much, in the mind of Herodotus, the facts of the centuries preceding his own, unrecorded as they were by any contemporary authority, tended to cast themselves into a sort of religious drama; the threads of the historical web being in part put together, in part orignally spun, for the purpose of setting forth the religious sentiment and doctrine woven in as a pattern. The Pythian priestess predicts to Gyges that the crime which he had committed in assassinating his master would be expiated by his fifth descendant, though, as Herodotus tells us, no one took any notice of this prophecy until it was at last fulfilled: we see thus the history of the first Mermnad king is made up after the catastrophe of the last. There was something in the main facts of the history of Crœsus profoundly striking to the Greek mind, a king at the summit of wealth and power—pious in the extreme and munificent toward the gods—the first destroyer of Hellenic liberty in Asia—then precipitated, at once and on a sudden, into the abyss of ruin. The sin of the first parent helped much toward the solution of this perplexing problem, as well as to exalt the credit of the oracle, when made to assume the shape of an unnoticed prophecy. In the affect-ing story of Solon and Crœsus, the Lydian king is punished with an acute domestic affliction because he thought himself the happiest of mankind—the gods not suffering any one to be arrogant except themselves; and the warning of Solon is made to recur to Crœsus after he has become the prisoner of Cyrus, in the narrative of Herodotus. To the same vein of thought belongs the story, just recounted, of the relations of Crœsus with the Delphian oracle. An account is provided, satisfactory to the religious feelings of the Greeks, how and why he was ruined—but nothing less than the overruling and omnipotent Mœræ could be invoked to explain so stupendous a result. It is rarely that these supreme goddesses—or hyper-goddesses, since the gods themselves must submit to them— are brought into such distinct light and action. Usually they are kept in the dark, or are left to be understood as the unseen stumbling block in cases of extreme incomprehensibility; and it is difficult clearly to determine (as in the case of some com-plicated political constitutions) where the Greeks conceived sovereign power to reside, in respect to the government of the world. But here the sovereignty of the Mœræ, and the sub-ordinate agency of the gods, are unequivocally set forth. The gods are still extremely powerful, because the Mœræ comply with their requests up to a certain point, not thinking it proper to be wholly inexorable; but their compliance is carried no farther than they themselves choose; nor would they, even in deference to Apollo, alter the original sentence of punishment for the sin of Gyges in the person of his fifth descendant— a sentence, moreover, which Apollo himself had formerly prophesied shortly after the sin was committed, so that, if the Mœræ had listened to his intercession on behalf of Crœsus, his own prophetic credit would have been endangered. Their unalterable resolution has predetermined the ruin of Crœsus, and the grandeur of the event is manifested by the circum-stance that even Apollo himself cannot prevail upon them to alter it, or to grant more than a three years' respite. The religious element must here be viewed as giving the form, the historical element as giving the matter only, and not the whole matter, of the story. These two elements will be found conjoined more or less throughout most of the history of Herodotus, though as we descend to later times, we shall find the latter element in constantly increasing proportion. His conception of history is extremely different from that of Thucydides, who lays down to himself the true scheme and purpose of the historian, common to him with the philosopher—to recount and interpret the past, as a rational aid toward prevision of the future.

In the short abstract which we now possess of the lost work of Ctesias, no mention appears of the important conquest of Babylon. His narrative, indeed, as far as the abstract enables us to follow it, diverges materially from that of Herodotus, and must have been founded on data altogether different.

"I shall mention (says Herodotus) these conquests which gave Cyrus most trouble, and are most memorable: after he had subdued all the rest of the continent, he attacked the Assyrians." Those who recollect the description of Babylon and its surrounding territory, will not be surprised to learn that the capture of it gave the Persian aggressor much trouble. Their only surprise will be, how it could ever have been taken at all—or indeed how a hostile army could have even reached it. Herodotus informs us that the Babylonian queen Nitocris (mother of that very Labynetus who was king when Cyrus attacked the place) apprehensive of invasion from the Medes after their capture of Nineveh, had executed many laborious works near the Euphrates for the purpose of obstructing their approach. Moreover there existed what was called the wall of Media (probably built by her, but certainly built prior to the Persian conquest), one hundred feet high and twenty feet thick, across the entire space of seventy-five miles which joined the Tigris with one of the canals of the Euphrates: while the canals themselves, as we may see by the march of the ten thousand Greeks after the battle of Cunaxa, presented means of defence altogether insuperable by a rude army such as that of the Persians. On the east, the territory of Babylonia was defended by the Tigris, which cannot be forded lower than the ancient Nineveh or the modern Mosul. In addition to these ramparts, natural as well as artificial, to protect the territory— populous, cultivated, productive, and offering every motive to its inhabitants to resist even the entrance of an enemy—we are told that the Babylonians were so thoroughly prepared for the inroad of Cyrus that they had accumulated within their walls a store of provisions for many years. Strange as it may seem, we must suppose that the king of Babylon, after all the cost and labor spent in providing defences for the territory, voluntarily neglected to avail himself of them, suffered the invader to tread down the fertile Babylonia without resistance, and merely drew out the citizens to oppose him when he arrived under the walls of the city—if the statement of Herodotus is correct. And we may illustrate this unaccountable omission by that which we know to have happened in the march of the younger Cyrus to Cunuxa against his brother Artaxerxes Mnemon. The latter had caused to be dug, expressly in preparation for this invasion, a broad and deep ditch (thirty feet wide and eight feet deep) from the wall of Media to the river Euphrates, a distance of twelve parasangs or forty-five English miles, leaving only a passage of twenty feet broad close alongside of the river. Yet when the invading army arrived at this important pass, they found not a man there to defend it, and all of them marched without resistance through the narrow inlet. Cyrus the younger, who had up to that moment felt assured that his brother would fight, now supposed that he had given up the idea of defending Babylon: instead of which, two days afterward, Artaxerxes attacked him on an open plain of ground where there was no advantage of position on either side; though the invaders were taken rather unawares in consequence of their extreme confidence arising from recent unopposed entrance within the artificial ditch. This anecdote is the more valuable as an illustration, because all its circumstances are transmitted to us by a discerning eye-witness. And both the two incidents here brought into comparison demonstrate the recklessness, changefulness, and incapacity of calculation belonging to the Asiatic mind of that day—as well as the great command of hands possessed by these kings, and their prodigal waste of human labor. Vast walls and deep ditches are an inestimable aid to a brave and well-commanded garrison; but they cannot be made entirely to supply the want of bravery and intelligence.

In whatever manner the difficulties of approaching Babylon may have been overcome, the fact that they were overcome by Cyrus is certain. On first setting out for this conquest, he was about to cross the river Gyndes (one of the affluents from the east which joins the Tigris near the modern Bagdad, and along which lay the high road crossing the pass of Mount Zagros from Babylon to Ekbatana) when one of the sacred white horses, which accompanied him, entered the river in pure wantonness and tried to cross it by himself. The Gyndes resented this insult and the horse was drowned: upon which Cyrus swore in his wrath that he would so break the strength of the river as that women in future should pass it without wetting their knees. Accordingly he employed his entire army, during the whole summer season, in digging three hundred and sixty artificial channels to disseminate the unit of the stream. Such, according to Herodotus, was the incident which postponed for one year the fall of the great Babylon. But in the next spring Cyrus and his army were before the walls, after having defeated and driven in the population who came out to fight. These walls were artificial mountains (three hundred feet high, seventy-five feet thick, and forming a square of fifteen miles to each side), within which the besieged defied attack, and even blockade, having previously stored up several years' provision. Through the midst of the town, however, flowed the Euphrates. That river which had been so laboriously trained to serve for protection, trade and sustenance to the Babylonians, was now made the avenue of their ruin. Having left a detachment of his army at the two points where the Euphrates enters and quits the city, Cyrus retired with the remainder to the higher part of its course, where an ancient Babylonian queen had prepared one of the great lateral reservoirs for carrying off in case of need the superfluity of its water. Near this point Cyrus caused another reservoir and another canal of communication to be dug, by means of which he drew off the water of the Euphrates to such a degree it became not above the height of a man's thigh. The period chosen was that of a great Babylonian festival, when the whole population were engaged in amusement and revelry. The Persian troops left near the town, watching their opportunity, entered from both sides along the bed of the river, and took it by surprise with scarcely any resistance. At no other time, except during a festival, could they have done this (says Herodotus) had the river been ever so low, for both banks throughout the whole length of the town were provided with quays, with continuous walls, and with gates at the end of every street which led down to the river at right angles so that if the population had not been disqualified by the influences of the moment, they would have caught the assailants in the bed of the river "as in a trap," and overwhelmed them from the walls alongside. Within a square of fifteen miles to each side, we are not surprised to hear that both the extremities were already in the power of the besiegers before the central population heard of it, and while they were yet absorbed in unconscious festivity.

Such is the account given by Herodotus of the circumstances which placed Bablyon—the greatest city of Western Asia—in the power of the Persians. To what extent the information communicated to him was incorrect or exaggerated, we cannot now decide. The way in which the city was treated would lead us to suppose that its acquisition cannot have cost the conqueror either much time or much loss. Cyrus comes into the list as king of Babylon, and the inhabitants with their whole territory become tributary to the Persians, forming the richest satrapy in the empire; but we do not hear that the people were otherwise ill-used, and it is certain that the vast walls and gates were left untouched. This was very different from the way in which the Medes had treated Nineveh, which seems to have been ruined and for a long time absolutely uninhabited, though reoccupied on a reduced scale under the Parthian empire; and very different also from the way in which Babylon itself was treated twenty years afterward by Darius, when reconquered after a revolt.

The importance of Babylon, marking as it does one of the peculiar forms of civilization belonging to the ancient world in a state of full development, gives an interest even to the half-authenticated stories respecting its capture. The other exploits ascribed to Cyrus—his invasion of India, across the desert of Arachosia—and his attack upon the Massagetæ, Nomads ruled by Queen Tomyris and greatly resembling the Scythians, across the mysterious river which Herodotus calls Araxes—are too little known to be at all dwelt upon.   In the latter he is said to have perished, his army being defeated in a bloody battle.   He was buried at Pasargadæ, in his native province of Persis proper, where his tomb was honored and watched until the breaking up of the empire, while his memory was held in profound veneration among the Persians.   Of his real exploits we know little or nothing, but in what we read respecting him there seems, though amid constant fighting, very little cruelty.   Xenophon has selected his life as the subject of a moral romance which for a long time was cited as authentic history, and which even now serves as an authority, express or implied, for disputable and even incorrect conclusions.   His extraordinary activity and conquests admit of no doubt.   He left the Persian empire extending from Sogdiana and the rivers Jaxartes and Indus eastward, to the Hellespont and the Syrian coast westward, and his successors made no permanent addition to it except that of Egypt.   Phenicia and Judæa were dependencies of Babylon, at the time when he conquered it, with their princes and grandees in Babylonian captivity.   As they seem to have yielded to him, and became his tributaries without difficulty; so the restoration of their captives was conceded to them.   It was from Cyrus that the habits of the Persian kings took commencement, to dwell at Susa in the winter, and Ekbatana during the summer; the primitive territory of Persis, with its two towns of Persepolis and Pasargadæ, being reserved for the burial-place of the kings and the religious sanctuary of the empire.   How or when the conquest of Susiana was made, we are not informed.   It lay eastward of the Tigris, between Babylonia and Persis proper, and its people, the Kissians, as far as we can discern, were of Assyrian and not of Aryan race. The river Choaspes near Susa was supposed to furnish the only water fit for the palate of the great king, and it is said to have been carried about with him wherever he went.

While the conquests of Cyrus contributed to assimilate the distinct types of civilization in Western Asia—not by elevating the worse, but by degrading the better—upon the native Persians themselves they operated as an extraordinary stimulus, provoking alike their pride, ambition, cupidity, and warlike

propensities. Not only did the territory of Persis proper pay
no tribute to Susa or Ekbatana—being the only district so
exempted between the Jaxartes and the Mediterranean—but
the vast tributes received from the remaining empire were distributed to a great degree among its inhabitants. Empire to
them meant—for the great men, lucrative satrapies or pachalics,
with powers altogether unlimited, pomp inferior only to that of
the great king, and standing armies which they employed at
their own discretion sometimes against each other—for the
common soldiers, drawn from their fields or flocks, constant
plunder, abundant maintenance, and an unrestrained license,
either in the suite of one of the satraps, or in the large permanent troops which moved from Susa to Ekbatana with the
Great King. And if the entire population of Persis proper did
not migrate from their abodes to occupy some of those more
inviting spots which the immensity of the imperial dominion
furnished—a dominion extending (to use the language of Cyrus
the younger before the battle of Cunaxa) from the region of
insupportable heat to that of insupportable cold—this was only
because the early kings discouraged such a movement, in order
that the nation might maintain its military hardihood and be in
a situation to furnish undiminished supplies of soldiers. The
self-esteem and arrogance of the Persians were no less remarkable than their avidity for sensual enjoyment. They were fond
of wine to excess; their wives and their concubines were both
numerous; and they adopted eagerly from foreign nations new
fashions of luxury as well as of ornament. Even to novelties
in religion, they were not strongly averse. For though disciples of Zoroaster, with Magi as their priests and as indispensable companions of their sacrifices, worshipping sun, moon,
earth, fire, etc., and recognizing neither image, temple, nor
altar—yet they had adopted the voluptuous worship of the goddess Mylitta from the Assyrians and Arabians. A numerous
male offspring was the Persian's boast. His warlike charater
and consciousness of force were displayed in the education of
these youths, who were taught, from five years old to twenty,
only three things—to ride, to shoot with the bow, and to speak
the truth. To owe money, or even to buy and sell, was
accounted among the Persians disgraceful—a sentiment which

they defended by saying that both the one and the other imposed the necessity of telling falsehood. To exact tribute from subjects, to receive pay or presents from the king, and to give away without forethought whatever was not immediately wanted, was their mode of dealing with money. Industrial pursuits were left to the conquered, who were fortunate if by paying a fixed contribution and sending a military contingent when required, they could purchase undisturbed immunity for their remaining concerns. They could not thus purchase safety for the family hearth, since we find instances of noble Grecian maidens torn from their parents for the harem of the satrap.

To a people of this character, whose conceptions of political society went no farther than personal obedience to a chief, a conqueror like Cyrus would communicate the strongest excitement and enthusiasm of which they were capable. He had found them slaves, and made them masters: he was the first and greatest of national benefactors, as well as the most forward of leaders in the field: they followed him from one conquest to another, during the thirty years of his reign, their love of empire growing with the empire itself. And this impulse of aggrandizement continued unabated during the reigns of his three next successors—Cambyses, Darius, and Xerxes—until it was at length violently stifled by the humiliating defeats of Platæa and Salamis; after which the Persians became content with defending themselves at home and playing a secondary game.

RISE OF CONFUCIUS, THE CHINESE SAGE

B.C. 550

R. K. DOUGLAS

Confucius is the Latinized name of Kung Futusze, or "Master Kung," whose work in China did much to educate the people in social and civic virtues. He began as a political reformer at a time when the empire was cut up into a number of petty and discordant principalities. As a practical statesman and administrator, he urged the necessity of reform upon the princes whom one after another he served. His advice was invariably disregarded, and as he said "no intelligent ruler arose in his time." His great maxims of submission to the emperor or supreme head of the state he based on the analogous duty of filial obedience in a household, and his very spirit of piety prevented him from taking independent measures for redressing the evils and oppressions of his distracted country.

His moral teachings are not based on any specific religious foundation, but they have become the settled code of Chinese life, of which submissiveness to authority, industry, frugality, and fair dealing as prescribed by Confucian ethics are general characteristics. The political doctrines of this great reformer were eventually adopted, and his teaching and example brought about a peaceful and gradual, but complete revolution, in the Chinese Empire, whose consolidation into a simple kingdom was the practical result of this sage's influence.

A T the time of which we write the Chinese were still clinging to the banks of the Yellow River, along which they had first entered the country, and formed, within the limits of China proper, a few states on either shore lying between the 33d and 38th parallels of latitude, and the 106th and 119th of longitude. The royal state of Chow occupied part of the modern province of Honan. To the north of this was the powerful state of Tsin, embracing the modern province of Shanse and part of Chili; to the south was the barbarous state of Ts'oo, which stretched as far as the Yang-tsze-kiang; to the east, reaching to the coast, were a number of smaller states, among which those of Ts'e, Loo, Wei, Sung, and Ching were the chief and to the west of the Yellow River was the state of Ts'in, which was destined eventually to gain the mastery over the contending principalities.

On the establishment of the Chow dynasty, King Woo had apportioned these fiefships among members of his family, his adherents, and the descendants of some of the ancient virtuous kings. Each prince was empowered to administer his government as he pleased so long as he followed the general lines indicated by history; and in the event of any act of aggression on the part of one state against another, the matter was to be reported to the king of the sovereign state, who was bound to punish the offender. It is plain that in such a system the elements of disorder must lie near the surface; and no sooner was the authority of the central state lessened by the want of ability shown by the successors of kings Woo, Ching, and K'ang, than constant strife broke out between the several chiefs. The hand of every man was against his neighbor, and the smaller states suffered the usual fate, under like circumstances, of being encroached upon and absorbed, notwithstanding their appeals for help to their common sovereign. The House of Chow having been thus found wanting, the device was resorted to of appointing one of the most powerful princes as a presiding chief, who should exercise royal functions, leaving the king only the title and paraphernalia of sovereignity. In fact, the China of this period was governed and administered very much as Japan was up till about twenty years ago. For Mikado, Shogun, and ruling Daimios, read king, presiding chief, and princes, and the parallel is as nearly as possible complete. The result of the system, however, in the two countries was different, for apart from the support received by the Mikado from the belief in his heavenly origin, the insular position of Japan prevented the possibility of the advent of elements of disorder from without, whereas the principalities of China were surrounded by semi-barbarous states, the chiefs of which were engaged in constant warfare with them.

Confucius' deep spirit of loyalty to the House of Chow forbade his following in the Book of History the careers of the sovereigns who reigned between the death of Muh in B.C. 946 and the accession of P'ing in 770. One after another these kings rose, reigned, and died, leaving each to his successor an ever-increasing heritage of woe. During the reign of Seuen (827–781) a gleam of light seems to have shot through the pervading darkness. Though falling far short of the excellencies of the founders of the dynasty, he yet strove to follow, though at a long interval, the examples they had set him; and according to the Chinese belief, as an acknowledgment from Heaven of his efforts in the direction of virtue, it was given him to sit upon the throne for nearly half a century.

His successor, Yew, "the Dark," appears to even less advantage. No redeeming acts relieve the general disorder of his reign, and at the instigation of a favorite concubine he is said to have committed acts which place him on a level with Kee and Show. Earthquakes, storms, and astrological portents appeared as in the dark days at the close of the Hea and Shang dynasties. His capital was surrounded by the barbarian allies of the Prince of Shin, the father of his wife, whom he had dismissed at the request of his favorite, and in an attempt to escape he fell a victim to their weapons.

With this event the Western Chow dynasty was brought to a close.

Here, also, the Book of History comes to an end, and the Spring and Autumn Annals by Confucius takes up the tale of iniquity and disorder which overspread the land. No more dreadful record of a nation's struggles can be imagined than that contained in Confucius's history. The country was torn by discord and desolated by wars. Husbandry was neglected, the peace of households was destroyed, and plunder and rapine were the watchwords of the time.

Such was the state of China at the time of the birth of Confucius (B.C. 551). Of the parents of the Sage we know but little, except that his father, Shuh-leang Heih, was a military officer, eminent for his commanding stature, his great bravery, and immense strength, and that his mother's name was Yen Ching-tsai. The marriage of this couple took place when Heih was seventy years old, and the prospect, therefore, of his having an heir having been but slight, unusual rejoicings commemorated the birth of the son, who was destined to achieve such everlasting fame.

Report says that the child was born in a cave on Mount Ne, whither Ching-tsai went in obedience to a vision to be confined. But this is but one of the many legends with which Chinese historians love to surround the birth of Confucius. With the same desire to glorify the Sage, and in perfect good faith, they narrate how the event was heralded by strange portents and miraculous appearances, how genii announced to Ching-tsai the honor that was in store for her, and how fairies attended at his nativity.

Of the early years of Confucius we have but scanty record. It would seem that from his childhood he showed ritualistic tendencies, and we are told that as a boy he delighted to play at the arrangement of vessels and postures of ceremony. As he advanced in years he became an earnest student of history, and looked back with love and reverence to the time when the great and good Yaou and Shun reigned in

" A golden age, fruitful of golden deeds."

At the age of fifteen "he bent his mind to learning," and when he was nineteen years old he married a lady from the state of Sung. As has befallen many other great men, Confucius' married life was not a happy one, and he finally divorced his wife, not, however, before she had borne him a son.

Soon after his marriage, at the instigation of poverty, Confucius accepted the office of keeper of the stores of grain, and in the following year he was promoted to be guardian of the public fields and lands. It was while holding this latter office that his son was born, and so well known and highly esteemed had he already become that the reigning duke, on hearing of the event, sent him a present of a carp, from which circumstance the infant derived his name, Le ("a carp"). The name of this son seldom occurs in the life of his illustrious father, and the few references we have to him are enough to show that a small share of paternal affection fell to his lot. "Have you heard any lessons from your father different from what we have all heard?" asked an inquisitive disciple of him. "No," replied Le, "he was standing alone once when I was passing through the court below with hasty steps, and said to me, ' Have you read the Odes?' On my replying, ' Not yet,' he added, ' If you do not learn the Odes, you will not be fit to con-verse with.' Another day, in the same place and the same way, he said to me, ' Have you read the rules of Propriety?' On my replying, ' Not yet,' he added, ' If you do not learn the rules of Propriety, your character cannot be established.' " "I asked one thing," said the enthusiastic disciple, "and I have learned three things. I have learned about the Odes; I have learned about the rules of Propriety; and I have learned that the superior man maintains a distant reserve toward his son."

At the age of twenty-two we find Confucius released from the toils of office, and devoting his time to the more congenial task of imparting instruction to a band of admiring and earnest students. With idle or stupid scholars he would have nothing to do. "I do not open the truth," he said, "to one who is not eager after knowledge, nor do I help any one who is not anx-ious to explain himself. When I have presented one corner of a subject, and the listener cannot from it learn the other three, I do not repeat my lesson."

When twenty-eight years old Confucius studied archery, and in the following years took lessons in music from the cele-brated master, Seang. At thirty he tells us "he stood firm," and about this time his fame mightily increased, many noble youths enrolled themselves among his disciples; and on his expressing a desire to visit the imperial court of Chow to confer on the subject of ancient ceremonies with Laou Tan, the founder of the Taouist sect, the reigning duke placed a carriage and horses at his disposal for the journey.

The extreme veneration which Confucius entertained for the founders of the Chow dynasty made the visit to Lo, the capital, one of intense interest to him. With eager delight he wandered through the temple and audience-chambers, the place of sacrifices and the palace, and having completed his inspec-tion of the position and shape of the various sacrificial and ceremonial vessels, he turned to his disciples and said, "Now I understand the wisdom of the duke of Chow, and how his house attained to imperial sway." But the principal object of his visit to Chow was to confer with Laou-tsze; and of the interview between these two very dissimilar men we have vari-ous accounts. The Confucian writers as a rule merely mention the fact of their having met, but the admirers of Laou-tsze affirm that Confucius was very roughly handled by his more ascetic contemporary, who looked down from his somewhat higher standpoint with contempt on the great apostle of antiquity. It was only natural that Laou-tsze, who preached that stillness and self-emptiness were the highest attainable objects, should be ready to assail a man whose whole being was wrapt up in ceremonial observances and conscious well-doing. The very measured tones and considered movements of Confucius, coupled with a certain admixture of that pride which apes humility, must have been very irritating to the metaphysically-minded treasurer. And it was eminently char-acterisic of Confucius, that notwithstanding the great provoca-tion given him on this occasion, he abstained from any rejoin-der. We nowhere read of his engaging in a dispute. When an opponent arose, it was in keeping with the doctrine of Con-fucius to retire before him. "A sage," he said, "will not enter a tottering state nor dwell in a disorganized one. When right principles of government prevail he shows himself, but when they are prostrated he remains concealed." And carrying out the same principle in private life, he invariably refused to wrangle.

It was possibly in connection with this incident that Con-fucius drew the attention of his disciples to the metal statue of a man with a triple clasp upon his mouth, which stood in the ancestral temple at Lo. On the back of the statue were inscribed these words: "The ancients were guarded in their speech, and like them we should avoid loquacity. Many words invite many defeats. Avoid also engaging in many busi-nesses, for many businesses create many difficulties."

"Observe this, my children," said he, pointing to the in-scription. "These words are true, and commend themselves to our reason."

Having gained all the information he desired in Chow, he returned to Loo, where pupils flocked to him until, we are told, he was surrounded by an admiring company of three thousand disciples His stay in Loo was, however, of short duration, for the three principal clans of the state, those of Ke, Shuh, and Mang, after frequent contests between themselves, en-

gaged in a war with the reigning duke, and overthrew his
armies. Upon this the duke took refuge in the state of T'se,
whither Confucius followed him. As he passed along the road
he saw a woman weeping at a tomb, and having compassion
on her, he sent his disciple Tsze-loo to ask her the cause of her
grief. "You weep as if you had experienced sorrow upon sorrow," said Tsze-loo. "I have," said the woman, "my father-in-
law was killed here by a tiger, and my husband also; and now
my son has met the same fate." "Why, then, do you not
remove from the place?" asked Confucius. "Because here
there is no oppressive government," replied the woman. On
hearing this answer, Confucius remarked to his disciples, "My
children remember this, oppressive government is fiercer than
a tiger."

Possibly Confucius was attracted to T'se by a knowledge
that the music of the emperor Shun was still preserved at the
court. At all events, we are told that having heard a strain of
the much-desired music on his way to the capital, he hurried
on, and was so ravished with the airs he heard that for three
months he never tasted flesh. "I did not think," said he,
"that music could reach such a pitch of excellence."

Hearing of the arrival of the Sage, the duke of T'se—King,
by name—sent for him, and after some conversation, being
minded to act the part of a patron to so distinguished a visitor,
offered to make him a present of the city of Lin-k'ew with its
revenues. But this Confucius declined, remarking to his disciples, "A superior man will not receive rewards except for
services done. I have given advice to the duke King, but he
has not followed it as yet, and now he would endow me with
this place. Very far is he from understanding me." He still,
however, discussed politics with the duke, and taught him that
"There is good government when the prince is prince, and the
minister is minister; when the father is father, and the son is
son." "Good," said the duke; "if, indeed, the prince be not
prince, the minister not minister, and the son not son, although
I have my revenue, can I enjoy it?"

Though Duke King was by no means a satisfactory pupil,
many of his instincts were good, and he once again expressed
a desire to pension Confucius, that he might keep him at hand;

but Gan Ying, the Prime Minister, dissuaded him from his purpose. "These scholars," said the minister, "are impracticable, and cannot be imitated. They are haughty and conceited of their own views, so that they will not rest satisfied in inferior positions. They set a high value on all funeral ceremonies, give way to their grief, and will waste their property on great funerals, so that they would only be injurious to the common manners. This Kung Footsze has a thousand peculiarities. It would take ages to exhaust all he knows about the ceremonies of going up and going down. This is not the time to examine into his rules of propriety. If you wish to employ him to change the customs of T'se, you will not be making the people your primary consideration." This reasoning had full weight with the duke, who the next time he was urged to follow the advice of Confucius, cut short the discussion by the remark, "I am too old to adopt his doctrines."

Under these circumstances Confucius once more returned to Loo, only however to find that the condition of the state was still unchanged; disorder was rife; and the reins of government were in the hands of the head of the strongest party for the time being. This was no time for Confucius to take office, and he devoted the leisure thus forced upon him to the compilation of the "Book of Odes" and the "Book of History."

But in process of time order was once more restored, and he then felt himself free to accept the post of magistrate of the town of Chung-too, which was offered him by the duke King.

He now had an opportunity of putting his principles of government to the test, and the result partly justified his expectations. He framed rules for the support of the living, and for the observation of rites for the dead; he arranged appropriate food for the old and the young; and he provided for the proper separation of men and women. And the results were, we are told, that, as in the time of King Alfred, a thing dropped on the road was not picked up; there was no fraudulent carving of vessels; coffins were made of the ordained thickness; graves were unmarked by mounds raised over them; and no two prices were charged in the markets. The duke, surprised at what he saw, asked the sage whether his rule of government could be applied to the whole state. "Certainly," replied Confucius, "and not only to the state of Loo, but to the whole empire." Forthwith, therefore, the duke made him Assistant-Superintendent of Works, and shortly afterwards appointed him Minister of Crime. Here, again, his success was complete. From the day of his appointment crime is said to have disappeared, and the penal laws remained a dead letter.

Courage was recognized by Confucius as being one of the great virtues, and about this period we have related two instances in which he showed that he possessed both moral and physical courage to a high degree. The chief of the Ke family, being virtual possessor of the state, when the body of the exiled Duke Chaou was brought from T'se for interment, directed that it should be buried apart from the graves of his ancestors. On Confucius becoming aware of his decision, he ordered a trench to be dug round the burying-ground which should enclose the new tomb. "Thus to censure a prince and signalize his faults is not according to etiquette," said he to Ke. "I have caused the grave to be included in the cemetery, and I have done so to hide your disloyalty." And his action was allowed to pass unchallenged.

The other instance referred to was on the occasion, a few years later, of an interview between the dukes of Loo and T'se, at which Confucius was present as master of ceremonies. At his instigation an altar was raised at the place of meeting, which was mounted by three steps, and on this the dukes ascended, and having pledged one another proceeded to discuss a treaty of alliance. But treachery was intended on the part of the duke of T'se, and at a given signal a band of savages advanced with beat of drum to carry off the duke of Loo. Some such stratagem had been considered probable by Confucius, and the instant the danger became imminent he rushed to the altar and led away the duke. After much disorder, in which Confucius took a firm and prominent part, a treaty was concluded, and even some land on the south of the river Wan, which had been taken by T'se, was by the exertions of the Sage restored to Loo. On this recovered territory the people of Loo, in memory of the circumstance, built a city and called it, "The City of Confession."

But to return to Confucius as the Minister of Crime.

Though eminently successful, the results obtained under his system were not quite such as his followers have represented them to have been. No doubt crime diminished under his rule, but it was by no means abolished. In fact, his biographers mention a case which must have been peculiarly shocking to him. A father brought an accusation against his son, in the expectation, probably, of gaining his suit with ease before a judge who laid such stress on the virtues of filial piety. But to his surprise, and that of the on-lookers, Confucius cast both father and son into prison, and to the remonstrances of the head of the Ke clan answered, "Am I to punish for a breach of filial piety one who has never been taught to be filially minded? Is not he who neglects to teach his son his duties, equally guilty with the son who fails in them? Crime is not inherent in human nature, and therefore the father in the family, and the government in the state, are responsible for the crimes committed against filial piety and the public laws. If a king is careless about publishing laws, and then peremptorily punishes in accordance with the strict letter of them, he acts the part of a swindler; if he collect the taxes arbitrarily without giving warning, he is guilty of oppression; and if he puts the people to death without having instructed them, he commits a cruelty."

On all these points Confucius frequently insisted, and strove both by precept and example to impart the spirit they reflected on all around him. In the presence of his prince we are told that his manner, though self-possessed, displayed respectful uneasiness. When he entered the palace, or when he passed the vacant throne, his countenance changed, his legs bent under him, and he spoke as though he had scarcely breath to utter a word. When it fell to his lot to carry the royal sceptre, he stooped his body as though he were not able to bear its weight. If the prince came to visit him when he was ill, he had himself placed with his head to the east, and lay dressed in his court clothes with his girdle across them. When the prince sent him a present of cooked meat, he carefully adjusted his mat and just tasted the dishes; if the meat were uncooked, he offered it to the spirits of his ancestors, and any animal which was thus sent him he kept alive.

At the village festivals he never preceded, but always followed after the elders. To all about him he assumed an appearance of simplicity and sincerity. To the court officials of the lower grade he spoke freely, and to superior officers his manner was bland but precise. Even at the wild gatherings which accompanied the annual ceremony of driving away pestilential influences, he paid honor to the original meaning of the rite, by standing in court robes on the eastern steps of his house, and received the riotous exorcists as though they were favored guests. When sent for by the prince to assist in receiving a royal visitor, his countenance appeared to change. He inclined himself to the officers among whom he stood, and when sent to meet the visitor at the gate, "he hastened forward with his arms spread out like the wings of a bird." Recognizing in the wind and the storm the voice of Heaven, he changed countenance at the sound of a sudden clap of thunder or a violent gust of wind.

The principles which underlie all these details relieve them from the sense of affected formality which they would otherwise suggest. Like the sages of old, Confucius had an overweening faith in the effect of example. "What do you say," asked the chief of the Ke clan on one occasion, "to killing the unprincipled for the good of the principled?" "Sir," replied Confucius, "in carrying on your government why should you employ capital punishment at all? Let your evinced desires be for what is good and the people will be good." And then quoting the words of King Ching, he added, "The relation between superiors and inferiors is like that between the wind and the grass. The grass must bend when the wind blows across it." Thus in every act of his life, whether at home or abroad, whether at table or in bed, whether at study or in moments of relaxation, he did all with the avowed object of being seen of men and of influencing them by his conduct. And to a certain extent he gained his end. He succeeded in demolishing a number of fortified cities which had formed the hotbeds of sedition and tumult; and thus added greatly to the power of the reigning duke. He inspired the men with a spirit of loyalty and good faith, and taught the women to be chaste and docile. On the report of the tranquillity prevailing in Loo, strangers flocked into the state, and thus was fulfilled the old criterion of good government which was afterward repeated by Confucius, "the people were happy, and strangers were attracted from afar."

But even Confucius found it impossible to carry all his theories into practice, and his experience as Minister of Crime taught him that something more than mere example was necessary to lead the people into the paths of virtue. Before he had been many months in office, he signed the death-warrant of a well-known citizen named Shaou for disturbing the public peace. This departure from the principle he had so lately laid down astonished his followers, and Tsze-kung—the Simon Peter as he has been called among his disciples—took him to task for executing so notable a man. But Confucius held to it that the step was necessary. "There are five great evils in the world," said he: "a man with a rebellious heart who becomes dangerous; a man who joins to vicious deeds a fierce temper; a man whose words are knowingly false; a man who treasures in his memory noxious deeds and disseminates them; a man who follows evil and fertilizes it. All these evil qualities were combined in Shaou. His house was a rendezvous for the disaffected; his words were specious enough to dazzle any one; and his opposition was violent enough to overthrow any independent man."

But notwithstanding such departures from the lines he had laid down for himself, the people gloried in his rule and sang at their work songs in which he was described as their savior from oppression and wrong.

Confucius was an enthusiast, and his want of success in his attempt completely to reform the age in which he lived never seemed to suggest a doubt to his mind of the complete wisdom of his creed. According to his theory, his official administration should have effected the reform not only of his sovereign and the people, but of those of the neighboring states. But what was the practical result? The contentment which reigned among the people of Loo, instead of instigating the duke of T'se to institute a similar system, only served to rouse his jealousy. "With Confucius at the head of its government," said he, "Loo will become supreme among the states, and T'se, which is nearest to it, will be swallowed up. Let us propitiate it by a surrender of territory." But a more provident statesman suggested that they should first try to bring about the disgrace of the Sage.

With this object he sent eighty beautiful girls, well skilled in the arts of music and dancing, and a hundred and twenty of the finest horses which could be procured, as a present to the duke King. The result fully realized the anticipation of the minister. The girls were taken into the duke's harem, the horses were removed to the ducal stables, and Confucius was left to meditate on the folly of men who preferred listening to the songs of the maidens of T'se to the wisdom of Yaou and Shun. Day after day passed and the duke showed no signs of returning to his proper mind. The affairs of state were neglected, and for three days the duke refused to receive his ministers in audience.

"Master," said Tsze-loo, "it is time you went." But Confucius, who had more at stake than his disciple, was disinclined to give up the experiment on which his heart was set. Besides, the time was approaching when the great sacrifice to Heaven at the solstice, about which he had had so many conversations with the duke, should be offered up, and he hoped that the recollection of his weighty words would recall the duke to a sense of his duties. But his gay rivals in the affections of the duke still held their sway, and the recurrence of the great festival failed to awaken his conscience even for the moment. Reluctantly therefore Confucius resigned his post and left the capital.

But though thus disappointed of the hopes he entertained of the duke of Loo, Confucius was by no means disposed to resign his role as the reformer of the age. "If any one among the princes would employ me," said he, "I would effect something considerable in the course of twelve months, and in three years the government would be perfected." But the tendencies of the times were unfavorable to the Sage. The struggle for supremacy which had been going on for centuries between the princes of the various states was then at its height, and though there might be a question whether it would finally result in the victory of Tsin, or of Ts'oo, or of Ts'in, there could be no doubt that the sceptre had already passed from the hands of the ruler of Chow. To men therefore who were fighting over the possessions of a state which had ceased to live, the idea of employing a minister whose principal object would have been to breathe life into the dead bones of Chow, was ridiculous. This soon became apparent to his disciples, who being even more concerned than their master at his loss of office, and not taking so exalted a view as he did of what he considered to be a heaven-sent mission, were inclined to urge him to make concessions in harmony with the times. "Your principles," said Tsze-kung to him, "are excellent, but they are unacceptable in the empire, would it not be well therefore to bate them a little?" "A good husbandman," replied the Sage, "can sow, but he cannot secure a harvest. An artisan may excel in handicraft, but he cannot provide a market for his goods. And in the same way a superior man can cultivate his principles, but he cannot make them acceptable."

But Confucius was at least determined that no efforts on his part should be wanting to discover the opening for which he longed, and on leaving Loo he betook himself to the state of Wei. On arriving at the capital, the reigning duke received him with distinction, but showed no desire to employ him. Probably expecting, however, to gain some advantage from the counsels of the Sage in the art of governing, he determined to attach him to his court by the grant of an annual stipend of sixty thousand measures of grain—that having been the value of the post he had just resigned in Loo. Had the experiences of his public life come up to the sanguine hopes he had entertained at its beginning, Confucius would probably have declined this offer as he did that of the Duke of T'se some years before, but poverty unconsciously impelled him to act up to the advice of Tsze-kung and to bate his principles of conduct somewhat. His stay, however, in Wei was of short duration. The officials at the court, jealous probably of the influence they feared he might gain over the duke, intrigued against him, and Confucius thought it best to bow before the coming storm. After living on the duke's hospitality for ten months, he left the capital, intending to visit the state of Ch'in.

It chanced, however, that the way thither led him through the town of Kwang, which had suffered much from the filibustering expeditions of a notorious disturber of the public peace, named Yang-Hoo. To this man of ill-fame Confucius bore a striking resemblance, so much so that the townspeople, fancying that they now had their old enemy in their power, surrounded the house in which he lodged for five days, intending to attack him. The situation was certainly disquieting, and the disciples were much alarmed. But Confucius's belief in the heaven-sent nature of his mission raised him above fear. "After the death of King Wan," said he, "was not the cause of truth lodged in me? If Heaven had wished to let this sacred cause perish, I should not have been put into such a relation to it. Heaven will not let the cause of truth perish, and what therefore can the people of Kwang do to me?" Saying which he tuned his lyre, and sang probably some of those songs from his recently compiled Book of Odes which breathed the wisdom of the ancient emperors.

From some unexplained cause, but more probably from the people of Kwang discovering their mistake than from any effect produced by Confucius' ditties, the attacking force suddenly withdrew, leaving the Sage free to go wherever he listed. This misadventure was sufficient to deter him from wandering farther a-field, and, after a short stay at Poo, he returned to Wei. Again the duke welcomed him to the capital, though it does not appear that he renewed his stipend, and even his consort Nan-tsze forgot for a while her intrigues and debaucheries at the news of his arrival. With a complimentary message she begged an interview with the Sage, which he at first refused; but on her urging her request, he was fain obliged to yield the point. On being introduced into her presence, he found her concealed behind a screen, in strict accordance with the prescribed etiquette, and after the usual formalities they entered freely into conversation.

Tsze-loo was much disturbed at this want of discretion, as he considered it, on the part of Confucius, and the vehemence of his master's answer showed that there was a doubt in his own mind whether he had not overstepped the limits of sage-like propriety. "Wherein I have done improperly," said he, "may Heaven reject me! may Heaven reject me!" This incident did not, however, prevent him from maintaining friendly relations with the court, and it was not until the duke by a public act showed his inability to understand the dignity of the role which Confucius desired to assume, that he lost all hope of finding employment in the state of his former patron. On this occasion the duke drove through the streets of his capital seated in a carriage with Nan-tsze, and desired Confucius to follow in a carriage behind. As the procession passed through the market-place, the people perceiving more clearly than the duke the incongruity of the proceeding, laughed and jeered at the idea of making virtue follow in the wake of lust. This completed the shame which Confucius felt at being in so false a position.

"I have not seen one," said he, "who loves virtue as he loves beauty." To stay any longer under the protection of a court which could inflict such an indignity upon him was more than he could do, and he therefore once again struck southward toward Ch'in.

After his retirement from office it is probable that Confucius devoted himself afresh to imparting to his followers those doctrines and opinions which we shall consider later on. Even on the road to Ch'in we are told that he practised ceremonies with his disciples beneath the shadow of a tree by the wayside in Sung. In the spirit of Laou-tsze, Hwuy T'uy, an officer in the neighborhood, was angered at his reported "proud air and many desires, his insinuating habit and wild will," and attempted to prevent him entering the state. In this endeavor, however, he was unsuccessful, as were some more determined opponents, who two years later attacked him at Poo, when he was on his way to Wei. On this occasion he was seized, and though it is said that his followers struggled manfully with his captors, their efforts did not save him from having to give an oath that he would not continue his journey to Wei. But in spite of his oath, and in spite of the public slight which had previously been put upon him by the duke of Wei, an irresistible attraction drew him toward that state, and he had no sooner escaped from the clutches of his captors than he continued his journey.

This deliberate forfeiture of his word in one who had commanded them to "hold faithfulness and sincerity as first principles," surprised his disciples; and Tsze-kung, who was generally the spokesman on such occasions, asked him whether it was right to violate the oath he had taken. But Confucius, who had learned expediency in adversity, replied, "It was an oath extracted by force. The spirits do not hear such."

But to return to Confucius flying from his enemies in Sung. Finding his way barred by the action of Hwan T'uy, he proceeded westward and arrived at Ch'ing, the capital of the state of the same name. Thither it would appear his disciples had preceded him, and he arrived unattended at the eastern gate of the city. But his appearance was so striking that his followers were soon made aware of his presence. "There is a man," said a townsman to Tsze-kung, "standing at the east gate with a forehead like Yaou, a neck like Kaou Yaou, his shoulders on a level with those of Tsze-ch'an, but wanting below the waist three inches of the height of Yu, and altogether having the forsaken appearance of a stray dog." Recognizing his master in this description, Tsze-kung hastened to meet him, and repeated to him the words of his informant. Confucius was much amused, and said: "The personal appearance is a small matter; but to say I was like a stray dog—capital! capital!"

The ruling powers in Ch'ing, however, showed no disposition to employ even a man possessing such marked characteristics, and before long he removed to Ch'in, where he remained a year. From Ch'in he once more turned his face toward Wei, and it was while he was on this journey that he was detained at Poo, as mentioned above. Between Confucius and the duke of Wei there evidently existed a personal liking, if not friendship. The duke was always glad to see him and ready to converse with him; but Confucius's unbounded admiration for those whose bones, as Laou-tsze said, were mouldered to dust, and especially for the founders of the Chow dynasty, made it impossible for the duke to place him in any position of importance. At the same time Confucius seems always to have hoped that he would be able to gain the duke over to his views; and thus it came about that the Sage was constantly attracted to the court of Duke Ling, and as often compelled to exile himself from it.

On this particular occasion, as at all other times, the duke received him gladly, but their conversations, which had principally turned on the act of peaceful government, were now directed to warlike affairs. The duke was contemplating an attack on Poo, the inhabitants of which, under the leadership of Hwan T'uy, who had arrested Confucius, had rebelled against him. At first Confucius was quite disposed to support the duke in his intended hostilities; but a representation from the duke that the probable support of other states would make the expedition one of considerable danger, converted Confucius to the opinion evidently entertained by the duke, that it would be best to leave Hwan T'uy in possession of his ill-gotten territory. Confucius's latest advice was then to this effect, and the duke acted upon it.

The duke was now becoming an old man, and with advancing age came a disposition to leave the task of governing to others, and to weary of Confucius' high-flown lectures. He ceased "to use" Confucius, as the Chinese historians say, and the Sage was therefore indignant, and ready to accept any offer which might come from any quarter. While in this humor he received an invitation from Pih Hih, an officer of the state of Tsin who was holding the town of Chung-mow against his chief, to visit him, and he was inclined to go. It is impossible to study this portion of Confucius' career without feeling that a great change had come over his conduct. There was no longer that lofty love of truth and of virtue which had distinguished the commencement of his official life. Adversity, instead of stiffening his back, had made him pliable. He who had formerly refused to receive money he had not earned, was now willing to take pay in return for no other services than the presentation of courtier-like advice on occasions when Duke Ling desired to have his opinion in support of his own; and in defiance of his oft-repeated denunciation of rebels, he was now ready to go over to the court of a rebel chief, in the hope possibly of being able through his means "to establish," as he said on another occasion, "an Eastern Chow."

Again Tsze-loo interfered, and expostulated with him on

his inconsistency. "Master," said he, "I have heard you say that when a man is guilty of personal wrong-doing, a superior man will not associate with him. If you accept the invitation of this Pih Hih, who is in open rebellion against his chief, what will people say?" But Confucius, with a dexterity which had now become common with him, replied: "It is true I have said so. But is it not also true that if a thing be really hard, it may be ground without being made thin; and if it be really white, it may be steeped in a black fluid without becoming black? Am I a bitter gourd? Am I to be hung up out of the way of being eaten?" But nevertheless Tsze-loo's remonstrances prevailed, and he did not go.

His relations with the duke did not improve, and so dissatisfied was he with his patron that he retired from the court. As at this time Confucius was not in the receipt of any official income, it is probable that he again provided for his wants by imparting to his disciples some of the treasures out of the rich stores of learning which he had collected by means of diligent study and of a wide experience. Every word and action of Confucius were full of such meaning to his admiring followers that they have enabled us to trace him into the retirement of private life. In his dress, we are told, he was careful to wear only the "correct" colors, viz., azure, yellow, carnation, white and black, and he scrupulously avoided red as being the color usually affected by women and girls. At the table he was moderate in his appetite but particular as to the nature of his food and the manner in which it was set before him. Nothing would induce him to touch any meat that was "high" or rice that was musty, nor would he eat anything that was not properly cut up or accompanied with the proper sauce. He allowed himself only a certain quantity of meat and rice, and though no such limit was fixed to the amount of wine with which he accompanied his frugal fare, we are assured that he never allowed himself to be confused by it. When out driving, he never turned his head quite round, and in his actions as well as in his words he avoided all appearance of haste.

Such details are interesting in the case of a man like Confucius, who has exercised so powerful an influence over so large a proportion of the world's inhabitants, and whose instructions, far from being confined to the courts of kings, found their loudest utterances in intimate communings with his disciples, and in the example he set by the exact performance of his daily duties.

The only accomplishment which Confucius possessed was a love of music, and this he studied less as an accomplishment than as a necessary part of education. "It is by the odes that the mind is aroused," said he. "It is by the rules of propriety that the character is established. And it is music which completes the edifice."

But having tasted the sweets of official life, Confucius was not inclined to resign all hope of future employment, and the duke of Wei still remaining deaf to his advice, he determined to visit the state of Tsin, in the hope of finding in Chaou Keen-tsze, one of the three chieftains who virtually governed that state, a more hopeful pupil. With this intention he started westward, but had got no farther than the Yellow River when the news reached him of the execution of Tuh Ming and Tuh Shun-hwa, two men of note in Tsin. The disorder which this indicated put a stop to his journey; for had not he himself said "that a superior man will not enter a tottering state." His disappointment and grief were great, and looking at the yellow waters 'as they flowed at his feet, he sighed and muttered to himself: "Oh how beautiful were they; this river is not more majestic than they were! and I was not there to avert their fate!"

So saying he returned to Wei, only to find the duke as little inclined to listen to his lectures, as he was deeply engaged in warlike preparations. When Confucius presented himself at court, the duke refused to talk on any other subject but military tactics, and forgetting, possibly on purpose, that Confucius was essentially a man of peace, pressed him for information on the art of manœuvreing an army. "If you should wish to know how to arrange sacrificial vessels," said the Sage, "I will answer you, but about warfare I know nothing."

Confucius was now sixty years old, and the condition of the states composing the empire was even more unfavorable for the reception of his doctrines than ever. But though depressed by fortune, he never lost that steady confidence in himself and his mission, which was a leading characteristic of his career, and when he found the duke of Wei deaf to his advice, he removed to Ch'in, in the hope of there finding a ruler who would appreciate his wisdom.

In the following year he left Ch'in with his disciples for Ts'ae, a small dependency of the state of Ts'oo. In those days the empire was subjected to constant changes. One day a new state carved out of an old one would appear, and again it would disappear, or increase in size, as the fortunes of war might determine. Thus while Confucius was in Ts'ae, a part of Ts'oo declared itself independent, under the name of Ye, and the ruler usurped the title of duke. In earlier days such rebellion would have called forth a rebuke from Confucius; but it was otherwise now, and, instead of denouncing the usurper as a rebel, he sought him as a patron. The duke did not know how to receive his visitor, and asked Tsze-loo about him. But Tsze-loo, possibly because he considered the duke to be no better than Pih Hih, returned him no answer. For this reticence Confucius found fault with him, and said, "Why did you not say to him, 'He is simply a man who, in his eager pursuit of knowledge, forgets his food; who, in the joy of its attainments, forgets his sorrows; and who does not perceive that old age is coming on?'"

But whatever may have been the opinion of Tsze-loo, Confucius was quite ready to be on friendly terms with the duke, who seems to have had no keener relish for Confucius' ethics than the other rulers to whom he had offered his services. We are only told of one conversation which took place between the duke and the Sage, and on that occasion the duke questioned him on the subject of government. Confucius' reply was eminently characteristic of the man. Most of his definitions of good government would have sounded unpleasantly in the ears of a man who had just thrown off his master's yoke and headed a successful rebellion, so he cast about for one which might offer some excuse for the new duke by attributing the fact of his disloyalty to the bad government of his late ruler. Quoting the words of an earlier sage, he replied, "Good government obtains when those who are near are made happy, and those who are far off are attracted."

Returning from Ye to Ts'ae, he came to a river which, being unbridged, left him no resource but to ford it. Seeing two men whom he recognized as political recluses ploughing in a neighboring field, he sent the ever-present Tsze-loo to inquire of them where best he could effect a crossing. "Who is that holding the reins in the carriage yonder?" asked the first addressed, in answer to Tsze-loo's inquiry. "Kung Kew," replied the disciple. "Kung Kew, of Loo?" asked the ploughman. "Yes," was the reply. "*He* knows the ford," was the enigmatic answer of the man as he turned to his work; but whether this reply was suggested by the general belief that Confucius was omniscient, or by way of a parable to signify that Confucius possessed the knowledge by which the river of disorder, which was barring the progress of liberty and freedom, might be crossed, we are only left to conjecture. Nor from the second recluse could Tsze-loo gain any practical information. "Who are you, sir?" was the somewhat peremptory question which his inquiry met with. Upon his answering that he was a disciple of Confucius, the man, who might have gathered his estimate of Confucius from the mouth of Laou-tsze, replied: "Disorder, like a swelling flood, spreads over the whole empire, and who is he who will change it for you? Rather than follow one who merely withdraws from this court to that court, had you not better follow those who (like ourselves) withdraw from the world altogether?" These words Tsze-loo, as was his wont, repeated to Confucius, who thus justified his career: "It is impossible to associate with birds and beasts as if they were the same as ourselves. If I associate not with people, with mankind, with whom shall I associate? If right principles prevailed throughout the empire, there would be no necessity for me to change its state."

Altogether Confucius remained three years in Ts'ae,—three years of strife and war, during which his counsels were completely neglected. Toward their close, the state of Woo made an attack on Ch'in, which found support from the powerful state of Ts'oo on the south. While thus helping his ally, the Duke of Ts'oo heard that Confucius was in Ts'ae, and determined to invite him to his court. With this object he sent messengers bearing presents to the Sage, and charged them with a message begging him to come to Ts'oo. Confucius readily accepted the invitation, and prepared to start. But the news of the transaction alarmed the ministers of Ts'ae and Ch'in. "Ts'oo," said they, "is already a powerful state, and Confucius is a man of wisdom. Experience has proved that those who have despised him have invariably suffered for it, and, should he succeed in guiding the affairs of Ts'oo, we should certainly be ruined. At all hazards we must stop his going." When, therefore, Confucius had started on his journey, these men despatched a force which hemmed him in in a wild bit of desert country. Here, we are told, they kept him a prisoner for seven days, during which time he suffered severe privations, and, as was always the case in moments of difficulty, the disciples loudly bewailed their lot and that of their master.

"Has the superior man," said Tsze-loo, "indeed, to endure in this way?" "The superior man may indeed have to suffer want," replied Confucius, "but it is only the mean man who, when he is in straits, gives way to unbridled license." In this emergency he had recourse to a solace which had soothed him on many occasions when fortune frowned: he played on his lute and sang.

At length he succeeded in sending word to the duke of Ts'oo of the position he was in. At once the duke sent ambassadors to liberate him, and he himself went out of his capital to meet him. But though he welcomed him cordially, and seems to have availed himself of his advice on occasions, he did not appoint him to any office, and the intention he at one time entertained of granting him a slice of territory was thwarted by his ministers, from motives of expediency. "Has your majesty," said this officer, "any servant who could discharge the duties of ambassador like Tsze-kung? or any so well qualified for a premier as Yen Hwuy? or any one to compare as a general with Tsze-loo? Did not kings Wan and Woo, from their small states of Fung and Kaou, rise to the sovereignty of the empire? And if Kung Kew once acquired territory, with such disciples to be his ministers, it will not be to the prosperity of Ts'oo."

This remonstrance not only had the immediate effect which

was intended, but appears to have influenced the manner of the duke toward the Sage, for in the interval between this and the duke's death, in the autumn of the same year, we hear of no counsel being either asked or given. In the successor to the throne Confucius evidently despaired of finding a patron, and he once again returned to Wei.

Confucius was now sixty-three, and on arriving at Wei he found a grandson of his former friend, the duke Ling, holding the throne against his own father, who had been driven into exile for attempting the life of his mother, the notorious Nantsze. This chief, who called himself the duke Chuh, being conscious how much his cause would be strengthened by the support of Confucius, sent Tsze-loo to him, saying, "The Prince of Wei has been waiting to secure your services in the administration of the state, and wishes to know what you consider is the first thing to be done." "It is first of all necessary," replied Confucius, "to rectify names." "Indeed," said Tsze-loo, "you are wide of the mark. Why need there be such rectification?" "How uncultivated you are, Yew," answered Confucius; "a superior man shows a cautious reserve in regard to what he does not know. If names be not correct, language is not in accordance with the truth of things. If language be not in accordance with the truth of things, affairs cannot be carried on successfully. When affairs cannot be carried on successfully, proprieties and music will not flourish. When proprieties and music do not flourish, punishments will not properly be awarded. When punishments are not properly awarded, the people do not know how to move hand or foot. Therefore the superior man considers it necessary that names should be used appropriately, and that his directions should be carried out appropriately. A superior man requires that his words should be correct."

The position of things in Wei was naturally such as Confucius could not sanction, and, as the duke showed no disposition to amend his ways, the Sage left his court, and lived the remainder of the five or six years, during which he sojourned in the state, in close retirement.

He had now been absent from his native state of Loo for fourteen years, and the time had come when he was to return to it. But, by the irony of fate, the accomplishment of his long-felt desire was due, not to his reputation for political or ethical wisdom, but to his knowledge of military tactics, which he heartily despised. It happened that at this time Yen Yew, a disciple of the Sage, being in the service of Ke K'ang, conducted a compaign against T'se with much success. On his triumphal return, Ke K'ang asked him how he had acquired his military skill. "From Confucius," replied the general. "And what kind of man is he?" asked Ke K'ang. "Were you to employ him," answered Yen Yew, "your fame would spread abroad; your people might face demons and gods, and would have nothing to fear or to ask of them. And if you accepted his principles, were you to collect a thousand altars of the spirits of the land it would profit you nothing." Attracted by such a prospect, Ke K'ang proposed to invite the Sage to his court. "If you do," said Yen Yew, "mind you do not allow mean men to come between you and him."

But before Ke K'ang's invitation reached Confucius an incident occurred which made the arrival of the messengers from Loo still more welcome to him. K'ung Wan, an officer of Wei, came to consult him as to the best means of attacking the force of another officer with whom he was engaged in a feud. Confucius, disgusted at being consulted on such a subject, professed ignorance, and prepared to leave the state, saying as he went away: "The bird chooses its tree; the tree does not choose the bird." At this juncture Ke K'ang's envoys arrived, and without hesitation he accepted the invitation they brought. On arriving at Loo, he presented himself at court, and in reply to a question of the duke Gae on the subject of government, threw out a strong hint that the duke might do well to offer him an appointment. "Government," he said, "consists in the right choice of ministers." To the same question put by Ke K'ang he replied, "Employ the upright and put aside the crooked, and thus will the crooked be made upright."

At this time Ke K'ang was perplexed how to deal with the prevailing brigandage. "If you, sir, were not avaricious, though you might offer rewards to induce people to steal, they would not." This answer sufficiently indicates the estimate formed by Confucius of Ke K'ang and therefore of the duke Gae, for so entirely were the two of one mind that the acts of Ke K'ang appear to have been invariably indorsed by the duke. It was plainly impossible that Confucius could serve under such a regime, and instead, therefore, of seeking employment, he retired to his study and devoted himself to the completion of his literary undertaking.

He was now sixty-nine years of age, and if a man is to be considered successful only when he succeeds in realizing the dream of his life, he must be deemed to have been unfortunate. Endowed by nature with a large share of reverence, a cold rather than a fervid disposition, and a studious mind, and reared in the traditions of the ancient kings, whose virtuous achievements obtained an undue prominence by the obliteration of all their faults and failures, he believed himself capable of effecting far more than it was possible for him or any other man to accomplish. In the earlier part of his career, he had in Loo an opportunity given him for carrying his theories of government into practice, and we have seen how they failed to do more than produce a temporary improvement in the condition of the people under his immediate rule. But he had a lofty and steady confidence in himself and in the principles which he professed, which prevented his accepting the only legitimate inference which could be drawn from his want of success. The lessons of his own experience were entirely lost upon him, and he went down to his grave at the age of seventy-two firmly convinced as of yore that if he were placed in a position of authority "in three years the government would be perfected."

Finding it impossible to associate himself with the rulers of Loo, he appears to have resigned himself to exclusion from office. His wanderings were over:

> "And as a hare, when hounds and horns pursue,
> Pants to the place from whence at first he flew,"

he had lately been possessed with an absorbing desire to return once more to Loo. This had at last been brought about, and he made up his mind to spend the remainder of his days in his native state. He had now leisure to finish editing the *Shoo King*, or *Book of History*, to which he wrote a preface; he also "carefully digested the rites and ceremonies determined by the wisdom of the more ancient sages and kings; collected and arranged the ancient poetry; and undertook the reform of music." He made a diligent study of the *Book of Changes*, and added a commentary to it, which is sufficient to show that the original meaning of the work was as much a mystery to him as it has been to others. His idea of what would probably be the value of the kernel encased in this unusually hard shell, if it were once rightly understood, is illustrated by his remark, "that if some years could be added to his life, he would give fifty of them to the study of the *Book of Changes* and that then he expected to be without great faults."

In the year B.C. 482 his son Le died, and in the following year he lost by death his faithful disciple Yen Hwuy. When the news of this last misfortune reached him, he exclaimed, "Alas! Heaven is destroying me!" A year later a servant of Ke K'ang caught a strange one-horned animal while on a hunting excursion, and as no one present could tell what animal it was, Confucius was sent for. At once he declared it to be a K'e-lin, and legend says that its identity with the one which appeared before his birth was proved by its having the piece of ribbon on its horn which Ching-tsae tied to the weird animal which presented itself to her in a dream on Mount Ne. This second apparition could only have one meaning, and Confucius was profoundly affected at the portent. "For whom have you come?" he cried, "for whom have you come?" and then, bursting into tears, he added, "The course of my doctrine is run, and I am unknown."

"How do you mean that you are unknown?" asked Tsze-kung. "I don't complain of Providence," answered the Sage, "nor find fault with men that learning is neglected and success is worshipped. Heaven knows me. Never does a superior man pass away without leaving a name behind him. But my principles make no progress, and I, how shall I be viewed in future ages?"

At this time, notwithstanding his declining strength and his many employments, he wrote the *Ch'un ts'ew*, or *Spring and Autumn Annals*, in which he followed the history of his native state of Loo, from the time of the duke Yin to the fourteenth year of the duke Gae, that is, to the time when the appearance of the K'e-lin warned him to consider his life at an end.

This is the only work of which Confucius was the author, and of this every word is his own. His biographers say that "what was written, he wrote, and what was erased, was erased by him." Not an expression was either inserted or altered by any one but himself. When he had completed the work, he handed the manuscript to his disciples, saying, "By the *Spring and Autumn Annals* I shall be known, and by the *Spring and Autumn Annals* I shall be condemned." This only furnishes another of the many instances in which authors have entirely misjudged the value of their own works.

In the estimation of his countrymen even, whose reverence for his every word would incline them to accept his opinion on this as on every subject, the *Spring and Autumn Annals* holds a very secondary place, his utterances recorded in the *Lun yu*, or *Confucian Analects*, being esteemed of far higher value, as they undoubtedly are. And indeed the two works he compiled, the *Shoo king* and the *She king*, hold a very much higher place in the public regard than the book on which he so prided himself. To foreigners, whose judgments are unhampered by his recorded opinion, his character as an original historian sinks into insignificance, and he is known only as a philosopher and statesman.

Once again only do we hear of Confucius presenting himself at the court of the duke after this. And this was on the occasion of the murder of the duke of T'se by one of his officers. We must suppose that the crime was one of a gross nature, for it raised Confucius' fiercest anger, and he who never wearied of singing the praises of those virtuous men who overthrew the thrones of licentious and tyrannous kings, would have had no room for blame if the murdered duke had been like unto Kee or Show. But the outrage was one which Confucius felt should be avenged, and he therefore bathed and presented himself at court.

"Sir," said he, addressing the duke, "Ch'in Hang has slain his sovereign; I beg that you will undertake to punish him." But the duke was indisposed to move in the matter, and pleaded the comparative strength of T'se. Confucius, however, was not to be so silenced. "One-half of the people of T'se," said he, "are not consenting to the deed. If you add to the people of Loo one-half of the people of T'se, you will be sure to overcome." This numerical argument no more affected the duke than the statement of the fact, and wearying with Confucius' importunity, he told him to lay the matter before the chiefs of the three principal families of the state. Before this court of appeal, whither he went with reluctance, his cause fared no better, and the murder remained unavenged.

At a period when every prince held his throne by the strength of his right arm, revolutions lost half their crime, and must have been looked upon rather as trials of strength than as disloyal villanies. The frequency of their occurrence, also, made them less the subjects of surprise and horror. At the time of which we write, the states in the neighborhood of Loo appear to have been in a very disturbed condition. Immediately following on the murder of the duke of T'se, news was brought to Confucius that a revolution had broken out in Wei. This was an occurrence which particularly interested him, for when he returned from Wei to Loo he left Tsze-loo and Tsze-kaou, two of his disciples, engaged in the official service of the state. "Tsze-kaou will return," was Confucius' remark, when he was told of the outbreak, "but Tsze-loo will die." The prediction was verified. For when Tsze-kaou saw that matters were desperate he made his escape; but Tsze-loo remained to defend his chief, and fell fighting in the cause of his master. Though Confucius had looked forward to the event as probable, he was none the less grieved when he heard that it had come about, and he mourned for his friend, whom he was so soon to follow to the grave.

One morning, in the spring of the year B.C. 478, he walked in front of his door, mumbling as he went:

> "The great mountain must crumble;
> The strong beam must break;
> And the wise man withers away like a plant."

These words came as a presage of evil to the faithful Tsze-kung. "If the great mountain crumble," said he, "to what shall I look up? If the strong beam break, and the wise man wither away, on whom shall I lean? The master, I fear, is going to be ill." So saying, he hastened after Confucius into the house. "What makes you so late?" said Confucius, when the disciple presented himself before him; and then he added, "According to the statutes of Hea, the corpse was dressed and coffined at the top of the eastern steps, treating the dead as if he were still the host. Under the Yin, the ceremony was performed between the two pillars, as if the dead were both host and guest. The rule of Chow is to perform it at the top of the western steps, treating the dead as if he were a guest. I am a man of Yin, and last night I dreamed that I was sitting, with offerings before me, between the two pillars. No intelligent monarch arises; there is not one in the empire who will make me his master. My time is come to die." It is eminently characteristic of Confucius that in his last recorded speech and dream, his thoughts should so have dwelt on the ceremonies of bygone ages. But the dream had its fulfilment. That same day he took to his bed, and after a week's illness he expired.

On the banks of the river Sze, to the north of the capital city of Loo, his disciples buried him, and for three years they mourned at his grave. Even such marked respect as this fell short of the homage which Tsze-kung, his most faithful disciple, felt was due to him, and for three additional years that loving follower testified by his grief his reverence for his master. "I have all my life had the heaven above my head," said he, "but I do not know its height; and the earth under my feet, but I know not its thickness. In serving Confucius, I am like a thirsty man, who goes with his pitcher to the river and there drinks his fill, without knowing the river's depth."

ROME ESTABLISHED AS A REPUBLIC

INSTITUTION OF TRIBUNES

B.C. 510-494

HENRY GEORGE LIDDELL

The republic of Rome was the outcome of a sudden revolution caused by the crimes of the House of Tarquin, an Etruscan family who had reached the highest power at Rome. The indignation raised by the rape of Lucretia by Sextus Tarquinius, and the suicide of the outraged lady at Collatia, moved her father, in conjunction with Lucius Junius Brutus and Publius Valerius, to start a rebellion. The people were assembled by curiæ, or wards, and voted that Tarquinius Superbus should be stripped of the kingly power, and that he and all his family should be banished from Rome.

This was accordingly done; and, instead of kings, consuls were appointed to wield the supreme power. These consuls were elected annually at the *comitia centuriata*, and they had sovereign power granted them by a vote of the *comitia curiata*. The first consuls chosen were Lucius Junius Brutus and Lucius Tarquinius Collatinus.

What is known as the Secession to the Sacred Hill took place when the plebeians of Rome, in the early days of the Republic, indignant at the oppression and cruelty of the patricians, left the city en masse and gathered with hostile manifestations at a hill, Mons Sacer, some distance from Rome. It was here Menenius Agrippa conciliated them by reciting the famous fable of " The Belly and the Members." After this the people were induced to come to terms with the patricians and to return to the city.

The people had, however, gained a great advantage by their bold defiance of the consular and patrician class, who had practically been supeme in the state, had been oppressive money-lenders, and had controlled the decisions of the law courts. It was not in vain that the people now demanded that as the two consuls were practically elected to further the interests of the upper class, so they, the plebeians, should have the election of two tribunes to protect them from wrong and oppression. These new officers were duly appointed, and eventually their number was increased to ten. Their power was almost absolute, but it never seems to have been abused, and this fact is a proof of the native moderation of the ancient Romans. There have been many constitutional struggles in the history of modern times, but nothing like the plebeian tribunate has ever appeared, and it is a question if the institution could have existed for a month, in any country of modern times, with the salutary influences which it exercised in early Rome.

TARQUIN had made himself king by the aid of the patricians, and chiefly by means of the third or Lucerian tribe, to which his family belonged. The burgesses of the Gentes were indignant at the curtailment of their privileges by the popular reforms of Servius, and were glad to lend themselves to any overthrow of his power. But Tarquin soon kicked away the ladder by which he had risen. He abrogated, it is true, the hated Assembly of the Centuries; but neither did he pay any heed to the Curiate Assembly, nor did he allow any new members to be chosen into the senate in place of those who were removed by death or other causes; so that even those who had helped him to the throne repented them of their deed. The name of Superbus, or the Proud, testifies to the general feeeling against the despotic rule of the second Tarquin.

It was by foreign alliances that he calculated on supporting his despotism at home. The Etruscans of Tarquinii, and all its associate cities, were his friends; and among the Latins also he sought to raise a power which might counterbalance the senate and people of Rome.

The wisdom of Tarquinius Priscus and Servius had united all the Latin name to Rome, so that Rome had become the sovereign city of Latium. The last Tarquin drew those ties still closer. He gave his daughter in marriage to Octavius Mamilius, chief of Tusculum, and favored the Latins in all things. But at a general assembly of the Latins at the Ferentine Grove, beneath the Alban Mount, where they had been accustomed to meet of olden time to settle their national affairs, Turnus Herdonius of Aricia rose and spoke against him. Then Tarquinius accused him of high treason, and brought false witnesses against him; and so powerful with the Latins was the king that they condemned their countryman to be drowned in the Ferentine water, and obeyed Tarquinius in all things.

With them he made war upon the Volscians and took the

city of Suessa, wherein was a great booty. This booty he applied to the execution of great works in the city, in emulation of his father and King Servius. The elder Tarquin had built up the side of the Tarpeian rock and levelled the summit, to be the foundation of a temple of Jupiter, but he had not completed the work. Tarquinius Superbus now removed all the temples and shrines of the old Sabine gods which had been there since the time of Titus Tatius; but the goddess of Youth and the god Terminus kept their place, whereby was signified that the Roman people should enjoy undecaying vigor, and that the boundaries of their empire should never be drawn in. And on the Tarpeian height he built a magnificent temple, to be dedicated jointly to the great gods of the Latins and Etruscans, Jupiter, Juno, and Minerva; and this part of the Saturnian Hill was ever after called the Capitol or the Chief Place, while the upper part was called the Arx or Citadel.

He brought architects from Etruria to plan the temple, but he forced the Roman people to work for him without hire.

One day a strange woman appeared before the king and offered him nine books to buy; and when he refused them she went away and burned three of the nine books and brought back the remaining six and offered to sell them at the same price that she had asked for the nine; and when he laughed at her and again refused, she went as before and burned three more books, and came back and asked still the same price for the three that were left. Then the king was struck by her pertinacity, and he consulted his augurs what this might be; and they bade him by all means buy the three, and said he had done wrong not to buy the nine, for these were the books of the Sibyl and contained great secrets. So the books were kept underground in the Capitol in a stone chest, and two men (*duumviri*) were appointed to take charge of them, and consult them when the state was in danger.

The only Latin town that defied Tarquin's power was Gabii; and Sextus, the king's youngest son, promised to win this place also for his father. So he fled from Rome and presented himself at Gabii; and there he made complaints of his father's tyranny and prayed for protection. The Gabians believed him, and took him into their city, and they trusted him, so that in time he was made commander of their army. Now his father suffered him to conquer in many small battles, and the Gabians trusted him more and more. Then he sent privately to his father, and asked what he should do to make the Gabians submit. Then King Tarquin gave no answer to the messenger, but, as he walked up and down his garden, he kept cutting off the heads of the tallest poppies with his staff. At last the messenger was tired, and went back to Sextus and told him what had passed. But Sextus understood what his father meant, and he began to accuse falsely all the chief men, and some of them he put to death and some he banished. So at last the city of Gabii was left defenceless, and Sextus delivered it up to his father.

While Tarquin was building his temple on the Capitol, a strange portent offered itself; for a snake came forth and devoured the sacrifices on the altar. The king, not content with the interpretation of his Etruscan soothsayers, sent persons to consult the famous oracle of the Greeks at Delphi, and the persons he sent were his own sons Titus and Aruns, and his sister's son, L. Junius, a young man who, to avoid his uncle's jealousy, feigned to be without common sense, wherefore he was called Brutus or the Dullard. The answer given by the oracle was that the chief power of Rome should belong to him of the three who should first kiss his mother; and the two sons of King Tarquin agreed to draw lots which of them should do this as soon as they returned home. But Brutus perceived that the oracle had another sense; so as soon as they landed in Italy he fell down on the ground as if he had stumbled, and kissed the earth, for she (he thought) was the true mother of all mortal things.

When the sons of Tarquin returned with their cousin, L. Junius Brutus, they found the king at war with the Rutulians of Ardea. Being unable to take the place by storm, he was forced to blockade it; and while the Roman army was encamped before the town the young men used to amuse themselves at night with wine and wassail. One night there was a feast, at which Sextus, the king's third son, was present, as also Collatinus, the son of Egerius, the king's uncle, who had been made governor of Collatia. So they soon began to dis-

pute about the worthiness of their wives; and when each maintained that his own wife was worthiest, "Come, gentlemen,"
said Collatinus, "let us take horse and see what our wives are
doing; they expect us not, and so we shall know the truth."
All agreed, and they galloped to Rome, and there they found
the wives of all the others feasting and revelling: but when
they came to Collatia they found Lucretia, the wife of Collatinus, not making merry like the rest, but sitting in the midst
of her handmaids carding wool and spinning; so they all
allowed that Lucretia was the worthiest.

Now Lucretia was the daughter of a noble Roman, Spurius
Lucretius, who was at this time prefect of the city; for it was
the custom, when the kings went out to war, that they left a
chief man at home to administer all things in the king's name,
and he was called prefect of the city.

But it chanced that Sextus, the king's son, when he saw
the fair Lucretia, was smitten with lustful passion; and a few
days after he came again to Collatia, and Lucretia entertained
him hospitably as her husband's cousin and friend. But at
midnight he arose and came with stealthy steps to her bedside:
and holding a sword in his right hand, and laying his left hand
upon her breast, he bade her yield to his wicked desires; for if
not, he would slay her and lay one of her slaves beside her, and
would declare that he had taken them in adultery. So for
shame she consented to that which no fear would have wrung
from her: and Sextus, having wrought this deed of shame, returned to the camp.

Then Lucretia sent to Rome for her father, and to the
camp at Ardea for her husband. They came in haste. Lucretius brought with him P. Valerius, and Collatinus brought L.
Junius Brutus, his cousin. And they came in and asked if all
was well. Then she told them what was done: "but," she said,
"my body only has suffered the shame, for my will consented
not to the deed. Therefore," she cried, "avenge me on the
wretch Sextus. As for me, though my heart has not sinned, I
can live no longer. No one shall say that Lucretia set an example of living in unchastity." So she drew forth a knife and
stabbed herself to the heart.

When they saw that, her father and her husband cried

aloud; but Brutus drew the knife from the wound, and holding
it up, spoke thus: "By this pure blood I swear before the gods
that I will pursue L. Tarquinius the Proud and all his bloody
house with fire, sword, or in whatsoever way I may, and that
neither they nor any other shall hereafter be king in Rome."
Then he gave the knife to Collatinus and Lucretius and Valerius, and they all swore likewise, much marvelling to hear such
words from L. Junius the Dullard. And they took up the body
of Lucretia, and carried it into the Forum, and called on the
men of Collatia to rise against the tyrant. So they set a guard
at the gates of the town, to prevent any news of the matter
being carried to King Tarquin: and they themselves, followed
by the youth of Collatia, went to Rome. Here Brutus, who
was chief captain of the knights, called the people together,
and he told them what had been done, and called on them by
the deed of shame wrought against Lucretius and Collatinus
—by all that they had suffered from the tyrants—by the
abominable murder of good King Servius—to assist them in
taking vengeance on the Tarquins. So it was hastily agreed
to banish Tarquinius and his family. The youth declared
themselves ready to follow Brutus against the king's army, and
the seniors put themselves under the rule of Lucretius, the
prefect of the city. In this tumult, the wicked Tullia fled from
her house, pursued by the curses of all men, who prayed that
the avengers of her father's blood might be upon her.

When the king heard what had passed, he set off in all
haste for the city. Brutus also set off for the camp at Ardea;
and he turned aside that he might not meet his uncle the king.
So he came to the camp at Ardea, and the king came to Rome.
And all the Romans at Ardea welcomed Brutus, and joined
their arms to his, and thrust out all the king's sons from the
camp. But the people of Rome shut the gates against the
king, so that he could not enter. And King Tarquin, with
his sons Titus and Aruns, went into exile and lived at Cære in
Etruria. But Sextus fled to Gabii, where he had before held
rule, and the people of Gabii slew him in memory of his former
cruelty.

So L. Tarquinius Superbus was expelled from Rome, after
he had been king five-and-twenty years. And in memory of

this event was instituted a festival called the " Regifugium" or " Fugalia," which was celebrated every year on the 24th day of February.

To gratify the plebeians, the patricians consented to restore, in some measure at least, the popular institutions of King Servius; and it was resolved to follow his supposed intention with regard to the supreme government—that is, to have two magistrates elected every year, who were to have the same power as the king during the time of their rule. These were in after days known by the name of Consuls; but in ancient times they were called " Prætors" or Judges. They were elected at the great Assembly of Centuries; and they had sovereign power conferred upon them by the assembly of the Curies. They wore a robe edged with violet color, sat in their chairs of state called curule chairs, and were attended by twelve lictors each. These lictors carried fasces, or bundles of rods, out of which arose an axe, in token of the power of life and death possessed by the consuls as successors of the kings. But only one of them at a time had a right to this power; and, in token thereof, his colleague's fasces had no axes in them. Each retained this mark of sovereign power (*Imperium*) for a month at a time.

The first consuls were L. Junius Brutus and L. Tarquinius Collatinus.

The new consuls filled up the senate to the proper number of three hundred; and the new senators were called " Conscripti," while the old members retained their old name of " Patres." So after this the whole senate was addressed by speakers as " Patres, Conscripti." But in later times it was forgotten that these names belonged to different sorts of persons, and the whole senate was addressed as by one name, " Patres Conscripti."

The name of king was hateful. But certain sacrifices had always been performed by the king in person; and therefore, to keep up form, a person was still chosen, with the title of "Rex Sacrorum " or "Rex Sacrificulus," to perform these offerings. But even he was placed under the authority of the chief pontifex.

After his expulsion, King Tarquin sent messengers to Rome to ask that his property should be given up to him, and the senate decreed that his prayer should be granted. But the king's ambassadors, while they were in Rome, stirred up the minds of the young men and others who had been favored by Tarquin, so that a plot was made to bring him back. Among those who plotted were Titus and Tiberius, the sons of the Consul Brutus; and they gave letters to the messengers of the king. But it chanced that a certain slave hid himself in the place where they met, and overheard them plotting; and he came and told the thing to the consuls, who seized the messengers of the king with the letters upon their persons, authenticated by the seals of the young men. The culprits were immediately arrested; but the ambassadors were let go, because their persons were regarded as sacred. And the goods of King Tarquin were given up for plunder to the people.

Then the traitors were brought up before the consuls, and the sight was such as to move all beholders to pity; for among them were the sons of L. Junius Brutus himself, the first consul, the liberator of the Roman people. And now all men saw how Brutus loved his country; for he bade the lictors put all the traitors to death, and his own sons first; and men could mark in his face the struggle between his duty as a chief magistrate of Rome and his feelings as a father. And while they praised and admired him, they pitied him yet more.

Then a decree of the senate was made that no one of the blood of the Tarquins should remain in Rome. And since Collatinus, the consul, was by descent a Tarquin, even he was obliged to give up his office and return to Collatia. In his room, P. Valerius was chosen consul by the people.

This was the first attempt to restore Tarquin the Proud.

When Tarquin saw that the plot at home had failed, he prevailed on the people of Tarquinii and Veii to make war with him against the Romans. But the consuls came out against them; Valerius commanding the main army, and Brutus the cavalry. And it chanced that Aruns, the king's son, led the cavalry of the enemy. When he saw Brutus he spurred his horse against him, and Brutus declined not the combat. So they rode straight at each other with levelled spears; and so fierce was the shock, that they pierced each other through from breast to back, and both fell dead.

Then, also, the armies fought, but the battle was neither won nor lost. But in the night a voice was heard by the Etruscans, saying that the Romans were the conquerors. So the enemy fled by night; and when the Romans arose in the morning, there was no man to oppose them. Then they took up the body of Brutus, and departed home, and buried him in public with great pomp, and the matrons⁀of Rome mourned him for a whole year, because he had avenged the injury of Lucretia.

And thus the second attempt to restore King Tarquin was frustrated.

After the death of Brutus, Publius Valerius ruled the people for a while by himself, and he began to build himself a house upon the ridge called Velia, which looks down upon the Forum. So the people thought that he was going to make himself king; but when he heard this, he called an assembly of the people, and appeared before them with his fasces lowered, and with no axes in them, whence the custom remained ever after, that no consular lictors wore axes within the city, and no consul had power of life and death except when he was in command of his legions abroad. And he pulled down the beginning of his house upon the Velia, and built it below that hill. Also he passed laws that every Roman citizen might appeal to the people against the judgment of the chief magistrates. Wherefore he was greatly honored among the people, and was called " Poplicola," or " Friend of the People."

After this Valerius called together the great Assembly of the Centuries, and they chose Sp. Lucretius, father of Lucretius, to succeed Brutus. But he was an old man, and in not many days he died. So M. Horatius was chosen in his stead.

The temple on the Capitol which King Tarquin began had never yet been consecrated. Then Valerius and Horatius drew lots which should be the consecrator, and the lot fell on Horatius. But the friends of Valerius murmured, and they wished to prevent Horatius from having the honor; so when he was now saying the prayer of consecration, with his hand upon the doorpost of the temple, there came a messenger, who told him that his son was just dead, and that one mourning for a son could not rightly consecrate the temple. But Horatius kept his hand upon the doorpost, and told them to see to the burial of his son, and finished the rites of consecration. Thus did he honor the gods even above his own son.

In the next year Valerius was again made consul, with T. Lucretius; and Tarquinius, despairing now of aid from his friends at Veii and Tarquinii, went to Lars Porsenna of Clusium, a city on the river Clanis, which falls into the Tiber. Porsenna was at this time acknowledged as chief of the twelve Etruscan cities; and he assembled a powerful army and came to Rome. He came so quickly that he reached the Tiber and was near the Sublician Bridge before there was time to destroy it; and if he had crossed it the city would have been lost. Then a noble Roman, called Horatius Cocles, of the Lucerian tribe, with two friends—Sp. Lartius, a Ramnian, and T. Herminius, a Titian—posted themselves at the far end of the bridge, and defended the passage against all the Etruscan host, while the Romans were cutting it off behind them. When it was all but destroyed, his two friends retreated across the bridge, and Horatius was left alone to bear the whole attack of the enemy. Well he kept his ground, standing unmoved amid the darts which were showered upon his shield, till the last beams of the bridge fell crashing into the river. Then he prayed, saying, "Father Tiber, receive me and bear me up, I pray thee." So he plunged in, and reached the other side safely; and the Romans honored him greatly: they put up his statue in the Comitium, and gave him as much land as he could plough round in a day, and every man at Rome subscribed the cost of one day's food to reward him.

Then Porsenna, disappointed in his attempt to surprise the city, occupied the Hill Janiculum, and besieged the city, so that the people were greatly distressed by hunger. But C. Mucius, a noble youth, resolved to deliver his country by the death of the king. So he armed himself with a dagger, and went to the place where the king was used to sit in judgment. It chanced that the soldiers were receiving their pay from the king's secretary, who sat at his right hand splendidly apparelled; and as this man seemed to be chief in authority, Mucius thought that this must be the king; so he stabbed him to the heart. Then the guards seized him and dragged him before the king, who was greatly enraged, and ordered them to burn him alive if he would not confess the whole affair. Then Mucius stood before the king and said: "See how little thy tortures can avail to make a brave man tell the secrets committed to him"; and so saying, he thrust his right hand into the fire of the altar, and held it in the flame with unmoved countenance. Then the king marvelled at his courage, and ordered him to be spared, and sent away in safety: "for," said he, "thou art a brave man, and hast done more harm to thyself than to me." Then Mucius replied: "Thy generosity, O king, prevails more with me than thy threats. Know that three hundred Roman youths have sworn thy death: my lot came first. But all the rest remain, prepared to do and suffer like myself." So he was let go, and returned home, and was called "Scævola," or "The Left-handed," because his right hand had been burnt off.

King Porsenna was greatly moved by the danger he had escaped, and perceiving the obstinate determination of the Romans, he offered to make peace. The Romans gladly gave ear to his words, for they were hard pressed, and they consented to give back all the land which they had won from the Etruscans beyond the Tiber. And they gave hostages to the king in pledge that they would obey him as they had promised, ten youths and ten maidens. But one of the maidens, named Clœlia, had a man's heart, and she persuaded all her fellows to escape from the king's camp and swim across the Tiber. At first King Porsenna was wroth; but then he was much amazed, even more than at the deeds of Horatius and Mucius. So when the Romans sent back Clœlia and her fellow-maidens— for they would not break faith with the king—he bade her return home again, and told her she might take whom she pleased of the youths who were hostages; and she chose those who were yet boys, and restored them to their parents.

So the Roman people gave certain lands to young Mucius, and they set up an equestrian statue to the bold Clœlia at the top of the Sacred Way. And King Porsenna returned home; and thus the third and most formidable attempt to bring back Tarquin failed.

When Tarquin now found that he had no hopes of further

assistance from Porsenna and his Etruscan friends, he went and dwelt at Tusculum, where Mamilius Octavius, his son-in-law, was still chief.   Then the thirty Latin cities combined together and made this Octavius their dictator, and bound themselves to restore their old friend and ally, King Tarquin, to the sovereignty of Rome.

P. Valerius, who was called "Poplicola," was now dead, and the Romans looked about for some chief worthy to lead them against the army of the Latins.   Poplicola had been made consul four times, and his compeers acknowledged him as their chief, and all men submitted to him as to a king.   But now the two consuls were jealous of each other; nor had they power of life and death within the city, for Valerius (as we saw) had taken away the axes from the fasces.   Now this was one of the reasons why Brutus and the rest made two consuls instead of one king: for they said that neither one would allow the other to become tyrant; and since they only held office for one year at a time, they might be called on to give account of their government when their year was at an end.

Yet though this was a safeguard of liberty in times of peace, it was hurtful in time of war, for the consuls chosen by the people in their great assemblies were not always skilful generals; or if they were so, they were obliged to lay down their command at the year's end.

So the senate determined, in cases of great danger, to call upon one of the consuls to appoint a single chief, who should be called "dictator," or master of the people.   He had sovereign power (*Imperium*) both in the city and out of the city, and the fasces were always carried before him with the axes in them, as they had been before the king.   He could only be appointed for six months, but at the end of the time he had to give no account.   So that he was free to act according to his own judgment, having no colleague to interfere with him at the present, and no accusations to fear at a future time.   The dictator was general-in-chief, and he appointed a chief officer to command the knights under him, who was called "master of the horse."

And now it appeared to be a fit time to appoint such a chief, to take the command of the army against the Latins.   So the first dictator was T. Lartius, and he made Spurius Cassius his master of the horse. This was in the year B.C. 499, eight years after the expulsion of Tarquin.

But the Latins did not declare war for two years after. Then the senate again ordered the consul to name a master of the people, or dictator; and he named Aul. Postumius, who appointed T. Æbutius(one of the consuls of that year) to be his master of the horse. So they led out the Roman army against the Latins, and they met at the Lake Regillus, in the land of the Tusculans. King Tarquin and all his family were in the host of the Latins; and that day it was to be determined whether Rome should be again subject to the tyrant and whether or not she was to be chief of the Latin cities.

King Tarquin himself, old as he was, rode in front of the Latins in full armor; and when he descried the Roman dictator marshalling his men, he rode at him; but Postumius wounded him in the side, and he was rescued by the Latins. Then also Æbutius, the master of the horse, and Oct. Mamilius, the dictator of the Latins, charged one another, and Æbutius was pierced through the arm, and Mamilius wounded in the breast. But the Latin chief, nothing daunted, returned to battle, followed by Titus, the king's son, with his band of exiles. These charged the Romans furiously, so that they gave way; but when M. Valerius, brother of the great Poplicola, saw this, he spurred his horse against Titus, and rode at him with spear in rest; and when Titus turned away and fled, Valerius rode furiously after him into the midst of the Latin host, and a certain Latin smote him in the side as he was riding past, so that he fell dead, and his horse galloped on without a rider. So the band of exiles pressed still more fiercely upon the Romans, and they began to flee.

Then Postumius the dictator lifted up his voice and vowed a temple to Castor and Pollux, the great twin heroes of the Greeks, if they would aid him; and behold there appeared on his right two horsemen, taller and fairer than the sons of men, and their horses were as white as snow. And they led the dictator and his guard against the exiles and the Latins, and the Romans prevailed against them; and T. Herminius the Titian, the friend of Horatius Cocles, ran Mamilius, the dictator of the Latins, through the body, so that he died; but when he was stripping the arms from his foe, another ran him through, and he was carried back to the camp, and he also died. Then also Titus, the king's son, was slain, and the Latins fled, and the Romans pursued them with great slaughter, and took their camp and all that was in it. Now Postumius had promised great rewards to those who first broke into the camp of the Latins, and the first who broke in were the two horsemen on white horses; but after the battle they were nowhere to be seen or found, nor was there any sign of them left, save on the hard rock there was the mark of a horse's hoof, which men said was made by the horse of one of those horsemen.

But at this very time two youths on white horses rode into the Forum at Rome. They were covered with dust and sweat and blood, like men who had fought long and hard, and their horses also were bathed in sweat and foam: and they alighted near the Temple of Vesta, and washed themselves in a spring that gushes out hard by, and told all the people in the Forum how the battle by the Lake Regillus had been fought and won. Then they mounted their horses and rode away, and were seen no more.

But Postumius, when he heard it, knew that these were Castor and Pollux, the great twin brethren of the Greeks, and that it was they who fought so well for Rome at the Lake Regillus. So he built them a temple, according to his vow, over the place where they had alighted in the Forum. And their effigies were displayed on Roman coins to the latest ages of the city.

This was the fourth and last attempt to restore King Tarquin. After the great defeat of Lake Regillus, the Latin cities made peace with Rome, and agreed to refuse harborage to the old king. He had lost all his sons, and, accompanied by a few faithful friends, who shared his exile, he sought a last asylum at the Greek city of Cumæ in the Bay of Naples, at the court of the tyrant Aristodemus. Here he died in the course of a year, fourteen years after his expulsion.

We shall now record, not only the slow steps by which the Romans recovered dominion over their neighbors, but also the long-continued struggle by which the plebeians raised themselves to a level with the patricians, who had again become the dominant caste at Rome. Mixed up with legendary tales as the history still is, enough is nevertheless preserved to excite the admiration of all who love to look upon a brave people pursuing a worthy object with patient but earnest resolution, never flinching, yet seldom injuring their good cause by reck‧less violence. To an Englishman this history ought to be especially dear, for more than any other in the annals of the world does it resemble the long-enduring constancy and sturdy determination, the temperate will and noble self-control, with which the Commons of his own country secured their rights. It was by a struggle of this nature, pursued through a century and a half, that the character of the Roman people was molded into that form of strength and energy, which threw back Hannibal to the coasts of Africa, and in half a century more made them masters of the Mediterranean shore.

There can be no doubt that the wars that followed the expulsion of the Tarquins, with the loss of territory that accompanied them, must have reduced all orders of men at Rome to great distress. But those who most suffered were the plebeians. The plebeians at that time consisted entirely of landholders, great and small, and husbandmen, for in those times the practice of trades and mechanical arts was considered unworthy of a freeborn man. Some of the plebeian familes were as wealthy as any among the patricians; but the mass of them were petty yeoman, who lived on the produce of their small farm, and were solely dependent for a living on their own limbs, their own thrift and industry. Most of them lived in the villages and small towns, which in those times were thickly sprinkled over the slopes of the Campagna.

The patricians, on the other hand, resided chiefly within the city. If slaves were few as yet, they had the labor of their clients available to till their farms; and through their clients also they were enabled to derive a profit from the practice of trading and crafts, which personally neither they nor the plebeians would stoop to pursue. Besides these sources of profit, they had at this time the exclusive use of the public land, a subject on which we shall have to speak more at length hereafter. At present, it will be sufficient to say, that the public land now spoken of had been the crown land or regal domain, which on the expulsion of the kings had been forfeited to the state. The patricians being in possession of all actual power, engrossed possession of it, and seem to have paid a very small quit-rent to the treasury for this great advantage.

Besides this, the necessity of service in the army, or militia —as it might more justly be called—acted very differently on the rich landholder and the small yeoman. The latter, being called out with sword and spear for the summer's campaign, as his turn came round, was obliged to leave his farm uncared for, and his crop could only be reaped by the kind aid of neighbors; whereas the rich proprietor, by his clients or his hired laborers, could render the required military service without robbing his land of his own labor. Moreover, the territory of Rome was so narrow, and the enemy's borders so close at hand, that any night the stout yeoman might find himself reduced to beggary, by seeing his crops destroyed, his cattle driven away, and his homestead burnt in a sudden foray. The patricians and rich plebeians were, it is true, exposed to the same contingencies. But wealth will always provide some defence; and it is reasonable to think that the larger proprietors provided places of refuge, into which they could drive their cattle and secure much of their property, such as the peel-towers common in our own border counties. Thus the patricians and their clients might escape the storm which destroyed the isolated yeoman.

To this must be added that the public land seems to have been mostly in pasturage, and therefore the property of the patricians must have chiefly consisted in cattle, which was more easily saved from depredation than the crops of the plebeian. Lastly, the profit derived from the trades and business of their clients, being secured by the walls of the city, gave to the patricians the command of all the capital that could exist in a state of society so simple and crude, and afforded at once a means of repairing their own losses, and also of obtaining a dominion over the poor yeoman.

For some time after the expulsion of the Tarquins it was necessary for the patricians to treat the plebeians with liberality. The institutions of "the Commons' King," King Servius, suspended by Tarquin, were, partially at least, restored: it is said even that one of the first consuls was a plebeian, and that he chose several of the leading plebeians into the senate. But after the death of Porsenna, and when the fear of the Tarquins ceased, all these flattering signs disappeared. The consuls seem still to have been elected by the Centuriate Assembly, but the Curiate Assembly retained in their own hands the right of conferring the *Imperium*, which amounted to a positive veto on the election by the larger body. All the names of the early consuls, except in the first year of the Republic, are patrician. But if by chance a consul displayed popular tendencies, it was in the power of the senate and patricians to suspend his power by the appointment of a dictator. Thus, practically, the patrician burgesses again became the *Populus*, or body politic of Rome.

It must not here be forgotten that this dominant body was an exclusive caste; that is, it consisted of a limited number of noble families, who allowed none of their members to marry with persons born out of the pale of their own order. The child of a patrician and a plebeian, or of a patrician and a client, was not considered as born in lawful wedlock; and however proud the blood which it derived from one parent, the child sank to the condition of the parent of lower rank. This was expressed in Roman language by saying, that there was no " Right of Connubium " between patricians and any inferior classes of men. Nothing can be more impolitic than such restrictions; nothing more hurtful even to those who count it their privilege. In all exclusive or oligarchical *pales*, families become extinct, and the breed decays both in bodily strength and mental vigor. Happily for Rome, the patricians were unable long to maintain themselves as a separate caste.

Yet the plebeians might long have submitted to this state of social and political inferiority, had not their personal distress and the severe laws of Rome driven them to seek relief by claiming to be recognized as members of the body politic.

The severe laws of which we speak were those of debtor and creditor. If a Roman borrowed money, he was expected to enter into a contract with his creditor to pay the debt by a certain day; and if on that day he was unable to discharge his obligation, he was summoned before the patrician judge, who was authorized by the law to assign the defaulter as a bondsman to his creditor—that is, the debtor was obliged to pay by his own labor the debt which he was unable to pay in money. Or if a man incurred a debt without such formal contract, the rule was still more imperious, for in that case the law itself fixed the day of payment; and if after a lapse of thirty days from that date the debt was not discharged, the creditor was empowered to arrest the person of his debtor, to load him with chains, and feed him on bread and water for another thirty days; and then, if the money still remained unpaid, he might put him to death, or sell him as a slave to the highest bidder; or, if there were several creditors, they might hew his body in pieces and divide it. And in this last case the law provided with scrupulous providence against the evasion by which the Merchant of Venice escaped the cruelty of the Jew; for the Roman law said that "whether a man cut more or less [than his due], he should incur no penalty." These atrocious provisions, however, defeated their own object, for there was no more unprofitable way in which the body of a debtor could be disposed of.

Such being the law of debtor and creditor, it remains to say that the creditors were chiefly of the patrician caste, and the debtors almost exclusively of the poorer sort among the plebeians. The patricians were the creditors, because from their occupancy of the public land, and from their engrossing the profits to be derived from trade and crafts, they alone had spare capital to lend. The plebeian yeomen were the debtors, because their independent position made them, at that time, helpless. Vassals, clients, serfs, or by whatever name dependents are called, do not suffer from the ravages of a predatory war like free landholders, because the loss falls on their lords or patrons. But when the independent yeoman's crops are destroyed, his cattle "lifted," and his homestead in ashes, he must himself repair the loss. This was, as we have said, the condition of many Roman plebeians. To rebuild their houses and restock their farms they borrowed; the patricians were their creditors; and the law, instead of protecting the small holders, like the law of the Hebrews, delivered them over into serfdom or slavery.

Thus the free plebeian population might have been reduced

to a state of mere dependency, and the history of Rome might have presented a repetition of monotonous severity, like that of Sparta or of Venice.[1] But it was ordained otherwise. The distress and oppression of the plebeians led them to demand and to obtain political protectors, by whose means they were slowly but surely raised to equality of rights and privileges with their rulers and oppressors. These protectors were the famous Tribunes of the Plebs. We will now repeat the no less famous legends by which their first creation was accounted for.

It was, by the common reckoning, fifteen years after the expulsion of the Tarquins (B.C. 494), that the plebeians were roused to take the first step in the assertion of their rights. After the battle of Lake Regillus, the plebeians had reason to expect some relaxation of the law of debt, in consideration of the great services they had rendered in the war. But none was granted. The patrician creditors began to avail themselves of the severity of the law against their plebeian debtors. The discontent that followed was great, and the consuls prepared to meet the storm. These were Appius Claudius, the proud Sabine nobleman who had lately become a Roman, and who now led the high patrician party with all the unbending energy of a chieftain whose will had never been disputed by his obedient clansmen; and P. Servilius, who represented the milder and more liberal party of the Fathers.

It chanced that an aged man rushed into the Forum on a market-day, loaded with chains, clothed with a few scanty rags, his hair and beard long and squalid; his whole appearance ghastly, as of one oppressed by long want of food and air. He was recognized as a brave soldier, the old comrade of many who thronged the Forum. He told his story, how that in the late wars the enemy had burned his house and plundered his little farm; that to replace his losses he had borrowed money of a patrician, that his cruel creditor (in default of payment) had thrown him into prison,[2] and tormented him with chains and scourges. At this sad tale, the passions of the people rose high.

---

[1] A well-known German historian calls the Spartans by the name of "stunted Romans." There is much resemblance to be traced.

[2] Such prisons were called *ergastula*, and afterward became the places for keeping slaves in.

Appius was obliged to conceal himself, while Servilius undertook to plead the cause of the plebeians with the senate.

Meantime news came to the city that the Roman territory
was invaded by the Volscian foe. The consuls proclaimed a
levy; but the stout yeomen, one and all, refused to give in their
names and take the military oath. Servilius now came forward
and proclaimed by edict that no citizen should be imprisoned
for debt so long as the war lasted, and that at the close of the
war he would propose an alteration of the law. The plebeians
trusted him, and the enemy was driven back. But when the
popular consul returned with his victorious soldiers, he was denied a triumph, and the senate, led by Appius, refused to make
any concession in favor of the debtors.

The anger of the plebeians rose higher and higher, when
again news came that the enemy was ravaging the lands of
Rome. The senate, well knowing that the power of the consuls would avail nothing, since Appius was regarded as a tyrant, and Servilius would not choose again to become an instrument for deceiving the people, appointed a dictator to lead the
citizens into the field. But to make the act as popular as might
be, they named M. Valerius, a descendant of the great Poplicola. The same scene was repeated over again. Valerius protected the plebeians against their creditors while they were at
war, and promised them relief when war was over. But when
the danger was gone by, Appius again prevailed; the senate
refused to listen to Valerius, and the dictator laid down his
office, calling gods and men to witness that he was not responsible for his breach of faith.

The plebeians whom Valerius had led forth were still under
arms, still bound by their military oath, and Appius, with the
violent patricians, refused to disband them. The army, therefore, having lost Valerius, their proper general chose two of
themselves, L. Junius Brutus and L. Sicinius Bellutus by
name, and under their command they marched northward and
occupied the hill which commands the junction of the Tiber
and the Anio. Here, at a distance of about two miles from
Rome, they determined to settle and form a new city, leaving
Rome to the patricians and their clients. But the latter were
not willing to lose the best of their soldiery, the cultivators of

the greater part of the Roman territory, and they sent repeated embassies to persuade the seceders to return. They, however, turned a deaf ear to all promises, for they had too often been deceived. Appius now urged the senate and patricians to leave the plebeians to themselves. The nobles and their clients, he said, could well maintain themselves in the city without such base aid.

But wiser sentiments prevailed. T. Lartius, and M. Valerius, both of whom had been dictators, with Menenius Agrippa, an old patrician of popular character, were empowered to treat with the people. Still their leaders were unwilling to listen, till old Menenius addressed them in the famous fable of the "Belly and the Members":

"In times of old," said he, "when every member of the body could think for itself, and each had a separate will of its own, they all, with one consent, resolved to revolt against the belly. They knew no reason, they said, why they should toil from morning till night in its service, while the belly lay at its ease in the midst of all, and indolently grew fat upon their labors. Accordingly they agreed to support it no more. The feet vowed they would carry it no longer; the hands that they would do no more work; the teeth that they would not chew a morsel of meat, even were it placed between them. Thus resolved, the members for a time showed their spirit and kept their resolution; but soon they found that instead of mortifying the belly they only undid themselves: they languished for a while, and perceived too late that it was owing to the belly that they had strength to work and courage to mutiny."

The moral of this fable was plain. The people readily applied it to the patricians and themselves, and their leaders proposed terms of agreement to the patrician messengers. They required that the debtors who could not pay should have their debts cancelled, and that those who had been given up into slavery should be restored to freedom. This for the past. And as a security for the future, they demanded that two of themselves should be appointed for the sole purpose of protecting the plebeians against the patrician magistrates, if they acted cruelly or unjustly toward the debtors. The two officers thus to be appointed were called "Tribunes of the Plebs." Their persons were to be sacred and inviolable during their year of office, whence their office is called *sacrosancta Potestas*. They were never to leave the city during that time, and their houses were to be open day and night, that all who needed their aid might demand it without delay.

This concession, apparently great, was much modified by the fact that the patricians insisted on the election of the tribunes being made at the Comitia of the Centuries, in which they themselves and their wealthy clients could usually command a majority. In later times, the number of the tribunes was increased to five, and afterward to ten. They were elected at the Comitia of the tribes. They had the privilege of attending all sittings of the senate, though they were not considered members of that famous body. Above all, they acquired the great and perilous power of the veto, by which any one of their number might stop any law, or annul any decree of the senate without cause or reason assigned. This right of veto was called the "Right of Intercession."

On the spot where this treaty was made, an altar was built to Jupiter, the causer and banisher of fear, for the plebeians had gone thither in fear and returned from it in safety. The place was called Mons Sacer, or the Sacred Hill, forever after, and the laws by which the sanctity of the tribunitian office was secured were called the *Leges Sacratæ.*

The tribunes were not properly magistrates or officers, for they had no express functions or official duties to discharge. They were simply representatives and protectors of the plebs. At the same time, however, with the institution of these protective officers, the plebeians were allowed the right of having two ædiles chosen from their own body, whose business it was to preserve order and decency in the streets, to provide for the repair of all buildings and roads there, with other functions partly belonging to police officers, and partly to commissioners of public works.

THE BATTLE OF MARATHON

B.C. 490

SIR EDWARD SHEPHERD CREASY

Marathon ! A name to conjure up such visions of glory as few battle-fields have ever shown. Heroism and determination on the part of the Athenians, supported by the small but ever noble band of Platæans who came to their aid ; who can read the repulse of the Persians on this ever memorable plain without experiencing a thrill of admiration and delight at the achievement? The whole world since that battle has looked upon it as a victory of the under dog. Many of the great engagements of modern times have been likened unto it. For long it has been the syno-nym of brave despair; the conquering of an enemy many times superior in numbers to its opponent.

This attempt of the Persians on the Greeks was not the first against them. That took place B.C. 493 under Mardonius. This commander had reduced Ionia, dethroned the despots, and established democracy throughout the land. After this he turned his attention to Eretria and Athens, taking his army across the straits in vessels. But the ships of war and transports were wrecked by a mighty headwind as they rounded Mount Athos. Many were driven ashore, about three hundred of them were totally lost, and some twenty thousand men perished in the catas-trophe.

All the trouble between the Persians and Greeks arose over the cap-ture of Sardis by the Ionians, B.C. 500. The city was burned, and then the Ionians retreated. It was to avenge this that Persia determined on a punitive expedition against the Greeks. The Ionians and Milesian men were mostly slain by the Persians, the women and children léd into captivity, and the temples in the cities burned and razed to the ground.[1]

In the battle of Marathon, which succeeded these events, we have a vivid picture presented to us in Creasy's glowing words:

TWO thousand three hundred and forty years ago a council of Athenian officers was summoned on the slope of one of the mountains that look over the plain of Marathon, on the eastern coast of Attica. The immediate subject of their meet-

[1] The year following the fall of the Ionic city of Miletus the poet Phrynichus made it the subject of a tragedy. On bringing it on the stage he was fined one thousand drachmæ for having recalled to them their own misfortunes.—SMITH.

ing was to consider whether they should give battle to an
enemy that lay encamped on the shore beneath them; but on
the result of their deliberations depended, not merely the fate
of two armies, but the whole future progress of human civilization.

There were eleven members of that council of war. Ten
were the generals who were then annually elected at Athens,
one for each of the local tribes into which the Athenians were
divided. Each general led the men of his own tribe, and each
was invested with equal military authority. But one of the
archons was also associated with them in the general command
of the army. This magistrate was termed the " Polemarch" or
War-ruler. He had the privilege of leading the right wing of
the army in battle, and his vote in a council of war was equal
to that of any of the generals. A noble Athenian named Callimachus was the war-ruler of this year, and, as such, stood
listening to the earnest discussion of the ten generals. They
had, indeed, deep matter for anxiety, though little aware how
momentous to mankind were the votes they were about to give,
or how the generations to come would read with interest the
record of their discussions. They saw before them the invading forces of a mighty empire, which had in the last fifty years
shattered and enslaved nearly all the kingdoms and principal
cities of the then known world. They knew that all the resources of their own country were comprised in the little army
intrusted to their guidance. They saw before them a chosen
host of the great king, sent to wreak his special wrath on that
country and on the other insolent little Greek community which
had dared to aid his rebels and burn the capital of one of his
provinces. That victorious host had already fulfilled half its
mission of vengeance.

Eretria, the confederate of Athens in the bold march against
Sardis nine years before, had fallen in the last few days; and
the Athenian generals could discern from the heights the island
of Ægilia, in which the Persians had deposited their Eretrian
prisoners, whom they had reserved to be led away captives into
Upper Asia, there to hear their doom from the lips of King
Darius himself. Moreover, the men of Athens knew that in
the camp before them was their own banished tyrant, who was

seeking to be reinstated by foreign cimeters in despotic sway over any remnant of his countrymen that might survive the sack of their town, and might be left behind as too worthless for leading away into Median bondage.

The numerical disparity between the force which the Athenian commanders had under them, and that which they were called on to encounter, was hopelessly apparent to some of the council. The historians who wrote nearest to the time of the battle do not pretend to give any detailed statements of the numbers engaged, but there are sufficient data for our making a general estimate. Every free Greek was trained to military duty; and, from the incessant border wars between the different states, few Greeks reached the age of manhood without having seen some service. But the muster-roll of free Athenian citizens of an age fit for military duty never exceeded thirty thousand, and at this epoch probably did not amount to two-thirds of that number. Moreover, the poorer portion of these were unprovided with the equipments, and untrained to the operations of the regular infantry. Some detachments of the best-armed troops would be required to garrison the city itself and man the various fortified posts in the territory, so that it is impossible to reckon the fully equipped force that marched from Athens to Marathon, when the news of the Persian landing arrived, at higher than ten thousand men.[1]

With one exception, the other Greeks held back from aiding them. Sparta had promised assistance, but the Persians had landed on the sixth day of the moon, and a religious scruple delayed the march of Spartan troops till the moon should have reached its full. From one quarter only, and that from a most unexpected one, did Athens receive aid at the moment of her great peril.

Some years before this time the little state of Platæa in Bœotia, being hard pressed by her powerful neighbor, Thebes, had asked the protection of Athens, and had owed to an Athe-

---

[1] The historians, who lived long after the time of the battle, such as Justin, Plutarch, and others, give ten thousand as the number of the Athenian army. Not much reliance could be placed on their authority if unsupported by other evidence; but a calculation made for the number of the Athenian free population remarkably confirms it.

nian army the rescue of her independence. Now when it was noised over Greece that the Mede had come from the uttermost parts of the earth to destroy Athens, the brave Platæans, unsolicited, marched with their whole force to assist the defence, and to share the fortunes of their benefactors.

The general levy of the Platæans amounted only to a thousand men; and this little column, marching from their city along the southern ridge of Mount Cithæron, and thence across the Attic territory, joined the Athenian forces above Marathon almost immediately before the battle. The reënforcement was numerically small, but the gallant spirit of the men who composed it must have made it of tenfold value to the Athenians, and its presence must have gone far to dispel the cheerless feeling of being deserted and friendless, which the delay of the Spartan succors was calculated to create among the Athenian ranks.[1]

This generous daring of their weak but true-hearted ally was never forgotten at Athens. The Platæans were made the civil fellow-countrymen of the Athenians, except the right of exercising certain political functions; and from that time forth in the solemn sacrifices at Athens, the public prayers were offered up for a joint blessing from Heaven upon the Athenians, and the Platæans also.

After the junction of the column from Platæa, the Athenian commanders must have had under them about eleven thousand fully armed and disciplined infantry, and probably a large number of irregular light-armed troops; as, besides the poorer citizens who went to the field armed with javelins, cutlasses, and targets, each regular heavy-armed soldier was attended in the

---

[1] Mr. Grote observes that " this volunteer march of the whole Platæan force to Marathon is one of the most affecting incidents of all Grecian history," In truth, the whole career of Platæa, and the friendship, strong, even unto death, between her and Athens form one of the most affecting episodes in the history of antiquity. In the Peloponnesian war the Platæans again were true to the Athenians against all risks, and all calculation of self-interest: and the destruction of Platæa was the consequence. There are few nobler passages in the classics than the speech in which the Platæan prisoners of war, after the memorable siege of their city, justify before their Spartan executioners their loyal adherence to Athens.

camp by one or more slaves, who were armed like the inferior freemen. Cavalry or archers the Athenians (on this occasion) had none, and the use in the field of military engines was not at that period introduced into ancient warfare.

Contrasted with their own scanty forces, the Greek commanders saw stretched before them, along the shores of the winding bay, the tents and shipping of the varied nations who marched to do the bidding of the king of the Eastern world. The difficulty of finding transports and of securing provisions would form the only limit to the numbers of a Persian army. Nor is there any reason to suppose the estimate of Justin exaggerated, who rates at a hundred thousand the force which on this occasion had sailed, under the satraps Datis and Artaphernes, from the Cilician shores against the devoted coasts of Euboea and Attica. And after largely deducting from this total, so as to allow for mere mariners and camp followers, there must still have remained fearful odds against the national levies of the Athenians.

Nor could Greek generals then feel that confidence in the superior quality of their troops, which ever since the battle of Marathon has animated Europeans in conflicts with Asiatics, as, for instance, in the after struggles between Greece and Persia, or when the Roman legions encountered the myriads of Mithradates and Tigranes, or as is the case in the Indian campaigns of our own regiments. On the contrary, up to the day of Marathon the Medes and Persians were reputed invincible. They had more than once met Greek troops in Asia Minor, in Cyprus, in Egypt, and had invariably beaten them.

Nothing can be stronger than the expressions used by the early Greek writers respecting the terror which the name of the Medes inspired, and the prostration of men's spirits before the apparently resistless career of the Persian arms. It is, therefore, little to be wondered at that five of the ten Athenian generals shrank from the prospect of fighting a pitched battle against an enemy so superior in numbers and so formidable in military renown. Their own position on the heights was strong and offered great advantages to a small defending force against assailing masses. They deemed it mere foolhardiness to descend into the plain to be trampled down by the Asiatic horse, overwhelmed with the archery, or cut to pieces by the invincible veterans of Cambyses and Cyrus.

Moreover, Sparta, the great war state of Greece, had been applied to, and had promised succor to Athens, though the religious observance which the Dorians paid to certain times and seasons had for the present delayed their march. Was it not wise, at any rate, to wait till the Spartans came up, and to have the help of the best troops in Greece, before they exposed themselves to the shock of the dreaded Medes?

Specious as these reasons might appear, the other five generals were for speedier and bolder operations. And, fortunately for Athens and for the world, one of them was a man, not only of the highest military genius, but also of that energetic character which impresses its own type and ideas upon spirits feebler in conception.

Miltiades was the head of one of the noblest houses at Athens. He ranked the Æacidæ among his ancestry, and the blood of Achilles flowed in the veins of the hero of Marathon. One of his immediate ancestors had acquired the dominion of the Thracian Chersonese, and thus the family became at the same time Athenian citizens and Thracian princes. This occurred at the time when Pisistratus was tyrant of Athens. Two of the relatives of Miltiades—an uncle of the same name, and a brother named Stesagoras—had ruled the Chersonese before Miltiades became its prince. He had been brought up at Athens in the house of his father, Cimon,[1] who was renowned throughout Greece for his victories in the Olympic chariot-races, and who must have been possessed of great wealth.

The sons of Pisistratus, who succeeded their father in the tyranny at Athens, caused Cimon to be assassinated; but they treated the young Miltiades with favor and kindness and when his brother Stesagoras died in the Chersonese, they sent him out there as lord of the principality. This was about twenty-eight years before the battle of Marathon, and it is with his arrival in the Chersonese that our first knowledge of the career and character of Miltiades commences. We find, in the first act recorded of him, the proof of the same resolute and unscrupulous spirit that marked his mature age. His brother's

[1] Herodotus.

authority in the principality had been shaken by war and revolt: Miltiades determined to rule more securely. On his
arrival he kept close within his house, as if he was mourning
for his brother. The principal men of the Chersonese, hearing
of this, assembled from all the towns and districts, and went
together to the house of Miltiades, on a visit of condolence.
As soon as he had thus got them in his power, he made them
all prisoners. He then asserted and maintained his own absolute authority in the peninsula, taking into his pay a body of
five hundred regular troops, and strengthening his interest by
marrying the daughter of the king of the neighboring Thracians.

When the Persian power was **exten**ded to the Hellespont
and its neighborhood, Miltiades, as prince of the Chersonese,
submitted to King Darius; and **he was** one of the numerous
tributary rulers who led their contingents of men to serve in
the Persian army, in the expedition against Scythia. Miltiades
and the vassal Greeks of Asia Minor were left by the Persian
king in charge of the bridge across the Danube, when the invading army crossed that river, and plunged into the wilds of
the country that now is Russia, in vain pursuit of the ancestors
of the modern Cossacks. On learning the reverses that Darius
met with in the Scythian wilderness, Miltiades proposed to his
companions that they should break the bridge down and leave
the Persian king and his army to perish by famine and the
Scythian arrows. The rulers of the Asiatic Greek cities,
whom Miltiades addressed, shrank from this bold but ruthless
stroke against the Persian power, and Darius returned in
safety.

But it was known what advice Miltiades had given, and the
vengeance of Darius was thenceforth specially directed against
the man who had counselled such a deadly blow against his
empire and his person. The occupation of the Persian arms
in other quarters left Miltiades for some years after this in
possession of the Chersonese; but it was precarious and interrupted. He, however, availed himself of the opportunity which
his position gave him of conciliating the good-will of his fellow-
countrymen at Athens, by conquering and placing under the
Athenian authority the islands of Lemnos and Imbros, to

which Athens had ancient claims, but which she had never previously been able to bring into complete subjection.

At length, in B.C. 494, the complete suppression of the Ionian revolt by the Persians left their armies and fleets at liberty to act against the enemies of the Great King to the west of the Hellespont. A strong squadron of Phœnician galleys was sent against the Chersonese. Miltiades knew that resistance was hopeless, and while the Phœnicians were at Tenedos, he loaded five galleys with all the treasure that he could collect, and sailed away for Athens. The Phœnicians fell in with him, and chased him hard along the north of the Ægean. One of his galleys, on board of which was his eldest son Metiochus, was actually captured. But Miltiades, with the other four, succeeded in reaching the friendly coast of Imbros in safety. Thence he afterward proceeded to Athens, and resumed his station as a free citizen of the Athenian commonwealth.

The Athenians, at this time, had recently expelled Hippias the son of Pisistratus, the last of their tyrants. They were in the full glow of their newly recovered liberty and equality; and the constitutional changes of Clisthenes had inflamed their republican zeal to the utmost. Miltiades had enemies at Athens; and these, availing themselves of the state of popular feeling, brought him to trial for his life for having been tyrant of the Chersonese. The charge did not necessarily import any acts of cruelty or wrong to individuals: it was founded on no specific law; but it was based on the horror with which the Greeks of that age regarded every man who made himself arbitrary master of his fellow-men, and exercised irresponsible dominion over them.

The fact of Miltiades having so ruled in the Chersonese was undeniable; but the question which the Athenians assembled in judgment must have tried, was whether Miltiades, although tyrant of the Chersonese, deserved punishment as an Athenian citizen. The eminent service that he had done the state in conquering Lemnos and Imbros for it, pleaded strongly in his favor. The people refused to convict him. He stood high in public opinion. And when the coming invasion of the Persians was known, the people wisely elected him one of their generals for the year.

Two other men of high eminence in history, though their renown was achieved at a later period than that of Miltiades, were also among the ten Athenian generals at Marathon. One was Themistocles, the future founder of the Athenian navy, and the destined victor of Salamis. The other was Aristides, who afterward led the Athenian troops at Platæa, and whose integrity and just popularity acquired for his country, when the Persians had finally been repulsed, the advantageous preëminence of being acknowledged by half of the Greeks as their imperial leader and protector. It is not recorded what part either Themistocles or Aristides took in the debate of the council of war at Marathon. But, from the character of Themistocles, his boldness, and his intuitive genius for extemporizing the best measures in every emergency—a quality which the greatest of historians ascribes to him beyond all his contemporaries—we may well believe that the vote of Themistocles was for prompt and decisive action. On the vote of Aristides it may be more difficult to speculate. His predilection for the Spartans may have made him wish to wait till they came up; but, though circumspect, he was neither timid as a soldier nor as a politician, and the bold advice of Miltiades may probably have found in Aristides a willing, most assuredly it found in him a candid, hearer.

Miltiades felt no hesitation as to the course which the Athenian army ought to pursue; and earnestly did he press his opinion on his brother generals. Practically acquainted with the organization of the Persian armies, Miltiades felt convinced of the superiority of the Greek troops, if properly handled; he saw with the military eye of a great general the advantage which the position of the forces gave him for a sudden attack, and as a profound politician he felt the perils of remaining inactive, and of giving treachery time to ruin the Athenian cause.

One officer in the council of war had not yet voted. This was Callimachus, the War-ruler. The votes of the generals were five and five, so that the voice of Callimachus would be decisive.

On that vote, in all human probability, the destiny of all the nations of the world depended. Miltiades turned to him, and in simple soldierly eloquence—the substance of which we may read faithfully reported in Herodotus, who had conversed with the veterans of Marathon—the great Athenian thus adjured his countrymen to vote for giving battle:

"It now rests with you, Callimachus, either to enslave Athens, or, by assuring her freedom, to win yourself an immortality of fame, such as not even Harmodius and Aristogiton have acquired; for never, since the Athenians were a people, were they in such danger as they are in at this moment. If they bow the knee to these Medes, they are to be given up to Hippias, and you know what they then will have to suffer. But if Athens comes victorious out of this contest, she has it in her to become the first city of Greece. Your vote is to decide whether we are to join battle or not. If we do not bring on a battle presently, some factious intrigue will disunite the Athenians, and the city will be betrayed to the Medes. But if we fight, before there is anything rotten in the state of Athens, I believe that, provided the gods will give fair play and no favor, we are able to get the best of it in an engagement."

The vote of the brave War-ruler was gained, the council determined to give battle; and such was the ascendency and acknowledged military eminence of Miltiades, that his brother generals one and all gave up their days of command to him, and cheerfully acted under his orders. Fearful, however, of creating any jealousy, and of so failing to obtain the vigorous coöperation of all parts of his small army, Miltiades waited till the day when the chief command would have come round to him in regular rotation before he led the troops against the enemy.

The inaction of the Asiatic commanders during this interval appears strange at first sight; but Hippias was with them, and they and he were aware of their chance of a bloodless conquest through the machinations of his partisans among the Athenians. The nature of the ground also explains in many points the tactics of the opposite generals before the battle, as well as the operations of the troops during the engagement.

The plain of Marathon, which is about twenty-two miles distant from Athens, lies along the bay of the same name on the northeastern coast of Attica. The plain is nearly in the form of a crescent, and about six miles in length. It is about two miles broad in the centre, where the space between the mountains and the sea is greatest, but it narrows toward either extremity, the mountains coming close down to the water at the horns of the bay. There is a valley trending inward from the middle of the plain, and a ravine comes down to it to the southward. Elsewhere it is closely girt round on the land side by rugged limestone mountains, which are thickly studded with pines, olive-trees and cedars, and overgrown with the myrtle, arbutus, and the other low odoriferous shrubs that everywhere perfume the Attic air.

The level of the ground is now varied by the mound raised over those who fell in the battle, but it was an unbroken plain when the Persians encamped on it. There are marshes at each end, which are dry in spring and summer and then offer no ob- struction to the horseman, but are commonly flooded with rain and so rendered impracticable for cavalry in the autumn, the time of year at which the action took place.

The Greeks, lying encamped on the mountains, could watch every movement of the Persians on the plain below, while they were enabled completely to mask their own. Miltiades also had, from his position, the power of giving battle whenever he pleased, or of delaying it at his discretion, unless Datis were to attempt the perilous operation of storming the heights.

If we turn to the map of the Old World, to test the com- parative territorial resources of the two states whose armies were now about to come into conflict, the immense preponder- ance of the material power of the Persian king over that of the Athenian republic is more striking than any similar contrast which history can supply. It has been truly remarked that, in estimating mere areas Attica, containing on its whole surface only seven hundred square miles, shrinks into insignificance if compared with many a baronial fief of the Middle Ages, or many a colonial allotment of modern times. Its antagonist, the Persian, empire, comprised the whole of modern Asiatic and much of modern European Turkey, the modern kingdom of Persia and the countries of modern Georgia, Armenia, Balkh, the Punjaub, Afghanistan, Beloochistan, Egypt and Tripoli.

Nor could a European, in the beginning of the fifth century before our era, look upon this huge accumulation of power beneath the sceptre of a single Asiatic ruler with the indifference with which we now observe on the map the extensive dominions of modern Oriental sovereigns; for, as has been already remarked, before Marathon was fought, the prestige of success and of supposed superiority of race was on the side of the Asiatic against the European. Asia was the original seat of human societies, and long before any trace can be found of the inhabitants of the rest of the world having emerged from the rudest barbarism, we can perceive that mighty and brilliant empires flourished in the Asiatic continent. They appear before us through the twilight of primeval history, dim and indistinct, but massive and majestic, like mountains in the early dawn.

Instead, however, of the infinite variety and restless change which has characterized the institutions and fortunes of European states ever since the commencement of the civilization of our continent, a monotonous uniformity pervades the histories of nearly all Oriental empires, from the most ancient down to the most recent times. They are characterized by the rapidity of their early conquests, by the immense extent of the dominions comprised in them, by the establishment of a satrap or pashaw system of governing the provinces, by an invariable and speedy degeneracy in the princes of the royal house, the effeminate nurslings of the seraglio succeeding to the warrior sovereigns reared in the camp, and by the internal anarchy and insurrections which indicate and accelerate the decline and fall of these unwieldy and ill-organized fabrics of power.

It is also a striking fact that the governments of all the great Asiatic empires have in all ages been absolute despotisms. And Heeren is right in connecting this with another great fact, which is important from its influence both on the political and the social life of Asiatics. "Among all the considerable nations of Inner Asia, the paternal government of every household was corrupted by polygamy: where that custom exists, a good political constitution is impossible. Fathers, being converted into domestic despots, are ready to pay the same abject obedience to their sovereign which they exact from their family and dependents in their domestic economy."

We should bear in mind, also, the inseparable connection

between the state religion and all legislation which has always prevailed in the East, and the constant existence of a powerful sacerdotal body, exercising some check, though precarious and irregular, over the throne itself, grasping at all civil administration, claiming the supreme control of education, stereotyping the lines in which literature and science must move, and limiting the extent to which it shall be lawful for the human mind to prosecute its inquiries.

With these general characteristics rightly felt and understood it becomes a comparatively easy task to investigate and appreciate the origin, progress and principles of Oriental empires in general, as well as of the Persian monarchy in particular. And we are thus better enabled to appreciate the repulse which Greece gave to the arms of the East, and to judge of the probable consequences to human civilization, if the Persians had succeeded in bringing Europe under their yoke, as they had already subjugated the fairest portions of the rest of the then known world.

The Greeks, from their geographical position, formed the natural van-guard of European liberty against Persian ambition; and they preëminently displayed the salient points of distinctive national character which have rendered European civilization so far superior to Asiatic. The nations that dwelt in ancient times around and near the northern shores of the Mediterranean Sea were the first in our continent to receive from the East the rudiments of art and literature, and the germs of social and political organizations. Of these nations the Greeks, through their vicinity to Asia Minor, Phœnicia, and Egypt, were among the very foremost in acquiring the principles and habits of civilized life; and they also at once imparted a new and wholly original stamp on all which they received. Thus, in their religion, they received from foreign settlers the names of all their deities and many of their rites, but they discarded the loathsome monstrosities of the Nile, the Orontes, and the Ganges; they nationalized their creed, and their own poets created their beautiful mythology. No sacerdotal caste ever existed in Greece.

So, in their governments, they lived long under hereditary kings, but never endured the permanent establishment of absolute monarchy. Their early kings were constitutional rulers, governing with defined prerogatives. And long before the Persian invasion, the kingly form of government had given way in almost all the Greek states to republican institutions, presenting infinite varieties of the blending or the alternate predominance of the oligarchical and democratical principles. In literature and science the Greek intellect followed no beaten track, and acknowledged no limitary rules. The Greeks thought their subjects boldly out; and the novelty of a speculation invested it in their minds with interest, and not with criminality.

Versatile, restless, enterprising, and self-confident, the Greeks presented the most striking contrast to the habitual quietude and submissiveness of the Orientals; and, of all the Greeks, the Athenians exhibited these national characteristics in the strongest degree. This spirit of activity and daring, joined to a generous sympathy for the fate of their fellow-Greeks in Asia, had led them to join in the last Ionian war, and now mingling with their abhorrence of the usurping family of their own citizens, which for a period had forcibly seized on and exercised despotic power at Athens, nerved them to defy the wrath of King Darius, and to refuse to receive back at his bidding the tyrant whom they had some years before driven out.

The enterprise and genius of an Englishman have lately confirmed by fresh evidence, and invested with fresh interest, the might of the Persian monarch who sent his troops to combat at Marathon. Inscriptions in a character termed the Arrow-headed, or Cuneiform, had long been known to exist on the marble monuments at Persepolis, near the site of the ancient Susa, and on the faces of rocks in other places formerly ruled over by the early Persian kings. But for thousands of years they had been mere unintelligible enigmas to the curious but baffled beholder; and they were often referred to as instances of the folly of human pride, which could indeed write its own praises in the solid rock, but only for the rock to outlive the language as well as the memory of the vainglorious inscribers.

The elder Niebuhr, Grotefend, and Lassen, had made some guesses at the meaning of the cuneiform letters; but Major Rawlinson of the East India Company's service, after years of labor, has at last accomplished the glorious achievement of fully revealing the alphabet and the grammar of this long unknown tongue. He has, in particular, fully deciphered and expounded the inscription on the sacred rock of Behistun, on the western frontiers of Media. These records of the Achæmenidæ have at length found their interpreter; and Darius himself speaks to us from the consecrated mountain, and tells us the names of the nations that obeyed him, the revolts that he suppressed, his victories, his piety, and his glory.

Kings who thus seek the admiration of posterity are little likely to dim the record of their successes by the mention of their occasional defeats; and it throws no suspicion on the narrative of the Greek historians that we find these inscriptions silent respecting the overthrow of Datis and Artaphernes, as well as respecting the reverses which Darius sustained in person during his Scythian campaigns. But these indisputable monuments of Persian fame confirm, and even increase the opinion with which Herodotus inspires us of the vast power which Cyrus founded and Cambyses increased; which Darius augmented by Indian and Arabian conquests, and seemed likely, when he directed his arms against Europe, to make the predominant monarchy of the world.

With the exception of the Chinese empire, in which, throughout all ages down to the last few years, one-third of the human race has dwelt almost unconnected with the other portions, all the great kingdoms, which we know to have existed in ancient Asia, were, in Darius' time, blended into the Persian. The northern Indians, the Assyrians, the Syrians, the Babylonians, the Chaldees, the Phœnicians, the nations of Palestine, the Armenians, the Bactrians, the Lydians, the Phrygians, the Parthians, and the Medes, all obeyed the sceptre of the Great King: the Medes standing next to the native Persians in honor, and the empire being frequently spoken of as that of the Medes, or as that of the Medes and Persians. Egypt and Cyrene were Persian provinces; the Greek colonists in Asia Minor and the islands of the Ægean were Darius' subjects; and their gallant but unsuccessful attempts to throw off the Persian yoke had only served to rivet it more strongly, and to increase the general belief that the Greeks could not stand before the Persians in a field of battle. Darius' Scythian war, though unsuccessful in its immediate object, had brought about the subjugation of Thrace and the submission of Macedonia. From the Indus to the Peneus, all was his.

We may imagine the wrath with which the lord of so many nations must have heard, nine years before the battle of Marathon, that a strange nation toward the setting sun, called the Athenians, had dared to help his rebels in Ionia against him, and that they had plundered and burned the capital of one of his provinces. Before the burning of Sardis, Darius seems never to have heard of the existence of Athens; but his satraps in Asia Minor had for some time seen Athenian refugees at their provincial courts imploring assistance against their fellow-countrymen.

When Hippias was driven away from Athens, and the tyrannic dynasty of the Pisistratidæ finally overthrown in B.C. 510, the banished tyrant and his adherents, after vainly seeking to be restored by Spartan intervention, had betaken themselves to Sardis, the capital city of the satrapy of Artaphernes. There Hippias—in the expressive words of Herodotus—began every kind of agitation, slandering the Athenians before Artaphernes, and doing all he could to induce the satrap to place Athens in subjection to him, as the tributary vassal of King Darius. When the Athenians heard of his practices, they sent envoys to Sardis to remonstrate with the Persians against taking up the quarrel of the Athenian refugees.

But Artaphernes gave them in reply a menacing command to receive Hippias back again if they looked for safety. The Athenians were resolved not to purchase safety at such a price, and after rejecting the satrap's terms, they considered that they and the Persians were declared enemies. At this very crisis the Ionian Greeks implored the assistance of their European brethren, to enable them to recover their independence from Persia. Athens, and the city of Eretria in Eubœa, alone consented. Twenty Athenian galleys, and five Eretrian, crossed the Ægean Sea, and by a bold and sudden march upon Sardis, the Athenians and their allies succeeded in capturing the capital city of the haughty satrap who had recently menaced them with servitude or destruction. They were pursued, and defeated on their return to the coast, and Athens took no further part in the Ionian war; but the insult that she had put upon the Persian power was speedily made known throughout that empire, and was never to be forgiven or forgotten.

In the emphatic simplicity of the narrative of Herodotus, the wrath of the Great King is thus described: "Now when it was told to King Darius that Sardis had been taken and burned by the Athenians and Ionians, he took small heed of the Ionians, well knowing who they were, and that their revolt would soon be put down; but he asked who, and what manner of men, the Athenians were. And when he had been told, he called for his bow; and, having taken it, and placed an arrow on the string, he let the arrow fly toward heaven; and as he shot it into the air, he said, 'Oh! supreme God, grant me that I may avenge myself on the Athenians.' And when he had said this, he appointed one of his servants to say to him every day as he sat at meat, 'Sire, remember the Athenians.' "

Some years were occupied in the complete reduction of Ionia. But when this was effected, Darius ordered his victorious forces to proceed to punish Athens and Eretria, and to conquer European Greece. The first armament sent for this purpose was shattered by shipwreck, and nearly destroyed off Mount Athos. But the purpose of King Darius was not easily shaken. A larger army was ordered to be collected in Cilicia, and requisitions were sent to all the maritime cities of the Persian empire for ships of war, and for transports of sufficient size for carrying cavalry as well as infantry across the Ægean. While these preparations were being made, Darius sent heralds round to the Grecian cities demanding their submission to Persia. It was proclaimed in the market-place of each little Hellenic state—some with territories not larger than the Isle of Wight—that King Darius, the lord of all men, from the rising to the setting sun,[1] required earth and water to be delivered to his heralds, as a symbolical acknowledgment that he was head and master of the country. Terror-stricken at the power of Persia and at the severe punishment that had recently been inflicted on the refractory Ionians, many of the continental Greeks and nearly all the islanders submitted, and

[1] Æschines.

gave the required tokens of vassalage. At Sparta and Athens an indignant refusal was returned—a refusal which was disgraced by outrage and violence against the persons of the Asiatic heralds.

Fresh fuel was thus added to the anger of Darius against Athens, and the Persian preparations went on with renewed vigor. In the summer of B.C. 490, the army destined for the invasion was assembled in the Aleian plain of Cilicia, near the sea. A fleet of six hundred galleys and numerous transports was collected on the coast for the embarkation of troops, horse as well as foot. A Median general named Datis, and Artaphernes, the son of the satrap of Sardis, and who was also nephew of Darius, were placed in titular joint-command of the expedition. The real supreme authority was probably given to Datis alone, from the way in which the Greek writers speak of him.

We know no details of the previous career of this officer; but there is every reason to believe that his abilities and bravery had been proved by experience, or his Median birth would have prevented his being placed in high command by Darius. He appears to have been the first Mede who was thus trusted by the Persian kings after the overthrow of the conspiracy of the Median magi against the Persians immediately before Darius obtained the throne. Datis received instructions to complete the subjugation of Greece, and especial orders were given him with regard to Eretria and Athens. He was to take these two cities, and he was to lead the inhabitants away captive, and bring them as slaves into the presence of the Great King.

Datis embarked his forces in the fleet that awaited them, and coasting along the shores of Asia Minor till he was off Samos, he thence sailed due westward through the Ægean Sea for Greece, taking the islands in his way. The Naxians had, ten years before, successfully stood a siege against a Persian armament, but they now were too terrified to offer any resistance, and fled to the mountain tops, while the enemy burned their town and laid waste their lands. Thence Datis, compelling the Greek islanders to join him with their ships and men, sailed onward to the coast of Eubœa. The little town of Carystus essayed resistance, but was quickly over-powered.

He next attacked Eretria. The Athenians sent four thousand men to its aid; but treachery was at work among the Eretrians; and the Athenian force received timely warning from one of the leading men of the city to retire to aid in saving their own country, instead of remaining to share in the inevitable destruction of Eretria. Left to themselves, the Eretrians repulsed the assaults of the Persians against their walls for six days; on the seventh they were betrayed by two of their chiefs, and the Persians occupied the city. The temples were burned in revenge for the firing of Sardis, and the inhabitants were bound, and placed as prisoners in the neighboring islet of Ægilia, to wait there till Datis should bring the Athenians to join them in captivity, when both populations were to be led into Upper Asia, there to learn their doom from the lips of King Darius himself.

Flushed with success, and with half his mission thus accomplished, Datis reëmbarked his troops, and, crossing the little channel that separates Eubœa from the mainland, he encamped his troops on the Attic coast at Marathon, drawing up his galleys on the shelving beach, as was the custom with the navies of antiquity. The conquered islands behind him served as places of deposit for his provisions and military stores. His position at Marathon seemed to him in every respect advantageous, and the level nature of the ground on which he camped was favorable for the employment of his cavalry, if the Athenians should venture to engage him. Hippias, who accompanied him, and acted as the guide of the invaders, had pointed out Marathon as the best place for a landing, for this very reason. Probably Hippias was also influenced by the recollection that forty-seven years previously, he, with his father Pisistratus, had crossed with an army from Eretria to Marathon, and had won an easy victory over their Athenian enemies on that very plain, which had restored them to tyrannic power. The omen seemed cheering. The place was the same, but Hippias soon learned to his cost how great a change had come over the spirit of the Athenians.

But though "the fierce democracy" of Athens was zealous

and true against foreign invader and domestic tyrant, a faction existed in Athens, as at Eretria, who were willing to purchase a party triumph over their fellow-citizens at the price of their country's ruin. Communications were opened between these men and the Persian camp, which would have led to a catastrophe like that of Eretria, if Miltiades had not resolved and persuaded his colleagues to resolve on fighting at all hazards.

When Miltiades arrayed his men for action, he staked on the arbitrament of one battle not only the fate of Athens, but that of all Greece; for if Athens had fallen, no other Greek state, except Lacedæmon, would have had the courage to resist; and the Lacedæmonians, though they would probably have died in their ranks to the last man, never could have successfully resisted the victorious Persians and the numerous Greek troops which would have soon marched under the Persian satraps, had they prevailed over Athens.

Nor was there any power to the westward of Greece that could have offered an effectual opposition to Persia, had she once conquered Greece, and made that country a basis for future military operations. Rome was at this time in her season of utmost weakness. Her dynasty of powerful Etruscan kings had been driven out; and her infant commonwealth was reeling under the attacks of the Etruscans and Volscians from without, and the fierce dissensions between the patricians and plebeians within. Etruria, with her *lucumos* and serfs, was no match for Persia. Samnium had not grown into the might which she afterward put forth; nor could the Greek colonies in South Italy and Sicily hope to conquer when their parent states had perished. Carthage had escaped the Persian yoke in the time of Cambyses, through the reluctance of the Phœnician mariners to serve against their kinsmen.

But such forbearance could not long have been relied on, and the future rival of Rome would have become as submissive a minister of the Persian power as were the Phœnician cities themselves. If we turn to Spain; or if we pass the great mountain chain, which, prolonged through the Pyrenees, the Cevennes, the Alps, and the Balkan, divides Northern from Southern Europe, we shall find nothing at that period but mere savage Finns, Celts, Slavs, and Teutons. Had Persia

beaten Athens at Marathon, she could have found no obstacle
to prevent Darius, the chosen servant of Ormuzd, from advancing his sway over all the known Western races of mankind.
The infant energies of Europe would have been trodden out
beneath universal conquest, and the history of the world, like
the history of Asia, have become a mere record of the rise and
fall of despotic dynasties, of the incursions of barbarous
hordes, and of the mental and political prostration of millions
beneath the diadem, the tiara, and the sword.

Great as the preponderance of the Persian over the Athenian power at that crisis seems to have been, it would be unjust
to impute wild rashness to the policy of Miltiades and those
who voted with him in the Athenian council of war, or to look
on the after-current of events as the mere fortunate result of
successful folly. As before has been remarked, Miltiades,
while prince of the Chersonese, had seen service in the Persian
armies; and he knew by personal observation how many elements of weakness lurked beneath their imposing aspect of
strength. He knew that the bulk of their troops no longer
consisted of the hardy shepherds and mountaineers from Persia
proper and Kurdistan, who won Cyrus's battles; but that unwilling contingents from conquered nations now filled up the
Persian muster-rolls, fighting more from compulsion than from
any zeal in the cause of their masters. He had also the
sagacity and the spirit to appreciate the superiority of the
Greek armor and organization over the Asiatic, notwithstanding former reverses. Above all, he felt and worthily
trusted the enthusiasm of those whom he led.

The Athenians whom he led had proved by their newborn
valor in recent wars against the neighboring states that
"liberty and equality of civic rights are brave spirit-stirring
things, and they, who, while under the yoke of a despot, had
been no better men of war than any of their neighbors, as soon
as they were free, became the foremost men of all; for each
felt that in fighting for a free commonwealth, he fought for
himself, and whatever he took in hand, he was zealous to do
the work thoroughly." So the nearly contemporaneous historian describes the change of spirit that was seen in the Athenians after their tyrants were expelled; and Miltiades knew

that in leading them against the invading army, where they had Hippias, the foe they most hated, before them, he was bringing into battle no ordinary men, and could calculate on no ordinary heroism.

As for traitors, he was sure that, whatever treachery might lurk among some of the higher born and wealthier Athenians, the rank and file whom he commanded were ready to do their utmost in his and their own cause. With regard to future attacks from Asia, he might reasonably hope that one victory would inspirit all Greece to combine against the common foe; and that the latent seeds of revolt and disunion in the Persian empire would soon burst forth and paralyze its energies, so as to leave Greek independence secure.

With these hopes and risks, Miltiades, on the afternoon of a September day, B.C. 490, gave the word for the Athenian army to prepare for battle. There were many local associations connected with those mountain heights which were calculated powerfully to excite the spirits of the men, and of which the commanders well knew how to avail themselves in their exhortations to their troops before the encounter. Marathon itself was a region sacred to Hercules. Close to them was the fountain of Macaria, who had in days of yore devoted herself to death for the liberty of her people. The very plain on which they were to fight was the scene of the exploits of their national hero, Theseus; and there, too, as old legends told, the Athenians and the Heraclidæ had routed the invader, Eurystheus.

These traditions were not mere cloudy myths or idle fictions, but matters of implicit earnest faith to the men of that day, and many a fervent prayer arose from the Athenian ranks to the heroic spirits who, while on earth, had striven and suffered on that very spot, and who were believed to be now heavenly powers, looking down with interest on their still beloved country, and capable of interposing with superhuman aid in its behalf.

According to old national custom, the warriors of each tribe were arrayed together; neighbor thus fighting by the side of neighbor, friend by friend, and the spirit of emulation and the consciousness of responsibility excited to the very utmost.

The War-ruler, Callimachus, had the leading of the right wing; the Platæans formed the extreme left; and Themistocles and Aristides commanded the centre. The line consisted of the heavy-armed spearmen only; for the Greeks—until the time of Iphicrates—took little or no account of light-armed soldiers in a pitched battle, using them only in skirmishes, or for the pursuit of a defeated enemy. The panoply of the regular infantry consisted of a long spear, of a shield, helmet, breastplate, greaves, and short sword.

Thus equipped, they usually advanced slowly and steadily into action in a uniform phalanx of about eight spears deep. But the military genius of Miltiades led him to deviate on this occasion from the commonplace tactics of his countrymen. It was essential for him to extend his line so as to cover all the practicable ground, and to secure himself from being outflanked and charged in the rear by the Persian horse. This extension involved the weakening of his line. Instead of a uniform reduction of its strength, he determined on detaching principally from his centre, which, from the nature of the ground, would have the best opportunities for rallying, if broken; and on strengthening his wings so as to insure advantage at those points; and he trusted to his own skill and to his soldiers' discipline for the improvement of that advantage into decisive victory.[1]

In this order, and availing himself probably of the inequalities of the ground, so as to conceal his preparations from the enemy till the last possible moment, Miltiades drew up the eleven thousand infantry whose spears were to decide this crisis in the struggle between the European and the Asiatic worlds. The sacrifices by which the favor of heaven was sought, and its will consulted, were announced to show propitious omens. The trumpet sounded for action, and, chanting the hymn of

[1] It is remarkable that there is no other instance of a Greek general deviating from the ordinary mode of bringing a phalanx of spearmen into action until the battles of Leuctra and Mantinea, more than a century after Marathon, when Epaminondas introduced the tactics which Alexander the Great in ancient times, and Frederick the Great in modern times, made so famous, of concentrating an overpowing force to bear on some decisive point of the enemy's line, while he kept back, or, in military phrase, refused the weaker part of his own.

battle, the little army bore down upon the host of the foe. Then, too, along the mountain slopes of Marathon must have resounded the mutual exhortation which Æschylus, who fought in both battles, tells us was afterward heard over the waves of Salamis: "On, sons of the Greeks! Strike for the freedom of your country! strike for the freedom of your children and of your wives—for the shrines of your fathers' gods, and for the sepulchres of your sires. All—all are now staked upon the strife."

Instead of advancing at the usual slow pace of the phalanx, Miltiades brought his men on at a run. They were all trained in the exercise of the *palæstra*, so that there was no fear of their ending the charge in breathless exhaustion; and it was of the deepest importance for him to traverse as rapidly as possible the mile or so of level ground that lay between the mountain foot and the Persian outposts, and so to get his troops into close action before the Asiatic cavalry could mount, form, and manœuvre against him, or their archers keep him long under fire, and before the enemy's generals could fairly deploy their masses.

"When the Persians," says Herodotus, "saw the Athenians running down on them, without horse or bowmen, and scanty in numbers, they thought them a set of madmen rushing upon certain destruction." They began, however, to prepare to receive them, and the Eastern chiefs arrayed, as quickly as time and place allowed, the varied races who served in their motley ranks. Mountaineers from Hyrcania and Afghanistan, wild horsemen from the steppes of Khorassan, the black archers of Ethiopia, swordsmen from the banks of the Indus, the Oxus, the Euphrates and the Nile, made ready against the enemies of the Great King.

But no national cause inspired them except the division of native Persians; and in the large host there was no uniformity of language, creed, race or military system. Still, among them there were many gallant men, under a veteran general; they were familiarized with victory, and in contemptuous confidence their infantry, which alone had time to form, awaited the Athenian charge. On came the Greeks, with one unwavering line of leveled spears, against which the light targets,

the short lances and cimeters of the Orientals offered weak
defence. The front rank of the Asiatics must have gone down
to a man at the first shock. Still they recoiled not, but strove
by individual gallantry and by the weight of numbers to make
up for the disadvantages of weapons and tactics, and to bear
back the shallow line of the Europeans. In the centre, where
the native Persians and the Sacæ fought, they succeeded in
breaking through the weakened part of the Athenian phalanx;
and the tribes led by Aristides and Themistocles were, after a
brave resistance, driven back over the plain, and chased by the
Persians up the valley toward the inner country. There the
nature of the ground gave the opportunity of rallying and
renewing the struggle.

Meanwhile, the Greek wings, where Miltiades had concen-
trated his chief strength, had routed the Asiatics opposed to
them; and the Athenian and Platæan officers, instead of pursuing the fugitives, kept their troops well in hand, and, wheel-
ing round, they formed the two wings together. Miltiades
instantly led them against the Persian centre, which had hitherto been triumphant., but which now fell back, and prepared
to encounter these new and unexpected assailants. Aristides
and Themistocles renewed the fight with their reorganized
troops, and the full force of the Greeks was brought into close
action with the Persian and Sacean divisions of the enemy.
Datis' veterans strove hard to keep their ground, and evening
was approaching before the stern encounter was decided.

But the Persians, with their slight wicker shields, destitute
of body armor, and never taught by training to keep the even
front and act with the regular movement of the Greek infantry, fought at heavy disadvantage with their shorter and
feebler weapons against the compact array of well-armed
Athenian and Platæan spearmen, all perfectly drilled to perform each necessary evolution in concert, and to preserve a uniform and unwavering line in battle. In personal courage and
in bodily activity the Persians were not inferior to their adver-
saries. Their spirits were not yet cowed by the recollection
of former defeats; and they lavished their lives freely, rather
than forfeit the fame which they had won by so many victories. While their rear ranks poured an incessant shower of

arrows over the heads of their comrades, the foremost Persians kept rushing forward, sometimes singly, sometimes in desperate groups of ten or twelve, upon the projecting spears of the Greeks, striving to force a lane into the phalanx, and to bring their cimeters and daggers into play. But the Greeks felt their superiority, and though the fatigue of the long-continued action told heavily on their inferior numbers, the sight of the carnage that they dealt upon their assailants nerved them to fight still more fiercely on.

At last the previously unvanquished lords of Asia turned their backs and fled, and the Greeks followed, striking them down, to the water's edge,[1] where the invaders were now hastily launching their galleys, and seeking to embark and fly. Flushed with success, the Athenians attacked and strove to fire the fleet. But here the Asiatics resisted desperately, and the principal loss sustained by the Greeks was in the assault on the ships. Here fell the brave War-ruler Callimachus, the general Stesilaus, and other Athenians of note. Seven galleys were fired; but the Persians succeeded in saving the rest. They pushed off from the fatal shore; but even here the skill of Datis did not desert him, and he sailed round to the western coast of Attica, in hopes to find the city unprotected, and to gain possession of it from some of the partisans of Hippias.

Miltiades, however, saw and counteracted his manœuvre. Leaving Aristides, and the troops of his tribe, to guard the spoil and the slain, the Athenian commander led his conquering army by a rapid night-march back across the country to Athens. And when the Persian fleet had doubled the Cape of Sunium and sailed up to the Athenian harbor in the morning, Datis saw arrayed on the heights above the city the troops before whom his men had fled on the preceding evening. All hope of further conquest in Europe for the time was abandoned, and the baffled armada returned to the Asiatic coasts.

[1] The flying Mede, his shaftless broken bow;
The fiery Greek, his red pursuing spear;
Mountains above, Earth's, Ocean's plain below,
Death in the front, Destruction in the rear!
Such was the scene.—BYRON.

After the battle had been fought, but while the dead bodies were yet on the ground, the promised reënforcement from Sparta arrived. Two thousand Lacedæmonian spearmen, starting immediately after the full moon, had marched the hundred and fifty miles between Athens and Sparta in the wonderfully short time of three days. Though too late to share in the glory of the action, they requested to be allowed to march to the battle-field to behold the Medes. They proceeded thither, gazed on the dead bodies of the invaders, and then praising the Athenians and what they had done, they returned to Lacedæmon.

The number of the Persian dead was sixty-four hundred; of the Athenians, one hundred and ninety-two. The number of the Platæans who fell is not mentioned; but, as they fought in the part of the army which was not broken, it cannot have been large.

The apparent disproportion between the losses of the two armies is not surprising when we remember the armor of the Greek spearmen, and the impossibility of heavy slaughter being inflicted by sword or lance on troops so armed, as long as they kept firm in their ranks.[1]

The Athenian slain were buried on the field of battle. This was contrary to the usual custom, according to which the bones of all who fell fighting for their country in each year were deposited in a public sepulchre in the suburb of Athens called the "Ceramicus." But it was felt that a distinction ought to be made in the funeral honors paid to the men of Marathon, even as their merit had been distinguished over that of all other Athenians. A lofty mound was raised on the plain of Marathon, beneath which the remains of the men of Athens who fell in the battle were deposited. Ten columns were erected on the spot, one for each of the Athenian tribes; and on the monumental column of each tribe were graven the names of those of its members whose glory it was to have fallen in the great battle of liberation. The antiquarian Pausanias read those names there six hundred years after the

---

[1] Mitford well refers to Crecy, Poictiers, and Agincourt as instances of similar disparity of loss between the conquerors and the conquered.

time when they were first graven.[1] The columns have long perished, but the mound still marks the spot where the noblest heroes of antiquity repose.

A separate tumulus was raised over the bodies of the slain Platæans, and another over the light-armed slaves who had taken part and had fallen in the battle.[2] There was also a separate funeral monument to the general to whose genius the victory was mainly due. Miltiades did not live long after his achievement at Marathon, but he lived long enough to experience a lamentable reverse of his popularity and success. As soon as the Persians had quitted the western coasts of the Ægean, he proposed to an assembly of the Athenian people that they should fit out seventy galleys, with a proportionate force of soldiers and military stores, and place it at his disposal; not telling them whither he meant to lead it, but promising them that if they would equip the force he asked for, and give him discretionary powers, he would lead it to a land where there was gold in abundance to be won with ease.

The Greeks of that time believed in the existence of eastern realms teeming with gold, as firmly as the Europeans of the sixteenth century believed in El Dorado of the West. The Athenians probably thought that the recent victor of Marathon, and former officer of Darius, was about to lead them on a secret expedition against some wealthy and unprotected cities of treasure in the Persian dominions. The armament was voted and equipped, and sailed eastward from Attica, no one but Miltiades knowing its destination until the Greek isle of paros was reached, when his true object appeared. In former years, while connected with the Persians as prince of the Chersonese, Miltiades had been involved in a quarrel with

---

[1] Pausanias states, with implicit belief, that the battle-field was haunted at night by supernatural beings, and that the noise of combatants and the snorting of horses were heard to resound on it. The superstition has survived the change of creeds, and the shepherds of the neighborhood still believe that spectral warriors contend on the plain at midnight, and they say that they have heard the shouts of the combatants and the neighing of the steeds.

[2] It is probable that the Greek light-armed irregulars were active in the attack on the Persian ships, and it was in this attack that the Greeks suffered their principal loss.

one of the leading men among the Parians, who had injured his credit and caused some slights to be put upon him at the court of the Persian satrap Hydarnes. The feud had ever since rankled in the heart of the Athenian chief, and he now attacked Paros for the sake of avenging himself on his ancient enemy.

His pretext, as general of the Athenians, was, that the Parians had aided the armament of Datis with a war-galley. The Parians pretended to treat about terms of surrender, but used the time which they thus gained in repairing the defective parts of the fortifications of their city, and they then set the Athenians at defiance. So far, says Herodotus, the accounts of all the Greeks agree. But the Parians in after years told also a wild legend, how a captive priestess of a Parian temple of the Deities of the Earth promised Miltiades to give him the means of capturing Paros; how, at her bidding, the Athenian general went alone at night and forced his way into a holy shrine, near the city gate, but with what purpose it was not known; how a supernatural awe came over him, and in his flight he fell and fractured his leg; how an oracle afterward forbade the Parians to punish the sacrilegious and traitorous priestess, "because it was fated that Miltiades should come to an ill end, and she was only the instrument to lead him to evil." Such was the tale that Herodotus heard at Paros. Certain it was that Miltiades either dislocated or broke his leg during an unsuccessful siege of the city, and returned home in evil plight with his baffled and defeated forces.

The indignation of the Athenians was proportionate to the hope and excitement which his promises had raised. Xanthippas, the head of one of the first families in Athens, indicted him before the supreme popular tribunal for the capital offence of having deceived the people. His guilt was undeniable, and the Athenians passed their verdict accordingly. But the recollections of Lemnos and Marathon, and the sight of the fallen general, who lay stretched on a couch before them, pleaded successfully in mitigation of punishment, and the sentence was commuted from death to a fine of fifty talents. This was paid by his son, the afterward illustrious Cimon, Miltiades dying, soon after the trial, of the injury which he had received at Paros.

The melancholy end of Miltiades, after his elevation to such a height of power and glory, must often have been recalled to the minds of the ancient Greeks by the sight of one in particular of the memorials of the great battle which he won. This was the remarkable statue—minutely described by Pausanias—which the Athenians, in the time of Pericles, caused to be hewn out of a huge block of marble, which, it was believed, had been provided by Datis, to form a trophy of the anticipated victory of the Persians. Phidias fashioned out of this a colossal image of the goddess Nemesis, the deity whose peculiar function was to visit the exuberant prosperity both of nations and individuals with sudden and awful reverses. This statue was placed in a temple of the goddess at Rhamnus, about eight miles from Marathon. Athens itself contained numerous memorials of her primary great victory. Panenus, the cousin of Phidias, represented it in fresco on the walls of the painted porch; and, centuries afterward, the figures of Miltiades and Callimachus at the head of the Athenians were conspicuous in the fresco. The tutelary deities were exhibited taking part in the fray. In the background were seen the Phœnician galleys, and, nearer to the spectator, the Athenians and the Platæans—distinguished by their leather helmets—were chasing routed Asiatics into the marshes and the sea. The battle was sculptured also on the Temple of Victory in the Acropolis, and even now there may be traced on the frieze the figures of the Persian combatants with their lunar shields, their bows and quivers, their curved cimeters, their loose trousers, and Phrygian tiaras.

These and other memorials of Marathon were the produce of the meridian age of Athenian intellectual splendor, of the age of Phidias and Pericles; for it was not merely by the generation whom the battle liberated from Hippias and the Medes that the transcendent importance of their victory was gratefully recognized. Through the whole epoch of her prosperity, through the long Olympiads of her decay, through centuries after her fall, Athens looked back on the day of Marathon as the brightest of her national existence.

By a natural blending of patriotic pride with grateful piety, the very spirits of the Athenians who fell at Marathon were deified by their countrymen. The inhabitants of the district of Marathon paid religious rites to them, and orators solemnly invoked them in their most impassioned adjurations before the assembled men of Athens. "Nothing was omitted that could keep alive the remembrance of a deed which had first taught the Athenian people to know its own strength, by measuring it with the power which had subdued the greater part of the known world. The consciousness thus awakened fixed its character, its station, and its destiny; it was the spring of its later great actions and ambitious enterprises."

It was not indeed by one defeat, however signal, that the pride of Persia could be broken, and her dreams of universal empire dispelled. Ten years afterward she renewed her attempts upon Europe on a grander scale of enterprise, and was repulsed by Greece with greater and reiterated loss. Larger forces and heavier slaughter than had been seen at Marathon signalized the conflicts of Greeks and Persians at Artemisium, Salamis, Platæa, and the Eurymedon. But, mighty and momentous as these battles were, they rank not with Marathon in importance. They originated no new impulse. They turned back no current of fate. They were merely confirmatory of the already existing bias which Marathon had created. The day of Marathon is the critical epoch in the history of the two nations. It broke forever the spell of Persian invincibility, which had previously paralyzed men's minds. It generated among the Greeks the spirit which beat back Xerxes, and afterward led on Xenophon, Agesilaus, and Alexander, in terrible retaliation through their Asiatic campaigns. It secured for mankind the intellectual treasures of Athens, the growth of free institutions, the liberal enlightenment of the Western world, and the gradual ascendency for many ages of the great principles of European civilization.

EXPLANATORY REMARKS ON SOME OF THE CIRCUMSTANCES OF THE BATTLE OF MARATHON

Nothing is said by Herodotus of the Persian cavalry taking any part in the battle, although he mentions that Hippias recommended the Persians to land at Marathon, because the plain was favorable for cavalry evolutions. In the life of Miltiades which is usually cited as the production of Cornelius Nepos, but which I believe to be of no authority whatever, it is said that Miltiades protected his flanks from the enemy's horse by an abatis of felled trees. While he was on the high ground he would not have required this defence, and it is not likely that the Persians would have allowed him to erect it on the plain.

But, in truth, whatever amount of cavalry we suppose Datis to have had with him on the day of Marathon, their inaction in the battle is intelligible, if we believe the attack of the Athenian spearmen to have been as sudden as it was rapid. The Persian horse-soldier, on an alarm being given, had to take the shackles off his horse, to strap the saddle on, and bridle him, besides equipping himself (Xenophon), and when each individual horseman was ready, the line had to be formed; and the time that it takes to form the Oriental cavalry in line for a charge has, in all ages, been observed by Europeans.

The wet state of the marshes at each end of the plain, in the time of year when the battle was fought, has been adverted to by Wordsworth,[1] and this would hinder the Persian general from arranging and employing his horsemen on his extreme wings, while it also enabled the Greeks, as they came forward, to occupy the whole breadth of the practicable ground with an unbroken line of leveled spears, against which, if any Persian horse advanced, they would be driven back in confusion upon their own foot.

Even numerous and fully arrayed bodies of cavalry have been repeatedly broken, both in ancient and modern warfare, by resolute charges of infantry. For instance, it was by an attack of some picked cohorts that Cæsar routed the Pompeian cavalry—which had previously defeated his own—and won the battle of Pharsalia.

[1] *Greece.*

INVASION OF GREECE BY PERSIANS UNDER XERXES

DEFENCE OF THERMOPYLÆ

B.C. 480

HERODOTUS

The invasion of Greece by Xerxes is the subject of the great history written in nine books by Herodotus. His object is to show the pre-eminence of Greece, whose fleets and armies defeated the forces of the Persians after these latter had triumphed over the most powerful nations of the earth. Xerxes collected a vast army from all parts of the empire. The Phœnicians furnished him with an enormous fleet, and he made a bridge of a double line of boats across the Hellespont and cut a canal through the peninsula of Mount Athos. He reached Sardis in the autumn of B.C. 481, and the next year his army crossed the bridge of boats, taking seven days and seven nights for the transit. The number of his fighting men was over two millions and a half. His ships of war were twelve hundred and seven in number, and he had three thousand smaller vessels for carrying his land forces and supplies. At the narrow pass of Thermopylæ, in the northeast of Greece, this immense army was checked for a while by the heroic Leonidas and his three hundred Spartans, who, however, perished in their attempt to prevent the Persian's attack on Athens, which city was almost entirely destroyed by the invaders. The sea-fight of Salamis was won by the Greeks against enormous odds; and in the battle of Platæa, B.C. 479, the defeat of the Persians by the Greek land forces was made more complete by the death of Mardonius, the most renowned general of Xerxes.

THE Greeks, when they arrived at the Isthmus, consulted on the message they had received from Alexander, in what way and in what places they should prosecute the war. The opinion which prevailed was that they should defend the pass at Thermopylæ; for it appeared to be narrower than that into Thessaly, and at the same time nearer to their own territories; for the path by which the Greeks who were taken at Thermopylæ were afterward surprised, they knew nothing of, till, on their arrival at Thermopylæ, they were informed of it by the Trachinians. They accordingly resolved to guard this pass, and not suffer the barbarian to enter Greece; and that the naval force should sail to Artemisium, in the territory of Histiæotis, for these places are near one another, so that they could hear what happened to each other. These spots are thus situated.

In the first place, Artemisium is contracted from a wide space of the Thracian sea into a narrow frith, which lies between the island of Sciathus and the continent of Magnesia. From the narrow frith begins the coast of Eubœa, called Artemisium, and in it is a temple of Diana. But the entrance into Greece through Trachis, in the narrowest part, is no more than a half *plethrum* in width: however, the narrowest part of the country is not in this spot, but before and behind Thermopylæ; for near Alpeni, which is behind, there is only a single carriage-road, and before, by the river Phœnix, near the city of Anthela, is another single carriage-road. On the western side of Thermopylæ is an inaccessible and precipitous mountain, stretching to Mount Œta, and on the eastern side of the way is the sea and a morass. In this passage there are hot baths, which the inhabitants call "Chytri," and above these is an altar to Hercules. A wall had been built in this pass, and formerly there were gates in it. The Phocians built it through fear, when the Thessalians came from Thesprotia to settle in the Æolian territory which they now possess: apprehending that the Thessalians would attempt to subdue them, the Phocians took this precaution; at the same time, they diverted the hot water into the entrance, that the place might be broken into clefts, having recourse to every contrivance to prevent the Thessalians from making inroads into their country. Now this old wall had been built a long time, and the greater part of it had already fallen through age; but they determined to rebuild it, and in that place to repel the barbarian from Greece. Very near this road there is a village called Alpeni; from this the Greeks expected to obtain provisions.

Accordingly, these situations appeared suitable for the Greeks; for they, having weighed everything beforehand, and considered that the barbarians would neither be able to use their numbers nor their cavalry, there resolved to await the invader of Greece. As soon as they were informed that the Persian was in Pieria, breaking up from the Isthmus some of them proceeded by land to Thermopylæ, and others by sea to Artemisium.

The Greeks, therefore, being appointed in two divisions, hastened to meet the enemy; but, at the same time, the Delphians, alarmed for themselves and for Greece, consulted the oracle, and the answer given them was, "that they should pray to the winds, for that they would be powerful allies to Greece."

The Delphians, having received the oracle, first of all communicated the answer to those Greeks who were zealous to be free; and as they very much dreaded the barbarians, by giving that message they acquired a claim to everlasting gratitude. After that, the Delphians erected an altar to the winds at Thyia, where there is an inclosure consecrated to Thyia, daughter of Cephisus, from whom this district derives its name, and conciliated them with sacrifices; and the Delphians, in obedience to that oracle, to this day propitiate the winds.

The naval force of Xerxes, setting out from the city of Therma, advanced with ten of the fastest sailing ships straight to Scyathus, where were three Grecian ships keeping a lookout: a Trœzenian, an Æginetan, and an Athenian. These, seeing the ships of the barbarians at a distance, betook themselves to flight.

The Trœzenian ship, which Praxinus commanded, the barbarians pursued and soon captured; and then, having led the handsomest of the marines to the prow of the ship, they slew him, deeming it a good omen that the first Greek they had taken was also very handsome. The name of the man that was slain was Leon, and perhaps he in some measure reaped the fruits of his name.

The Æginetan ship, which Asonides commanded, gave them some trouble; Pytheas, son of Ischenous, being a marine on board, a man who on this day displayed the most consummate valor; who, when the ship was taken, continued fighting until he was entirely cut to pieces. But when, having fallen (he was not dead, but still breathed), the Persians who served on board the ships were very anxious to save him alive, on

account of his valor, healing his wounds with myrrh, and binding them with bandages of flaxen cloth; and when they returned to their own camp, they showed him with admiration
to the whole army, and treated him well; but the others, whom
they took in this ship, they treated as slaves.

Thus, then, two of the ships were taken; but the other,
which Phormus, an Athenian, commanded, in its flight ran
ashore at the mouth of the Peneus, and the barbarians got
possession of the ship, but not of the men; for as soon as the
Athenians had run the ship aground, they leaped out, and,
proceeding through Thessaly, reached Athens. The Greeks
who were stationed at Artemisium were informed of this event
by signal-fires from Sciathus; and being informed of it, and
very much alarmed, they retired from Artemisium to Chalcis,
intending to defend the Euripus, and leaving scouts on the
heights of Eubœa. Of the ten barbarian ships, three approached the sunken rock called Myrmex, between Sciathus
and Magnesia. Then the barbarians, when they had erected
on the rock a stone column, which they had brought with
them, set out from Therma, now that every obstacle had been
removed, and sailed forward with all their ships, having waited
eleven days after the king's departure from Therma. Pam-
mon, a Scyrian, pointed out to them this hidden rock, which
was almost directly in their course. The barbarians, sailing
all day, reached Sepias in Magnesia, and the shore that lies
between the city of Casthanæa and the coast of Sepias.

As far as this place and Thermopylæ, the army had
suffered no loss, and the numbers were at that time, as I find
by calculations, of the following amount: of those in ships
from Asia, amounting to one thousand two hundred and seven,
originally the whole number of the several nations was two
hundred forty-one thousand four hundred men, allowing two
hundred to each ship; and on these ships thirty Persians,
Medes, and Sacæ served as marines, in addition to the native
crews of each; this farther number amounts to thirty-six thousand two hundred and ten. To this and the former number I
add those that were on the *penteconters*[1] supposing eighty
men on the average to be on board of each. Three thousand

[1] Fifty-oared ships.

of these vessels were assembled; therefore the men on board them must have been two hundred and forty thousand. This, then, was the naval force from Asia, the total being five hundred and seventeen thousand six hundred and ten. Of infantry there were seventeen hundred thousand, and of cavalry eighty thousand; to these I add the Arabians who drove camels, and the Libyans who drove chariots, reckoning the number at twenty thousand men. Accordingly, the numbers on board the ships and on the land, added together, make up two millions three hundred and seventeen thousand six hundred and ten. This, then, is the force which, as has been mentioned, was assembled from Asia itself, exclusive of the servants that followed, and the provision ships, and the men that were on board them.

But the force brought from Europe must still be added to this whole number that has been summed up; but it is necessary to speak by guess. Now the Grecians from Thrace, and the islands contiguous to Thrace, furnished one hundred and twenty ships; these ships give an amount of twenty-four thousand men. Of land-forces, which were furnished by Thracians, Pæonians, the Eordi, the Bottiæans, the Chalcidian race, Brygi, Pierians, Macedonians, Perrhæbi, Ænianes, Dolopians, Magnesians, and Achæans, together with those who inhabit the maritime parts of Thrace—of these nations I suppose that there were three hundred thousand men, so that these *myriads*, added to those from Asia, make a total of two millions six hundred and forty one thousand six hundred and ten fighting men!

I think that the servants who followed them, and with those on board the provision ships and other vessels that sailed with the fleet, were not fewer than the fighting men, but more numerous; but supposing them to be equal in number to the fighting men, they make up the former number of *myriads*.[1] Thus Xerxes, son of Darius, led five millions two hundred and eighty-three thousand two hundred and twenty men to Sepias and Thermopylæ!

This, then, was the number of the whole force of Xerxes. But of women who made bread, and concubines, and eunuchs,

[1] In Greek numeration, ten thousand.

no one could mention the number with accuracy; nor of draught-cattle and other beasts of burden; nor of Indian dogs that followed could any one mention the number, they were so many; therefore I am not astonished that the streams of some rivers failed, but rather it is a wonder to me how provisions held out for so many *myriads*; for I find by calculation, if each man had a *chœnix* of wheat daily, and no more, one hundred and ten thousand three hundred and forty *medimni* must have been consumed every day; and I have not reckoned the food for the women, eunuchs, beasts of burden, and dogs. But of these *myriads* of men, not one of them, for beauty and stature, was more entitled than Xerxes himself to possess the supreme command.

When the fleet, having set out, sailed and reached the shore of Magnesia that lies between the city of Casthanæa and the coast of Sepias, the foremost of the ships took up their station close to land, others behind rode at anchor—the beach not being extensive enough—with their prows toward the sea, and eight deep. Thus they passed the night; but at daybreak, after serene and tranquil weather, the sea began to swell, and a heavy storm with a violent gale from the east—which those who inhabit these parts call a "Hellespontine"—burst upon them; as many of them then as perceived the gale increasing, and who were able to do so from their position, anticipated the storm by hauling their ships on shore, and both they and their ships escaped. But such of the ships as the storm caught at sea it carried away, some to the parts called Ipni, near Pelion, others to the beach; some were dashed on Cape Sepias itself; some were wrecked at Melibœa, and others at Casthanæa. The storm was indeed irresistible.

The barbarians, when the wind had lulled and the waves had subsided, having hauled down their ships, sailed along the continent; and having doubled the promontory of Magnesia, stood directly into the bay leading to Pagasæ. There is a spot in this bay of Magnesia where it is said Hercules was abandoned by Jason and his companions when he had been sent from the Argo for water, as they were sailing to Colchis, in Asia, for the golden fleece; and from there they purposed to put out to sea after they had taken in water. From this circumstance, the name of "Aphetæ" was given to the place. In this place, then, the fleet of Xerxes was moored.

Fifteen of these ships happened to be driven out to sea some time after the rest, and somehow saw the ships of the Greeks at Artemisium. The barbarians thought that they were their own, and sailing on, fell among their enemies. They were commanded by Sandoces, son of Thaumasius, governor of Cyme, of Æolia. He, being one of the royal judges, had been formerly condemned by King Darius (who had detected him in the following offence), to be crucified. Sandoces gave an unjust sentence, for a bribe; but while he was actually hanging on the cross, Darius, considering within himself, found that the services he had rendered to the royal family were greater than his faults. Darius, therefore, having discovered this, and perceiving that he, himself, had acted with more expedition than wisdom, released him. Having thus escaped being put to death by Darius, he survived; but now, sailing down among the Grecians, he was not to escape a second time; for when the Greeks saw them sailing toward them, perceiving the mistake they had committed, they bore down upon them and easily took them.

King Xerxes encamped in the Trachinian territory of Malis, and the Greeks in the pass. This spot is called by most of the Greeks, "Thermopylæ," but by the inhabitants and neighbors, "Pylæ." Both parties, then, encamped in these places. The one was in possession of all the parts toward the north as far as Trachis, and the others, of the parts which stretch toward the south and meridian of this continent.

The following were the Greeks who awaited the Persians in this position. Of Spartans, three hundred heavy-armed men; of Tegeans and Mantineans, one thousand (half of each); from Orchomenus in Arcadia, one hundred and twenty; and from the rest of Arcadia, one thousand (there were so many Arcadians); from Corinth, four hundred; from Phlius, two hundred men; and from Mycenæ, eighty. These came from Peloponnesus. From Bœotia, of Thespians seven hundred; and of Thebans, four hundred.

In addition to these, the Opuntian Locrians, being invited, came with all their forces, and a thousand Phocians; for the

Greeks themselves had invited them, representing by their embassadors that "they had arrived as forerunners of the others, and that the rest of the allies might be daily expected; that the sea was protected by them, being guarded by the Athenians, the Æginetæ, and others, who were appointed to the naval service; and that they had nothing to fear, for that it was not a god who invaded Greece, but a man; and that there never was, and never would be, any mortal who had not evil mixed with *his prosperity* from his very birth, and to the greatest of them the greatest *reverses happen;* that it must therefore needs be that he who is marching against us, being a mortal, will be disappointed in his expectation." They, having heard this, marched with assistance to Trachis.

These nations had separate generals for their several cities, but the one most admired, and who commanded the whole army, was a Lacedæmonian, Leonidas, son of Anaxandrides, son of Leon, son of Eurycratides, son of Anaxander, son of Eurycates, son of Polydorus, son of Alcamenes, son of Teleclus, son of Archelaus, son of Agesilaus, son of Doryssus, son of Leobotes, son of Echestratus, son of Agis, son of Eurysthenes, son of Aristodemus, son of Aristomachus, son of Cleodæus, son of Hyllus, son of Hercules, who had unexpectedly succeeded to the throne of Sparta.

For, as he had two elder brothers, Cleomenes and Dorieus, he was far from any thought of the kingdom. However, Cleomenes having died without male issue, and Dorieus being no longer alive—having ended his days in Sicily—the kingdom thus devolved upon Leonidas; both because he was older than Cleombrotus—for he was the youngest son of Anaxandrides—and also because he had married the daughter of Cleomenes. He then marched to Thermopylæ, having chosen the three hundred men allowed by law, and such as had children. On his march he took with him the Thebans, whose numbers I have already reckoned, and whom Leontiades, son of Eurymachus, commanded. For this reason Leonidas was anxious to take with him the Thebans alone of all the Greeks, because they were strongly accused of favoring the Medes: he therefore summoned them to the war, wishing to know whether they would send their forces with him, or would openly renounce the alliance of the Grecians; but they, though other-wise minded, sent assistance.

The Spartans sent these troops first with Leonidas, in order that the rest of the allies, seeing them, might take the field, and might not go over to the Medes if they heard that they were delaying; but afterward—for the Carnean festival was then an obstacle to them—they purposed, when they had kept the feast, to leave a garrison in Sparta and to march immediately with their whole strength. The rest of the con-federates likewise intended to act in the same manner; for the Olympic games occurred at the same period as these events. As they did not, therefore, suppose that the engagement at Thermopylæ would so soon be decided, they despatched an advance-guard.

The Greeks at Thermopylæ, when the Persians came near the pass, being alarmed, consulted about a retreat; accordingly, it seemed best to the other Peloponnesians to retire to Pelo-ponnesus, and guard the Isthmus; but Leonidas, perceiving the Phocians and Locrians were very indignant at this propo-sition, determined to stay there, and to despatch messengers to the cities, desiring them to come to their assistance, they being too few to repel the army of the Medes.

While they were deliberating on these matters, Xerxes sent a scout on horseback, to see how many they were and what they were doing; for while he was still in Thessaly, he had heard that a small army had been assembled at that spot, and as to their leaders, that they were Lacedæmonians, and Leonidas, who was of the race of Hercules. When the horse-man rode up to the camp, he reconnoitred, and saw not indeed the whole camp, for it was not possible that they should be seen who were posted within the wall, which having rebuilt they were now guarding; but he had a clear view of those on the outside, whose arms were piled in front of the wall. At this time the Lacedæmonians happened to be posted outside; and some of the men he saw performing gymnastic exercises, and others combing their hair. On beholding this he was astonished, and ascertained their number, and having in-formed himself of everything accurately, he rode back at his leisure, for no one pursued him and he met with general contempt. On his return he gave an account to Xerxes of all that he had seen.

When Xerxes heard this, he could not comprehend the truth that the Grecians were preparing to be slain and to slay to the utmost of their power; but, as they appeared to behave in a ridiculous manner, he sent for Demaratus, son of Ariston, who was then in the camp, and when he was come into his presence Xerxes questioned him as to each particular, wishing to understand what the Lacedæmonians were doing. Demaratus said: "You before heard me when we were setting out against Greece, speak of these men, and when you heard, you treated me with ridicule though I told you in what way I foresaw these matters would issue; for it is my chief aim, O king, to adhere to the truth in your presence; hear it, therefore, once more. These men have to fight with us for the pass and are now preparing themselves to do so; for such is their custom when they are going to hazard their lives, then they dress their heads; but be assured if you conquer these men and those that remain in Sparta, there is no other nation in the world that will dare to raise its hand against you, O king! for you are now to engage with the noblest kingdom and city of all among the Greeks and with the most valiant men." What was said seemed incredible to Xerxes and he asked again, "how, being so few in number, they could contend with his army." He answered: "O king, deal with me as with a liar if these things do not turn out as I say!"

By saying this he did not convince Xerxes. He therefore let four days pass, constantly expecting that they would be taking themselves to flight; but on the fifth day, as they had not retreated, but appeared to him to stay through arrogance and rashness, he, being enraged, sent the Medes and Cissians against them, with orders to take them alive, and bring them into his presence. When the Medes bore down impetuously upon the Greeks, many of them fell; others followed to the charge, and were not repulsed, though they suffered greatly; but they made it evident to every one, and not least of all to the king himself, that they were indeed many men, but few soldiers. The engagement lasted through the day.

When the Medes were roughly handled, they thereupon

retired, and the Persians whom the king called "Immortal," and whom Hydarnes commanded, taking their place advanced to the attack thinking that they indeed would easily settle the business. But when they engaged with the Grecians they succeeded no better than the Medic troops, but just the same; as they fought in a narrow space and used shorter spears than the Greeks, they were unable to avail themselves of their numbers. The Lacedæmonians fought memorably in other respects, showing that they knew how to fight with men who knew not, and whenever they turned their backs they retreated in close order, but the barbarians, seeing them retreat, followed with a shout and clamor; then they, being overtaken, wheeled round so as to front the barbarians, and having faced about, overthrew an inconceivable number of the Persians, and then some few of the Spartans themselves fell, so that when the Persians were unable to gain anything in their attempt on the pass by attacking in troops and in every possible manner, they retired.

It is said that during these onsets of the battle, the king, who witnessed them, thrice sprang from his throne, being alarmed for his army. Thus they strove at that time. On the following day the barbarians fought with no better success; for considering that the Greeks were few in number, and expecting that they were covered with wounds and would not be able to raise their heads against them any more, they renewed the contest. But the Greeks were marshalled in companies and according to their several nations, and each fought in turn, except only the Phocians; they were stationed at the mountain to guard the pathway. When, therefore, the Persians found nothing different from what they had seen on the preceding day, they retired.

While the king was in doubt what course to take in the present state of affairs, Ephialtes, son of Eurydemus, a Malian, obtained an audience of him (expecting that he should receive a great reward from the king), and informed him of the path which leads over the mountain to Thermopylæ, and by that means caused the destruction of those Greeks who were stationed there; but afterward, fearing the Lacedæmonians, he fled to Thessaly, and when he had fled, a price was set on his head by the Pylagori when the Amphictyons were assembled at Pylæ; but some time after, he went down to Anticyra and was killed by Athenades, a Trachinian.

Another account is given, that Onetes, son of Phanagoras, a Carystian, and Corydallus of Anticyra, were the persons who gave this information to the king and conducted the Persians round the mountains; but to me, this is by no means credible; for, in the first place, we may draw the inference from this circumstance, that the Pylagori of the Grecians set a price on the head, not of Onetes and Corydallus, but of Ephialtes the Trachinian, having surely ascertained the exact truth; and, in the next place, we know that Ephialtes fled on that account. Onetes, indeed, though he was not a Malian, might be acquainted with this path if he had been conversant with the country; but it was Ephialtes who conducted them round the mountain by the path, and I charge him as the guilty person.

Xerxes, since he was pleased with what Ephialtes promised to perform, being exceedingly delighted, immediately despatched Hydarnes and the troops that Hydarnes commanded, and he started from the camp about the hour of lamp-lighting. The native Malians discovered this pathway, and having discovered it, conducted the Thessalians by it against the Phocians at the time when the Phocians, having fortified the pass by a wall, were under shelter from an attack. From that time it appeared to have been of no service to the Malians.

This path is situated as follows: it begins from the river Asopus, which flows through the cleft; the same name is given both to the mountain and to the path, "Anopæa," and this Anopæa extends along the ridge of the mountain and ends near Alpenus, which is the first city of the Locrians toward the Malians, and by the rock called "Melampygus," and by the seats of the Cercopes, and there the path is the narrowest.

Along this path, thus situate, the Persians, having crossed the Asopus, marched all night, having on their right the mountains of the Œtæans, and on their left those of the Trachinians; morning appeared, and they were on the summit of the mountain. At this part of the mountain, as I have already mentioned, a thousand heavy-armed Phocians kept guard, to defend their own country and to secure the pathway—for the lower pass was guarded by those before mentioned—and the Phocians had voluntarily promised Leonidas to guard the path across the mountain.

The Phocians discovered them after they had ascended, in the following manner; for the Persian ascended without being observed, as the whole mountain was covered with oaks; there was a perfect calm, and, as was likely, a considerable rustling taking place from the leaves strewn under foot, the Phocians sprang up and put on their arms, and immediately the barbarians made their appearance. But when they saw men clad in armor they were astonished, for, expecting to find nothing to oppose them, they fell in with an army; thereupon Hydarnes, fearing lest the Phocians might be Lacedæmonians, asked Ephialtes of what nation the troops were, and being accurately informed, he drew up the Persians for battle. The Phocians, when they were hit by many and thick-falling arrows, fled to the summit of the mountain, supposing that they had come expressly to attack them, and prepared to perish. Such was their determination. But the Persians, with Ephialtes and Hydarnes, took no notice of the Phocians but marched down the mountain with all speed.

To those of the Greeks who were at Thermopylæ, the augur Megistias, having inspected the sacrifices, first made known the death that would befall them in the morning; certain deserters afterward came and brought intelligence of the circuit the Persians were taking. These brought the news while it was yet night; and, thirdly, the scouts running down from the heights as soon as day dawned, *brought the same intelligence.* Upon this the Greeks held a consultation, and their opinions were divided; some would not hear of abandoning their post, and others opposed that view. After this, when the assembly broke up, some of them departed, and being dispersed, betook themselves to their several cities; but others of them prepared to remain there with Leonidas.

It is said that Leonidas himself sent them away, being anxious that they should not perish, but that he and the Spartans who were there could not honorably desert the post which

they originally came to defend. For my own part, I am rather
inclined to think that Leonidas, when he perceived that the
allies were averse and unwilling to share the danger with him,
bade them withdraw, but that he considered it dishonorable
for himself to depart; on the other hand, by remaining there,
great renown would be left for him and the prosperity of
Sparta would not be obliterated, for it had been announced to
the Spartans by the Pythian, when they consulted the oracle
concerning this war as soon as it commenced, "that either
Lacedæmon must be overthrown by the barbarians, or their
king perish." This answer she gave in hexameter verses, to
this effect: "To you, O inhabitants of spacious Lacedæmon!
either your vast glorious city shall be destroyed by men
sprung from Perseus, or, if not so, the confines of Lacedæmon
shall mourn a king deceased, of the race of Hercules. For
neither shall the strength of bulls nor of lions withstand him with
force opposed to force, for he has the strength of Jove, and I
say he shall not be restrained before he has certainly obtained
one of these for his share." I think, therefore, that Leonidas,
considering these things and being desirous to acquire glory
for the Spartans alone, sent away the allies, rather than that
those who went away differed in opinion, and went away in
such an unbecoming manner.

The following in no small degree strengthens my conviction
on this point; for not only *did he send away* the others, but it
is certain that Leonidas also sent away the augur who followed
the army, Megistias the Acarnanian, who was said to have
been originally descended from Melampus, the same who announced, from an inspection of the victims, what was about to
befall them, in order that he might not perish with them. He
however, though dismissed, did not himself depart but sent
away his son who served with him in the expedition, being his
only child.

The allies that were dismissed, accordingly departed, and
obeyed Leonidas, but only the Thespians and the Thebans
remained with the Lacedæmonians; the Thebans, indeed, remained unwillingly and against their inclination, for Leonidas
detained them, treating them as hostages; but the Thespians
willingly, for they refused to go away and abandon Leonidas

and those with him, but remained and died with them. Demophilus, son of Diadromas, commanded them.

Xerxes, after he had poured out libations at sunrise, having waited a short time, began his attack about the time of full market, for he had been so instructed by Ephialtes; for the descent from the mountain is more direct and the distance much shorter than the circuit and ascent. The barbarians, therefore, with Xerxes, advanced, and the Greeks with Leonidas, marching out as if for certain death, now advanced much farther than before into the wide part of the defile, for the fortification of the wall had protected them, and they on the preceding days, having taken up their position in the narrow part, fought there; but now engaging outside the narrows, great numbers of the barbarians fell; for the officers of the companies from behind, having scourges, flogged every man, constantly urging them forward; in consequence, many of them, falling into the sea, perished, and many more were trampled alive under foot by one another and no regard was paid to any that perished, for the Greeks, knowing that death awaited them at the hands of those who were going round the mountain, being desperate and regardless of their own lives, displayed the utmost possible valor against the barbarians.

Already were most of their javelins broken and they had begun to despatch the Persians with their swords. In this part of the struggle fell Leonidas, fighting valiantly, and with him other eminent Spartans, whose names, seeing they were deserving men, I have ascertained; indeed, I have ascertained the names of the whole three hundred. On the side of the Persians also, many other eminent men fell on this occasion, and among them two sons of Darius, Abrocomes and Hyperanthes, born to Darius of Phrataguna, daughter of Artanes; but Artanes was brother to king Darius, and son of Hystaspes, son of Arsames. He, when he gave his daughter to Darius, gave him also all his property, as she was his only child.

Accordingly, two brothers of Xerxes fell at this spot fighting for the body of Leonidas, and there was a violent struggle between the Persians and Lacedæmonians, until at last the Greeks rescued it by their valor and four times repulsed the enemy. Thus the contest continued until those with Ephialtes came up. When the Greeks heard that they were approaching, from this time the battle was altered; for they retreated to the narrow part of the way, and passing beyond the wall came and took up their position on the rising ground all in a compact body with the exception of the Thebans. The rising ground is at the entrance where the stone lion now stands to the memory of Leonidas. On this spot, while they defended themselves with swords—such as had them still remaining—and with hands and teeth, the barbarians overwhelmed them with missiles, some of them attacking them in front, having thrown down the wall, and others surrounding and attacking them on every side.

Though the Lacedæmonians and Thespians behaved in this manner, yet Dieneces, a Spartan, is said to have been the bravest man. They relate that he made the following remark before they engaged with the Medes, having heard a Trachinian say that when the barbarians let fly their arrows they would obscure the sun by the multitude of their shafts, so great was their number; but he, not at all alarmed at this, said, holding in contempt the numbers of the Medes, that "their Trachinian friend told them everything to their advantage, since if the Medes obscure the sun, they would then have to fight in the shade and not in the sun." This, and other sayings of the same kind, they relate that Dieneces the Lacedæmonian left as memorials.

Next to him, two Lacedæmonian brothers, Alpheus and Maron, sons of Orisiphantus, are said to have distinguished themselves most; and of the Thespians, he obtained the greatest glory whose name was Dithyrambus, son of Harmatides.

In honor of the slain, who were buried on the spot where they fell, and of those who died before they who were dismissed by Leonidas went away, the following inscription has been engraved over them: "Four thousand from Peloponnesus once fought on this spot with three hundred *myriads!*"[1] This inscription was made for all; and for the Spartans in particular: "Stranger, go tell the Lacedæmonians that we lie here,

---

[1] Three millions.

obedient to their commands!" This was for the Lacedæmonians; and for the prophet, the following: "This is the monument of the illustrious Megistias, whom once the Medes, having passed the river Sperchius, slew; a prophet who, at the time well knowing the impending fate, would not abandon the leaders of Sparta!"

The Amphictyons are the persons who honored them with these inscriptions and columns, with the exception of the inscription to the prophet; that of the prophet Megistias, Simonides, son of Leoprepes, caused to be engraved, from personal friendship.

CHRONOLOGY OF UNIVERSAL HISTORY

EMBRACING THE PERIOD COVERED IN THIS VOLUME

B.C. 5867–B.C. 451

JOHN RUDD, LL.D.

CHRONOLOGY OF UNIVERSAL HISTORY

Embracing the Period Covered in This Volume

B.C. 5867–B.C. 451

JOHN RUDD, LL.D.

Events treated at length are here indicated in large type; the numerals following give volume and page.

Separate chronologies of the various nations, and of the careers of famous persons, will be found in the INDEX VOLUME, with volume and page references showing where the several events are fully treated.

All dates are approximate up to B.C. 776, the beginning of the Olympiads.

B.C.

5867. Menes, the first human ruler recorded in history, unites the two kingdoms of Egypt under one crown; introduces the cult of Apis; founds the city of Memphis; rears the great temple of Ptah. See "DAWN OF CIVILIZATION," i, 1.

5000. Babylonia is invaded by a race of Semites; they conquer the land and become the Babylonians of history.

4500 (before). A patesi (priest-ruler), by name En-shag-kush-anna, is King of Kengi, Southern Babylonia; Sungir, which later gave the name Sumer to the whole district, is his capital.

4400. Shirpurla, Mesopotamia, subjugated by Mesilim, King of Kish.

4200. The hero of Shirpurla, E-anna-tum, throws off the Kish yoke and takes the title of king. He is successful in conflicts with Erech, Ur, and Larsa. Walls are erected and canals dug by him.

3700. The great Pyramid of Gizeh erected. This was during the IV or Pyramid dynasty; so called because its chief monarchs built the three great pyramids.

Beautiful Queen Nitocris, of the VI dynasty, reigned about this time. She is said to have avenged the killing of her brother, King of Egypt, by inviting his murderers to a banquet held in a subterranean chamber. Into this the river was turned, and they all miserably perished.

3000. Nineveh, colonized from Babylonia, ruled by subject princes of that country.

2800. Probable date of the foundation of the Chinese empire.

2500. Rise of the kingdom of Elam. Asshurbanipal (Sardanapalus), King of Nineveh, records an invasion of Chaldæa, or Babylonia, by the Elamites, B.C. 2300. The records of clay recently unearthed show that Cyrus was originally king of Elam. See " CONQUESTS OF CYRUS THE GREAT," i, 250.

2458. Zoroaster (Zarathushtra) founds the religion known by his name. Ancient tradition has it that he was a Median king who conquered Babylon about B.C. 2458. M. Haug assigns the date as not later than B.C. 2300. Be the time when he lived what it may, it is certain that, as the Persian national religion, it dates little further back than B.C. 559 and up to A.D. 641. The four elements—fire, air, earth, and water, especially the first—were recognized as the only proper objects of human reverence.

2300. A chart of the heavens in China.

2250. Commencement of the reign of Hammurabi, King of Babylonia; the earliest compilation of a code of laws was made in this reign. See "COMPILATION OF THE EARLIEST CODE," i, 14.

2200-1700. Dominion of the Hyksos, or Shepherd kings, in Egypt. It is not improbable that Abraham made his well-known journey to Egypt during the early reign of these kings. Joseph's visit occurred near the close of their power.

2200. Hereditary monarchy founded in China.

1700-1250. The new empire of Egypt attains the period of its greatest splendor and power. Meneptah, about 1320 (1322), has been generally accepted as the Pharaoh of the Exodus.

1500. Independence of Assyria as the rising of a kingdom apart from Babylonia; the rise of Nineveh.

1450-1300. The Hittite realm in Syria attains its greatest power. The Egyptians knew the Hittites as the Khita or Khatta. Recent discoveries indicate that they formed a civilized and powerful nation. Many inscriptions and rock sculptures in Asia Minor, formerly inexplicable, are now attributed to the Hittites of the Bible.

1330. Rameses II of Egypt; the Sesostris of the Greeks.

1300. Shalmaneser I reigns in Assyria.

1250. The Phœnicians, closely allied in language to the Hebrews, begin their colonizing career.

1235. Probable date of the consolidation of Athens. See " THESEUS FOUNDS ATHENS," i, 45.

1200. Exodus of Israel from Egypt.

" FORMATION OF THE CASTES IN INDIA." See i, 52.

1184. " FALL OF TROY." See i, 70.

1122. Wou Wang becomes emperor of China.

1120. Beginning of the reign of Tiglath-Pileser, King of Assyria.

1100. Dorian migration into the Peloponnesus.

1095 (1055; 1080 common chronology). Hebrews establish the monarchy. Saul the first king.

1058 (1033). At Gilboa, Saul is defeated by the Philistines. David becomes king in Judah.

1017 (998). Accession of Solomon as king of the Hebrews. The Temple at Jerusalem is built in this reign. See "ACCESSION OF SOLOMON," i, 92.

1015. Smyrna founded.

977 (953). Israel and Judah become separate kingdoms, following the revolt of the Ten Tribes under Jeroboam.

973 (949). Jerusalem captured by Sheshonk, King of Egypt.

958 (929). Asa ascends the throne of Judah.

931 (899). Omri's accession in Israel.

917 (873). Jehoshaphat begins his reign in Judah.

900 (853). The Syrians defeat and slay Ahab, King of Israel, at Ramoth-Gilead.

Divambar conquers Armenia, Persia, Syria, and adjacent lands.

887 (843). The throne of Israel usurped by Jehu.

850. The Tyrians colonize Carthage.

811 (792). Uzziah succeeds to the throne of Judah.

800. The canal and tunnel of Negoub constructed to convey the waters of the Zab River to Nineveh.

800 (850). Sparta: Probable date of the legislation of Lycurgus.

790 (825). Jeroboam II becomes King of Israel.

789. First destruction of Nineveh: death of Sardanapalus. See "FIRST DESTRUCTION OF NINEVEH," i, 105.

776. Beginning of the Olympiads. Olympiad in ancient Greece meant the space of four years between one celebration of the Olympic games and another. In this year it began as a system of chronology.

772* (748). End of Jehu's dynasty in Israel.

753 (common chronology). "FOUNDATION OF ROME." See i, 116.

750.* The Corinthians found Syracuse.

743–724. First great war between Sparta and Messenia: the latter is subjugated.

734.* Syria becomes subject to Tiglath-Pileser II of Assyria.

731.* Tiglath-Pileser II subjects Chaldea.

727* (728). Hezekiah ascends the throne of Judah.

722.* King Sargon of Assyria conquers Samaria; he puts an end to the kingdom of Israel. Captivity of the Ten Tribes.

701. Siege of Jerusalem by Sennacherib; he encounters the Egyptian and Ethiopian forces; his expedition into Syria fails.

697. Accession of Manasseh to the throne of Judah.

685–668. The second war between Sparta and Messenia.

660.* Prince Jimmu establishes Yamato as the capital of Japan. See "PRINCE JIMMU FOUNDS JAPAN'S CAPITAL," i, 140.

650.* The whole of Egypt united under Psammetichus I, founder of the XXVI dynasty. He frees Egypt from Assyrian rule and opens the country to the Greeks.

645–628. The Messenians make an unsuccessful attempt to throw off the yoke of Sparta.

* Date uncertain.

640. Birth of Thales, one of the Seven Wise Men of Greece. He taught the spherical form of the earth and the true causes of lunar eclipses; discovered the electricity of amber. The Seven Sages, or Wise Men, are commonly made up of Thales, Solon, Bias, Chilo, Cleobulus, Periander, and Pittacus.

Media becomes independent of Assyria; she appears as a single united kingdom.

625. Media, Assyria, and Syria have a great irruption of Scythians in their borders.

623. "FOUNDATION OF BUDDHISM." See i, 160.

621* (624). Date of the legislation of Draco, at Athens.

612. Conspiracy of Cylon at Athens.

609.* Josiah is slain at Megiddo, when Necho, the Egyptian King, crushes the power of Judah.

607.* Nineveh taken by the Medes and Babylonians, who overthrow the Assyrian monarchy.

605.* Nebuchadnezzar defeats Necho at Carchemish. Necho maintained a powerful fleet; the Phœnician ships under his order rounded the Cape of Good Hope. Herodotus says that twice during this voyage the crews, fearing a lack of food, after landing, drew their ships on shore, sowed grain and waited for a harvest. It will be noticed that this was over two thousand years before Vasco da Gama, to whom is usually given the credit of first circumnavigating Africa.

597.* Jerusalem captured by Nebuchadnezzar, who carries away the principal inhabitants.

595. The Delphic Games in Greece. See "PYTHIAN GAMES AT DELPHI," i, 181.

594. Adoption of the Constitution of Solon at Athens. See "SOLON'S EARLY GREEK LEGISLATION," i, 203.

586.* Nebuchadnezzar captures and destroys Jerusalem; puts an end to the kingdom of Judah. The Babylonish captivity.

570.* Egypt attacked by Nebuchadnezzar, who dethrones Hophra (Apries); he places Amasis on the throne.

560. Tyranny of Pisistratus at Athens. The Grecian poor were still getting poorer, notwithstanding Solon's legislation; they clamored for relief, placed Pisistratus at their head, and passed a decree allowing him to have a bodyguard of fifty men armed with clubs. Pisistratus then threw off all disguise and established himself in the Acropolis as tyrant of Athens.

550.* Cyrus, at the head of the Persians, destroys the Median monarchy. See "CONQUESTS OF CYRUS THE GREAT," i, 250.

550.* "RISE OF CONFUCIUS, THE CHINESE SAGE." See i, 270.

546. Crœsus, King of Lydia, overthrown by Cyrus. See "CONQUESTS OF CYRUS THE GREAT," i, 250.

540.* Calimachus invents the Corinthian order of architecture.

* Date uncertain.

538. Conquest of Babylon by Cyrus. See "CONQUESTS OF CYRUS THE GREAT," i, 250.

529. Death of Cyrus: Cambyses succeeds him on the throne of Persia.

527. Hippias and Hipparchus succeed their father, Pisistratus, at Athens, in the government of that city.

525 (527). Conquest of Egypt by Cambyses, King of Persia. He completely subdued it, and, after an attempted rising, crushed Egypt with merciless severity. Cambyses treated the Egyptian deities, priests, and temples with insult and contempt.

Æschylus, Greek tragic poet, born.

522. Pseudo-Smerdis usurps the Persian throne. Cambyses had slain his brother Bardes, whom Herodotus calls Smerdis. A Magian, Gaumata by name, resembling Bardes in appearance, impersonated the murdered prince. A revolution ensued and, owing to the death of Cambyses by his own hand, Pseudo-Smerdis became master of the empire.

521. Darius I, by defeating Pseudo-Smerdis, who had reigned eight months, ascends the Persian throne.

521-516. The Temple at Jerusalem, which had been destroyed by the Babylonians, rebuilt.

520.* Birth of Pindar, the chief lyric poet of Greece. He was in the prime of life when Salamis and Thermopylæ were fought. His poems have as groundwork the legends which form the Grecian religious literature.

516.* Invasion of Scythia by Darius, King of Persia, who seems to have acted according to an oriental idea of right, in that he claimed to punish the Scythians for an invasion of Media at some previous time.

514. Hipparchus, of Athens, assassinated by Harmodius and Aristogiton.

514.* Birth of Themistocles, a famous Athenian commander and statesman. He was largely instrumental in increasing the navy; induced the Athenians to leave Athens for Salamis and the fleet, and brought about the victory of Salamis.

510. Hippias expelled from Athens. The democratic party is headed by Clisthenes, the master-spirit of the revolution inaugurated for the overthrow of the despotic and hated sons of Pisistratus. The Athenian democracy was reorganized by Clisthenes.

510. The Crotonians destroy Sybaris. Croton and Sybaris were two ancient Greek cities situated on the Gulf of Tarentum, Southern Italy. Little is known of them except their luxury, fantastic self-indulgence, and extravagant indolence, for which qualities their names remain a synonyme.

510. Expulsion of the Tarquins from Rome. Founding of the Republic; consulship instituted. See "ROME ESTABLISHED AS A REPUBLIC," i, 300.

506.* The Persians subject Macedonia, and extend their dominion

* Date uncertain.

over Thrace. The Thracians occupied the region between the rivers Strymon and Danube. They were more Asiatic than European in character and religion.

500* (501, 502). Rising of the Greek colonies in Ionia against the Persians. Harpagus, who had saved Cyrus in his infancy from his grandfather, while governor of Lydia reduced the cities of the coast. Town after town submitted. The Tieans abandoned theirs, retiring to Abdera in Thrace; the Phocians, after settling in Corsica, whence they were driven by the Carthaginians and Tyrrhenians, went to Italy and later founded Massalia (Marseilles) on the coast of Gaul. Thus the Greek colonies became a portion of the Persian empire. The insurrection of the Ionians continued for six years, the fate of the revolt turning at last on the siege of Miletus.

499* (500). Ionian expedition against Sardis. The city was taken and during the pillage was accidentally burned. The Ionian forces were utterly inadequate to hold Sardis; and their return was not effected without a serious defeat by the pursuing army of Persians.

497.* The Latins are defeated by the Romans at Lake Regillus.

495. Birth of Sophocles.

494. The naval battle of Lade, in which the Persians defeat the Asiatic Greeks. Fall of Miletus.

494 (492). First secession of the plebeians from Rome. Creation of the tribunes of the people. See "ROME ESTABLISHED AS A REPUBLIC," i, 300.

493 (491). The Latins are compelled by the Romans to enter into a league with Rome, which is threatened by the Etruscans, Volscians, and the Æquians. The Latins obtained the name of Roman citizens; the title disguised a real subjection, since the men who bore it had the obligation of citizens without the rights.

492.* Mardonius heads the first Persian expedition against Greece.

490. Battle of Marathon, in which Darius' Persian host is overwhelmingly defeated by Miltiades. See "THE BATTLE OF MARATHON," i, 322.

489. Condemnation and death of Miltiades. See "THE BATTLE OF MARATHON," i, 322.

486. Darius Hystaspes, of Persia, is succeeded on the throne by his son Xerxes.

League of Rome with the Hernici.

484.* Birth of Herodotus, the "Father of History."

483. Aristides, one of the ten leaders of the Greeks at Marathon, ostracized through the jealousy of Themistocles.

480. Second Persian invasion of Greece, this time by Xerxes. Defence of Thermopylæ by Leonidas. See "DEFENCE OF THERMOPYLÆ," i, 354. Naval battle of Artemisium. Athens burned. The Persian fleet vanquished by Themistocles and Eurybiades at Salamis. Retreat of Xerxes.

* Date uncertain.

The Carthaginians attempt the conquest of the Greek cities of Sicily. Gelon, the tyrant of Syracuse, defeats their army at Himera.

Birth of Euripides, the celebrated Greek tragic poet.*

479. The Greeks, under the command of Pausanias, at the battle of Platæa, crush the Persian army under the lead of Mardonius. Leotychides and Xanthippus gain a simultaneous victory over the Persian fleet at Mycale. End of the Persian invasion of Greece.

478. The tyranny of Hieron, brother of Gelon, begins at Syracuse. He was noted as a patron of literature.

477. The predominance in Greece passes from Sparta to Athens, by the formation of the Confederacy of Delos.

474. Hieron, of Syracuse, defeats the Etruscans near Cumæ.

471. Themistocles exiled from Athens, the Spartan faction having plotted his ruin, alleging his complicity with the enemy.

Birth of Thucydides.*

470 (471). The Publilian law passed in Rome; the plebeians accorded the right of initiating legislation in their assemblies. See "ROME ESTABLISHED AS A REPUBLIC," i, 300.

469.* Birth of Socrates.

468.* Democracy triumphs in the cities of Sicily.

466. Naval victory of the Greeks, under Cimon, over the Persians at Eurymedon. B.C. 470 Cimon had reduced Eion, after a gallant defence by Boges, the Persian governor, who, rather than surrender, cast all his gold and silver into the river Strymon, raised a huge pile of wood, and on it placed the bodies of his wives, children, and slaves—all of whom he had slain—then, having set fire thereto, he flung himself into the flames and perished.

The Revolt of Naxos crushed by Cimon during the expedition against the Persians.

Fall of the tyrants at Syracuse.

465. Murder of Xerxes I, by Artabanus, captain of his guard; accession of Artaxerxes I to the Persian throne.

464. Sparta destroyed by an earthquake which shook the whole of Laconia, opened great chasms in the ground, rolled down huge masses from the peaks of Taygetus, and threw Sparta into a heap of ruins. Not more than five houses are said to have remained standing. Twenty thousand persons lost their lives by the shock. The flower of the Spartan youth was slain by the overthrow of the building in which they were exercising.

464-455. The Messenian helots rise against the Spartans, taking advantage of the confusion caused by the earthquake. This was the beginning of the third Messenian war.

463. Mycenæ is reduced by the Argives, who enslave or drive away its inhabitants.

460. Birth of Hippocrates, in the island of Cos, who became known as the "Father of Medicine."

* Date uncertain.

458.* Jews return from Babylonia to Jerusalem, under Ezra.

Esther, the Jewess, pleases King Ahasuerus and is made queen in place of Vashti. This was the origin of the Jewish festival of Purim, celebrated on the 14th and 15th of the month Adar (March).

Beginning of the Long Walls of Athens; built to protect the communication of the city with its port. One, four miles long, ran to the harbor of Phalerum, and others, four and one-half miles long, to the Piræus.

457. Beginning of war of Corinth, Sparta, and Ægina with Athens: Battle of Tanagra, in which the Athenians were defeated.

456. Athenian victory at Œnophyta; the Bœotians defeated by Myronides, who also secures the submission of Phocis and Locris.

455. End of the third Messenian war.

451. Ion of Chios, historian and tragedian, exhibits his first drama.

*Date uncertain.

END OF VOLUME I